THE CHESAPEAKE COMMAND

The adventures of Rory Dunbrody, CSN,
and Tobias St. John, USN

Second Edition

a novel by Les Eldridge

Printed in the United States of America.

ISBN# 978-0-9794847-2-8

To Mary,
and to Pat, Katie, Tiffany and Jason

AUTHOR'S NOTE TO THE READER:

"He who expects a perfect work to see, longs for what never was, and ne'er shall be" – Dryden

"History is just a bag of tricks we play on the dead." - Voltaire

The Chesapeake Command, second edition is fiction, but most of its characters actually existed. I have tried to be true to their characteristics as we know them from history. They were involved in most of the events that take place in the novel, but occasionally I have collapsed time (and merged the accomplishments of actual characters) in the interest of the story.

For the reader who is not a sailor, nor Irish, nor yet Hawaiian, it may help to scan the newly-added glossary. As the story eventually tracks two often separate story lines, the new chapter list or table of contents identifies the primary character (Rory, Tobias) in each.

When my rights to the 2005 first edition automatically reverted to me in early 2008, my current publisher suggested a second edition to bring The Chesapeake Command into conformity with Gray Raiders, Green Seas and The Wake of the Woonsocket regarding size, print quality and addenda (table of contents, historical note, ship list, character list and glossary). This edition accomplishes those goals and expands and corrects certain aspects of the first edition text.

Les Eldridge

ABOUT THE AUTHOR:

Les Eldridge has retired from careers as a college administrator, county commissioner, corporate executive, mediator, and administrative law hearings officer.

ALSO BY LES ELDRIDGE:

In the Dunbrody-St. John Series -

The Chesapeake Command (2005)

Gray Raiders, Green Seas (2007)

The Wake of the Woonsocket (2008)

The Wilkes Expedition, Puget Sound and the Oregon Country (1987), a history, co-authored by Frances Barkan (also editor), and Drew Crooks.

ACKNOWLEDGEMENTS

My special thanks to those critical readers who read and edited the manuscripts of these editions, Jane Laclergue (second edition), Professors Thomas Rainey and S. Rudolph Martin of The Evergreen State College, Evergreen Professor Lowell "Duke" Kuehn and Don Lennartson, my teaching colleagues, and my long-time friends and colleagues Sherie Story and Don Law. My heartfelt thanks to my wife Mary Eldridge who read, edited and produced many a manuscript copy. My friend and kumu, Laulipolipo'okanahele (Nova-Jean Mackenzie) often prevented me from falling into the abyss of dumbhaoleness. Mahalo to my friend, Herb Kawainui Ka'ne for his support and assistance. My thanks to Pat Soden and Chuck Fowler for their excellent advice. My presubmission editor Heather Lodge greatly improved the manuscript and my morale.

In preparing this second edition, Kevin Herridge of the Algiers Historical Society was greatly helpful. Thanks to Catherine Tuck and owner James of the Crown and Anchor in Algiers Point (Old Algiers) for arranging a seminar with Mr. Herridge. Concierge Eva Gallerani of the Hotel Monteleone in New Orleans' French Quarter guided me to many valuable sources, including the Historic New Orleans Williams Research facility, and Mary Ellen McGuire of the Jackson Square Tourism Office was a fount of information. The Mason County (WA) Historical Society assured me conclusively that Jimmie Pickett was raised in Mason County. Thanks to Susan Rohrer of the Washington State Historical Society for introducing me to Dr. John Cloud of the National Oceanographic and Atmospheric Administration (NOAA) who then provided me details of the US Coast Survey in the Civil War from the fine history written by NOAA's Skip Theberge. My friend and photographer Lloyd Wright was indispensable. Leeward Coast Press, in the persons of Layout and Graphics Editor Patrick Eldridge and Publisher Robert Payne, made it all come together.

CONTENTS

To aid the reader in tracking our two heroes, the table of contents denotes the principal character of each chapter.

Map #1) The San Juan Islands & Puget's Sound

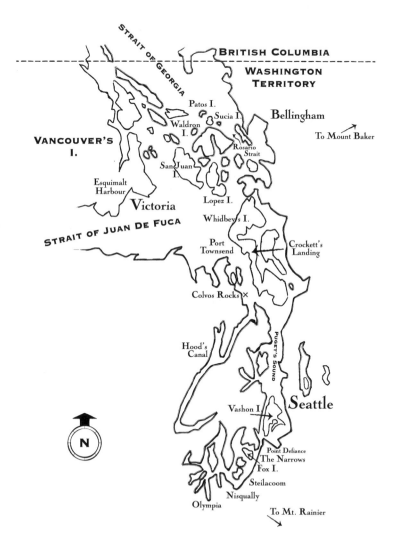

Map #2)   Camp Pickett and Cattle Point

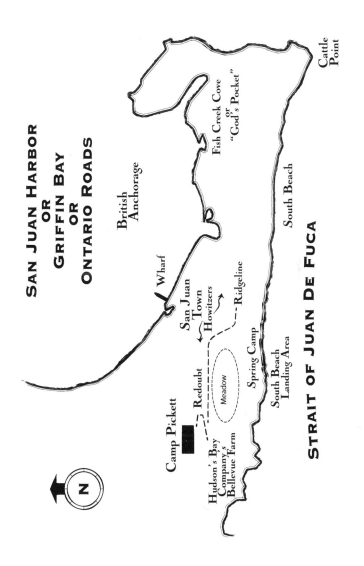

SAN JUAN HARBOR
OR
GRIFFIN BAY
OR
ONTARIO ROADS

Cattle
Point

Fish Creek Cove
or
"God's Pocket"

British
Anchorage

South Beach

Wharf

San Juan
Town
Howitzers

Ridgeline

STRAIT OF JUAN DE FUCA

Camp Pickett

Redoubt

Meadow

Spring Camp

South Beach
Landing Area

Hudson's Bay
Company's
Bellevue Farm

N

x

Map #3)   The Haida Raid

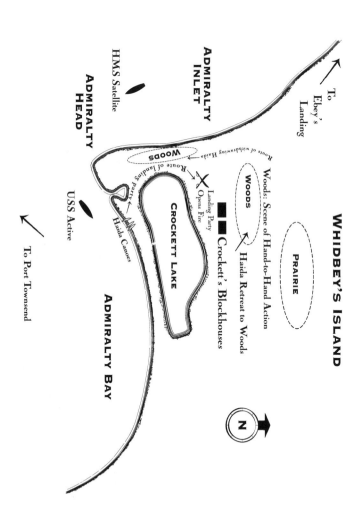

Map #4) Northeastern North Carolina

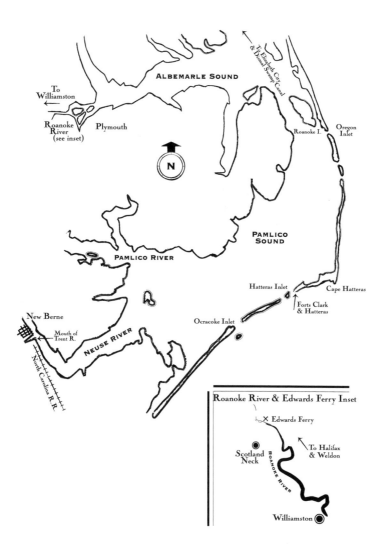

ALBEMARLE SOUND

To
Williamston

To Elizabeth City
& Dismal Swamp Canal

Roanoke
River
(see inset)

Plymouth

Roanoke I.

Oregon
Inlet

N

PAMLICO
SOUND

PAMLICO RIVER

Hatteras Inlet

Cape Hatteras

New Berne

Mouth of
Trent R.

NEUSE RIVER

Ocracoke Inlet

Forts Clark
& Hatteras

North Carolina R. R.

Roanoke River & Edwards Ferry Inset

Edwards Ferry

Scotland
Neck

To Halifax
& Weldon

ROANOKE RIVER

Williamston

Map #5) New Orleans & The Head of the Passes

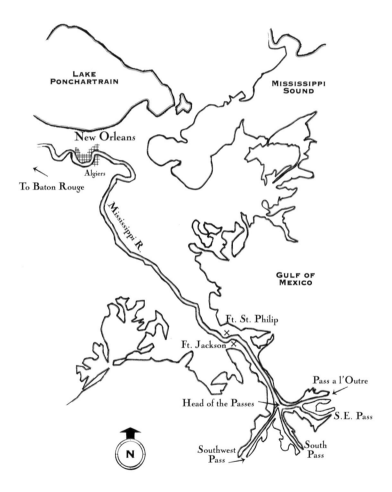

Map #6)
Northern Lesser Antilles

St. Kitts &
Nevis

Antigua

Montserrat

Guadeloupe

Iles des Saints

Marie Gallante

Dominica

St. John's

ANTIGUA

Shirley Heights

English Harbour & Nelson's Dockyard

N

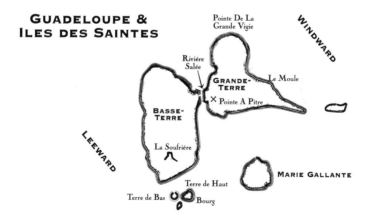

**GUADELOUPE &
ILES DES SAINTES**

Pointe De La
Grande Vigie

WINDWARD

Riviére
Salée

**GRANDE-
TERRE**

Le Moule

✕ Pointe A Pitre

**BASSE-
TERRE**

LEEWARD

La Soufriére

Terre de Haut

MARIE GALLANTE

Terre de Bas

Bourg

Map #7) Lower Chesapeake Bay

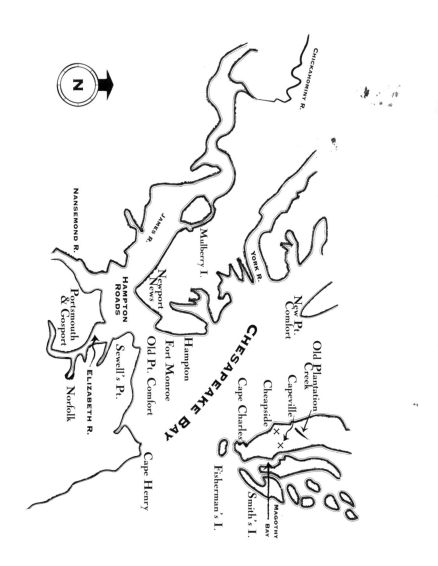

N

CHICKAHOMINY R.

NANSEMOND R.

JAMES R.

Mulberry I.

YORK R.

Newport
News

New Pt.
Comfort

HAMPTON
ROADS

Portsmouth
& Gosport

Sewell's Pt.

ELIZABETH R.

Norfolk

Hampton

Fort Monroe

Old Pt. Comfort

CHESAPEAKE BAY

Cape Henry

Cape Charles

Old Plantation
Creek

Capeville

Cheapside

Fisherman's I.

Smith's I.

MAGOTHY
BAY

Map #8) Charleston, Port Royal
& The Savannah River

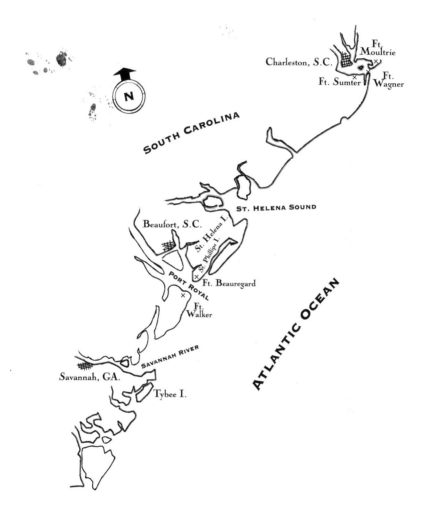

Charleston, S.C.

Ft. Moultrie

Ft. Sumter

Ft. Wagner

N

SOUTH CAROLINA

ST. HELENA SOUND

Beaufort, S.C.

St. Helena I.

St. Phillip I.

PORT ROYAL

Ft. Beauregard

Ft. Walker

ATLANTIC OCEAN

SAVANNAH RIVER

Savannah, GA.

Tybee I.

CHAPTER 1
THE HAIDA CANOE
AUGUST 1859

"Fire!" The swivel gun barked in the bow of the USS *Active's* launch. Rory glanced at Tobias St. John, the acting master, as he sighted through his pelorus, an instrument he used to measure the bearing of an on-shore rock from the launch.

"Mark!" Tobias called, noting the angle to the Waldron Island rock they used as their "fixed point" in their charting calculations. It was a boulder six feet high, left by a glacier retreating at the end of the last ice age, ten thousand years before.

Rory gave command to his oarsmen: "Stand by to give way together. Give way all!" The surge of each stroke rocked Midshipman Rory Dunbrody back and forth as he clutched the tiller bar. The eight oarsmen of the U.S. Coast Survey steamer *Active's* launch drove their blades through the choppy waters off Waldron Island, thickly forested with Douglas Fir. "Mr. St. John, has the cutter signaled?"

"Aye, Mr. Dunbrody, they've timed the flash and the report and marked their shore point angle."

"Well, now, we have our triangle's dimensions," said Rory, smiling at his fellow-officer. Knowing the speed of sound, and considering the flash of the cannon as the moment the sound of the gun started toward them, they could calculate the length of the triangle's three bases by sound. The angles from the boats to the rock ashore would complete their calculation. It was a method perfected by Charles Wilkes, the cartographer who commanded the famed U.S. Exploring Expedition from 1838 to 1842.

"Sure, now, Captain Wilkes' patented 'running survey' charting method makes this quick work," said Rory, lapsing in jest into a broader version of his usual mild Connemara brogue.

"Oh, yes, mon, you may be sure of dat," replied Tobias in kind; using his native Antiguan accent to which he could turn at will.

The two officers were virtually equal in rank in the U.S. Navy of 1859. A master's mate held a warrant from the navy. The Master, a commissioned rank below lieutenant since 1837, and his mates were the navigational specialists of the American Navy and its cousin, the Royal Navy. Tobias, as master's mate, was serving in the master's billet aboard the Coast Survey steamer as acting master. Although the traditional title, "Sailing Master" had been abolished when masters became commissioned rather than warrant officers, the title was still used as a courtesy.

Lieutenants' billets were few in the rank-top-heavy USN. But watch-keeping officers were in great demand, so midshipmen like Rory were encouraged to pass the Lieutenant's Examinations. As "passed midshipmen," they were able to assume the duties of commissioned lieutenants.

"Mr. St. John, signal the cutter to return to *Active*." The two boats had been surveying President's Channel, away from the *Active* for two days.

"Aye, aye, sir," replied Tobias. Rory commanded the ship's boat in its surveying duties while Tobias handled the technical details of their task. The side-wheel paddle steamer *Active*, assigned to the U.S. Coast Survey, was hull-down, northeast from the launch toward the eastern reaches of the Gulf of Georgia. As the cutter pulled out of sight, the topmast of the *Active* was visible, framed by the low islands of Patos and Sucia, with the still-snowcapped Cascade Mountains of Washington Territory towering over the ship.

From behind Saturna Island to the north, the launch's crew heard a chilling sound - the harmonic rhythmic chant of a Haida tribe canoe crew at full paddle.

The Haida Indians, whose home was far to the north in the Queen Charlotte Islands, were notorious for their paddling prowess and feared for their frequent raids on settlers and the southern Salish tribes.

Rory felt his stomach spasm, a visceral "thump" in the face of the oncoming Haida crew. *Shall we run, or challenge? Boldness is better,* he decided.

"Helm's a'starboard," called Rory, preparing his oarsmen for a sharp left turn toward the approaching Haida. Rory hoped firing the swivel gun would serve to drive off the Haida. The bow oar McGinty, a new and inexperienced addition to the *Active's* crew, failed to react to the warning command. His blade "crabbed", catching the water as it was squared up and forced the oar handle into his chest, lifting him off the thwart and neatly depositing him over the side and into the bone-chilling waters of the Gulf, fifty degrees Fahrenheit even in August.

"Tobias, take the helm," Rory cried as he instinctively and impetuously dove overboard, splashing toward McGinty's oar, now floating near the thrashing bow oarsman. "He can't swim a stroke!"

As he struggled to move McGinty's oar toward the struggling seaman, he swore at himself. *And aren't I the idjit, trying to save a man when I can hardly swim, meself!*

Instantly gauging the one-mile distance to the oncoming Haida, Tobias barked to the stroke-oar. "Hardcastle! Take the helm while I save these two." The lean and muscular six-foot-two ex-whaler dove overboard and with his powerful Caribbean stroke, swiftly reached the floundering Rory who was desperately trying to shove the floating twelve-foot sweep oar into the grasp of the unfortunate McGinty.

"Hold on to the sweep, Rory," implored Tobias, "while I get McGinty." Rory watched and marveled as Tobias crooked an arm beneath McGinty's chin and grasped the sweep to which Rory clung. Tobias kicked powerfully and swam toward the launch. Hardcastle steered the launch to provide a lee from the northwest wind. "Starboard side!" cried Hardcastle, "Help these men over the gun'l." .

Retching and gasping from his encounter with the frigid waters, Rory peered over the gunwale at the approaching northern raiders. "Load the swivel and fire!" he commanded. "We've only wad and powder loaded, but they don't know that." As Tobias and Rory heaved themselves over the gunwale, the two bow oarsmen tossed and shipped their oars in the center of the launch, and turned to fire the swivel gun.

"They're still coming, sir," said Hardcastle.

"You bow men, break out the round shot and load. Smartly, now!" Rory turned to Tobias. "There must be sixteen of them to our ten. I'm inclined to keep right for them, firing as we go, and try to ram and capsize them."

"I hope we can put a ball into them before collision, Rory. They're paddling a canoe made from a single log. We're the vulnerable ones in a collision." Tobias could see a musket being brandished in the Haida canoe. *If some of them stop to fire muskets, it gives us more shots with the swivel,* he thought. "I'll lay out cutlasses beside each man and load your Navy Six and mine." The 1851 Colt 'Navy' .36 caliber six-shot revolver was also the standard cavalry weapon of the day, light and easy to handle. Tobias bounded, thwart-by-thwart, to the foresheets and gathered the ten cutlasses stored there.

The distance separating canoe and launch diminished quickly; a quarter mile, then a shot from the swivel gun, two hundred yards, and then, finally, providentially, a half-pounder shot from the swivel that struck home, killing the aftermost paddler and the steeringman of the Haida canoe. The cedar canoe, absent her steering paddle, slewed broadside to the launch at the moment of impact. The bow of the launch rode over the port gunwale of the canoe and forced the starboard gunwale under, spilling the Haida into the water.

"Bow men, cutlasses! Stern six, give way together!" The keel of the launch ground over the capsized canoe. Rory, Tobias, and the two bow men seized the cutlasses and stood ready to hack at any Haida hands attempting to grab the gunwale and swing aboard the launch, but the Indian raiders were too busy staying afloat and away from the oar blades of the six sailors still rowing.

"Stern six, maintain your stroke!" To Tobias, Rory said, "We'll leave these worthies to make their way ashore on their own. *Active* is hull up and churning our way."

"We didn't lose a man!"

"Thanks to you, St. John," said Rory, pronouncing Tobias' name "Sinjin", as did Tobias and his Antiguan family's former British slave masters. "You've saved two lives and we've driven off the raiders!"

"Aye, my friend, and you really ought to let me teach you to swim. It's such a useful skill in our line of endeavor!" Tobias threw a blanket from the launch's lazarette to Rory, and looked to the northeast horizon to find the *Active* bearing down on them with paddle wheels thrashing.

Captain James Alden, commanding the survey steamer USS *Active,* stood on his quarterdeck and smiled as he watched the soggy junior officers of his launch crew ascend the companionway to the paddlewheel cover platform, enter through the entry port, and come topside to the quarterdeck of his steamer to report. "You gentlemen find the sanitary facilities of this ship inadequate for your toilette?"

"No, sir," they replied in unison.

"Very well, then. Get yourselves dry and report to me in the great cabin in ten minutes." Alden watched with almost fatherly approval as the two officers went below. Even though Rory and Tobias were each from the lowest social orders of the day, their Coast Survey status would give a boost to their navy careers. The US Coast Survey was among the elite cartographic organizations in the world, and the navy and army officers selected for it were recognized for their professional excellence.

James Alden was no stranger to the waters of the San Juan Islands and Puget's Sound. In 1841, he had served as a very junior lieutenant on the four-year U.S. Exploring Expedition under command of the brilliant but irascible Charles Wilkes and had spent six months in Puget's Sound aboard the flotilla flagship, USS *Vincennes.* The San Juans, where Alden was now adding to Wilkes' nineteen-year-old charts, had first been named by 18th century Spanish explorers. Later, Wilkes charted the islands he called the "Navy Archipelago" and on his charts the islands bore names of U.S. warships, naval heroes, and Wilkes crewmembers, superimposed on many of the Spanish names. Waldron Island, off the port bow, had been named for Wilkes' purser.

Alden's view of his former commander was that he was a superb cartographer, an uneven dispenser of justice, and a man with a mercurial temper and rampant suspicion of subordinates. Alden was determined to emulate only the first of those characteristics. His own nature was prone, at times, to over-caution, and yet he treated his command as a private fiefdom in support of the navy, even 'though the *Active* was a U.S. Coast Survey ship, and its officers were on detached duty from the Navy to the Coast Survey. This tendancy drove his US Coast Survey boss George Davidson to distraction.

Tobias and Rory, dry and newly uniformed, knocked on the cabin door, guarded by a Marine sentry. "Enter!" called Alden. "Be seated, gentlemen. I want your report, and I need to tell you of new developments in these islands, and what they may mean for this ship."

"Aye, aye, sir," replied Rory. Rory recounted the day's charting, describing the sudden appearance of the Haida war canoe, McGinty's crab and the rescue. "I went overboard after him. I think I ought not to have done, sir, what with my propensity to sink, and all." He colored slightly at the admission.

"Mr. St. John, here, bein' more thoughtful, turned the helm over to Hardcastle, dove over, and rescued McGinty and me." Rory concluded with the story of the collision. "We rolled them over and rowed away."

Alden smiled. "You must allow stronger swimmers to gain the glory of rescue, Mr. Dunbrody," said the captain. "Well done, the both of you, and a happy ending."

"Yes, sir. I need to curtail my heroics, to be sure," Rory replied.

"It could have been otherwise, you know," Alden continued. "These fierce northern tribes are still raiding and killing settlers, and Washington's been a territory these six years. They're fine seamen, for all that, paddling seven hundred miles through dangerous waters."

"Hardcastle, the stroke oar, did a fine job at the helm, sir," said Tobias. "I'll ask the bo'sun to see that McGinty gets more work at the oars."

"Excellent, Mr. St. John," said Captain Alden. "Now, I must make you both aware of recent developments. I've already done so for the other officers. As you know, a most important aspect of our work here is to lay a solid foundation for our country's claim that Canal de Haro, the

Haro Strait, fits the requirement of the 'main channel' referenced in the 1846 treaty with Great Britain. That treaty established this portion of the border between the United States and British North America, but it failed to define the 'main channel'."

"Sir, don't the Bold Saxons claim that it's Rosario Strait that they agreed to, and that the San Juan Islands are theirs, as a result?" asked Rory, with a smile.

"Yes, they do, and keep your damn Irish politics out of it!" laughed the captain. "One would hardly guess you're North Carolina born, with that accent and attitude."

"Aye, sir, being raised by my uncles in Galway and Meath makes it difficult to drawl my way into the confidence of my fellow southern-born officers," Rory countered.

"Well," said Alden, "a damned pig has just made our task more immediate. In mid-June, an American settler on San Juan, Mr. Cutlar, shot the boar of Mr. Griffin, a British neighbor and Hudson's Bay Company agent, for rooting potatoes in his garden. The British government sent a Vancouver Island magistrate to arrest Cutlar, and the Whatcom County commissioners sent their own magistrate to inform the British they had no jurisdiction on American soil. Our own General Harney heard about the pig while in Bellingham in early July, visited San Juan, and decided to put the army on the Island. The general is well-known for quick shots from the hip!"

"Have we landed troops, sir?" Tobias asked.

"Yes, on the 26th. We've landed Company 'D', Ninth Infantry, about sixty troops. I don't have to tell you that until our State Department and their Foreign Office agree on which channel is the 'main' one, based on our chart work here, this issue is clouded and in dispute. Landing troops on San Juan while its ownership is in question is incendiary. It's part of our mission to prevent escalation of the dispute."

"Are we in contact, sir?" Tobias asked.

"Yes, St. John, through Captain Fauntleroy of the USS *Massachusetts*. We spoke her while you all were surveying. The general has leased her from the navy's West Coast command because of the Indian raids and the boundary dispute. Captain Fauntleroy relayed a request from Captain Pickett of the Ninth infantry for us to assist as a dispatch vessel."

"I hope he's a prudent officer, sir," said Tobias.

"I have my doubts, Mr. St. John," said Alden. "After speaking to Captain Fauntleroy, I went ashore to meet Pickett. He's determined to fight the British if they try to land on the island, no matter how superior their force. This is the same man who, after arriving on the island, announced that British subjects had no rights there, as it's American territory."

"He doesn't sound terribly diplomatic, sir. Has the Royal Navy reacted?" Rory asked.

"Her Majesty's Ships *Plumper, Satellite,* and *Tribune* are anchored in San Juan Harbor as we speak. The *Massachusetts* has gone to Townsend to embark Major Haller and Company I of the Fourth Infantry. The revenue cutter *Jeff Davis* has sailed to Steilacoom with Harney's request for Lieutenant Colonel Casey and three more companies of the Ninth Infantry to reinforce Pickett."

A knock at the cabin door heralded a black steward with bread and cheeses. "You gentlemen must be famished with your swim and engaging the enemy," said Alden. Alden's crew reflected the racial mix of the 1859 navy, seven to twelve percent black sailors, including landsmen, ordinary seamen, and a few able seamen, stokers and stewards, but fully integrated, unlike the all-white army. St. John, as a black warrant officer, was a rarity. The navy's monthly black recruiting limit of five percent did not prevent the cumulative number of black sailors from exceeding that monthly target level.

"Sir, making an ass of myself has given me quite an appetite, to be sure," said Rory, mentally kicking himself for his impulsive action.

"Now, young Mr. Dunbrody, you did the right thing in trying to save McGinty, you just used the wrong equipment: a non-buoyant officer!" The captain offered the food basket to his junior officers. "Help yourselves, gentlemen. Tomorrow, I'm off to Victoria to see Governor Douglas of the Crown Colony, and inform him of Pickett's determination. I'm hoping he'll see how volatile the confrontation is, and exercise restraint."

Rory hungrily seized both cheese and bread. "You know the governor, do you not, sir?"

"I've met him several times. He'll be protective of the Hudson's Bay Company farm on the island, as he's still an HBC officer, but I must try to persuade him to go slowly. I know Colonel Casey is concerned with General Harney's reputation for precipitous action, particularly in the face of this confrontation with Great Britain. Silas Casey's a master tactician, but far more cautious than Harney."

"How do we respond to Captain Pickett's request for dispatch assistance, sir?" Dunbrody asked.

"We're landing you as dispatch officer at first light. You're an experienced ordnance officer, and all he has are two howitzers until he can land the 32-pounders from the *Massachusetts*. I'm sure you'll be of use to him. And your first fourteen years were spent in Ireland. Three quarters of his command are Irish immigrants right off the boat. You may be able to glean information of use to Colonel Casey. I'm certain he and Harney will be at odds over the conduct of this dispute. If Pickett errs and provokes an international incident, I need a good officer on the scene with his wits about him to prevent disaster. I want the navy in the position of knowing all we can in order to keep the lid on a boiling pot."

"Aye, aye, sir, I'll be all eyes and ears, and very little mouth," Rory promised.

The two junior officers repaired to the wardroom where Rory began to pack a small sea bag. In the midst of packing he sat down at the wardroom table across from Tobias who was reading a chart.

"Tobias," said Rory, staring piercingly and seriously at St. John. "Rory," said St. John, staring back until a huge grin spread across his face.

"Dammit, Tobias," said Rory, "I'm being serious! You saved my life!"

Tobias leaned back and smiled warmly. "And nothing could make me happier, young friend. While you, like some great, gloomy nimbo-stratus cloud, are so serious you're giving me a case of the giggles! Rejoice! Relax! Collapse in a paroxysm of laughter! It will do you a world of good." The grin stayed on his finely chiseled face. His high cheekbones accentuated the mirth in his eyes.

Tobias was seven years older than Rory. His experience as both a whaler and then a naval officer, coupled with his prodigious mathematical skills and his appointment to the US Coast Survey, had propelled him far beyond the usual level for a black sailor in a largely white navy. His father had moved to New Bedford and Tobias had followed him into whaling after Quaker schooling. Tobias was then mentored by a senior naval officer who was a New Bedford neighbor, and who encouraged him to join the navy. Rising from the ranks to one of a handful of black warrant officers had exposed him to bigotry sometimes subtle, sometimes, not. He consequently approached life with a realistic, faintly amused, and somewhat world-weary attitude.

"I know, I know," said Rory. "I'm just settling down enough to be scared out of my wits. Sure, that's an unforgiving body of water out there. What was I thinking?"

"You're young and impetuous. It suits you well. Let's hope you grow out of it before your luck runs out. I'm glad I went after you, Rory. Life's more interesting with you present."

"Thanks, Tobias." Rory extended his hand and Tobias shook it warmly.

"My pleasure, shipmate. Somehow, this takes me back to when we met, chasing William Walker through the jungles of Nicaraqua. Now get packed. I have to finish recording our bearings and distances from today." Tobias returned his attention to his calculations.

Rory packed his sea bag, remembering the 1857 Nicaraguan episode when he met Tobias as their US Navy ships confronted the American adventurer William Walker, an elected president of Nicaragua. *That was a steamy battle,* he thought as he stowed his sea bag beneath his bunk, and ran back up the companionway to the deck. His preparations for his morning landing were complete. He smiled as he realized he now had a rare moment for quiet contemplation. He sauntered to the starboard rail and gazed across Haro Strait at the blue-black mountains of Vancouver's Island Crown Colony. His athleticism, in everything except swimming, had given him a confidence reflected in his wide-set eyes and firm chin framed by his dark hair. *Tobias is right*, he thought. *I should not dwell overmuch on each mistake I make. But, I believe I'll cling to my cynicism a bit longer. Hard not to, having witnessed the British and the Church leave the Irish people to the ravages of the Famine.*

The afternoon sun warmed Rory's face. He was unaware how much his love of life, his keen humor, and his occasional irreverence served as a counterbalance to the dismaying experiences of his youth in Ireland.

CHAPTER 2
BATTLE LINES ON SAN JUAN
AUGUST 1859

The bow of the *Active's* jolly boat grounded in the soft sand of San Juan Island's south shore the next morning. Rory stepped ashore, and the boat's coxswain shoved off from the beach and guided his four oarsmen back to the steamer.

Alden had opted to land Rory below the southern shore slope rising from South Beach. Buildings of the Hudson's Bay Company's Bellevue Farm were visible to the west as they approached the shore. Almost everyone in the northwest referred to the Hudson's Bay Company as 'HBC". Some maintained that the initials really stood for "here before Christ,"

On a meadow near a spring above the beach, Captain Pickett and his sixty infantry had pitched their tents, and were positioning their two inadequate howitzers upslope and north, facing the hundred guns of the Royal Navy anchored in San Juan Harbor. Their position, which the Americans called "Spring Camp," was exposed to the wind and weather of the Strait of Juan de Fuca. It was hidden from the British ships in San Juan Harbor by a ridge extending from a high point above the HBC farm to the promontory of Cattle Point.

"Advance, and be recognized!" called the sentry on the bluff south of Spring Camp in a quavering but recognizable Wexford brogue.

"Ah, sure, 'tis Passed Midshipman Dunbrody of the USS *Active,* and God bless all here!" Rory replied.

"Pass, friend," the sentry replied, glimpsing Rory's blue serge uniform jacket and his peaked naval cap with the fouled anchor insignia.

"And where might I be findin' Captain George 'Himself' Pickett?" Rory asked.

"Sure, in the first tent to your left, sor," said the sentry.

"And thank ye most kindly, private" said Rory, striding toward Pickett's tent and thoroughly enjoying his lapse into his boyhood accents for a brief moment.

"Sir, Passed Midshipman Dunbrody, USS *Active*, reporting for dispatches as ordered, sir!" Rory stood at attention in front of Pickett's tent and waited.

"Good morning to y'all, Midshipman. Give me just a moment, if you please," drawled a cordial Virginian voice from within the tent. Moments later, a mustachioed and goateed infantry captain stepped out of the tent. Rory saluted the shorter Pickett who smiled warmly, returned the salute and said, "At ease, Mr. Dunbrody. Stroll with me to the mess tent and we'll beg my cook for a cup of coffee. He's really in charge here."

Pickett led the way toward the mess tent. Rory followed, noting the placement of two field howitzers upslope from the row of tents, and the infantry officer's carefully curled, perfumed, shoulder-length hair below his uniform cap.

"O'Boyle, two cups of coffee to wrench us from our slumbers, and meet our naval dispatch officer, Mr. Dunbrody. He sounds a bit like you!" Of course, Pickett's drawl turned 'slumbers' into 'slumbahs', and 'our' into 'ouah'.

"Yes, captain, we can't have you wanderin' about the compound with yer eyes shut, now can we?" Mess Sergeant O'Boyle grinned at Rory. "And it's a pleasure to meet you, Mr. Dunbrody. From the looks of you, you come by your name honestly."

"And the map of Ireland looks to be written on your face too, Mess Sergeant." Rory responded.

The two officers sat at the mess table and sipped their coffee, enjoying the bright sunshine of a northwest August morning. After a few minutes Pickett cleared his throat. "This is not a comfortable tactical position, Mr. Dunbrody," he said with a regretful smile.

"No, sir," Rory said, "not with more than a hundred guns facing your howitzers. 'Tis a serious imbalance, and that's a fact, me being an ordnance expert, sir, as I'm sure you can tell." Rory said with a wink.

"Are you just?" Pickett grinned. "Then I'd like some serious advice from you, in that event."

"Well, sir, you can make a statement of principle with just two howitzers, but if you wish to make our British cousins a bit more cautious, you at least need the 32-pounders aboard the *Massachusetts,*" said Rory. "A couple of batteries from the Third Artillery in Fort Steilacoom wouldn't hurt, either. I'd put them on that height," he said, pointing northwest to an outcrop above the Hudson's Bay farm.

"An excellent observation, midshipman, but one which I'm unable to accommodate until Colonel Silas Casey's command arrives. You see, Mr. Dunbrody, Major Haller, a man not enthusiastic about George Edward Pickett, has been cruising about these waters the last few days with his "I" Company of the Fourth Infantry, aboard the *Massachusetts.* Every time he's offered to land and bring Captain Fauntleroy's eight 32pounders with him, I've turned him down. For one thing he outranks me, and I'd lose command of this challengin' and delicious confrontation with Her Majesty's forces!" Pickett sighed resignedly. "Furthermore, landing *Massachusetts'* main battery might goad the British into opening fire before we can place the guns."

"That's a possibility to ponder, sir, to be sure," said Rory.

"General Harney has informed me that he's ordered Lieutenant Colonel Casey of the Ninth Infantry to reinforce our position with his three companies from Fort Steilacoom. When they appear, Mr. Dunbrody, I'll take your advice and invite Major Haller ashore, with the guns from the ship. Now, oh ordnance expert, come help me determine the position of my eight new cannon when they eventually do land."

He stood and turned to lead Rory away but suddenly stopped. "Excuse me, I see my two lieutenants. I need to give them the orders of the day."

"Aye, aye, sir." While Pickett spoke to his officers, Rory thought to himself. *Our Captain Pickett may be less a firebrand than Haller and Casey fear and Harney hopes. He's diplomatic enough to avoid an escalation despite opportunity to the contrary. Still, he's enjoying his chance to twist the British Lion's tail.*

Pickett rejoined Rory with two infantry lieutenants trailing in his wake. "Mr. Dunbrody, meet Lieutenant John Howard and Lieutenant Klaus Dieter von Klopfenstein of my command."

"The captain tells me you're a fellow southerner, Mr. Dunbrody," said Howard, shaking Rory's hand.

"Sure, he's correct in that, lieutenant," Rory said.

Von Klopfenstein gazed fixedly at Rory. "Unt how is it, Herr Dunbrody, that you have not a southern accent but sound like what some of your countrymen call a 'mick'?"

"Sure, I was raised in County Galway until I entered our Naval Academy at the age of fourteen," Rory said, his attention caught by the pronounced dueling scar on von Klopfenstein's cheekbone.

"And are the Irish such a seafaring race?" said the Prussian with a trace of a sneer.

"My Irish are," replied Rory. "My Uncle Liam taught me to sail a Galway Hooker when I was six. Sailing a forty-foot, gaff-headed cutter hauling turf, cattle, and hay bales in the waters off Connemara and the Aran Islands is a fine sailing school. And my father is a North Carolina shipbuilder! What of your accent, lieutenant? What brings a Prussian to America's shores?"

"There are not-so-many promotion opportunities in the army of Prussia these days, my young Irish. Adventure on your frontier is more frequent than on the Baltic."

"You two share that situation," said Pickett. "The only reason a passed midshipman is not a lieutenant is a lack of promotion opportunity. We must not chide our naval friend, lieutenant, for we need his help in placing the guns from the *Massachusetts* when we ultimately land them." Picket spoke to von Klopfenstein in a mock admonishing tone.

"Come, Klaus," Lieutenant Howard said. "Morning formation is upon us."

"*Ja*, John," von Klopfenstein replied. As he rose, he spoke in an amused tone to Rory, his smirk replaced by a charming smile. "You see, Dunbrody, I now must turn from one Irishman to forty others. Most of our company has just come from your 'ould sod'. I wish they could shoot straighter!"

"If the British hear you, they'll be much quicker to land." Rory said.

"Yes, lieutenant," Pickett said, "let's hold our cards on poor marksmanship closer to the vest. I know y'all will whip them into shape, even 'though they can't hardly hit the ground with their hats at present. Come, Mr. Dunbrody, while they form the company, let's take a look at the hillcrest. You can tell me what I'll need to emplace Captain Fauntleroy's guns."

"Aye, aye, captain," Rory said, "you'll need to start with plenty of timber for gun platforms." The two men left the tent and climbed the slope toward the hillcrest, past its two forlorn howitzers, the morning sun glinting off the barrels.

"These guns you'll 'ultimately' be landing, captain, they're not the best the navy has, not like the new Parrotts, Dahlgrens, or Blakely rifles, to be sure. They're old smooth-bores, and they come on wooden carriages with small, wooden wheels, designed to recoil on a wooden deck, the recoil controlled by preventer block and tackle."

Pickett digested Rory's explanation. "So, we really must construct platforms!"

"Yes, sir," replied Rory, "and I can help with that. I had a similar task while serving with the Brazil Squadron in Greytown. As I mentioned, I suspect the northeast crest of the hill, where your howitzers are, may not be the best place for them. There's no cover, sir. Perhaps further upslope, on the height there above the Hudson's Bay Company farm that I pointed out."

"Excellent, Mr. Dunbrody. I'll ask for your assistance when Colonel Casey arrives and the *Massachusetts* disgorges the Major, his company, and her cannon!"

"It will be my pleasure, sir," Rory said. "Captain Alden has asked me to extend you every assistance."

"And how did you come by your affinity for ordnance,

Dunbrody?"

"I was fortunate, sir, to be taught by an inspiring instructor, John Taylor Wood, at the Naval Academy in 1854, when he was an assistant commandant. We'd been at the academy together, earlier. He was a first classman when I was a third classman, a 'Youngster', in 1852. He was a great influence in my career." Rory said.

"I know Lieutenant Wood!" Pickett exclaimed. "He's the nephew of Senator Jefferson Davis of Mississippi. A fine family! Our revenue cutter here in Puget Sound is named to honor the senator's service as a colonel in the Mexican War."

"Yes, sir. Mr. Wood was an excellent weapons instructor. I also had the opportunity, upon graduation, to encounter Commander John Randolph Tucker in Norfolk. I took the ordnance lessons I learned from Commander Tucker with me as I joined the Mediterranean Squadron in 1855."

"Well, Mr. Dunbrody, that is a fine gunnery pedigree, indeed. Your Commander Tucker's Randolph side are neighbors of the Picketts at Turkey Island, on the James."

Pickett looked intently at Rory. "Dunbrody, you've seen service in Europe, South America, the East Indies and the Northwest. And you're a navy man. I'd like you present this afternoon at a meeting with the British. They'll be confronting me over our temerity in landin' troops on 'British' soil. The commanders of all three warships will be there - Hornby of the *Tribune,* Prevost of the *Satellite,* and Richards of the *Plumper.* I'd be grateful for your nautical presence."

"As you wish, sir. It's always interesting to see British reaction to an Irish accent," Rory said.

"Yes, we don't want them too comfortable, notwithstanding their overwhelmin' force," Pickett mused.

"Sir, with your permission, I'd like to examine that upslope position for the guns near Bellevue Farm."

"Go right ahead, midshipman. I'm off to observe the company formation."

Rory climbed the gentle slope to the ridge above the Bellevue Farm and saw immediately a natural swale, perfect for a redoubt. A parapet could be constructed without serious obstacle. He glanced southwest toward the farm. A shepherd, an older man with dark skin and silver hair, stood near several ewes and lambs. Rory walked forward and greeted him. "A good morning to you, shepherd, and flock."

"*Aloha*, good sir," replied the shepherd, his Hawai'ian face lighted with the ready smile typical of his people. "You're a sea officer, by the cut of your jib. How did you come to be cast among so many soldiers?"

"And aren't you the well-spoken shepherd and a nautical one, at that? I'm just visiting ashore." Rory returned the Hawai'ian's smile.

"The missionaries who descended on my home islands did teach us English well, I'll give them that," said the shepherd. "And the Boston whale ships that arrived in Honolulu needing crewmen knew we were great sailors. *Sailamoku*, they called us in Pidgin. Before I grew too old to reef and steer, I practiced my English on my shipmates. Here, I practice my Haida and Chinook Jargon, but I've retired from the sea. A Hudson's Bay Company shepherd need not shorten sail in a full gale."

He would be handy to have as a translator on this station, thought Rory, recalling his Haida encounter. "Do the Haida come often?" He asked.

"Often to raid, and every summer, by the hundreds, to work for HBC on Vancouver's Island."

"So, the missionaries descended on your home, did they?"

"Like the locusts in their Bible. Our customs die with our people, and the land, *a'ina*, which no one can own, is taken and owned by them and their descendants," said the shepherd with a rueful expression.

"I've never been to your islands," said Rory, "but my shipmate has. He was a New Bedford whaler and is our navigator. He talks of Polynesian navigation skills with great awe. He heard stories of islanders from the west Pacific who steered only by the stars."

"And by the waves and clouds, as well," said the Hawai'ian.

"I must tell him I've found a *Kanaka*, as you're called here. He may come ashore to talk navigation."

"It's a word from our language, *Kanaka*. It means 'person'. But here it is meant to be an insult. I would be happy to talk to your friend. I may know him if he followed the whale."

"He is a negro," Rory said.

"Many whalers were *Pa ele*. I sailed with several. I am curious, sir, of your country's intent here on the island. I hope your soldier friends do not covet our farm. The HBC would not be pleased."

"Sure, it's my belief that the farm's in no danger. I'll bid you *aloha* now." Rory and the shepherd exchanged waves as Rory headed back to the camp.

Rory slept ashore that night after signaling the *Active* that he would be ashore for a day or two to aid in preparing for gun emplacements. Captain Alden signaled that he would return in forty-eight to seventy-two hours. After a morning working with Lieutenant Howard on potential gun sites, Rory joined Pickett in his tent to await the three Royal Navy captains. Verbal fireworks commenced as the meeting started.

"Captain Pickett, I must again vehemently protest your troops ashore on British territory." Captain Prevost of the *Satellite* had a face as red as his ship's ensign as he glowered at Pickett.

"And I consider it duplicitous, sir, to pretend they're here to defend the residents against Indian attack when your two guns are aimed northeast at us, and none aimed south, where they'd more likely land," Richards of the *Plumper* added.

"Gentlemen, before I respond, let me present Passed Midshipman Dunbrody of the USS *Active*, aiding us in carrying dispatches to my superior officers, at whose behest, I might add, I am here." Pickett glanced at Captain Geoffrey Hornby, the senior officer present, who thus far had said nothing.

Pickett's trying to defuse the tension with courtesy, thought Rory to himself as he rose and stood at attention. "A pleasure to meet you, gentlemen," he said in his best parade-ground voice.

"Captain Hornby" drawled Pickett, "I leave it to you, sir. Captain Richards noted I have but two howitzers. Would I have sent the *Massachusetts* on her way without disembarking the troops and guns aboard if my intent was to provoke conflict?"

"Well, sir," Hornby replied, "the fact remains that U.S. troops occupy British soil without one Royal Marine ashore to balance the situation."

"Captain, I'm sure my superiors would strongly dispute your characterization of San Juan Island as British," Pickett said. "But surely a factor in your decision not to have Marines ashore at this time is that you outnumber us so greatly. You need not put men ashore to prove your point."

"As you're here illegally, sir, why not have both Marines and your troops ashore to peacefully maintain the status quo until our superiors resolve the misunderstanding?" asked Hornby.

"I would need instruction from my superiors before I could allow such a landing, Captain," said Pickett.

"Damn it, sir, can you not see that is the solution most efficacious in preventing armed conflict?" Hornby said, his exasperation overcoming his determination to remain calm. "It will be on your head if I determine this confrontation demands protection of British honor!"

"Then, sir, at least can you provide me with a letter summarizing the points made here so I may show the colonel and general?" asked Pickett.

"You shall have it this evening," Hornby said. "Gentlemen, we must return to our ships. I can see no fruitful result from continuing here!" And with that, Hornby and his fellow captains stormed out of the tent and headed back across the ridge and down the slope to the San Juan Harbor wharf.

As the British officers left in a collective huff, Pickett pounded his fist on the table in exasperation and glanced at Rory, who had held the tent flap open for the departing Britons. "What did you think of that, Mr. Dunbrody?"

"Sir, I think that if they intended to land, they would have. I think they want to avoid an armed confrontation as much as we. I believe they're puzzled by General Harney's belligerency, sir. It's as if the general is ignoring an important reason *Active* and Captain Alden have been on station here since 1853. We're here to gather irrefutable evidence that Haro Strait is the border, and not Rosario, as the English claim. The 1846 Oregon Treaty language is ambiguous, thus the dispute. The general seems to ignore the fact of the disagreement, sir. That can be dangerous."

"Thank you, Dunbrody," Pickett said. "I confess I was unaware of the severity of the argument. Perhaps the general will clarify this in his response to my dispatch. By the way, I intend to dismantle the Fort Bellingham buildings and re-erect them here. I'll ask you to carry a dispatch via the *Active* to Colonel Casey at Steilacoom."

"Aye, aye, sir." Rory ventured a smile. "Sure, and your lads will be happier in buildings than tents, 'though most of them never lived this well in New York tenements or Dublin slums. I'll be ready to board *Active* as soon as we see her masthead."

"Captain Alden may appear as soon as tomorrow or the next day," Pickett said. "I'm expectin' a bevy of newspaper reporters from Victoria tomorrow. I may send them your way so I can attend to my duties."

"And aren't I just the lad to talk at length and say nothing at all, at all?" Rory laughed.

"You'll be doing me a great service, Dunbrody," Pickett said, "but you may wish yourself in a storm at sea, after a taste of the Fourth Estate! They can be the orneriest folks to deal with."

CHAPTER 3
THE FOURTH ESTATE
AUGUST 1859

The next morning Rory arose to another day of blue sky, sun and a ten-knot breeze from the southwest. As he packed his small sea bag in anticipation of *Active's* arrival, he heard a voice at the tent front. "Sir, Private O'Grady, sir. Captain Pickett sends his compliments and asks if you could meet the steamer from Victoria when she docks in an hour? He'll be at formation, and wishes you to meet the journalists."

Rory stuck his head through the tent flaps. "And will I be storin' up grace in Heaven for performin' such an odious task, now, O'Grady?"

"Ah, for certain, sor, and you dazzlin' 'em all the while with yer charts and soundin's and top gallants, and such," Private O'Grady replied with a broad smile.

"You're an articulate son of Erin," said Rory.

"Aye, sor, we came over in the Famine, but my mother could read and cipher. She got a good post as a housekeeper, and I got my lessons from Father Dominic at our parish in New York," said O'Grady.

"What d'ye think of all the Saxons in the bay, private?" asked Rory.

Well, sor, would they be wantin' a war here at the end of the world any more than we would, and over a pig? Not likely, sor." said O'Grady.

"I think you've the way of it, private," Rory said. "My respects to Captain Pickett and I'll be pleased to confront his ink-stained wretches."

An hour later, Rory stood near the makeshift wharf in San Juan Harbor as the steamer from Victoria secured to the wharf and disgorged her passengers. Several carried notepads.

"Gentlemen, Captain Pickett has asked me to inquire if I may be of service to you," Rory said as he approached a gaggle of notepad-carrying passengers from the steamer.

"Who might you be?" inquired the smallest of the lot. He wore a loud tartan waistcoat beneath his stained and wrinkled jacket. A porkpie derby half a size too small was perched on his head, and he pulled a pencil from behind his ear as if he were drawing a sword.

"Mr. Rory Dunbrody, of the United States Navy, at your service, sir."

"I'm Kendall of the *Victoria Gazette*. And where is Pickett?"

"Well, now, Mr. Kendall, the captain is forming his troops for reveille, and has asked me to answer your questions," Rory said.

"Are Great Britain and America on the verge of war, Mr. Dunbrody, was it?" asked Kendall with journalistic precision.

"One can hardly imagine these two great nations, cousins, if you will, sharing a common language, at war over a pig!" said Rory. "The United States Navy is here to gather factual information on which our respective governments may base their deliberations regarding the border."

"And the army of the United States?" asked another journalist.

"Merely to safeguard the U.S. citizens dwelling in the disputed area," said Rory, "as are Her Majesty's ships in the Bay for her subjects on the island."

"Not usual to hear the Irish ascribe such noble virtue to the RN," Kendall said with a sneer.

"I'm an American, sir, despite the brogue you hear, and my country intends to deal straightforwardly with yours."

"Well, then, while we have such a quotable source, wouldn't you agree that America has enough conflict brewing with the disputes between North and South in Congress, without creating another dispute with Great Britain?" asked Kendall.

"Sir, I assure you that a dispute with your nation is not a goal of my country. The officers and men of each country will do their duty here, and will leave the question of diplomacy to our respective governments. In fact, I understand the men of our respective commands have been mingling off-duty with considerable cordiality." The *Gazette*'s reporter looked at Rory with a mixed expression, amazement, and disgust.

"I thought you were a naval officer, not a glib politician!" Kendall exclaimed. "You've ignored my question about Congress by answering a question I haven't asked!"

"Sure and wasn't I raised in County Galway? You should not be expectin' a lad raised there to be tongue-tied, should you?"

"Where I was raised", said a bulky reporter with a pronounced Cockney accent and a look of disgust, "we'd hexpect the Irish to know their place and bash 'em good when they don't!"

"And tell me then, Mr. What's Yer Name, when we may see if that dog might hunt?" Rory's smile had faded.

"Broderick's me name, and I'll teach you manners any time."

In a sudden burst, Rory growled, "Sure, I'll be visitin' Victoria, without a doubt, and I'll look for you, y' great stupid lump!"

"Fight your fights later, Broderick," said Kendall, "we're here for a story. So, Mr. Dunbrody, you are not disputing Governor Douglas of British Columbia when he claims this island for the Crown?"

"I'm doing my duty as I must. The assertions of the governor and General Harney will be settled by those far above my pay grade, to be sure. And now I must report to Captain Pickett. Will y'be talkin' to the lads of the Ninth Infantry here? I'm sure you'd be discoverin' a fresh viewpoint of the Empire, and all". As the reporters scowled, Rory smiled sweetly at them and turned to make his way up the hill and over the ridge to Spring Camp.

"Dunbrody!" said Pickett as Rory reported. "How did you fare with the press?"

"I took a page from your book of last week, and spoke pleasantly and reassuringly at length, while saying nothing, sir."

"Well done, midshipman. My lookouts have just reported the topmast of *Active* in sight. I'll ask that you carry these dispatches to Colonel Casey, reporting on the establishment of the Bellingham buildings here, and cautioning him not to land troops and guns in San Juan Harbor under the guns of the British. I fear it would jar them from their tolerant mood. If he could land the troops and guns at night, up the South Beach bluff and out of sight of San Juan Harbor, the stores might be unloaded later at the wharf." Pickett handed Rory a packet, and returned his salute. Rory strode to his tent, slung his sea bag and walked over the crest and down the hill to the wharf to await *Active*.

It was just before sunset when Rory boarded the Coast Survey steamer. "Tobias, where has *Active* been the last week?" Rory unpacked his sea bag in his cubbyhole compartment off the officers' communal area, the wardroom. On a larger ship the wardroom would have been the province of the senior officers only, and the junior warrant officers and midshipmen would have lived around and in the gunroom. *Active* was too small for both. Tobias sat watching at the traditional large table in the center of the wardroom around which the officers ate and socialized.

"We've completed our charting of San Juan and Presidents' channels. There's no doubt, given the data, that Haro Strait is the main channel as referenced in the 1846 treaty. It's deeper than its competitors, and it separates Vancouver Island from U.S. territory." Tobias spoke in his usual New Bedford accent, his uniform tunic unbuttoned and his black skin glistening with sweat in the August heat of the unventilated wardroom. "How did you find our army cousins?"

"As amazing a few days as I've ever spent, my friend. Pickett was seriously uninformed about the severity of the border dispute. I suspect he's not given to serious study. From the way his camp is exposed to weather and gunfire, I can readily believe he graduated last in his class at West Point!"

Tobias grinned widely. "Easy enough for you to say, oh, first-in-your-class at Annapolis." Growing serious, he ventured, "If he's uninformed about the dispute, his superiors must be, also," said Tobias.

"Harney apparently is ignoring the possibility that anyone aside from the U.S. could mount a legitimate claim to San Juan Island," Rory responded. "The British are understandably irritated by that attitude. Fortunately, Pickett's had the good sense not to land reinforcements under the noses of Her Majesty's minions, and they've been able to be tolerant of our presence without their honor being besmirched enough to open fire."

"Are we on our way to Nisqually then, in our dispatch mode?" Tobias asked.

"Wouldn't be surprised, Tobias. I'm to report to Captain Alden in ten minutes. Pickett wants us to warn Colonel Casey not to land under the Sasanachs' noses, hoping not to provoke them."

"I'm continually amazed at the large number of words the Irish have for the English. Come below again when you're finished," Tobias said, "We've received mail from the San Francisco steamer. Your sister Siobhan sent a letter, and so did my father. Judging from the news in mine, the national debate is still heating up."

"Sure, and I'll be brief, then, with the captain. Oh, and I found a kindred spirit of yours in the guise of a Kanaka shepherd for the HBC. He was a whaler in his youth and knows about that wayfaring star-compass navigation you always marvel at. He said he'd be glad to talk to you. He also speaks the Haida language. That could be useful! Well, now, I'm off!" Rory bounded up the companionway aft of the wardroom, buttoning his tunic as he went.

"Passed Midshipman Dunbrody, reporting, sir." Rory stood at attention before Alden in the great cabin.

"Did you enjoy dry land, Mr. Dunbrody?" Alden asked.

"Lots of mud and rocks, sir, just like home in Connemara." When Rory had completed his report, Alden mused for a moment.

"I'm mindful, midshipman, that home is also New Berne, North Carolina. You seemed to get on well with your fellow southerner."

"Yes, sir, he seemed genuinely grateful for my gun-siting suggestions, and he's an affable fellow. He strikes me as a fun-loving type. His men seem to like him. Perhaps more shrewd than intelligent, and I think not duplicitous in his dealings with the British. His men seem skeptical about either side wanting to bring on war over a pig, sir."

"A good report, Dunbrody. With that hothead general on one hand and Major Haller's conspiracy theories on the other, we've a situation that bears watching. When I spoke to Governor Douglas in Victoria earlier this month, he was taken aback as I described Pickett's resolve to fight against any odds, but he was unyielding in pressing his case for British possession of the island. I think your presence on the island will help serve to keep a lid on this boiling pot! I'm inclined to recommend to Colonel Casey that we assign you as naval liaison to Pickett."

"Sir, you're taking a chance on my Irish temper with that spalpeen Prussian subaltern in the mix, dueling scar and all."

"I hesitate to ask what a 'spalpeen' is, and I concede the point on your temper. Still, you've been aboard almost a year. Usually, I can trust your judgment and demeanor. I don't suppose you disclosed to the Prussian your prowess with the sword?"

"No, sir, I chose to keep the memories of Grandfather Fearghus' saber drills to meself, not wantin' to provoke a contest. Von Klopfenstein's an odd sort, one moment affable, and the next, condescending and menacing."

"Well, Mr. Dunbrody, I'm sure you can deal with him. We'll see what Colonel Casey says about you serving as naval liaison when we encounter him. I'll have the officer of the watch set a course for Nisqually immediately."

Tobias was reading his letter from his father as Rory re-entered the wardroom. "My father says debate in Congress has gone beyond name calling, descending into canings of one member by another, and all of the members are armed while in their chamber." Tobias continued to read his father's letter aloud.

> *All Hell is breaking loose! The northern states are being accused of trying to destroy the agrarian South and the Southerners are accused of living from the sweat of an enslaved people. Next year's presidential campaign is shaping up to be a prelude to disunion, depending on whom the parties select as candidates.*

Tobias folded the letter and placed it in his letterbox. "That wasn't good news." He handed an envelope to Rory. "Here's your letter from your sister, Siobhan."

"Thanks, shipmate." Rory opened and read his letter swiftly. He summarized its contents for Tobias. "My brother, Timothy, has been promoted captain. His unit's at Fort Kearny. And Da's shipyard has just launched another schooner for the coastal trade."

"All's well in New Berne, it seems," said Tobias. "Now, tell me more about your Kanaka whaler. Before I joined the Navy, I spent many days in Lahaina and Honolulu aboard New Bedford whale ships. That's where I heard rumors of an ancient navigation method with neither chart nor instrument. The Hawai'ians are great sailors, and much sought after for the whaling crews."

"Well, now, our Hawai'ian friend has the white hair of a venerable elder, dark skin, and doesn't much care for missionaries."

"A natural result of exposure to the cream of the Protestant missionary corps, no doubt." Tobias sighed. "I've seen them in action as a whaler in Hawai'ian ports. They're quick to remove enjoyment from life, and threaten punishment to those who cling to joy."

"When was your last visit to the Hawai'ian isles?"

"On our way to Puget's Sound, Active stopped to visit Commander Wilkes' astronomical observatory site atop Mauna Kea. There are clear skies, indeed, at thirteen thousand feet. But it seems to me, Rory, that priest or pastor, the front-line clerics generally do good works. It's when the church hierarchies turn their attention to perpetuation and profit that the people suffer."

"Good evening, gentlemen," said First Lieutenant West, entering the wardroom. "Good to have you back aboard, Mr. Dunbrody, although I'm uncertain how long you'll be with us. Mr. St. John, here, has been looking forward to giving you back the watch-keeping duties he's assumed in your absence."

"Aye, sir, I'm not sure myself, but I'm happy to stand my watch, again, to be sure. I'm on the point of losing my sea-legs." Rory winked amiably. The steamer, as it had begun to cross the Strait of Juan de Fuca, had started to pitch and roll, as if to put Rory's sea legs to the test.

"Are you not more useful to this great country ashore, Rory?" Tobias asked. "From what I understand, the army and the British both need watching."

"It's been interesting, and that's a fact," said Rory. "Sir, I've told the captain, the army's worried that landing men and artillery in front of the Royal Navy might provoke a broadside or two."

"I suspect the Nisqually contingent will be circumspect when they land. Colonel Casey's nothing if not cautious," the first lieutenant replied. "Did I hear you gentlemen discussing the clouds of disunion?"

"Yes, sir, my father sends word from New Bedford of mutual distrust about to unravel the fabric of the Union," Tobias said.

"Ah, yes," said Lieutenant West, a thoughtful man given occasionally to pontification. "A complicated situation.

"Yes, sir, " Tobias said, "my father says each party's trying to win election by emotional appeals for or against abolition."

"Let's be thankful that our immediate duties call us from unpleasant contemplation," West said. "Mr. Dunbrody, you'll take the first dog watch, and Mr. St. John will be left with only one full-time task, piloting us up-Sound to Nisqually."

Passed Midshipman Phillip C. Johnson, officer of the watch, paused on the companionway. "Mr. West, sir, we're abeam Port Townsend. You asked to be called, sir."

"Thank you, Mr. Johnson. St. John, come with me to the quarterdeck and we'll talk about the tide in the Narrows and arrival time."

Rory returned to his sister's letter.

My Dearest Brother:

Brother Tim is worried about the talk of disunion. He's had the advantage of growing up in Carolina, as have I. But what a two-edged sword his upbringing is, with all the push-and-pull between his love of New Berne and North Carolina, and his love of the army and his valor in the Mexican War rewarded, and all.

Tim had started his army career in the North Carolina Militia and still had strong ties to his comrades there, even though an army Regular. Rory wondered how Tim would choose between the army and his North Carolina roots. *May we never have to make the choice,* he thought as he returned his sister's letter to his stationery case.

CHAPTER 4
THE WRECK AT COLVOS ROCKS
AUGUST 1859

USS *Active* had begun her run to Fort Steilacoom at sunset, crossing the Strait of Juan de Fuca in darkness, and in the face of a gathering westerly, the spawn of a summer low-pressure area approaching Washington Territory from the Gulf of Alaska. As *Active* entered Admiralty Inlet, she pitched and rolled in a quartering sea of five- to six-foot waves, the wave-tops whipped into a froth of whitecaps by the thirty-five-knot wind, now shifted to northwest.

"Our position, Mr. St. John?" Captain Alden shouted his question over the roar of the wind to Tobias who clung to a stanchion on the quarterdeck. One arm was curled around the stanchion, leaving both hands free for the new-fangled night-binoculars, easier to handle in rough weather than the night telescope.

"We're just south of Port Townsend, abaft to starboard, sir. It's about an hour to sunrise. We're abeam of Marrowstone Island, with Whidbey's Island to port. I've the glasses trained on the bearing for Colvos Rocks, south, southwest, a half south. I thought I saw a flare a minute ago through the spume, sir, and now I'm seeing a light where no light should be. We may have a ship in trouble, captain!"

"Very good, Mr. St. John, keep me apprised. Mr. Dunbrody, have the bo'sun stand by with a boat's crew, a leadsman, and a man with the heaving line. Have a detail below pay out a towing hawser."

"Aye, aye, sir." Rory welcomed the escape from the lashing spray and went below to find the boatswain.

The *Active* pitched and rolled in the northwest wind blowing at half-gale force. The *Active's* officers clung to stanchions, shrouds, and the taffrail on the quarterdeck as they tried to steady their night glasses on the steamer aground on Colvos Rocks. The *Active,* hove-to and trying to maintain a station to windward of the rocks, shuddered and pounded in the wrack of the storm in shoaling waters. Captain Alden called to Rory. "Mr. Dunbrody, take the launch and see if you can bring it alongside her. I can see some survivors in the lee of the deck cabin."

"Aye, aye, sir. Hardcastle, get the boats' crew to the lee side." Several men, under the tutelage of the boatswain, tailed on to the halyards controlling the main gaff, lifting the launch out of the chocks amidships, and then, hauling the gaff peak perpendicular to the gunwale, carefully lowered the launch over the lee side while two other line details controlled the boat's descent with lines to her bow and stern. The eight oarsmen and Rory went below to the paddle wheeler's entry port, emerging on the paddle wheel platform, then clambered down the hinged ladder and into the boat. They cast off the lines, rowing out of the lee and into the wind-whipped waves.

Drawing nearer to the grounded steamer as dawn began to light the scene, Rory saw her situation clearly for the first time. He glimpsed the name *Canute* through the spume and wrack as it appeared on the side of the deck cabin. Her bow was on the rocks and quartering into the north wind. Her stern was awash, and a succession of six-foot waves lifted and pounded her hull.

Twelve or thirteen crew and passengers crowded the small lee afforded by the deck cabin. "Port to back, starboard to row," called Rory to his crew. "We're going back, men! We'll never lay alongside in that pounding. We need a heaving line!" The launch returned to the lee side of *Active,* hooking on to the paddlewheel platform. Rory climbed the companionway and through the entry port, reporting to Allen on the quarterdeck.

"Sir, she's aground and pounding and I don't think she'll float if we tow her off. We need a swimmer, blocks and a shackle and clip. We can't get the boat along side in the sea. We'll have to get a line across, keep it taut as we can with the crew backing down, and use a bowline on a bight as a bo'sun's chair, with a line rove through two blocks to haul it back and forth. We'll be able to keep our bow into the wind. That'll help the oarsmen."

"How will you first haul the shackle and bowline to the wreck, Mr. Dunbrody?" The captain had to shout to be heard in the wind.

"We'll need a good man to go hand-over-hand across to help the crew set up and explain the process. A swimmer, in case he's washed off the line. And because of so many survivors, we'll need the cutter standing by to ferry them from the launch to *Active*. Otherwise, their exposure will be too lengthy and the launch too crowded."

"Very well, Mr. Dunbrody," he sighed, "make your selections and preparations. Mr. West, maintain station."

"Captain, I'm the strongest swimmer aboard. Let me go, please." Tobias stood at the quarterdeck rail before Alden, imploring him.

"Sure, and he's right, sir," said Rory. "Mr. St. John could make all the difference. And I'd be grateful for six extra men to haul the bowline from the *Canute* to the launch and back."

"Oh, very well, Mr. Dunbrody, see to it, if you please." Alden turned to shout the orders. "Have a care, Mr. St. John. Mr. Johnson, have the cutter standing by to take off the first group of survivors from the launch. Mr. Dunbrody, fire a flare when you're ready for the cutter."

"Aye, aye, sir." The launch's crew shoved off moments later, blankets, block and tackle, and spare seamen aboard. A gray dawn disclosed more details of the wrecked steamer. They took station thirty feet from the wreck, bow into the wind, and the eight oarsmen rowing to keep from losing ground. "Let me try the heaving line, Rory," said Tobias, "It's a skill left over from my whaling days."

"Very well, friend Tobias. Mind your balance, now." Bow into the wind, the oarsmen pulled steadily, to keep enough distance between launch and wreck.

Tobias stood in the stern, knees braced against the thwart, and whirled the line with the monkey fist spliced into the end 'round and 'round his head. Momentum having built, he let go. The heavy lead monkey fist carried the line forty feet across the waves and over the after edge of the *Canute*'s deckhouse. Eager hands seized it and made it fast to a stanchion on the port rail. The launch crew bent the thin heaving line to a stronger line and signaled the steamer's crew to haul it across. The launch crew line handlers secured that line to the launch's starboard stern bitt. The lifeline grew taut as the launch, bow in the wind, pulled away from the wreck to a forty-foot distance, tethered by the lifeline.

Tobias secured a second line around his waist, leaving both ends in the launch, with the bight around his waist holding a shackle, clip and block. Upside-down, his legs wrapped around the lifeline, the muscular Antiguan pulled himself hand-over-hand toward the wreck. Waves submerged him at regular intervals, and he timed his breathing accordingly.

"Pay out that line," called Rory to the launch crew in the stern sheets. The sailors eased the two ends of the second line around Tobias' waist so as not to impede his progress. He reached the wreck and was hauled in by the steamer's crew.

"Good God, man, you must be done in!" The *Canute*'s captain looked at Tobias with some wonderment. Tobias spoke to the drenched survivors as the *Canute* pounded in the breakers.

"You men, secure this block to that stanchion." A seaman took the block, with the second line rove through it, and anchored it to a port side stanchion. The launch crew clipped a shackle to the lifeline, attaching a knot known as a bowline on a bight. The knot formed two loops, one serving as a seat and the other as a back brace. They heaved on one end of the continuous line running through the first block, now secured aboard the wreck.

The looped knot served as a seat, the equivalent of a boatswain's chair. It was secured to the lifeline just run between wreck and launch by a sliding shackle. Two lines were attached to the shackle. One ran through the block or pulley now attached to the wreck's stanchion, and then back to the launch. The other ran from the shackle straight to the launch. The launch crew could move the looped "seat" back and forth from launch to wreck in either direction, depending upon which line they hauled in.

Turning to the *Canute's* captain, Tobias asked, "Sir, what happened?"

"The lifter on the port paddle cam fractured. We'd no power on the port side and couldn't hold her against the wind. Her back's about broke, I'll warrant!"

"How many passengers, sir?"

"Two men and two women. And the assistant engineer has a broken arm."

"We'll take the women and the assistant engineer first. None of them will have the strength to hold on to the line. I'll ride over with each. I'll rely on you to send the others, sir."

"Very well, mister," the captain said. "We'll get them off. I'm not losing anyone off my ship! I'll see you aboard, or I'll see you in Heaven!"

Tobias shouted to the survivors above the wind, holding the bowline on a bight. "Sit in this lower loop. Lean back against this upper loop and wrap your arms around it. Clutch the line just under the clip. You'll get wet, but it's only forty feet. I'll ride with the engineer and the women, and hold on for them. You first, Ma'am," he said to a small woman of middle years.

Tobias sat on the knot's lower loop and extended his arms to the woman, who smiled wanly, cast a look at the launch forty feet away, and sat in Tobias' lap, trembling, her eyes tightly shut. He put his right arm around her waist, his ankles around hers, and held the line below the clip with his left hand.

Rory, watching carefully, called "Haul away, line crew. Oarsmen, put your backs to it!" He knew this was the moment when his plan would prove itself, or fail as Alden had feared. The launch crew tailed on to line running through the launch's block, hauling Tobias and his charge through the waves as the eight oarsmen pulled with a will to tighten the lifeline. As they reached the launch, Tobias put his lips near the woman's ear. "You were very brave, ma'am, well done!" The line crew lifted the woman from Tobias' grasp and over the stern of the launch.

"Two more for me, Dunbrody, and then they'll come on their

own!" Rory acknowledged Tobias' shout with a wave and a broad smile.

"Run Mr. St. John back across, men." The haulers heaved on the other end of the continuous line and Tobias traversed the forty-foot gap, half submerged for much of it.

The two women huddled, shivering, below the gunwales of the launch with blankets and tarpaulin coats around them as Tobias brought the injured engineer across, and climbed over the stern transom himself, collapsing in a heap, exhausted. "I can go back, Rory," he declared, shivering and trying to warm himself. "Just give me a minute."

"Nonsense! Blanket for Mr. St. John, there," cried Rory, raising the flare pistol and firing the signal for the cutter to cast off from *Active*. "Avast hauling. Haulers, relieve the bow six. You relieved oars, commence hauling."

Four more survivors had reached the launch by the time the cutter lay across its bow. "Mr. Johnson, I'd be obliged if you'd take these seven survivors and Mr. St. John to *Active.*" Before Tobias could protest, Rory said, "No argument, now, Mr. St. John. I'm in command here, and you've been under water for the last half hour." The cutter's crew helped the survivors into the cutter. Midshipman Johnson's face was a mask of determination, tinged with fear, as he bought his boat around through the trough of the waves and into the wind, headed back to *Active*.

Rory shouted encouragement to his launch's crew, soaked to the skin, as they transferred the six remaining crewmembers of the *Canute*. As the fifth of the crew members, wearing the soggy remnants of an officer's uniform coat, was pulled in to the launch, he gasped to Rory, "the wreck is shifting, ja, you must hurry and get Captain Jacobson off!"

Rory looked up to see the wreck of the *Canute* slide off the rocks and into deep water, stern first. The captain gave a salute to Rory and then was lost to sight in the debris and the wind-whipped waves.

Rory turned to the last survivor. "Can the captain swim?"

"No, not a stroke," the officer replied in a marked Swedish accent. "He yoost would say, 'when my time comes, it comes.'"

"Mr. Dunbrody, the wreck's dragging us under!" Hardcastle, the lead seaman of the line-tending crew, had an axe in hand. "Cut those lines, Hardcastle," Rory ordered. "We'll take a short swing to see if the captain's afloat," Rory said to the Swede, "But I can't go far to loo'ard. This crew is too exhausted to make it very far back to windward. I'm sorry. We may be able to do a longer search from *Active*. The wind's dropping."

"What's your name, sir?" Rory asked the Swedish officer.

"Knudson, the chief engineer," he replied. "You've done everything you could and more, lieutenant," Knudson said, inadvertently promoting Rory to the rank he was qualified to hold.

In mid afternoon, *Active* headed south from Colvos Rocks in a diminishing sea, the wind having dropped to fifteen knots. Captain Alden had made an exhaustive search with *Active* in the waters to leeward of the rocks, after the boats and their crews had been recovered. Captain Jacobson was not to be found. Alden had turned his cabin over to the women survivors, while the male survivors were quartered in the wardroom. They had been fed, clothed, and were now sleeping, except for a rather distraught Chief Engineer Knudson. Lieutenant West had the watch, and Alden had been invited by the wardroom mess to share its hospitality while the women survivors used his cabin. Rory and Tobias, wearing dry clothes and wrapped in blankets, discussed the rescue as they warmed. Knudson listened intently.

"What a dam' fine commander that Captain Jacobson was," said Rory.

"True, my friend. He stayed aboard to the last man, in the tradition of the sea," said Tobias. "I hope I have the courage to do my duty thus when my time comes."

"You'll die in bed, in your seventies, with a jealous husband at your door," said Rory with a wry smile.

Captain Alden sat in the comfortable chair usually occupied by the president of the wardroom mess, the first lieutenant, Mr. West. "After watching Mr. St. John's endurance and strength today, Mr. Dunbrody, I'd agree with your prediction. You two young gentlemen should be proud of your performance today. You both look a bit downcast. You must realize you've done what few could do today."

"Sir, I think we're disappointed that we couldn't save Captain Jacobson," Rory responded.

"Aye, sir, he was so steadfast," said Tobias, "keeping his crew and passengers safe at his own risk."

"Ya, but as I told the lieutenant in the boat," said Knudson, "you all did everything that could be done. Captain Jacobson knew that. I know he was grateful. You're both fine seamen."

"Maritime enterprise, gentlemen, like politics, is the art of the possible." Alden smiled. "I appreciate you both having high expectations. You're allowed to lower them after the fact. Remember, we're dealing with the sea, which has more surprises than we can ever anticipate."

CHAPTER 5
RENDEZVOUS AT PT. DEFIANCE
AUGUST 1859

    As the ship ran south through the reaches of Puget Sound, Alden anchored to land the *Canute*'s survivors at the village of Seattle. Before Knudson left the ship, he had insisted that Rory and Tobias take his address. "The missus and I have a little place outside Trenton, New Jersey. If you're ever there, please come by. I want my wife to meet the men who saved me."

    As they headed south from Seattle's Elliott Bay, Tobias, ever the navigator, asked Alden, "Are most of the geographic names here in the Sound ones that were placed by the Wilkes Expedition, sir?"

    "Right you are, Mr. St. John. Elliott Bay, here, was named for a midshipman, Sam Elliott, and Colvos Rocks, where we carried out our rescue, was named for George Colvocoresses, a middie of Greek descent. Spelling was not Mr. Wilkes' strong point, so he shortened George's name to Colvos."

    It was slack tide in the morning sun as the *Active* rounded Point Defiance and headed into the Narrows, just miles north of the old Hudson's Bay Company post at Nisqually and Fort Steilacoom, home of the Ninth Infantry, the Fourth Infantry, and the Third Artillery. Tobias stood on the quarterdeck, pelorus in hand, as he checked his bearings in this most narrow part of Puget's Sound, bordered by towering bluffs thickly forested with fir, spruce, and madronna.

"We should continue this heading, Mr. Johnson," Tobias said to the officer of the watch.

"Very well, Mr. St. John," Johnson replied.

"Steamer in sight just abeam of Anderson Island," called the masthead lookout.

"Aye, aye," responded Johnson. He trained his telescope on the approaching vessel, amid the liberal sprinkling of forested islands dotting this part of the inland sea. "Looks like the *Julia*," he said to Tobias. "Would you be so kind as to inform the captain?"

"As you wish," Tobias said, and bounded below to the captain's cabin.

"Sir, the officer of the watch's respects, and the *Julia*'s in sight on a course for the Narrows. We're just abeam Fox Island, sir."

"Very well, Mr. St. John, I'll wager Colonel Casey and his command are aboard, in response to Harney's orders. I'll be on deck directly. Please ask Mr. Johnson to signal we've dispatches for Casey aboard, and call the first lieutenant."

The captain trained his glass on the approaching *Julia*, as Lieutenant West relieved the officer of the watch in anticipation of Alden leaving the ship. "Lieutenant West, I'll take the jolly boat from the davits, so we'll not need to unship the main boom for my gig."

"Aye, aye, sir," West replied. "Bo'sun, clear away the jolly boat and man the side!"

Alden turned to his officers, assembled behind him on the quarterdeck. "Well, gentlemen, Colonel Casey certainly has much of his command aboard. We'll heave to while I discuss the dispatches we carry with him. Dunbrody, stand by. It's likely we'll call for your presence." As the captain strode to the side and climbed into the waiting jolly boat, the sideboys in white gloves came to attention and the boatswain blew his call on his silver boatswain's pipe.

"I'll wager you'll be packing your sea bag again, friend," Tobias said.

"Time will tell," Rory said. "I'm just getting used to watch-standing again." Rory felt a thrill of anticipation and a sinking feeling in his stomach at the same time. Being charged by his superiors with keeping the lid on a boiling diplomatic confrontation was exhilarating, but daunting as well.

As Alden boarded the steamer *Julia*, her captain greeted him. "No sideboys in the Merchant Service, I'm afraid, captain," he said. "Colonel Casey asks that you join him in his stateroom." Alden made his way below through the deck crowded with infantrymen and artillerymen from Casey's command.

"Captain Alden, good morning!" Colonel Silas Casey rose from a table covered with paperwork and shook hands with Alden. "I understand you have dispatches from Captain Pickett, and I'd be grateful for your assessment of his situation. Please sit down. I'll ask the steward for coffee."

Alden quickly explained Pickett's concerns regarding the troop landings. Casey paused for a moment, and said, "Captain, I'll come right to the point. Major Haller is worried over the possibility that General Harney, a Southerner, may believe that conflict with the British would be helpful to those who advocate seceding from the Union. And Haller suspects that Pickett is a part of a conspiracy to create such a conflict, as Pickett has refused to let Haller land his troops from the Massachusetts. While your man Dunbrody's report indicates Pickett may just be doing his duty, I'd still like to have another set of eyes and ears there, particularly after I return to Steilacoom. Can you spare Dunbrody? And, can he do the job?"

"Colonel, I can spare him, although I suspect that the general is more hot-headed and self-aggrandizing than conspiratorial. As I reported, Dunbrody and Pickett seem to get on well, and Dunbrody, 'though Southern-born, and Irish-raised, understands well the importance of avoiding war with the British. He's a steady and capable officer."

"Excellent," said Casey. "Perhaps it's natural for me to trust an Irishman," he smiled. "My family's from County Tyrone. If you'd signal for him to join us, we'll give him his orders together."

"You're being summoned, Mr. Dunbrody." Lieutenant West lowered his telescope. "Take the jolly boat and report to the Captain on board the *Julia*."

"Aye, aye, sir." Rory stepped to the rail and waited for the jolly boat, making its way back to the *Active*.

Rory reported to Captain Alden and Colonel Casey in the captain's cabin of the *Julia*, removed from the noise and froth of the steamer's side-wheel paddles.

"Mr. Dunbrody, Colonel Casey has concluded that you should be assigned as naval liaison to the army at San Juan Island until the colonel is confident that the situation has stabilized." Alden nodded encouragingly at Rory. "I concur with the colonel's decision. You'll report to whoever commands the detachment there until further notice. That will be the colonel, initially, as soon as we can land his contingent."

Casey cleared his throat. "There are a number of reasons for this decision, Mr. Dunbrody. Your commanding officer tells me you clearly understand the need for prudent response to British involvement here. You're not in my command, and I need an objective source of information, especially during times when I will be off the island, attending to my other duties. Yet you get on well with Captain Pickett, you have an understandable skepticism of British motive, and you're well versed in gunnery. That will be extremely useful to me until Lieutenant Henry Robert, my senior engineering officer, can arrive next week, and, I'm sure you'll be helpful to him, as well."

"It's most kind of you, sir, to explain my assignment so thoroughly," Rory said.

"*Active* will proceed north with *Julia*," Alden told Rory. "We intend to arrive at daybreak and push this side-wheeler's bow as close to South Beach as possible. I'll ask you to assist the colonel's artillery battery officers here aboard *Julia* in landing their howitzers. You and I will return now to *Active*. You can pack your sea bag and reboard *Julia*. I'd be grateful if you'd spend the trip down-Sound discussing the details of the landing with the battery officers."

"Aye, aye, sir. And aren't I the expert, now, at sea bag packing?"

"You'll be a better man for it, Dunbrody," smiled Alden. "By your leave, colonel?"

"Thank you, captain. I'll see you at morning's light," said Casey.

The two paddle-wheel steamers chugged northward, down-Sound, with the verdant shores of Vashon Island to port. August evening sunlight glinted off the waves of the Sound and the peaks of the Olympic Mountains to the west, almost bereft of snow in mid- summer. Rory packed his three-foot sea bag. "I think, Tobias, I'll be needin' the larger bag for this shore duty," Rory said.

"Just make sure you build the parapet high enough to protect a cowering, six-foot Irishman," said Tobias from the wardroom table.

"Faith, and if I'm cowerin', can't we reduce the height considerable?"

"I presume you'll be riding any horse you can lay your hands on about the island in the manner your Uncle Francis taught you? How did your uncle come to be a great horseman?" Tobias asked.

"Sure, his is one of a thousand fine stables between Roscommon and Meath," Rory replied.

"*Adieu, mon ami.* Keep *Active* off the rocks." Rory climbed the companionway to the deck.

Passed Midshipman Johnson, officer of the deck, signaled *Julia* to heave to while Rory was transferred to the stern-wheeler. Each vessel backed its paddle wheels, and stopped its progress as effectively as a sailing ship backing its foresail. Rory lowered his sea bag to the jolly boat's crew. Saluting the officer of the deck and the national ensign, he disappeared down the companionway and out the entry port to the jolly boat below, glancing at the little village of Seattle on the forested shores of Elliott Bay, now abeam. Rory settled into the stern sheets of the jolly boat as it headed toward the *Julia*.

CHAPTER 6
THE GUNS OF SAN JUAN
AUGUST 1859

"Handsomely, now, damn your eyes, you men. You near dropped it through the launch!" Rory sighed with relief as a howitzer barrel of the Third U.S. Artillery, in a sling, plummeted and then stopped just feet from the *Active*'s launch alongside the *Julia*. "Mr. Johnson, would you be so kind as to ask Captain Alden for a detail of experienced seamen to assist the artillery and the *Julia*'s crew with unshipping these guns?"

The crew of the merchant steamer could not provide enough men to lift the howitzers into the boats. *Julia*'s captain suggested using the soldiers of the artillery battery already aboard. The soldiers unfortunately were inexperienced in the complex business of lowering a two-thousand-pound gun barrel into a fragile wooden launch alongside. They had eased the line, which was rove through the peak fitting on the *Julia*'s main gaff, in fits and starts. The whip end of the line bore a cradle in which a howitzer barrel was slung. As the soldiers lowered away, it jerked and dropped like a live thing.

"Easy, now, Mr. Bo'sun, just a few more feet and we'll send the launch on her way, instead of to Davy Jones." The small gap safely closed. The barrel securely in the launch, Rory turned to the *Julia*'s boatswain. "Avast heaving and stand the detail down, Bo'sun, 'til we can add some men from the *Active*."

Although steamers often did not rely on sail, their masts and spars were critical in launching and recovering ten-ton cutters and longboats, or, as in this case, the guns of Battery "A", Third Artillery.

"Captain's sending a detail," said Johnson.

"Thank you, Mr. Johnson. We'll be better off waiting than risking the loss of a boat."

The *Julia*'s bow was twenty-five yards from the South Beach shore in the morning fog common during Puget Sound summers. *Active* was anchored two hundred yards astern.

When *Active*'s additional men arrived, the unloading continued without mishap. Gangs of soldiers and sailors manhandled the howitzer components separately in improvised wooden sleds across the sand of the beach, on a path cleared through the driftwood, which choked the shoreline. At the base of the low cliff to the camp above, the barrels, wheels, and carriages were placed again in slings and dragged up the cliff, where they were assembled. The infantry and artillerymen, under supervision of the battery commander, with petty officers from *Active*, struggled up the South Beach cliff ravines while Rory oversaw the shipboard unloading.

The task was completed by mid-morning. *Active* and *Julia* steamed east and then north through Cattle Pass and around to San Juan Harbor, in the larger gulf off southeastern San Juan Island, which appeared on the Wilkes expedition charts as "Ontario Roads". The "Roads" were named for the Great Lakes battle with the British in the War of 1812, after which Commodore Perry sent his famous dispatch that began "we have met the enemy and they are ours." *Wilkes*, thought Rory, *did all he could with place names to make this an American inland sea.*

"Mr. St. John," roared Alden, "drop anchor a cable-length north of *Satellite*. Mr. West, fire an eleven-gun salute to recognize their squadron commander, Captain Hornby. And call away my gig."

"Aye, aye, sir," the acting master and the first lieutenant responded in unison.

"Mr. Dunbrody!"

"Sir?"

"Walk with me, Dunbrody." The captain moved to the starboard

side of the quarterdeck and the other officers made way for Alden and
Rory to afford them privacy. "You've met Captain Hornby, have you not?"

"Yes, sir, just briefly during a meeting with the other British
captains and Pickett."

"I'd like you to accompany me in my gig, then. I know you met
many British officers during your Mediterranean duty. We'll be cordial.
I'll courteously ask if I'd be interfering with his ship-to-shore traffic if
we secured to the wharf and unloaded supplies. I've also been asked by
Colonel Casey to request a meeting with him. Get your sword and your
best tunic."

"Aye, aye, sir." Rory ran below to change the threadbare jacket
he'd worn to carry out the transfer of the howitzers.

Alden turned to Lieutenant West. "Mr. West, signal *Julia* to
anchor north of us." As Alden strode to the side, the sideboys came to
attention, the pipe twittered, and Alden and Rory boarded the captain's
gig.

"Ahoy, the gig," called the officer of the deck aboard Her
Majesty's Ship *Tribune*.

"*Active*," replied Carter, the captain's coxswain, indicating in
naval shorthand that the boat contained the *Active*'s commanding officer.
Boatswain pipes twittered once again, this time aboard *Tribune*, as Captain
Hornby was called from his cabin and honors were afforded the two U.S.
Naval officers as they clambered up the *Tribune*'s entry-port ladder.

"Welcome aboard, sir," said a rather genial Geoffrey Phipps
Hornby, Post Captain, Royal Navy.

"Most gracious of you to receive us, sir, as we have arrived so
precipitously," countered Alden. "I am James Alden, commanding the
U.S. Coast Survey steamer *Active*, and your sterling reputation precedes
you, Captain Hornby. I believe you've met my senior passed midshipman,
Mr. Dunbrody."

"Very kind of you to say, captain, and indeed Mr. Dunbrody and
I have encountered one another."

"A very good morning to you, sir," Rory said.

"And to you, midshipman. Let me introduce Lieutenant
Tremaine, my first lieutenant. Gentlemen, let us repair to my cabin."

Hornby lead Tremaine and the two Americans below to his very well appointed quarters. The forested shores and meadows of Lopez Island were visible through the stern windows of the *Tribune*'s after cabin.

"Captain Hornby, I wish to ensure that securing my consort, *Julia*, to the wharf will not interfere with any operations you may be engaged in this afternoon. And my colleague, Lieutenant Colonel Casey, requests the kindness of a meeting with you aboard the *Tribune* this afternoon, or at your earliest convenience, to discuss troops ashore on the island." Alden waited for Hornby's response.

"Most courteous of you to ask about wharfing, Captain. Please avail yourself of the wharf at your convenience. As Mr. Dunbrody no doubt observed during his earlier stay, we're rather self-sufficient at anchor here, as a spring line off the anchor cable will suffice to bring our broadside to bear in a matter of moments. As to troops, have you landed more?"

"Sir, I shan't equivocate," Alden replied. "We landed two infantry companies and a battery of mountain howitzers this morning. Still, we're unarguably overmatched by your strength."

"I have no objection to meeting with Colonel Casey, 'tho I am nonplussed. Captain Pickett assured me days ago that my country's honor was unchallenged by reason of the great disparity between our relative strengths. What should I think now of the potential smudge upon Britain's escutcheon now that you've narrowed the gap?"

Hornby smiled the smile of a man with twelve hundred pounds of shot in each of his broadsides. "I'll meet with the colonel tomorrow at ten o'clock. Tell him four bells in the forenoon watch. I love a confused soldier. And I'll come ashore and meet at Spring Camp, as Pickett calls the meadow he's retreated to."

"Will I be encountering you once again, Mr. Dunbrody? You seem to keep cropping up."

"It's possible, sir. I've been assigned as naval liaison to the commander of the American forces ashore."

"I'm grateful for your courtesy, captain," said Alden. "*Active* will proceed on the afternoon tide. We've surveying to do."

"Until we next meet, then," Hornby said.

In the gig, Rory was silent. The evening breeze was just rising, rippling the harbor, and the early evening sun, about to drop behind the harbor ridge, reflected from the ripples like thousands of diamonds. "You look a bit pensive, midshipman," Alden said.

"Sir, I know how essential to the national interest it is to avoid war with Britain. This is a powder keg, sir. We've just escalated the tension in a potential conflict for which we're ill prepared. And that's just the tactical situation here. Nationally, it could be disaster!"

"I believe this is the first time I've seen you without a quip, Mr. Dunbrody!"

"Yes, sir, I neglected to pack my nonchalance."

"Well, you're right, Dunbrody. It's a dangerous set of circumstances, with too many players for comfort. You keep me informed, give Pickett and the colonel good advice, and maintain a professional relationship with the Royal Navy. If we're successful, and lucky, your career and mine may proceed unimpeded."

"Aye, aye, sir. I'll go ashore directly and report to Colonel Casey. Thank you for your confidence, sir. I'll not let you down."

Tobias was officer of the deck when Alden and Rory returned from *Tribune*. He pulled Rory aside. "Your short sojourn with us is ended, I'll warrant."

"Aye, it is. I'll just toss my sea bag in the gig and go ashore to prevent the outbreak of war. And aren't I quakin' with just the thought of it!"

"You'll do fine, Rory. Irish charm will always win out."

"Oh, aye, and look where charm has gotten your race and mine, Tobias. Once again, keep her off the rocks."

Ashore, Rory was announced at the command tent that had just been erected for Lieutenant Colonel Silas Casey. "Enter, Mr. Dunbrody." The colonel was seated with Captain Pickett. On the field table before them lay two Victoria newspapers. "Captain Pickett tells me you interviewed with reporters from Victoria. These resulting articles are fanning the flames of a shooting war!"

"Sir, I was very careful to maintain that we were merely protecting the rights of Americans on the island until the border question could be negotiated." Rory had a lump in the pit of his stomach.

"Yes, the papers acknowledge that as your statement, but go on to imply that your attitude would welcome a shooting war. They encourage the RN to open fire if we don't retire immediately." The colonel folded his arms and glared at Rory.

"Sir, the two reporters were hostile from the beginning. One of them threatened me physically."

"And did you respond, Dunbrody?" Pickett demanded.

"Captain Pickett, it was a question of my Irishness, not the U.S. presence on the island."

"Well, we'll hope the RN isn't unduly influenced by irresponsible journalism," said Casey. "Did Captain Hornby respond to my request for a meeting when you and Captain Alden spoke to him?"

"Yes sir, he suggested ten o'clock tomorrow morning."

"Very well, I'll want you to escort Captain Hornby to my tent when he lands on the wharf tomorrow."

"Aye, aye, sir." Rory saluted and exited the command tent. He entered his tent and threw himself on the cot, faulting himself for letting his temper with the reporters over-reach him.

The next morning Rory was waiting as Hornby's gig pulled alongside the wharf and discharged the British squadron commander and a midshipman carrying a chart case. "Good morning, sir," said Rory, saluting.

"And good morning to you, midshipman," Hornby said, smiling. "Are you here to keep me safe from pig hunters?"

Rory relaxed immediately. "Yes, sir, and leprechauns and spirits of the dread Haida, as well." He indicated the direction in which they were headed. "We've a bit of a stroll ahead before Colonel Casey's tent is hull-up, sir."

"Lead the way, then, Mr. Dunbrody. Meet Mr. Midshipman Preston of my command." The two junior officers shook hands as Preston awkwardly shifted the cumbersome chart case to do so. The three men trudged up the steep, grassy incline.

"An officer on the *Plumper* remembers you in the Mediterranean as a visitor aboard his ship," Hornby continued.

"Yes, sir, probably when I was assigned to the Mediterrean Squadron. I'd been there earlier, on a midshipman's cruise during the Crimean War. And we visited London, too. I was presented to Lord Cochrane himself." Rory remembered the thrill of meeting Lord Thomas Cochrane, famed for the record number of prizes he'd taken and for his single-ship actions as captain of HMS *Speedy* and other frigates in the Napoleonic wars. A fiery redhead, he'd angered superiors in the Royal Navy, and resigned to become an admiral in the fledgling navy of the Chileans rebelling against the Spaniards.

"And how did you find the dashing frigate captain and Chilean admiral?"

Rory chuckled. "Ah, sure and didn't we hit it off splendidly, bein' fellow Celts and all? He was actually quite kind to a young middie, sir."

"Yes, he's assuredly a legend in two navies." Hornby gave Rory a quizzical look. "Do you intensify that brogue on purpose, midshipman? You seem to do it at will."

Rory thought for a moment, kicking at stones along the path as he pondered the question. "No, sir, it's not intentional. The defense of a subjugated race, without a doubt."

"There's nothing subjugated about the Irish in my command, Mr. Dunbrody. I wish I could multiply them in a fight."

"Kind of you to say, sir. I'm afraid I may have angered the Victoria press during my interview last week. I hope that didn't complicate things for the Royal Navy, sir. I assure you, the U.S. Navy is determined that our countries' dispute be settled by peaceful negotiation."

"Get in a spot of trouble, did you, midshipman?" Hornby smiled warmly. "Not to worry, the RN isn't influenced in its duty by backwoods newspapers. I believe you'll find your career's intact when the dust settles, if we can keep your army from going off at half-cock." He winked.

"Thank you, sir, I'll do my best. Here's the colonel's tent."

"Captain Hornby to see Colonel Casey," Rory announced to the sentry. Casey appeared at the door flap of the tent.

"Welcome, Captain Hornby," he said, straightening his jacket before extending a hand. "Captain Pickett and I are eager to meet with you. Please come in." As Hornby and Preston ducked through the opening of the tent, Casey added, "Mr. Dunbrody, please stand by to escort the captain back to the wharf when we've concluded."

"Aye, aye, colonel," Rory said. The navy response was virtually automatic, even to an army officer. Rory walked across the company street, once grass, now trodden-down dirt, to the mess tent, where he could watch for Hornby's emergence. He looked past the command tent, south and west across the broad Strait of Juan de Fuca, toward the Olympic Mountains.

"And the top o' the mornin' to ye, Sergeant O'Boyle. Could ye be sparin' a cup o' coffee for a sleepy sailor?"

"My pleasure entirely, sir. And perhaps we can be talkin' of days that are gone, while yer waiting for Their Honors, yonder?"

"Sure, isn't it grand to hear the brogue, and we so far from Erin?" Rory smiled and sat with his coffee and an eye toward Casey's tent.

"The mess sergeant is the best source of news in any unit," said Rory. "What's come to your ears of late, Sergeant?"

"Well, sir, Mr. Hubbs, the farmer out on Cattle Point, and a great friend of Captain Pickett, just returned from Victoria with news that the Austrians have lost a major battle to the French at Solferino."

"Ah, and the Austrians being British allies, another reason for the Saxons not to engage in yet another conflict," Rory mused.

"So Mr. Hubbs thought, at any rate, sir." O'Boyle replied.

"Captain Pickett seems a popular commander?"

"To be sure, Mr. Dunbrody. Always with a good story, and a word for the men. A youthful exuberance, y' might say, although he's in his mid-thirties."

Voices raised in anger within the tent could occasionally be heard, even across the Company Street. At last, Hornby appeared at the tent front, his aide behind him. Rory hurried to his side.

"May I escort you to your gig, sir?" asked Rory.

"You may, Mr. Dunbrody. The sooner I'm out of here, the better." Hornby, clearly exasperated, set a rapid pace up to the ridge overlooking the harbor, and then down the hillside. Preston, struggling with the chart case, fell behind.

Rory broke the silence. "An unsatisfactory meeting, sir?"

Hornby cleared his throat.

"Your army colleagues think we have no right to be 'threatening' you all, in their words, with deadly force. When I noted that I'm under orders of my superior, Admiral Baynes, now in Esquimalt Harbor west of Victoria, they determined that they will go to him with a proposal to withdraw all but Pickett's original company if we'll withdraw our ships. They refuse to acknowledge that this dispute has two sides."

Hornby gave Rory a quizzical look. "I seem to be sharing an amount of detail unusual from a senior officer to a midshipman in the 'enemy camp'. Do you have this effect on others of your superiors?"

"It's my honest Irish face, sir. Rest assured, my orders from Captain Alden are to do everything possible to help resolve this situation peacefully."

"That's reassuring, Mr. Dunbrody. It's certain that the dispute over possession will be settled by the diplomats, not by the armed forces, unless we muck it up in the interim."

"Aye, sir, perhaps the admiral can explain the situation to our army commanders in terms they'll understand. Never underestimate the persuasiveness of a two-decker ship of the line like his *Ganges*." Rory winked good-naturedly. "Although," he continued, "she's really an anachronism next to a modern steam frigate like *Tribune*."

"Quite so, young man." Hornby stared off into the middle distance. The two strode rapidly along without speaking for a few moments.

"I've just heard, sir, of a French victory at Solferino. Yet another reason that we not be firing at one another."

"Too right, Mr. Dunbrody," Hornby sighed. Let's hope the diplomats can reasonably agree, if they ever reach the point of not being distracted by European events. In the meantime, it appears there's plenty of activity over at Spring Camp." Hornby had noticed scores of blue-coated soldiers were erecting tents, and the howitzer battery had been moved to the crest of the ridge overlooking San Juan Harbor, just above the point where Rory and Hornby were descending the trail to the dock.

"Yes, sir, my soldierly brethren are scurrying to and fro, as I will be as soon as I leave you. Now here's something remarkable, sir. The locals have taken to calling San Juan Harbor 'Griffin Bay' after Charles Griffin, the Hudson's Bay Company agent whose pig started all this. Amazin', the impact of commerce upon history, not to mention livestock!"

"Ah, Mr. Dunbrody, you've made me smile in spite of my mood." They had reached the dock, and the laboring Preston was able to catch up. "Thank you for your escort."

"You're most welcome, sir. Until we meet again." Rory saluted, and Hornby boarded his gig, as the American lighthouse tender, *Shubrick*, cleared Cattle Pass and steamed into the harbor. Rory looked up the hill toward the camp to see Pickett and Casey in full-dress uniform, epaulets flashing in the noonday sun, descending the trail at the quick-step.

"We're off to see Admiral Baynes in Esquimalt, Dunbrody. I'd appreciate your thoughts on gun placement when we return." Casey waved at a boat from the *Shubrick*, rowing toward the wharf in response to a signal from the hillcrest.

"Aye, aye, sir. Smooth sailing, sir." Rory saluted and ascended the trail once more.

CHAPTER 7
THE "DIPLOMATS" RETURN FROM ESQUIMALT
AUGUST 1859

The *Shubrick* returned after nightfall. Pickett found Rory in the mess tent in an after-dinner discussion with the lieutenants of D Company. George Edward Pickett did not look pleased.

"What a colossal waste of time. It grieves me just to think on it!"

"What went wrong, sir?" Lieutenant Howard asked.

"The colonel requested the admiral to join us aboard *Shubrick*. The admiral responded with an invitation to meet aboard *Ganges*. Neither one would budge, so, we weighed anchor and returned." Pickett sighed with exasperation.

"With respect, sir, was the colonel aware that naval custom calls for the junior officer to meet aboard the senior's vessel?" Rory wore an expression of complete diffidence.

"What ever his knowledge, Dunbrody, he's in a mood now to brook no criticism. He's sending *Shubrick* at first light to Fort Steilacoom for the remaining three batteries of the Third, and he's sending the *Jeff Davis* to find the *Massachusetts*, to land her armament and Major Haller's company."

"The additional men will come in handy, to be sure, sir. Landing those beastly 32-pounders from the *Massachusetts* will require a temporary pier across the sand of the beach, ramps from the boats, and lots of muscle. It will be landing the howitzers times ten, sir."

"Did you consult with the battery officers regarding gun placement, Dunbrody?"

"Indeed, I did, captain. They agreed with my original suggestion to you, sir, that is, establishing a redoubt further upslope above the Hudson's Bay Company farm. From what you tell us about today's occurrence, I'll wager we'll be seeing the colonel's sappers and their lieutenant, Mr. Robert, sooner rather than later. I'm sure the colonel will want his judgment on the emplacements."

"It won't be long, Dunbrody, and your efforts here will bear fruit," drawled Pickett. "I'll consult with the colonel about movin' the guns, and movin' the camp north to a part of the heights more protected from the elements. Carry on, gentlemen."

Casey's efforts to contact the *Massachusetts* were successful. Within a few days, Major Haller's Company "I" of the Fourth Infantry had landed from the *Massachusetts*. Eight 32-pounder cannon were transferred from the *Massachusetts* to the South Beach and thence up the bluff with the aid of the slings and the hastily-built wooden "sleds", all under Rory's supervision. Three additional batteries of the Third Artillery arrived from Nisqually, and ten engineer troops under the command of Lieutenant Henry M. Robert.

Colonel Casey's tent was crowded, with three senior officers and a younger lieutenant seated around the small table which held a map of the Cattle Point area. The sentry held the tent flap aside while Rory entered and reported.

"Mr. Dunbrody, meet Major Haller of the Fourth, and Lieutenant Robert, my engineering officer." Colonel Casey smiled as Rory shook hands with the two new arrivals to San Juan Harbor. "Lieutenant Robert will be officer-in-charge of the gun emplacements, Dunbrody, now that you've been kind enough to move them to Spring Camp. Lieutenant Robert concurs with your recommendation for the location of the redoubt. I'd like you to assist him in the construction of the gun emplacements, and mounting the guns. I'll be moving the entire camp to the ground just north of the redoubt."

"I look forward to assisting the lieutenant, sir." Rory smiled and nodded deferentially at Robert, who acknowledged with a polite bow of his head.

Major Haller cleared his throat. "Mr. Dunbrody, I have serious misgivings about British intentions. Captain Pickett here tells me you've been in conversation with Captain Hornby. I'm interested in your assessment of their next move, from the perspective of the navy." Haller stared aggressively at Rory.

"Sir, they've just allowed us to bring our complement to four hundred sixty men and twelve cannon, plus three howitzer batteries, without firing on us. I infer from this that when Admiral Baynes recently arrived, he gave orders that the British would not fire first. The proof of my theory, sir, will come when we begin emplacement. If I were in Hornby's shoes, I would not allow our heavy cannon to be protected by embrasure and parapet unless I'd been ordered not to shoot first."

"I hope you're right, Dunbrody," said Casey. "We may find out tomorrow. Lieutenant Robert, please proceed with the redoubt construction immediately."

"Yes, sir," Robert replied. "Mr. Dunbrody, let's walk to the redoubt and start our planning. By your leave, sir." And with that, the two junior officers left the tent and walked uphill to the redoubt site where the 32-pounders would soon sit, trained on the British ships.

"Your youth was spent in Ireland was it, sir?" asked Robert as they climbed.

"Indeed, sir, 'though I'm North Carolina-born. And you, from the northwest, Ohio or Illinois?"

"You've a good ear, sir," Robert replied. "I grew up in the Northwest, but I was born in South Carolina. As you are in a lieutenant's billet aboard your ship, and we're a pair of Carolinians, and as we'll be working side by side for weeks, I suggest a first-name basis."

"My pleasure, sir – Henry," said Rory.

"Excellent, Rory," Henry said. "I'd like to get those 32-pounders on platforms as soon as possible."

"We can begin moving them from Spring Camp immediately," Rory said. "I suggest we construct the platforms out of sight of the British, with the recoil tackle in place, and then move the guns to the platforms all at once. We'll need to ask Captain Fauntleroy for the *Massachusetts'* experienced gun crews to mount the guns on the platforms. We used them to mount the guns on the carriages after we hauled them up the bluff. The artillery lads can assist, and learn the nature of naval gunnery at the same time. Then, we can construct the parapet and embrasures."

"I agree, Rory. We've unloaded many thousand board-feet of cut planks from the steamers over the last few days. The infantry can turn-to, as well. We'll complete the platforms, mount the guns, and have picks and shovels at the ready to build the parapets. Then we'll see if we get broadsides or enigmatic stares from the British."

Henry clapped Rory on the shoulder as they walked to the high edge of the ground that would constitute the redoubt. He identified four emplacements facing San Juan Harbor, and four commanding the South Beach.

Two full days of construction had yielded eight gun platforms, complete with rings securing the tackle that controlled the recoil of each cannon firing a 32-pound cannon ball from the two-ton muzzle-loaders. The carriages, without the guns, were placed on the platforms. The platforms had been placed in slight depressions behind the ridge of the redoubt overlooking the harbor and the Strait of Juan de Fuca. Teams of soldiers stood with shovels ready to erect protective parapets once the cannon were moved to the platforms. Gangs of sailors from the American ships stood ready to move the cannon to the platforms. If they could raise the parapet to an adequate height without British interference, they could complete the redoubt at a more leisurely pace over the next few weeks.

At Robert's signal the thirty-twos were moved up ramps to the platforms as gun crews from the navy tailed on to the slings cradling the guns. The gangs of sailors lifted the guns onto the carriages. Simultaneously, squads of soldiers began moving earth to raise the parapets.

A group of officers stood just down-slope and to the north of the redoubt. Fauntleroy of the *Massachusetts*, Alden of the *Active*, Lieutenant West, and Acting Master Tobias St. John were among them.

"Captain Alden, can you see any activity aboard the ships?"

Colonel Casey, his telescope to his eye like the rest of the officers, scanned the three vessels.

"Nothing unusual, Colonel," Alden replied. "One of them, *Satellite*, has her guns shotted and run out, but without gun crews. That's a practice of this squadron. But you can see the officers on their respective quarterdecks, watching us watch them."

Rory turned to Lieutenant Robert. "I couldn't help notice that the lads of the Third Artillery neglected to bring along their caissons."

"True enough. They expect only to emplace the guns," said Robert, pointing to the three howitzer batteries just down-slope from the redoubt, and trained on the harbor.

"Well, now," Rory said with a smile, 'twill be difficult to limber up and make for the woods should the lobsterbacks land, without horses and caissons and all. I guess they'll die by their guns."

Two hours passed. The soldiers and sailors, under the direction of Henry and Rory, labored to raise the parapets to a secure height. The officers stood, desultorily, talking in pairs or in small groups and pausing occasionally to cast their telescopes on the frigate, corvette, and gunboat in the harbor. In mid-afternoon, Lieutenant Robert approached the group that included Colonel Casey.

"Colonel, sir. The parapet is at a height sufficient to protect the gun crews." Henry smiled at his commander.

Casey stepped toward the redoubt and in a parade command voice, called: "Soldiers and seamen of this command, well done!" A cheer rose from the ranks of the laboring men. The troops and sailors, most of whom were stripped to the waist, waved their picks and shovels aloft.

"And won't they be thinkin' twice before firin' broadsides now, lieutenant?" Rory grinned at Henry. "Congratulations, Henry! I do believe we've brought this off!"

"I suspect you're right, Rory. A celebration may be in order!" The two junior officers turned toward the harbor and took one last look at the British squadron, for reassurance.

A hastily expanded shanty housed old San Juan Town's foremost public house, a dubious distinction. The town had sprung up overnight after the landing of the first American troops in late July. Several tables in the pub were filled with officers from Casey's command, as the establishments of the town were, so far, off limits to enlisted men. Rory, Tobias, and Henry sat with Lieutenant West.

"Gentlemen, a toast to the status quo." Rory lifted his tankard and the others responded.

"And to a damn fine job by our sapper and our gunner." Tobias grinned at Henry and Rory.

"Hear, hear," from Lieutenant West. "We must find something additional to toast, gentlemen. I'm nearly dry. To our wives and sweethearts. May they never meet!"

"An old toast, Henry," Rory explained, "borrowed from our Royal Navy cousins."

Henry laughed. "You navy types have all the luck, moving from place to place and woman to woman constantly, all in the line of duty."

"Would that it were true, sir," Tobias said. "*Active*'s been on station here since '53, moving from Nisqually to Bellingham, and damn few women do we see, save for the Indians. We're too busy fending off their men folk's raiding parties to make overtures to them."

Henry turned to Tobias. "Mr. St. John. Pardon my curiosity, but how did you come to a navy life? With apologies, sir, but we've no colored in the army, yet I've noticed many Negro sailors aboard the ships in Puget Sound."

"No apology needed, lieutenant," replied the acting master. "'Tis a question to vex an army man quite naturally, where colored do not serve. In the merchant service, Negroes are frequently one-third of a crew, and in the whalers of my homeport, New Bedford, as much as two-thirds. But to your question, sir, my father is a whaler, and I grew up aboard ship. When time came for my schooling at the Quaker Academy, my propensity for mathematics was discovered, and I took quickly to navigation as a practical application of my classroom work."

"And then the navy beckoned?" Henry asked, draining his tankard.

"Indeed, sir, after several years a whaling." Tobias said. "I find that life is taken less frequently in the navy than in whaling, and often less violently. But you, lieutenant, surely mathematics is your constant companion as an engineer?"

"My instructors at the Military Academy made sure of that. Fear and curiosity make a fine mix of motivation. And as you have found, the practical application of classroom knowledge is most satisfying."

Henry fixed a quizzical look on Tobias. "Rory tells me you do lunar distance method calculations?"

"Chronometers still being somewhat scarce, it's a useful alternative, along with deduced or "ded" reckoning, as the navy refers to it." Tobias said.

"The *Active* is never in doubt about its location with Mr. St. John aboard," said Lieutenant West, appreciatively. "Another round, gentlemen?"

"By your leave, sir, it's late, and I have the forenoon watch as we sail in the morning, now that Rory has joined the artillery." Tobias rose to leave.

"Very well, acting master," said West. "Lieutenant? Mr. Dunbrody?"

"Another round would be fine," Henry said, as Rory nodded. Pickett, Howard, and von Klopfenstein, seated nearby, rose and approached their table.

"May we join y'all, gentlemen?" Pickett drawled.

"Of course, sir, please do." West responded, gesturing toward the empty bench along one side of their table.

"I couldn't help but notice y'all have a nigra officer in your command," Lieutenant Howard said as he sat down. "I'm curious. Do y'all find that he can perform to the exactin' standards of your service?" Howard looked challengingly at the two navy officers.

"Acting Master St. John is a brilliant navigator and excellent officer, sir!" Rory said in a low intense voice as he rose from his chair. "If, sir, you are implying that his presence diminishes the excellence of the Naval Service in any way, I would take strong exception to your remark, sir!"

"Well, suh," replied Howard, "I did not mean to disparage your fine service in any way, but I trust that you do not imply, suh, that absence of nigras in the United States Army in any way diminishes its excellence!"

"Gentlemen, I see where this is going!" Pickett rose, as well. "You are each essential to my command. I will not tolerate a confrontation that jeopardizes our situation. Lieutenant Howard, I'm confident you meant no disrespect to the Naval Service. Am I correct?"

"Yes, Captain, you are, suh." Howard said.

"And Mr. Dunbrody, as my command's naval liaison, I'm sure you did not mean to disparage the army."

"No, sir. My brother is an army captain. I have the highest respect for your service."

"I am satisfied with your responses. Are each of you?"

"Yes, sir," they chorused, their response quite muted. Pickett's Mexican War reputation for valor served to overcome the zeal for "satisfaction" evidenced by both officers, a zeal engendered by the honor code of the time, calling for redress of perceived slights to one's honor. Dueling was common among the gentry of the period, and, in particular, among the officer class.

"I am more than satisfied that both of the officers involved in this contretemps will continue to be integral parts of this command, both havin' stood on the hillcrest and risked the chance of shot and shell without a thought. As did Mr. St. John," Pickett added, as an afterthought. When controversy intensified, Pickett tended to increase the depth of his Virginian drawl and his flowery speech.

"As you two hotheads have taken a deep breath, perhaps we can arrange a bit of practice with me. I need to cleanse the rust from my saber and foil." Von Klopfenstein smiled maliciously as he drank from his beer stein.

"Sure, and me customary cutlass drill aboard *Active* has been interrupted of late. 'Twould be a great boon for t'cross swords with a Proosian duelist, even in practice," said Rory, with a great look of innocence.

"As I would be honored to fence with so talented a colleague," echoed Lieutenant Howard, with somewhat less enthusiasm.

"Well, gentlemen, at a time both soon and convenient, we will have a little *salle,* will we not?" The Prussian looked like a cat choosing between two mice.

"I suggest in four days, when *Active* returns.' said Rory. "The sunshine in these islands is at its most beautiful in the mornings." Rory turned to Howard.

"I'm thinkin' it will be a lesson for us both," said Howard, dryly.

Four days later, morning came to San Juan Harbor sans fog, an occasional occurrence in the Gulf of Georgia in late August. The sunrise, high over snow-capped Mt. Baker to the east, glistened off the glaciers of its thirteen thousand-foot peak. The morning westerly breeze only touched the ships anchored in the harbor, although its ripples, as they gained intensity toward Lopez Island to the east, brightly reflected the morning light, framed by the dark green of Lopez's evergreen shores.

"Rise and shine, rise and shine, heave out and trice up," rang the calls of the boatswain's mates as they wakened *Active* for another day. Rory had slept aboard. He and Tobias were already awake and emerging from their berths aside of the wardroom. They greeted each other groggily.

"Scuttlebutt has it that you've labored to defend my competence and honor after I left our recent celebration, thank you very much," said Tobias with a quizzical expression.

"Sure, nothin' you couldn't have done yourself, if present, and you bein' the Renaissance man you are, and all."

"All very well," he said tersely, "but I'd prefer to call out my own devils."

"Well you might, but none shall disparage a shipmate of mine while I've life and breath."

"Thank you, Rory. " Rory reached to open the locker beneath his bunk in the six-by-four "stateroom" off the wardroom. He brought out his saber, a gift from his grandfather Fearghus Dillon, late of the Army of France, Dillon's Regiment.

"Will you spring any surprises on Klaus today?"

"Well, now, Tobias, didn't Grandfather Fearghus tell me not to be showin' me best techniques to a foeman in practice, lest he later become an enemy in fact?"

"Let's hope your grandfather taught you well enough to fool a Prussian duelist."

Rory attached his sheathed saber to his belt. "Come along and see for yourself. Lieutenant West and the captain are going ashore to watch, and most of the army brass will be there too. Henry told me that the Prussian has been inviting his army colleagues to witness a *salle de armes* with him as the teacher. And isn't he quite the swashbuckler, now?"

"Maybe I will, at that," said Tobias. "I'll nod politely to Lieutenant Howard, and wish him well in his *mensur*, as the French and Germans call these semi-mock duels. I'll remind him that *mensurs* usually produce those sought-after scars."

He laughed heartily. "It should be amusing, although I doubt the Quakers would approve."

CHAPTER 8
CROSSED SABERS
AUGUST 1859

The *piste*, or strip upon which the fencers would collide, was set on a level patch of ground back from the eastern hillcrest, in view of the harbor and the ships, British and American, anchored there. The peaks of the Cascade Range loomed in the distance. Fauntleroy of the *Massachusetts*, at Major Haller's urging, had invited the officers of the Royal Navy, and they in turn had brought several Royal Marine officers ashore. Rory noticed that Haller was going to great lengths to make the British welcome, as if to counter the supposed effects of the conspiracy to alienate Great Britain he'd envisioned on the part of General Harney and Pickett.

Dress uniforms were the order of the day on this bright Saturday morning. The blue and gold of both navies, and the dark and light blue of the American Army contrasted with the red coats and white trousers of the Royal Marines. Rory, von Klopfenstein, and Howard had dressed in the mess tent, and were similarly clad in padded jackets, grasping cage-mask helmets in their heavily gloved sword hands.

The Saints preserve me from making a fool of myself, thought Rory as he looked at the blue, scarlet and gold bank of uniformed men all staring intently at him. He struggled to overcome a sudden visceral fear of failure. *I can't be hurt with all this padding, so I'll put on the armor of insouciance,* he told himself, drawing several deep breaths and putting a smile on his face.

"We have no cutlasses, Herr Dunbrody. I hope sabers will do." The Prussian smiled as well, a smile at once menacing and disdaining to Rory's active imagination. Von Klopfenstein then drew his own blunt-tipped, dual-cutting edge sword, slightly curved at the tip. "Come, let us ensure the lengths are close enough to preclude advantage." He looked at Rory's weapon with a critical eye. "I see you have your own."

"Ah, sure, and didn't they give us cutlass and saber practice twice a week at the Academy?" Rory said. "But they made us wear our masks, and we were denied the chance for a fine duelin' scar like yours, lieutenant."

"Perhaps someday we can rectify that, Dunbrody. I shall face each of you in turn. Who shall be first?" He grinned cruelly at the two Americans.

"Surely the most senior should begin. Would ye not agree, Mr. Howard?" Rory smiled innocently at the army lieutenant.

"I'm willing to fight the first round," replied Howard.

"The saber lengths appear to be comparable, gentlemen." Von Klopfenstein stepped to the strip.

"To the *piste*, John, *danke. En garde!*"

Howard and the Prussian engaged. Howard attacked vigorously, hoping to surprise the technically superior Prussian. Von Klopfenstein's form seemed effortless, parrying and riposting amid the fury of Howard's initial attack. Howard rained blows about his opponent's head and torso. Saber fencing allowed the head to be a target, unlike foil and *e'pe'e*. Cutting and slashing, together with the occasional thrust, was the fabric of saber encounters.

Von Klopfenstein parried Howard's cuts and thrusts with apparent ease. His ripostes were perfectly timed, and after four hits or touches, Howard cried "Enough!" and lowered the point of his saber. "Klaus, you have given me a fine lesson, and I am well exercised for the day!"

"*Zer goot,*" Klaus responded. "Some water and I shall be ready for Herr Dunbrody." He seemed to be quite pleased with himself, almost friendly, after his bout with Howard. The spectators congregated in discrete groups. One such included Captain Hornby, Lieutenant Tremaine, Captain Alden, Tobias, and Captain Pickett.

"Captain Alden, I have a pound that says young Dunbrody will somehow manage the last touch." Geoffrey Hornby grinned cordially at the American officer.

"Captain, I could never bet against a member of my command. But, more to the point, I've learned never to bet against Dunbrody."

"I feel constrained to take that bet, sir, and show my confidence in my aide. But I confess that it don't seem as sure a bet as it should, on the surface of the question," Pickett responded with raised eyebrows. Pickett had doffed his uniform cap in the morning sun, and his perfumed ringlets swirled in the breeze from Juan de Fuca Strait.

"My Quaker father would not approve of my gamble, but I'm inclined to put a dollar on Captain Hornby's wager, sir," said Tobias to Pickett.

"Do y'all know somethin' we don't, Master St. John?" asked Pickett.

"No, sir, I just have a long association with Mr. Dunbrody."

They all turned to watch as the two officers approached the *piste*. They stood, sabers poised. Von Klopfenstein, in the role for this practice normally taken by the fencing master, cried "*Engarde, Allez!*" Rory began with a thrust to the upper left torso of his opponent, the quadrant known as the "prime". The Prussian parried and followed with a lightning riposte which Rory parried at only the last possible moment, and the rhythm of the fence began: again and again, slash, parry, riposte, counter riposte.

Von Klopfenstein was aggressive and precise, strong and unpredictable. Rory soon found himself alternately attacking and retreating under a veritable flurry of slashes to the head and upper torso by the German. Once, attempting to parry a slash at his head by raising his wrist to the "quint" position, Rory was unable to prevent a hit.

"*Touché.*" the Prussian called with a satisfied laugh. "I fear I shall wear you down, my young Irish. Did you encounter opponents like me in your cutlass drill?"

Rory realized that unless he resorted to one of the masterstrokes or secret moves, the *coups de maitre* taught him by his grandfather, the Prussian would clearly have the best of him. *That's not a bad outcome, of itself, but 'twill make him all the more insufferable*, Rory thought as he retreated under another barrage of cuts and slashes. Suddenly, as he retreated, Rory contrived to catch his right heel on the edge of the strip, and fall sideways to his right and the Prussian's left. Executing a variation of a horizontal *fleche*, Rory swung his saber to his left as he fell. The flat of his blade caught the Prussian in the ribs and knocked him, stumbling, sideways off the strip.

Rory leaped to his feet, lowered the point of his sword and bowed to von Klopfenstein, who had barely managed to keep his feet. "Sure, I'm fallin' all over meself, lieutenant," he said with a playful smile. "The whole thing's been a lesson to me, and I'm grateful for yer instruction."

The Prussian paused, becoming aware of the ill-concealed smiles on the faces of several of the spectators, including some from his own company. "Well, perhaps someday we have lesson two," he said, deciding to treat the outcome of the match as a victory. His knuckles were white as he gripped his saber, and as he glared at Rory, his inner seething was apparent.

Colonel Casey approached the three fencers, eager to ensure that no hard feelings manifested. Pickett had briefed him as to the genesis of the practice session. Casey was determined that Pickett's efforts to avoid a duel would not be in vain. "Splendid swordplay, Lieutenant von Klopfenstein, and a good effort by the two novices, as well."

"Humph. *Danke, mein colonel.*" Von Klopfenstein clicked his heels and bowed to Colonel Casey. The Prussian's struggle to put a good face on the outcome was obvious.

"Thank you, sir," Rory replied. "At least Lieutenant Howard was able to keep his feet under him. Sure, I think I'll be tryin' that approach me next time out." The laughter that Rory's remarks evoked from the crowd of officers drained away the tension of the moment.

"I think lunch is in order, gentlemen," said Casey as he turned and led the way to the mess tent, obviously relieved at the match's outcome.

"Captain Pickett, d'ye think we should agree to call our wager a draw, under the circumstances?" asked Hornby as they walked together toward the mess tent.

"Yes, suh, a fair outcome." Pickett replied. "My stars and garters, gentlemen, did you see that young midshipman? Why, he was positively horizontal. I thought he was fixin' t'fly!"

Rory and Henry Robert sat at a table to the back of the mess tent. "Mr. Midshipman Dunbrody, sor! I hear you're workin' up an appetite. Try some of my mock corned beef. I'll not be sharing with ye the details of the recipe, but I'll swear by the taste. You try some too, lieutenant." Mess Sergeant O'Boyle placed a serving bowl, utensils, and napkins in front of the two officers.

"And my thanks to ye, mess sergeant," Rory said. "'Tis an appetite I surely have."

"That was quite entertaining, Rory." Henry said after O'Boyle had moved back to the kitchen tent. "I'm always astounded at the order and the protocols of what otherwise seems a chaotic pastime."

"To be sure, fencing has its own rhythm. Doesn't it appeal to your engineer's sense of order, now?"

"As a matter of fact it reminds me of a project I've been ignoring of late," Henry said. "Off and on, for years, ever since my commission, I've been working on a set of rules for the conduct of meetings. As an engineer, I'm constantly appearing at meetings with settlers, with legislatures, with local governmental bodies. Church committees may be the worst! No two are conducted alike, and many of the chairmen have no idea of how to maintain order and progress to a conclusion. The time I've spent while inept chairmen allow circular arguments to gobble up time like you're gobbling that corned beef! If I had a penny for each wasted hour, I'd be a rich man!"

"Heaven save us, he's goin' t'organize us all!" Rory laughed so hard he choked on his corned beef.

"We've more important tasks than my set of rules to occupy us now, Rory. I'm satisfied with the gun emplacements, though. It should give the British pause, now that we have more than howitzers facing them."

"And facing them from behind a parapet, however incomplete. The Royal Navy knows what roundshot and grapeshot from a 32-pounder can do."

"The best thing we can do now is to let them see both our increased strength and our competence."

"True," said Rory, "and if I'm right that their real inclination is away from war to begin with, what better way to subtly underscore our point than to create diversions like today where we can bring them ashore without threat, and in plain view of our fortifications?"

"Why not have a day of contests among the sailors? Boat races, races to the mastheads, heaving those ropes of yours? The officers and soldiers could be spectators. Food, drink, music?"

"Sure, you're a most devious fellow, Henry." He clapped his companion on the shoulder. "What a grand idea! Let's talk to our superiors!"

CHAPTER 9
THE CONTEST
AUGUST 1859

Later that afternoon, when the British had returned to their
ships, Henry and Rory asked to see Colonel Casey and Captain Alden.
The two young officers explained their idea to their seniors.

"I like this idea, captain," said Casey to Alden. "I've just been
advised that Territorial Governor Gholson intends to visit at month's end,
as well as former Governor Stevens, the territorial delegate to Congress.
By then, we'll have moved from Spring Camp to the ground just north of
the redoubt. We intend to have a formal review of the troops. We could
augment the review with an afternoon of contests. I'll let Captain Pickett
know you two will be assisting him in planning and implementing the
festivities, if that meets with your approval as to Dunbrody's involvement,
Captain Alden."

"Colonel, Mr. Dunbrody is your liaison. He's here to assist you
as you see fit."

"Excellent, captain. We've only nine days before the visit of
the governors. We'll need to invite the British to participate as soon as
possible." Henry and Rory saluted, and left to begin their preparations.

Relations with the British were improving. Every Sunday,
Colonel Casey attended religious services aboard HMS *Satellite*. He and
Captain Prevost of the *Satellite* developed a firm and cordial acquaintance.

On the day of the visit from Governor Gholson, the troops passed in review with Colonel Casey, mounted, in the lead. The British held gun drills for the governor and then served high tea aboard *Tribune*. The governor and the officers of the British squadron then returned ashore to witness the boat races and line heaving competition. The chief referees were the boatswains of the *Massachusetts* and the *Tribune*.

Groups of officers stood along the shore of the harbor near the finish line, which was directly off the wharf, with the shanties of San Juan Town clustered behind them. Chairs had been brought for the governor and the senior officers. Off-duty American troops stood slightly up the hill from the shore, with a good view of the starting line off the mouth of the long shallow cove later known as Fish Creek Cove, or "God's Pocket", toward the end of the Cattle Point peninsula, some nine cable lengths, or almost a nautical mile distant.

The crews of the British and American ships anchored in the harbor lined the bulwarks as the six boat crews rowed by on their way to the start, and cheered for their favorites.

Captain Geoffrey Hornby left the senior officers and walked east along the shore, a telescope under his arm. As he came to the group where Rory stood, Hornby motioned to the young American. Rory fell in step with the British captain.

"Have you recovered from your saber exercise, Mr. Dunbrody?" Hornby asked.

"Aye, sir, but my dignity may be permanently damaged, endin' as I did by falling over my own feet."

"Few who knew you in the crowd seemed surprised that you managed to convert your stumble into an artful exit."

"Ah, sure, wasn't it just my friends bein' kind, sir? And you're the man to stay close to, today, sir, with your presence of mind to bring your telescope ashore." Rory looked at the boats receding in the distance. "Who d'ye fancy in the race, sir?"

"My wager's on my fine gig crew from the *Tribune*, Mr. Dunbrody. But whoever wins, the race itself will doubtless serve to better the chances for a peaceful outcome to this affair."

"Without a doubt, sir. We're fortunate that cooler heads seem to be prevailin'. Admiral Baynes and you exhibit great forbearance, and I believe Colonel Casey and even Major Haller are of the same mind, if you'll forgive me temerity for commentin' on my superior officers."

"Not at all, Midshipman. Junior officers' views are frequently useful, and yours, I've found, in particular. Now, if only we can calm our Governor Douglas…" Hornby's voice trailed off as he realized he was approaching indiscretion.

"Sure, I was just about t'say the same of General Harney, before I bit me tongue, just in time, sir."

Hornby smiled. "Yes, Governor Douglas tells me that the General has been trying to convince your government that the Hudson's Bay Company is hiring northern Indians to raid American settlements in Washington Territory. That won't calm our fiery Scot."

"When Washington City hears that, sir, they'll be havin' some strong words with the general. The trouble is, it takes five weeks for word to travel each way."

"Well, I'm sure it's difficult to sustain nine infantry and artillery companies in this tiny corner of the Territory. Let's hope our governments can quickly agree that mutual occupation by token forces is the solution until negotiation can begin. Rest assured you've done your country great service by your efforts in that regard, including today's festivities. It would surprise me if you weren't involved in conceiving this peaceful competition. Ah, the race is under way." Hornby raised the telescope. "Nothing in it, as yet. Care to take a look, Dunbrody, before I rejoin your governor's party?"

"Thank you, sir." Rory focused the telescope on the racing boats. "*Shubrick*'s dropping back, but no open water among the others, sir. Thank you again."

Don't mention it, midshipman. It's been my pleasure. I'm sure we'll speak again." Hornby turned and walked back up the beach.

Rory felt a glow of self-satisfaction at Hornby's compliments and approval, but checked his self-congratulations abruptly. *The fuse to the powder keg's not out yet, me boyo,* he told himself.

"That looked interesting," said Tobias as Rory rejoined the junior officers.

"He wanted my advice on how to bet, knowin' what great gamblers the Irish are. I'm thinkin' I'll move down the beach for a better view. Care to join me?"

Rory walked toward Cattle Point and the approaching boats, and Tobias fell in step beside him. "Did you know Harney's accusin' the HBC of inciting the Indians to raid our settlers?"

"He'll have all of us ready to open fire, with talk like that." Tobias said. "They'll be raiding with or without HBC involvement. It'll remain their tradition until we make it too costly for them. We need to better arm and train our boat crew, is my thought, Rory."

"And while we're on the subject of preparing for the enemy," he continued, "you know, Rory, do you not, that you've made a foe of Klaus, the saber-rattler?"

"Oh, aye, but unless and until he ever means business, I'll stay out of his way, thank you very much, I'm sure. And I'm sure he's at least uncertain as to my fencing talent, and, I hope, convinced I have next to none." He peered out toward the activity on the water. "Come, let's go toward the finish line. I'm afraid *Active*'s gig is a length down goin' into the last quarter mile." Rory and Tobias walked quickly up the beach toward the wharf and the shacks of San Juan Town that surrounded it.

Troops and sailors cheered as four gigs crossed the finish line with no open water between any of them; *Tribune, Satellite, Massachusetts* and *Active*. Captain Pickett looked up as the two junior officers approached, obviously excited and delighted with the contest.

"Gentlemen, ah'm impressed with the race y'all gave Her Majesty's sailors. Very commendable, I must say! Tell me about the next event."

"Well, sir, we've secured two lanyards tied to colored ribbons at the mainmasthead of the *Tribune*." Tobias pointed to the British frigate. "She has the tallest masts in the harbor, sir," he explained. "Each ship of the six has selected a topman to race up the ratlines, untie the lanyard and return to the deck. They'll go two at a time. First one down wins the heat. Two ships drew byes for the first heat. First heat winners race them in the semi-final, and those winners race for the championship."

"My heavens, man, they'll be exhausted!"

"It's easier than doing it in a gale, sir. And they do that all the time!" He shook his head in appreciation.

"The last event is the line toss. Six boats will anchor off the *Tribune*, equally distant from the frigate. Each ship's contestant will heave a line weighted with a monkey fist over the bulwark of the *Tribune*. After each toss, they'll anchor at a greater distance, until only one or two can make the toss.

"I'm refereeing the line toss with Lieutenant Tremaine of the *Tribune*, sir, so I'll beg you to excuse me. By your leave, sir." Tobias motioned to *Active's* jolly boat nearby to take him to the *Tribune*.

Pickett turned to Rory. "I think I'd just as soon take a forced march."

"Sure, they love this, sir. It breaks the monotony." Rory cleared his throat. "Sir, I heard former Governor Stevens visited yesterday. Did you see him?" Rory waited expectantly.

"Indeed I did, midshipman. He and I both served in the Mexican war."

"I've heard the Indians call him the 'hanging governor'. Is that because he had Chief Leschi of the Nisquallies hanged after the 1853 war here?"

"I'm unaware of what the Indians call Governor Stevens," Pickett glowered. "He did arrange the trial of Leschi for murder. But I was not present during the Indian War. I didn't arrive here until 1856 when Leschi's trials were still ongoing." Pickett fixed Rory with a decidedly unfriendly look.

"Sure, I thought y'might know, sir, you with a part-Indian son, and all."

Pickett's jaw set, and he drew himself up to his full height. "I will tell you two things, Dunbrody, calmly, suh, in recognition of the good relations we have had thus far. First, there are always two sides to a story. And I doubt me y'all have heard Governor Stevens' side. And second, talk of my children is greatly disturbin' t'me. I have lost one son, and two wives in childbirth, suh, and I grieve still."

"Sir, I am often too eager to defend those I see as the downtrodden. I did not mean to cause you pain, sir. I wish to serve you well while under your command. I apologize."

"Accepted, midshipman." Pickett's posture relaxed a bit. "I confess part of my pain is the necessity of boarding my son, Jimmie, with friends down in Arkada, in Sawamish County. I could not be an adequate parent and still carry out my duties here, so I very seldom see him. And I am aware that Colonel Casey felt strongly that Chief Leschi should have been accorded the status of a prisoner of war, not a murderer. Now I must rejoin the governor and the colonel."

Rory saluted and Pickett returned the salute as he turned to join the senior officers at the wharf. *There I go with my mouth again*, thought Rory. *When will I learn that others don't like being reminded that the world is unjust?*

Tobias and Lieutenant Tremaine stood on the quarterdeck of the *Tribune* as the finalists in the line toss stood in the bows of their cutters, fifty-five feet away. The masthead race had ended shortly before, when a surprisingly agile topman from the *Massachusetts* had risked burning the skin from his hands by sliding down a backstay of the *Tribune* at breakneck speed, barely beating the *Tribune*'s captain of the foretop.

The coxswain of *Plumper*'s captain's gig stood in the bow of her cutter. Anchored thirty feet away was *Active*'s launch. The stroke oar Hardcastle stood in the bow. The coxswain tossed first. Twirling the lead-weighted monkey fist at his line's end, he let go on the upswing. The line paid out behind the fist, which landed on the gunwale of the steam frigate, balanced precariously, and slid off into the water. An equal chorus of groans and cheers rose from the spectators.

"*Active*'s turn," cried the hundreds of voices of the American crews and the blue-coated soldiers watching ashore. Hardcastle paused dramatically, then began to twirl the fist, slowly, then faster and faster. As he let go, he lurched forward and caught himself, hands braced against the bow of the cutter. The fist rose, trailing the line, and cleared the *Tribune*'s gunwale cleanly. A roar went up from the spectators, and Hardcastle waved both arms in response.

"Splendid effort!" First Lieutenant Wickstrand Tremaine, RN, clapped Tobias on the shoulder. "A strong step toward an atmosphere of resolution of differences, I say, Mr. St. John!"

"Too right, Mr. Tremaine," Tobias replied in his best Antiguan British accent, learned and discarded long ago, but not forgotten.

CHAPTER 10
WAITING FOR WINFIELD SCOTT
OCTOBER 1859

The relaxation of tensions between the British and Americans on San Juan Island had continued. Personnel of both commands fraternized frequently in San Juan Town. Rory continued his liaison duties with Pickett.

Meanwhile, *Active* lay in Port Townsend Harbor on a short respite from surveying. Alden was generous with shore leave. Tobias, Lieutenant West, and Midshipman Johnson found themselves in a public house on the Port Townsend waterfront, in an alcove around the corner from the bar in the 'L' shaped tavern. Through a grimy window, they looked out on *Active* and other ships anchored in the harbor, with Marrowstone Island's high cliffs to the south, across the anchorage.

Water Street in Port Townsend, beneath a towering bluff, was a raucous and rowdy collection of curses, shouts, spilled beer, and drunkenness. The recent British Columbia gold strikes had flooded northern Washington Territory with hopeful miners on their way to the Fraser River and the Cariboo district, and with disappointed ones returning. The U.S. Customs House for Washington had been relocated to Port Townsend, and every foreign bottom entering Admiralty Inlet and Puget's Sound made the required stop there.

Midshipman Johnson had joined West and Tobias moments

earlier, breathless with the news that Lieutenant General Winfield Scott, commanding general of the U.S. Army, was in Puget Sound aboard the steamer *Northerner*, direct from the Isthmus of Panama. Above the din of the bar, he shouted to make himself heard.

"The first 'luff' of the *Jeff Davis* told me that they're to stand by as a dispatch ship between the general and Governor Douglas in Victoria. And the first lieutenant of the *Massachusetts* told him that the general tore into General Harney and Captain Pickett in Fort Vancouver before they sailed up here." Midshipman Johnson paused for breath. "He said General Scott relieved General Harney on the spot!"

"Where's the *Northerner* now?" asked Lieutenant West.

"They're at Olympia, sir, but they're expected here in Port Townsend any day." Johnson looked toward the harbor as if he hoped to see evidence of *Northerner*'s arrival silhouetted against the bluffs of the anchorage.

"Captain Pickett may have chosen the wrong time for court martial duty in Fort Vancouver," West observed. "I'll wager that Scott was mad enough at Harney that he had plenty left over for Captain George."

"All those lies Harney's been spreading about the Hudson's Bay Company inciting the northern tribes certainly didn't help his cause any," observed Tobias. "I wonder if word has reached Colonel Casey and Rory at Camp Pickett?"

"The news will arrive soon enough, I'll warrant," said Lieutenant West. "We'll no doubt be seeing the *Northerner* within a day or two at the most."

Indeed, the steamer with the general and his staff aboard arrived in Port Townsend a day and a half later. *Active*, *Massachusetts*, and *Jeff Davis* still lay at anchor, their bows, in the flood tide, riding toward the Cascade Range in the eastern distance over the wooded shores of Whidbey's Island. Tobias appeared at Captain Alden's cabin door. "Sir, signal from *Northerner*. *Active*'s captain repair on board."

"Thank you, Mr. St. John. Call away my gig, if you please. I think I shall use my six-oared boat to call upon the army's commander, rather than the jolly boat."

"Aye, aye, sir. Have you met the general before?"

"I've only seen him from a distance in Washington City, when I was assigned to the Navy Department. He's beloved as the hero of the War of 1812 and the Mexican War. And he's revered as the 'Great Pacificator' for his negotiations with the British at Buffalo and in Maine. But he must be in his seventies. My gig, Mr. St. John?"

"Yes, sir. Sorry, sir, I was mesmerized." Tobias left the cabin and returned on deck.

James Alden was ushered into the cabin of General Scott by Scott's aide, Lieutenant Colonel George Lay. "Thank you for being so prompt, Captain Alden. I need to ask a favor of you." The general, his considerable heft clad in army dress blue, was seated on a settee rather than a chair, to accommodate his bulk. The table in front of him was strewn with dispatches and drafts.

Scott began without pausing for formalities. "I intend to enter into correspondence and negotiations with Governor Douglas of British Columbia, through Colonel Lay, my aide, here. I need several vessels to carry him and the dispatches back and forth. I intend to move my headquarters to the *Massachusetts*, as she was my headquarters ship in the Mexican War. We'll be moving around the islands and the northern Sound. Would *Active* be available as a dispatch ship?"

"It would be my pleasure, General. We've already served that function for Captain Pickett and Colonel Casey. In fact, one of my officers serves as liaison to Colonel Casey, and has assisted him in the construction of the redoubt on San Juan Island, at the colonel's request."

"I didn't realize that. Is he a good man?"

"Yes, sir, one of my best officers. I believe the colonel selected him because he had established a good relationship with Captain Pickett and with the Royal Navy squadron commander."

"Hmmm. That could be useful." Scott looked solemnly at Alden. "See here, captain. I've talked to your Coast Survey supervisor, George Davidson. He cautions me that you like to go your own way, but he says you know your way around the islands, having been here with Wilkes. Anyone who can survive Wilkes is an exceptional man, indeed." He chuckled softly.

"I know part of your mission here is to develop surveys that will prove once and for all, that our claim of Haro Strait as the border is sound. I'm convinced we'll win the debate, but we must not come to blows while the debate continues. I'm going to call upon you and your young officer to help as my naval liaisons. What's his name?"

"Passed Midshipman Rory Dunbrody, general."

"Fine. Now I must tell you that I've relieved General Harney from command for the duration of my stay here. You and the Naval Service will deal only with my staff and me as army authority. And I'm here at the express command of Secretary of State Lewis Cass and President Buchanan."

"Aye, aye, sir. We're at your disposal." Alden remarked to himself at the fire in the old soldier's eyes as he outlined his orders. Scott may have decided to treat himself to fine cuisine as a substitute for the reward he'd sought in 1852 from the electorate as presidential candidate against Franklin Pierce, but he still had the command presence that had led his troops through the mountain passes and down the plains of Mexico.

"As soon as I shift my flag to *Massachusetts*, we'll be calling at San Juan Harbor. If you'd be kind enough to accompany us in *Active*, I'd like to meet your Mr. Dunbrody, and then have you carry a communication to Governor Douglas." The general smiled at Alden.

"Aye, aye, sir. We'll be prepared to proceed upon your signal."

The next morning, Scott transferred his headquarters to Captain Charles M. Fauntleroy's screw barque *Massachusetts*, still missing her main battery of 32-pounders ashore at San Juan. Together *Massachusetts* and *Active* moved across the Strait of Juan de Fuca and through Cattle Pass to San Juan Harbor. At the General's request, Alden sent Tobias ashore with Scott's summons to a meeting of the general, his staff, Alden, and Rory.

"Enough of this lollygagging about the shore, midshipman," Tobias cried out at Rory's tent flap. "The commanding general of the United States Army requests your presence."

"Sure, and can His Honor wait until I get me trousers on?" came the response.

"I'm sure he can, you slug-a-bed. I suspect you'll be returning to pack your sea bag, so use the jolly boat to reach the *Massachusetts*. I'll wait ashore for you, and we can return to our ships together. In the meantime, I believe I'll try to find that *Kanaka* you met."

"Tobias, what's going on?" Rory hopped from his tent, still dressing.

"The captain said the general wants you to accompany his staff when they meet with the British, as you and Hornby get on so well."

"Get on with ye! The commanding general wants my help? Saints presarve us!"

"The boat's at the wharf. I will see you later."

Tobias left the tent and walked south over the hillcrest toward the Bellevue Farm. There he found the Hawai'ian shepherd.

"*Aloha*," he called in greeting. "My friend tells me you were once a whaler."

"And he tells me you were one, too. I sailed on the *Pride of the Mystic*, Captain Jackson. Do you know her?"

"Out of New Bedford? Indeed I do. And do you know of star navigation, in the old way?"

"Yes, my father told me that long before Kamehameha, Hawai'ians used the wayfaring ways. And then we stopped. No one in Hawai'i remembers the old ways of star navigation. But my son, Kekoa, who is a whaler, wishes to learn, even though he uses sextant and 'ded' reckoning now. When he was in the western Pacific, he met master navigators, *palu*, who still used the old ways. It was in what you call the Caroline Islands, Satawal and Polowat. Now, he has learned of a Tahitian *palu*, a grandson of Tupaia, who sailed with Cook. Kekoa has gone to Raiatea to study with him."

"What is your name?" Tobias asked.

"I am Kele Kalama. Of course, here, they call me 'Kanaka Bill'."

"Kele, I am Tobias St. John. I must go now, but I would like to return from time to time to talk of star navigation."

"I would like that, Tobias. Talk of the old ways eases my homesickness. *A hui hou*." Kele waved as Tobias walked over the ridge and down the hill.

Rory pulled himself up the accommodation ladder near the

Massachusetts' main chains. After saluting the quarterdeck where the national ensign flew, and the officer of the deck stood, he was ushered below to General Scott's cabin. "Passed Midshipman Dunbrody, sir," he announced.

General Scott, Captain Alden, and a lieutenant colonel were seated in the great cabin of the sloop of war *Massachusetts.* The large stern windows of the cabin were set over a cushioned window seat that extended the width of the ship's transom. The general occupied a large portion of it. "Mr. Dunbrody, meet my aide, Colonel Lay."

Colonel Lay nodded as Rory said, "How do you do, sir."

"Captain Alden thinks your experience with Captain Hornby might be useful to us as we open negotiations with Governor Douglas. You've been ashore and seen firsthand the encounters between the army and the British. What's your assessment of the Royal Navy's attitude toward this occupation of San Juan? And, do they influence the governor?" Scott peered at Rory from beneath his snowy white eyebrows.

Rory was painfully conscious of the vast difference in rank between himself and the army's commander. His throat constricted, and he coughed, nervously. *Plunge ahead,* he thought.

"General, the RN's main goal seems to be avoiding hostilities so long as we don't outrageously besmirch British national honor. Admiral Baynes seems very determined not to provoke our garrison. Captain Hornby has encouraged his men to fraternize with ours at every opportunity, sir. But I know he's concerned about the governor's volatility. He's said as much, sir, and then caught himself before he was indiscrete in front of a junior officer."

"Very interesting, Dunbrody. You seem to have moved Captain Hornby to considerable candor," General Scott said with some amusement.

"Sure, sir, the English often have a soft spot for the Irish, so long as we know our place." Rory smiled in return.

"Do you find this useful, Colonel Lay, as you depart for Victoria?" The general turned to his aide.

"Yes, general, but I'd like to have Mr. Dunbrody travel with me to Victoria. It's conceivable that I'll encounter the admiral or his staff, and

Mr. Dunbrody would be useful in that event."

"Very well, colonel," Scott said. "Captain, I'll be grateful if you would transport the colonel and Mr. Dunbrody here to Victoria. And captain, as you met with Douglas in August, and as the colonel is traveling aboard your ship, I think it appropriate if you also accompany Colonel Lay on his visit to Governor Douglas. Another senior officer would be helpful, particularly one who is acquainted with Governor Douglas. Colonel, please draft an order for Colonel Casey detaching his naval liaison to my command temporarily. And my thanks to you, captain, for being so generous with your vessel and your midshipman."

"Aye, aye, general. Colonel, we'll be ready at your pleasure." Alden glanced at Rory. "Mr. Dunbrody, I'll take the gig back to *Active*. Are you in the jolly boat?"

"Yes, sir, Mr. St. John is still ashore waiting for me. When the colonel has my orders, I'll go ashore, pack my gear and be aboard immediately, sir."

The jolly boat eased alongside the wharf where Tobias stood waiting. "Off on another adventure, art thou?"

"As ever was. Let me run to camp and grab the sea bag." Rory climbed the slope to his tent. To his left, the soldiers of Colonel Casey's command still labored to increase the height of the parapet and add layers of thickness. Rory waved at Lieutenant Robert in the distance, still supervising the redoubt construction.

Rory and Tobias returned to *Active* as steam was being raised. When Colonel Lay arrived from *Massachusetts*, the boatswain carried out the captain's order to weigh anchor.

The *Active* was fitted with a steam capstan. No more barefoot sailors straining against the capstan bars for her. Unless, of course, the steam winch failed, as it frequently did. In those cases, it was out with the eight-foot capstan bars, eight of them, with three men on each. But with this arrangement, the steam winch sprockets were set and driven by the steam engine coupling and the process worked perfectly.

"Anchor's a'peak," cried the boatswain as the anchor, still on the sea bottom, stood on its crown, or point. "Anchor's aweigh," he called again, as the stock cleared the water surface. *Active* turned her bow toward

Cattle Point and around it to Victoria.

The *Active* rounded the rocks at the entrance to Victoria Harbor and steamed toward her anchorage, two cable lengths from the shore in front of the Crown Colony capitol building. The Crown Colony of Vancouver's Island was created under special grant of the Crown to be managed by the Hudson's Bay Company. The obvious potential for conflict of interest between a government and a for-profit corporation compounded the difficulties of the Colony's governor, James Douglas, for he was also a director of the HBC, and beholden to its board and its investors.

Governor Douglas greeted Colonel Lay, Captain Alden, and Rory at the door of his spacious office overlooking the harbor. Lay and Rory were above average height, but the Scottish governor towered over them at six foot four inches. He wore a black frock coat and a black stock a decade or two out of fashion, which contrasted handsomely with his full silver sideburns.

"Enter, gentlemen, and welcome," he said, but in his Scots burr, it sounded like 'eenterrr, gentlemen, and weeelcome.'

Colonel Lay introduced himself, Alden, and Rory. He apologized for General Scott's indisposition to travel. "Recovering from being thrown by a horse, governor," Lay explained.

"Och, no' at all," said Douglas. "We're delighted to have the 'Great Pacificator' present to aid us in this dispute. A pleasure to meet you, colonel. Captain Alden, it's a pleasure to see you again. And you, young Dunbrody, Captain Hornby has told me of you."

"Governor," said Colonel Lay, "the general has asked me to convey the decision of Secretary Cass, which decision he believes has the approval of Ambassador Lord Lyon and Foreign Secretary Lord Russell. We propose the joint occupation of the island with token forces of fewer than one hundred men each until such time as our governments can reach agreement on the border."

"I have given this much thought, gentlemen, and I am convinced that neither country should place forces on the island." Douglas sat back in his chair.

"Sir, that leads us back to the situation in place when all this began, residents of two nations and no effective force for order on the ground." Lay leaned forward. "And I'm sure you're as concerned as we that some defenses be in place for Indian raids, to defend your British subjects and our citizens alike."

"Gentlemen, I dinnae argue wi' yer contention that Lord Russell hae approved the joint occupation, but I must confirm it for m'self. But in the meantime, I cannae offer more than a withdrawal of all but one vessel if you remove all but your original company of infantry."

"Very well, Governor. We'll return to General Scott with your proposal. If it meets with his approval, we'll confirm the agreement with you. Perhaps it would be useful for Mr. Dunbrody and me to meet with the Royal Navy at that time. I believe we will have to seek the *Massachusetts* in Bellingham Bay. We should be able to respond in a day or two, should we not, captain?" Alden nodded affirmatively. The colonel rose and Alden and Rory rose with him.

"Excellent, gentlemen. I look forward to hearing your response. Admiral Baynes will have returned by that time, and I will convey your request to meet with him or his staff. Good day t'ye."

As the three officers sat in the stern sheets of the *Active*'s gig, Lay said, "Gentlemen, this is significant progress toward stabilizing this conflict."

"Very true, colonel," Alden responded. "Even if Douglas equivocates until the Foreign Office confirms the joint occupation, it's in effect a joint occupation now. One small force will be ashore and another afloat."

"Sure, captain, and when the decision is agreed to, the Royal Marines will come ashore, and the navy can be about its business." Rory smiled in anticipation.

"I'm confident General Scott will see this as a victory. Let's make all possible speed to Bellingham, captain."

"Aye, colonel, that we will." Alden glanced up at his ship as they approached, full of determination. "After all, what could go wrong now?"

The clear weather of the last week was giving way to typical northwest November clouds, rain, and wind gusts. The shacks of Bellingham town had lanterns lit, even in mid afternoon.

In the great cabin of the sloop of war *Massachusetts*, a very satisfied Lieutenant General Scott smiled beneath his bushy eyebrows. "Well, done, gentlemen! I concur with your view that this is the camel's nose under the tent of peaceful co-occupation. Please return to Victoria with my concurrence, and also ensure that Admiral Baynes agrees, even if it takes a side trip to Esquimalt." He nodded toward Alden. "We're certainly putting the sea miles on that side-wheeler of yours, captain."

"All in a good cause, sir," replied Alden.

"I do not intend to wait for Douglas' response in order to effect ours, gentlemen. Colonel Lay, before you visit Victoria, draft an order for Colonel Casey to withdraw all but Captain Pickett's Company immediately. I must say I have some trepidation about Pickett, but let's take this action now. It should serve to make a change of mind by Douglas much more difficult." Scott looked immensely pleased with himself.

CHAPTER 11
PEACE AMONG THE ISLANDS
OCTOBER 1859

Two days later the three officers sat once more in the Crown Colony governor's office. Douglas was joined by Captain Geoffrey Phipps Hornby, RN, and Rear Admiral R. Lambert Baynes, commander of Great Britain's Pacific Station, and Douglas' nominal superior in the British chain of command. Baynes, a slight balding lowland Scot with a reputation for cool-headedness, spoke to Rory in the informal exchange of pleasantries before the meeting began.

"Mr. Dunbrody, I'm Admiral Baynes. Captain Hornby has mentioned you often. Supervising the gun emplacements, have you been?"

"Assisting Lieutenant Robert, admiral, for the most part. But I should tell you, sir, there was a great cheer from the men still workin' on the parapets when General Scott's order was read, endin' their labors. They're packin' up to re-embark for Nisqually and Bellingham as we speak."

"A very measured and thoughtful response from the general, I must say," said Baynes.

"Indeed, sir, I quite agree," Rory said.

"Gentlemen, may we begin?" Douglas announced. "We're surprised, yet pleased at the alacrity with which General Scott has implemented our interim proposal whilst we wait to hear from the Foreign Office. Upon reflection, I am concerned about one aspect of the American response. Leaving an officer in charge who once declared that British subjects had no rights on the island, is troubling to me. With the number of fine officers available, can we not find one less precipitous and volatile than Captain Pickett?"

Now I know what could go wrong, Rory thought to himself.

"Governor, I will take the risk of assuming that the general will have no objection to your request," Lay responded.

Douglas cleared his throat. "Excellent, colonel. Admiral, would you be so kind as to offer the Royal Navy's response?" Douglas turned to Admiral Baynes, who had watched the exchange with a slightly amused expression, just a hint of a smile.

"Thank you, governor. Gentlemen, I'll now give Captain Hornby the order to return to Esquimalt with *Tribune* and *Plumper*, leaving only *Satellite* and Captain Prevost at San Juan Island. She can 'occupy' the harbor. We'll be ready to replace *Satellite* with a company of Marines as the governor directs."

"I believe this calls for a toast, gentlemen." The governor stepped to a sideboard and uncorked a decanter of port. When the glasses were filled, he said "We've all done a significant service to two great nations. To many more years of peace between Britain and America!"

After the toast, Lay said to Admiral Baynes, "The general will be directing that the 32-pounders in the redoubt be returned to the *Massachusetts* immediately."

"More work for Mr. Dunbrody, I believe." Baynes said, smiling as he replied.

"Sure, admiral, 'twill be my pleasure," said Rory.

As the officers filed out of the governor's office, Hornby took Rory aside. "Midshipman, I believe you and I have been party to a footnote in history. Thank you for your part in it."

"Captain, it's been a pleasure to watch up close. You're a man with great presence of mind. It's a lesson I'll long remember, sir. And perhaps I've made up for my ill-fated press interview."

"Thank you for the compliment, Dunbrody. And you've learned

an important lesson for a naval officer: Beware the fourth estate!" He laughed warmly. "Off you go, now."

As Rory caught up with Alden and Lay, the lieutenant colonel spoke to him. "Mr. Dunbrody, I'm aware that you and Captain Pickett have a firm professional friendship. This reassignment will surely be a blow to his confidence. Might I prevail upon you, after he receives his orders for Fort Bellingham, to assure him of your personal knowledge that his reassignment stemmed from diplomatic necessity?"

"As you wish, sir," Rory responded.

Douglas' request was more than acceptable to General Scott. On November 9, 1859, *Massachusetts* recovered her main battery, and embarked elements of the Third U.S. Artillery for Fort Steilacoom. USS *Active* and the *Julia* stood by to embark elements of the Fourth and Ninth Infantry regiments. HMS *Plumper* and HMS *Tribune* weighed anchor and proceeded to Esquimalt. Captain Lewis Cass Hunt and Company C of the Fourth Infantry were assigned garrison duty at Camp Pickett. Pickett and Company D were reassigned to Fort Bellingham. The "Great Pacificator" transferred his staff once again to the *Northerner* and embarked on the return voyage to the Isthmus of Panama.

On his way out of the Pacific Northwest, Scott wrote to Harney, urging him to relinquish command of the Department of Oregon to assume a higher command of the Department of the West. Any inducement Harney might have found in the suggestion was thoroughly diminished by Scott's voicing of his supposition that the British would ask for Harney's removal from Northwest command, and that President Buchanan would be relieved if Harney removed himself. That was enough to entrench Harney's resolve to stay put. Although General Scott had "put out one fire", the match to light another remained.

As Company D of the Fourth Infantry prepared to leave for Fort Bellingham, Rory found his way to Pickett's tent. "Good afternoon, sir," Rory said as the sentry held open the tent flap. "I've been reassigned to *Active*, sir. I wanted to tell you how much I've enjoyed my time as naval liaison to you and Colonel Casey."

"I'm grateful for your courtesy, Mr. Dunbrody. I've been reassigned myself, as you may know." "Yes, sir, that's another reason I'm here. The general had requested my presence at the negotiations with the British because of my frequent contact with Captain Hornby. When Colonel Lay acceded to Governor Douglas' request for a garrison unit other than yours, the colonel specifically pointed out that it was a question of diplomacy, and no reflection on your fine soldierly qualities. He asked me to emphasize that to you, sir. I know he wanted to do so himself, but you know how quickly General Scott left for the Isthmus."

"A pity my superiors lacked the courage and common courtesy to inform me in person," Pickett complained. "I appreciate your willin'ness to do their work for them."

"Captain Pickett, sir, I have every confidence that your career will continue to flourish. I hope our paths cross again."

"Very kind of you to say so, midshipman." Pickett was obviously disturbed by his removal and reassignment, but his gratitude for Rory's reassurances was real. "Drop by if *Active* comes to Bellin'ham," Pickett said.

CHAPTER 12
THE HAIDA RAID
SEPTEMBER, 1860

The officers who messed or dined in the wardroom of the USS *Active* were engaging with great enjoyment in a time-honored tradition: inviting their captain to dinner. The President of the Mess, First Lieutenant West, had invited Captain Alden to dine this Tuesday afternoon. Alden customarily dined in his cabin, sometimes with some of his officers as his guests. To be invited to join his officers in their mess was an occasion, a welcome break in the monotony of service on this remote frontier.

The dinner of roasted chicken, greens, corn, potatoes, and gravy, all purchased from the HBC's Puget Sound Agricultural Company, was behind them. Dessert had not yet been served. Discussion was lively, owing to the convocation of active, intelligent young men in a relaxed setting, and to the wine that had flowed freely, for the American Navy was still "wet".

"Mr. West, surely we need a song?" Alden smiled at his host.

"Absolutely right, captain. Mr. St. John, a nautical ballad, if you please."

"Aye, aye, Mr. West," Tobias replied, delighted at the chance to demonstrate his rich baritone. He launched into "Henry Martin", the song of the Scot "turned robber all on the salt sea, for to maintain his two brothers and he." And by the time he reached the third verse, with a "stout, lofty ship comin' a-bibbin' down on them, straightway," they were all, in their mind's eye, Scots pirates clearing for action. Music in the wardroom was a long and treasured custom and a bulwark against the boredom and monotony of shipboard life. Johnson and West, with passable baritones, and Rory's Irish tenor, carried the table through the song in support of Tobias' lead.

"Mr. St. John, a toast?" The captain smiled expectantly at Tobias who as the most junior officer, was expected to offer the initial toast.

"The United States of America." Glasses were lifted around the table, but the men remained seated as the low overhead made standing difficult.

"Captain, you've been ashore. Did you see Captain Pickett?" Tobias asked. The *Active* had just arrived at San Juan Town, having spent several months charting in the southern Sound.

"See him I did, and he's glad to be back. He seems somewhat nervous about what General Scott's reaction will be when he learns Harney has replaced Captain Hunt and C Company. But, he's getting on well with the Royal Marines who've established camp at Garrison Bay. I met their commander, Captain Bazalgette."

After the Royal Marines arrived in March, HMS *Satellite* had returned to Esquimalt. San Juan Harbor was now clear of British vessels.

"Pickett seems no longer to be a potential trigger for provoking a conflict with the British," said Tobias.

"I agree, Mr. St. John," said Alden. "It's primarily Harney and his actions we have to worry about."

"Sure, sir, won't General Scott have a fit when he hears? The HBC people in Nisqually said General Harney is still accusing Governor Douglas of inciting the northern Indians." Rory pulled out an old copy of the *Pioneer and Democrat*, the territorial capital's newspaper. "The Olympia paper is full of praise for Harney and Governor Gholson, and diatribes against HBC."

"That surely won't set well with General Scott." Lieutenant West, at the head of the table, reached for the wine decanter. "More wine, captain?"

"Yes, thank you, Mr. West," Alden said, distracted. He returned his attention to Rory. "You're right. When Scott learns that Hunt was replaced for his attempts to control the waves of whisky dealers flooding the Island, I predict Harney will be gone. And Scott should have learned in June as Hunt was relieved in April. I've no doubt Hunt let Scott know immediately. I'll wager orders from Scott will arrive any time this month."

"Pickett's worried about Harney's actions, too. There has just been a murder of a Haida woman at San Juan. Harney wants Pickett to keep northern Indians off the island by firing on them as they land. Pickett knows that will just create more raids."

Rory helped himself to another glass of wine. "As bad a situation as this is, it's worse in the east. My brother Tim just wrote from Fort Kearny. They're on the telegraph line and don't have to wait five weeks for news." Rory drew Tim's letter from his pocket, and the wardroom diners leaned forward as one man, eager to hear news of the tense situation in the east. "He says:

> *My Dear Brother:*
>
> *The major parties have just held their conventions. The Democrats nominated Stephen Douglas, who is not pro slavery enough for the southern Democrats, who walked out and nominated their own candidate, Breckenridge, on a "right to own slaves" platform. The Republicans nominated Abraham Lincoln. He is far too moderate for the South. Talk of secession is everywhere in the South. I fear I may soon have to choose between my army career and my native state and family. Being on the other side from Da and Siobhan would be a terrible thing. You may have to make the same choice. The country's going mad back there."*
>
> *As ever, your brother, Tim*

"True enough, Dunbrody," said West. "If Lincoln is elected, I predict that states will secede. And the Democrats splitting slates makes Lincoln's election a distinct possibility. Pardon me, gentlemen, if I've crossed the line and broken the prohibition against talking politics in the wardroom."

"I think we all may be forgiven, Mr. West," said Alden. "This situation may change our professional lives more than the effects of armor or exploding shells."

"Thank you, sir," West replied. "I suspect you're right. I missed mail call. Was there more?"

Midshipman Johnson chimed in: "Only if you count St. John's usual love letter from the mysterious Monique." This brought a volley of catcalls from around the cabin.

"Jealous of me, are you, young Johnson?" Tobias grinned at his tormentor.

"He gets a letter from her in every mailbag, sir. It's manifestly unfair." Johnson responded in kind.

"Who is this mystery woman, St. John?" asked the captain, who was not normally privy to the wardroom banter at mail delivery.

"Just an acquaintance from childhood, sir. She lives in Bourg on the island of Terre de Haut, south of Guadeloupe."

"It's no mere acquaintance, sir. When he grew up in Antigua, they were the talk of both islands." Rory was clearly enjoying teasing his friend.

"We were ten years old," Tobias protested.

"And you've seen her since on every whaling and navy voyage of yours that went anywhere near Guadeloupe," Rory said.

"Captain!" The officer of the deck shouted down the wardroom skylight. "Kanaka Bill has rowed out from shore and wants to talk to you."

"I'm coming up directly," Alden said. "Finish your wine, gentlemen. This shouldn't take long."

Kele Kalama, the whaler turned sheepherder, stood on the quarterdeck, his hat in his hand. "Captain, I just saw three Haida war canoes headed southwest toward Whidbey's Island with fifteen warriors in each. I thought you should know."

"Did they have weapons?"

"Yes, captain. I saw muskets and axes. They didn't look like a trading party."

"Have you told Captain Pickett?"

"I came to tell you first, captain. I know it takes time to get steam up. I'll go to the soldiers next."

"You did well, Kanaka Bill. The settlers at Ebey's Landing and Crockett's Lake will have trouble with a party that size, even if they can make it to their blockhouses. We must move quickly. I'll take the jolly boat. Please come with me."

"Gentlemen!" Alden shouted down the wardroom skylight. "On deck smartly, if you please!"

As his officers rapidly assembled before him on the quarterdeck, Alden formulated his plan. "Lieutenant West, I'd be obliged if you'd raise steam. Kanaka Bill reports forty-five Haida in three war canoes headed toward Whidbey. He and I will see Pickett. I'll ask for twenty men. Mr. West, I'll want all ten of our Marines and ten of our most experienced hands. We'll land at Ebey's Landing if we find the Haida there. If not, we'll proceed to Crockett's Lake. Captain Pickett can send a messenger to Garrison Bay to ask Captain Bazalgette for a contingent of Royal Marines as reinforcement. They may have to row to Victoria for a ship. I wish there were others here in the harbor. We could commandeer one." Alden quickly led Kele to the jolly boat and headed toward the wharf.

Alden and Kele made their way to Camp Pickett and Pickett's tent. Pickett came to the tent front to greet them. "Captain Alden, I'm delighted to see you again. It seems you've only just left."

"Captain Pickett, we've not a moment to lose. Kanaka Bill saw three Haida war canoes headed toward Whidbey just minutes ago. I'm here to ask you to assume command of twenty of my men and a like number of yours. I'll embark your detachment, and we'll search for signs of the Haida. Perhaps you could send a man to ask Bazalgette for reinforcements."

"A fine plan, suh! Give me twenty minutes and my contingent will meet you on the wharf."

"Thank you, Captain Pickett." Alden and Kele regained the jolly boat. "I'm guessing you'd like to go along, Kanaka Bill?" Alden said to the old navigator.

"I would be useful, Captain. I know Chinook Jargon and enough Haida to get along. And I have fought with clubs and axes before. These are weapons of the *Kanaka*. You will find that my eyes are still sharp and my legs still strong. *Mahalo.*"

As *Active* headed southeast across the Strait of Juan de Fuca, the soldiers, sailors, and Marines of the landing party looked to their weapons; cutlasses and muskets for the sailors, muskets and bayonets for the soldiers and Marines. The high sandy bluffs of Whidbey's Island soon came into view. Forty miles long, it was heavily forested with occasional meadows. On the west side, one- to two-hundred foot bluffs prevailed, sloping every few miles to low banks and wetlands along the shore.

Such a place was the landing in front of Crockett's Lake, a shallow marsh pond separated from the Sound by a sandspit. Here the *Active* turned east as did the shoreline of Admiralty Inlet, creating Admiralty Bay. There they saw three war canoes on the beach, and heard gunfire from inland, toward the northeast, where two blockhouses stood, connected by two stockade fences.

The officers stood on the quarterdeck. Alden called to West. "Lieutenant, take the way off her. We'll land the shore party here and then lay off the beach a cable length or two. Have our two starboard nine-pounders run out and ready. We'll make some gun practice upon those canoes."

Alden turned to Pickett. "With most boats, I'd send a party ashore with axes and chop a hole or two in the hulls, but those canoes are red cedar and spruce from Russian America. Tough wood, indeed. Don't be alarmed when you hear us firing. Mr. Dunbrody and Mr. St. John will command our detachment under your direction."

"Excellent, sir," Pickett replied. "I believe I'll attempt to drive them away from the blockhouses and to the woods. I imagine they'll eventually return to their canoes. We shall wheel left and trap them between us and the shore."

"Fine, Captain Pickett," Alden said. "We'll cruise up and down the shoreline. If you flush them, and we see them, I'll fire a flare. Send a runner and we'll direct him. Be careful as they find the canoes. The Haida will be resourceful when they discover their canoes destroyed. And they're attacking settlers in the blockhouses. This is probably a revenge raid. These northern tribesmen are intelligent, courageous and determined."

"Thank you, sir. I appreciate the alacrity with which we've

managed to engage the raiders." Pickett walked forward toward where his platoon had assembled on the foredeck. His two lieutenants, Howard and von Klopfenstein followed him.

"Kanaka Bill, stay with Mr. St. John while ashore." Alden told the shepherd.

The *Active* gently backed her paddle wheels, maintaining her position abeam of the beached canoes against a flooding tide. "Boats ready to launch, sir," said West.

"Very well, Mr. West. Take the way off her. We'll launch boats here. Take your bearings and maintain station."

"Aye, aye, sir," said West. "Clear away all boats." Sailors tailed on to the lines running to the main yard and fore yard through blocks and then to a cradle sling separating two lines, one running to the bow and one to the transom of the larger launch and longboat. "Let fall." Other sailors were launching the smaller boats from the davits.

The naval shore party, the Marines and the infantrymen and their officers, filled the waiting boats. As they headed for the beach, Alden turned the *Active* and lay two cable lengths, or four hundred yards, offshore.

Pickett stood on the beach with his four officers and his company first sergeant, Burke. "Sergeant, detail two men to remain with you and me as our runners. I'll ask each of you lieutenants and naval officers to lead a squad of ten men. We shall form in line and advance inland to the blockhouses. Kindly place your best men at the right and left flanks where they must be aware of any efforts to flank the formation."

As they advanced a mile inland in the shadow of woods to their left, west of the blockhouses, Tobias' squad glimpsed the roofs of the two-story blockhouses, the weathered wood framed by the gloomy darkness of the forest behind. The June sunlight shone on the lighter green of the treetops. The trees, a huge stand of Douglas fir, began a hundred yards inshore, just north of the blockhouses.

"The Haida are firing from cover, Tobias," said Kanaka Bill. "I can see three bodies close to the first blockhouse door. They look like settlers."

Tobias' squad was the middle left of the formation. Pickett had placed the two Fourth Infantry squads on the flanks. Rory commanded *Active*'s Marines, with their sergeant as second-in-command.

In contrast to Company D, the Marines were notoriously good shots. The Marines left the line of woods and then concealing themselves behind a low rise in the meadows south of the blockhouses, advanced to within fifty yards behind the Haidas' position. Pickett stepped to the front and raised his saber, the pre-arranged signal to halt, kneel, and prepare to fire. Simultaneously, a Haida firing from the west of the blockhouses glanced to his right and spotted the troops. As he cried out to his companions, Pickett gave command:

"Kneel! Present! Take aim! Fire!" Forty muskets discharged. The Haida, surprised from the side and rear of their position, wasted no time in scrambling to better cover. Desultory shots rang out from the settlers in the blockhouses as the Haida presented new targets. With ten Haida laying down covering fire, the remaining thirty-five ran for positions closer to the forest on the north side of the blockhouse.

Rory's Marines had made good practice of the Haida as they shifted position. Three lay dead just south of the blockhouse, double-pointed metal daggers in leather cases around their necks. "Sergeant, if we can keep those few Indians to our front pinned down, Lieutenant Howard's squad can flank them. Their comrades have lost their field of fire now that they're back of the blockhouse and a hundred yards farther away."

"Aye, aye, sir. I'll have the men keep up a continuous fire. We'll keep them busy," said Deihl, the sergeant of Marines.

"Sure, I'll be right back," said Rory, as he stooped and ran to Captain Pickett's command position. Pickett and the first sergeant, with two runners, were crouched behind a log. "Captain, I think my Marines can keep these Haida to our front busy, if you wish to have Lieutenant Howard flank them to our left and lay down enfilading fire, sir."

Pickett thought for a moment. "I'm grateful for your interestin' suggestion, midshipman. Maintain your position and lay down fire until I can move Lieutenant Howard as y'all suggest."

Rory stopped at Tobias' squad on his way back to the Marines. He explained to Tobias and Kele his plan and the need to keep the attention of the Haida rearguard to the front. In the distance, the boom of the *Active*'s nine-pounders could be heard as they fired at the beached war canoes. The troops to the shore side of the blockhouse commenced fire with their own accompaniment.

Howard's ten infantrymen ceased fire and crept toward a flanking position to the west of the blockhouses and the seven Haida to the south side of the blockhouse. Tobias' sailors and Rory's Marines, in the center, kept up a rolling fire. The settlers in the blockhouses fired sporadically but effectively at the Haida rearguard, keeping their heads down. The infantry of von Klopfenstein engaged the Haida main body who were firing from the edge of the forest.

The Haida rearguard scattered like buckshot when Howard's infantry opened fire from their right flank. "They're running for it!" Tobias shouted to his sailors as the Haida rearguard ran directly toward the blockhouses, hoping to run so close that the settlers couldn't depress their muskets sufficiently to hit them. This route was also the most direct one to the forest and their main body. The Marines were able to down all but three before they reached the relative safety of the forest.

Captain Pickett stepped to the front of his command. "Lieutenant Howard, take your men and Mr. St. John's into the forest and form a barrier to their westward march - men every five feet. Lieutenant von Klopfenstein, take your men and the Marines to the forest, on the right, staying under cover as much as y'all can. Wheel left and drive them west."

"On the double, gentlemen, if y'all please." Turning to Sergeant Burke, Pickett confided, "We'll only extend the line a hundred feet into the woods. The Haida may be fixin' to go around them, but in any event, they will be exhausted by the time they reach their canoes. I'm hopeful we can trap them against the shore and gain their surrender."

His saber and Colt 1851 .36-caliber Navy six-shot pistol at his side, Rory entered the gloom of the forest. The Haida had fired a few shots as the Marines and infantry had carefully approached the forest edge, but then had disappeared deeper into the underbrush. Sunlight only occasionally filtered through the canopy of fir boughs. The contrast made the shade even darker.

"Herr Dunbrody, if you will be so kind as to take your Marines into the wood, left turn, and form on me. We will see how you fight for real, will we not?"

"Aye, aye, Lieutenant. Sergeant Diehl, lead the file. Five feet between each man. Left turn. You'll be on the right flank. Have your last man form on me." Rory, pistol and saber now in hand, glanced toward von Klopfenstein on his left. *Sadistic ould sod, he is*, Rory thought to himself. His palms were sweating, and his throat was dry.

A grimacing face with ochre stripes and an upraised war club was Rory's next sight as a Haida warrior jumped from behind a fir and across the underbrush. Rory parried the swing of the club with his saber and fired the Navy Six against the Indian's chest. Knocked backward by the rush, Rory ducked to his right as a second Haida fired a shot over Rory's head.

Rory dodged behind a fir, emerged on its right side and ran directly toward the Haida who was reloading his musket. The warrior dropped the musket, and picked up and swung his war club in one motion as the point of Rory's saber entered his torso.

The club head missed Rory, but the handle caught his left shoulder and he dropped his pistol. Wrenching his saber from his foe's body, he slashed the Indian's neck in a deathblow. At that moment the Prussian ended his own bout with his Haida opponent with a saber cut to the face.

"You do not appear as clumsy as you did in our *salle*, Irish," the duelist said, between deep breaths.

"Sure, fear is a great motivator, now, Herr Lieutenant." Rory saw the vague shapes of several Haida moving away from them west into the forest. The Marines and infantry had driven others off, and two soldiers had been wounded. "They're a rear guard, I'm thinkin', lieutenant." Rory said.

"*Ja*, I think we can move forward carefully," von Klopfenstein replied. Musket fire from the west of their position marked Haida attempts to move toward their canoes. It was followed by silence, and the line of soldiers and Marines moved cautiously northward through the underbrush.

Tobias and Lieutenant Howard were also side-by-side at the center of their line of infantry and sailors. "I'm not satisfied they can't work their way around our inner flank," Tobias said to Howard.

"Still, suh, we must hold our position. But tell your men to be aware of movement in their rear," Howard responded.

Tobias heard a sound behind him and backed into the stalking Haida just as he swung his war club at the back of Tobias' head. The surprise move caused the Haida to miss, while Tobias swept his left leg back in a powerful circular Capoeira motion, clipping the Haida's legs out from under him. Snatching his cutlass from his belt, Tobias nearly severed the Indian's head before he could rise.

Howard was held in a headlock by another Haida, his dagger in his other hand, when Kele and Tobias seized the Indian from behind and threw him to the ground. Kele bludgeoned him with his own war club. Tobias drew his Navy Six and shot a third Haida through the heart as he leaped from behind a fir.

It was suddenly quiet in the forest. The fight had taken thirty seconds. "You were right, sir. They did encircle our flank. My thanks to both of you." Howard sat facing the rear, breathing heavily.

Pickett, with Howard's platoon, saw the shako of an infantryman moving toward him. "Hold your fire, men. It's our other half."

The officers quickly conferred. "I believe they've gone deeper into the wood to outflank us and make their way back to their canoes," Pickett said. "We're now closer to the canoes. Form a column of twos and let us greet them."

The American command emerged from the forest a half-mile north of the beach and immediately sighted the twenty-five remaining Haida just as they came upon their destroyed canoes. USS *Active* stood two hundred yards off the beach, nine-pounder cannon run out. A half-mile distant on Admiralty Inlet was HMS *Satellite*, with a bone in her teeth. The red coats of Captain Bazalgette's Royal Marines could be seen on her deck.

The Haida paused, unsure of their best course of action. *Active* fired a broadside, and the shot hummed just over the heads of the Indians and crashed into the incline behind them.

The forty men of Pickett's command had double-timed into position fifty yards from the Haida. "Column right, march! At the double. Halt! Left face. Front rank, kneel. Present, aim." Pickett paused in his commands. The Haida realized they faced forty muskets and two nine-pounders. "Kanaka Bill, I'd be obliged if you'd ask them to surrender," Pickett drawled.

Kele stepped forward and addressed them in their language and the Chinook Jargon. He promised a fair trial if they surrendered and death far from home and their rituals of the dead if they did not. Their chief came forward and replied.

"Sir," Kele translated to Pickett, "the chief is Jefferson of the Skidegate Haida. He says his young warriors wish to fight on, but that he is no 'fool man'. I told him that the 'George's' chief, Douglas, prized the work of the hundreds of Haida tribesmen HBC hires each summer, and might intervene at their trial on their behalf if they give up now. He asks for time to talk to his young warriors."

"Excellent, Kanaka Bill. Tell him we will give him time to convince his party." The Haida still held muskets and war clubs, but several young leaders had been killed in the fighting. Their canoes had been smashed by roundshot. Some stared defiantly, some looked at the ground in discouragement, some shouted and waved their muskets as Chief Jefferson spoke to them. Finally, they raised their hands in surrender.

"Lieutenant Howard, have your men gather their weapons." Pickett found Rory in the ranks of his Marine squad. "We'll shackle them for now and consult with the British as to their disposition. The raid was on American soil, but we've no facilities or ready tribunal that can quickly deal with them. After Colonel Casey's experience with the hanging of Chief Leschi, he may be reluctant to allow civilian justice to be involved. Perhaps our British friends may have some ideas."

The well-appointed great cabin of Her Britannic Majesty's steam corvette *Satellite* held six officers of two nations in conference, Captains Prevost, RN; Bazalgette, Royal Marines; Pickett, Fourth U.S. Infantry; Alden, USN; Lieutenant Tremaine, RN, first lieutenant of the *Satellite* now that Captain Hornby and *Tribune* had returned to England; and

Passed Midshipman Dunbrody, USN. The captive Haida were still ashore, guarded by Bazalgette's fresh Marines, while the combat-weary members of Pickett's combined command rested and tended their wounded. A detail of men from *Active* and *Satellite*, commanded by First Sergeant Burke, were gathering the bodies of the Americans killed during the engagement. The ships' cooks were preparing a meal for all, including the surviving men, women, and children of Crockett's Landing, now released from their blockhouse complex.

As the six officers sat around Captain Prevost's table, Prevost said to Rory, "While Captain Bazalgette was ashore, he spoke to Sergeant Diehl of your Marines. He said you and the Prussian dispatched three of the Haida in hand-to-hand action, and two were by your hand. They're a fierce lot. You did well. If you ever tire of Captain Alden's harsh discipline, I've a spot for an Irish officer aboard *Satellite*." Laughter rippled 'round the table, accompanied by congratulations.

Rory permitted himself a rare moment of self-approval and enjoyed the glow of accomplishment. Then, as usual, he silently cautioned himself not to let his guard down too far.

"And let me express my thanks, Captain Alden," said Pickett, "for Dunbrody's action and for that of Mr. St. John in savin' the life of Lieutenant Howard, also in desperate hand-to-hand combat. Your officers are most resourceful, suh."

Prevost brought the meeting to order. "Gentlemen, I have a surprise for you. We shipped a supernumerary in Victoria as we responded to Captain Bazalgette's request to transport his detachment." At that moment, the door from Prevost's sleeping cabin opened, and Governor Douglas stepped into the great cabin.

"Well done, gentlemen. The frontier is safer for your quick response. Captain Pickett, let me say how impressed I am with your leadership in this engagement. Your men were courageous. Your strategy was effective against a fierce adversary. And Captain Bazalgette has nought but praise for your cooperation on San Juan Island. I was wrong about you, sir." He crossed his arms across his chest. "I will not, however, extend that judgment to General Harney."

"Thank you, governor," said Pickett, "on behalf of our forces."

Pickett was obviously pleased, for his soldierly reputation was the thing he prized most.

"You're welcome, I'm sure. And may I add my delight that a Hudson's Bay employee, Kanaka Bill, distinguished himself in combat and in persuading the Haida to surrender."

"He did a fine job, governor," Alden agreed. "I watched from my quarterdeck. He stepped forward while they still had weapons in hand. Sheer courage!"

"Now, gentlemen, I propose a model of international cooperation." Douglas took his seat at the table. "I've been concerned at the potential for mischief each summer with such large numbers of northern Indians coming south to work for HBC: Haida, yes, but also Tlingits, Gitskans, other Tsimshians, Bella Coolas, many tribes and bands. I propose to disarm them all for the duration of their work here in the straits and Puget Sound."

Douglas continued. "I'm aware that Captain Pickett is concerned with the risks of taking the kind of aggressive action suggested by General Harney: barring them from the San Juans, throwing trespassers in gaol, that sort of thing. And that concern is compounded by having to hold twenty-five of them for Lord knows what felony under American law with inadequate facilities. So I offer our prison in Victoria until they're charged, arraigned, and tried. What say you?" Douglas sat back, having delivered his speech.

"Suh, that is indeed a generous and thoughtful offer. But I'm uncertain of what my superiors might say." Pickett sighed.

"Captain Pickett, if I may." Alden leaned forward to make his point. "You are the hero, the leader of this victory. You will be seen as such by the territorial governor, and by the press, who love you even now. You can do no wrong. Governor Gholson will thank you for saving him the embarrassment of potential jailbreak and perhaps some costs besides. And I shouldn't worry about the general. The wagering in my wardroom is that he'll receive orders to report to Winfield Scott in Washington City by the next post to answer for insubordination. No offense, Captain Pickett."

"None taken, suh." Pickett was smiling now, his path looking much clearer.

Tobias and Kele walked on the sand and pebbles of the beach at Crockett's Landing. "That was quite a chance you took, today, my friend," Tobias said. "The Haida still had weapons in hand when you stepped forward. I'm glad you speak their language so well."

"*Mahalo*, Tobias. As I mentioned, they come by the hundreds to work for HBC each summer so I have my own 'language school' each year. It came in handy today. Speaking many languages is such a gift. I've convinced my son of that. His English is good, and, of course, his Pidgin and Hawai'ian."

"I haven't heard you use Pidgin here."

"Oh, me *allee* same a' you Boston *haole sailamoku*. Me sail, killee whale, *pau hana, inu grog nui loa*!" Kele laughed with Tobias. "You must speak a patois, from da islands?"

"Oh yes, mon," said Tobias. "And I learned French from my lover, Monique. My friend, Rory, learned his French from his grandfather, who spoke it in the French Army. As you say, it's a gift."

"It was an honor to fight alongside you today, friend. *Mahalo nui loa*."

"And alongside you," replied Tobias. "*A hui hou* and *aloha*."

CHAPTER 13
SECESSION'S SHADOW
MARCH 1861

The wardroom table of the USS *Active* was the scene. The occasion? Mail call, the highlight of the month in the remote duty station known as Puget's Sound. The *Active* lay anchored off Fort Steilacoom, several miles north of the mouth of the Nisqually River. The Nisqually had a broad estuary with square miles of wetlands that served as periodic home to thousands of migratory birds. The fresh water it discharged into saltwater Nisqually Reach began its journey at the foot of Nisqually Glacier on towering Mount Rainier, named by George Vancouver, RN, for one of his patrons, Admiral Peter Rainier. The Puyallups and Nisquallies, nearby tribes, called the 14,410-foot peak Tahoma, 'mother of earth'.

"Listen to this!" Tobias waved his letter from home. "Father says that six more states have seceded since South Carolina in December; Mississippi, Florida, Alabama, Georgia, Louisiana, and Texas. How can the nation survive this?"

Rory added news from his letter. "Sister Siobhan writes that the Confederate States of America, in Congress assembled, have elected Jefferson Davis of Mississippi as provisional president."

"Where were they assembled, Rory?" Tobias asked.

"Montgomery, Alabama, apparently. I'm thinking it's a bit remote for the capital if the larger states like Virginia and North Carolina decide to secede." Rory read further. "Siobhan says brother Tim seems ready to resign his army commission when and if North Carolina secedes. Something about not lifting up his sword against neighbor and family. God save us all, what can my brother be thinking?"

Lieutenant West looked up from his reading at the head of the table. "Surely, Dunbrody, you can't be surprised by your brother's concern that must be shared by thousands of Americans."

"Ah, sure and aren't I the selfish one, worried that his moral crisis will move me where I don't wish to go," said Rory.

"Rory, there're three more letters in the mail bag. They were under a fold. They're all for you." Passed Midshipman Johnson handed Rory the bag.

"Oh, Jasus, and what else can go amiss? Here's a letter from Tim. Maybe he's found some sense." Rory began to read. "No, no hope there, at all, at all. Here's what he says." He read aloud to his fellow officers.

> *Dear Brother,*
> *I'm convinced our state will secede within weeks. What a quandary, my country or my family. Would that I were closer to home instead of stuck out here in Kansas. I'll just have to make the best of a bad choice. I imagine by the time you receive this, you will have learned of the seven states' secession, and find yourself in the same dilemma. As my Texan friends used to say, "every man's got to kill his own snakes."*
> *Your brother,*
> *Tim*

"If it isn't just the sound guidance I've been hopin' for! Brother Tim," moaned Rory, "calm and decisive as usual!" "Do I hear the diminishing of brotherly love?" Tobias asked.

"Not a bit of it," said Rory. "Himself is just a shade excitable. God bless'm, 'tis a grand brother he is. Holy Mary! This one is from the Confederate States of America."

"The seceding states are reaching out, Rory." said Midshipman Johnson. "I hesitated to mention it, but I got one, too, from the

Committee on Naval Affairs."

"Johnson, you're a Marylander. Do you think Maryland will secede?" Tobias leaned forward, half curious, half afraid. "Maryland is a slave state but deeply divided on the question of slavery," said Johnson.

"It's hard to imagine the federal government or the other northern states allowing Maryland to secede," said Lieutenant West. "If Virginia secedes, as it probably has by now, Washington City would be surrounded."

"Apparently, this Confederate Naval Committee is writing to officers from any state which may secede, whether it has or not," said Tobias. "What do they say, Rory?"

"It's dated February 14, from Montgomery." Rory read the letter.

> *Sir:*
> *On behalf of the Committee of Naval Affairs, I beg leave to request that you repair to this place, at your earliest convenience, to accept a commission in the Confederate States Navy, at a rank at least commensurate with your present one.*
> *Your Obedient Servant,*
> *C. M. Conrad, Chairman.*

"That's word for word like the one they sent me, Rory." Johnson leaned back, perplexed.

"Sure, 'tis a clever strategy, damn their eyes. Forcin' a choice between kith and kin, and the oath we took. There'll be many a southern-born officer starin' at the overhead these nights." Rory reached for the third letter. "God save us, here's one of those troubled souls, now. Lieutenant John Taylor Wood, my old instructor, as I live and breathe." Rory read to himself:

> *My Dear Dunbrody,*
> *I hope all is well with you on the Northwest frontier. It's a while since we discussed the latest innovations in gunnery. I'm writing because our talks always ranged beyond our profession to the condition of mankind. The talk of secession has me in misery as*

I suspect it has you, and I need to share my thoughts with someone outside my family. I've been contacted by the Confederate Naval Committee and asked to accept a commission in the Confederate States Navy. Senator Stephen Mallory of Florida has been named Confederate Secretary of the Navy. He's an excellent choice.

My northern-born father, the colonel, will stay with the Union, as we've begun to call the northern states. My southern-born mother will stand behind him. But my brother Robert has resigned his army commission this month (February) and been named General Braxton Bragg's Adjutant General in Montgomery.

My southern midshipmen are resigning and the decrease in the numbers of students may make my teaching role at the Academy unnecessary. I want to support the Union but cannot take up arms against the South. I am in misery, and I realize that our circumstances are similar. Please be assured of my certainty that as you confront this dilemma, you will do so with thoughtfulness and honor.

With great affection, I remain your obedient servant and friend,

J. T. Wood

"Ah, the poor divil. His Da's with the North, and his brother's gone t' Montgomery. 'Tis enough t' vex St. Peter, sure and all," said Rory. "I must write him back and commiserate."

"We've a lot of thinking to do, Rory." Johnson said.

"You're right, Phillip, and I implore both of you to take your time and talk this through. This is a turning point for all of us." Tobias heaved a sigh of near-despair at his shipmates' quandary.

The next morning Passed Midshipman Johnson was officer of the deck. Seaman McGinty stood lookout on the quarterdeck. "Shore boat coming off, sor," said McGinty. "Looks t' be an army officer in the stern sheets, sor."

"Very well, McGinty. Ask the duty boatswain's mate to report to me, please."

Honors were rendered Captain George Pickett as he came aboard

Active. "Would y'all be so kind as to ask Mr. Dunbrody t' have a word with me, midshipman?"

"Certainly, sir," Johnson responded. "I'm sure Mr. Dunbrody will be delighted to see you."

"Captain! What brings you to sea?" Rory smiled a welcome as he came on deck.

"I'm on my way to see my son, Jimmy. He's still staying in Arkada, west of here, with my friends the Collins family." He pulled Rory aside and added, *sotto voce*, "And I wanted to speak to you with candor about the secession."

"Of course, sir. I'll just be askin' for the jolly boat, sir, and we'll have a quiet stroll on the beach."

Side by side on the shore below Fort Steilacoom, Rory walked and talked with George Edward Pickett. "I was glad to see that you stayed on as American commander at San Juan after General Harney was relieved last year."

"I believe I was most fortunate that Genr'l Harney was replaced by my old friend, Colonel George Wright. We served together in the Mexican War. And we've been able to reduce the problems with the Haida with Governor Douglas' help. Captain Bazalgette and I have become good friends. He laughs at my stories, bless his heart."

"What will you do if Virginia secedes?"

Pickett sighed heavily. "I cannot lift mah sword against Virginia. It pains me greatly to think of leaving so many fine and dear comrades on the other side. You must be in the same conundrum, suh."

"The same intensity, to be sure. My ties to North Carolina may not be as strong as yours to Virginia, but my family is there, and my brother may well choose to stay with his birth-state. I'll not find ease with either choice." Rory sighed. "Sure, our world will not be the same, captain. I just heard from John Taylor Wood. He wrestles with the same demons."

"If Virginia secedes, I shall resign."

"Wouldn't it be a comfort, now, if my choice were so clear? May you find good fortune, Captain Pickett."

"I wish you the very same, suh."

CHAPTER 14
A PARTING OF THE WAYS
MARCH 1861

Two days later, Kele and Tobias stood at the edge of Fort Steilacoom's three-hundred-yard-long parade ground while Rory, astride the bay mount of the Third Artillery Regiment's adjutant, put the strapping animal through its paces. The two naval officers had encountered Kele on their walk to the fort and invited him to join them. Kele was visiting from the Hudson's Bay Company trading post at Nisqually, just a few miles to the south.

"Your friend is quite a rider," said Kele.

"He loves to ride," said Tobias. "His summers in Ireland were spent riding his uncle's horses. He's beset by a difficult choice in his life. I think the riding helps to clear his mind. I hope so. Kele, what brings you to Nisqually?"

"The HBC sends me to the trading post periodically for supplies for the herders on San Juan. I ride the *Beaver*, a ship nearly as old as am I." Tobias had seen the brigantine-rigged side-wheeler anchored in the Reach south from the *Active* as they had left the ship this morning. "She came around Cape Horn in your year 1834, the first steamer in the Pacific," Kele said.

"One sees her everywhere on the Sound," said Tobias. "How does she sail?"

"Slowly, except with the wind aft. But any tack or run is preferable to steam. She burns many cords of fir. Half of any trip is falling and splitting her fuel. Thank Heaven we've found coal on Vancouver's Island!"

Rory cantered up to the two men, the bay steaming from the exercise. "Working things out, are you?' Tobias asked. "I brought a basket of bread, cheese, and wine from the wardroom. Let's cool off in the tower yonder." Tobias pointed to the two-story water tower slightly behind the row of officers' quarters lining one side of the parade ground. "We'll have fewer spectators there." Rory's riding had been watched by officers' families from their verandas and by the soldiers of the post carrying out various fatigue details. Colonel Casey's quarters were three houses to their left.

The adjutant's groom appeared. "I'll cool him down now, sir, if you're finished."

"Thanks for taking him, corporal," said Rory, handing him the reins. "Please extend my thanks to the adjutant."

Climbing to the tower's second level, the three could see the snow-capped Mount Rainier as they looked left across the parade ground toward the chapel and the stables behind it. They leaned back on the benches and gazed at the parade ground turf and Mount Rainier's white and ice blue peak, towering and crystal clear in the rare March sunshine. Kele pointed to the fourteen thousand-foot summit. "Doctor Tolmie, the chief factor of the HBC post here, has climbed that mountain!"

"Och, the daft Scotsman. Who'd want to go that high, and in his right mind, and all?" Rory grinned at Kele.

"I think the vastness of the country inspires such feats. Yet, until the *haole* came, as in my islands, these hills and shores and plains were peopled by those who lived on the land but knew it could not be owned. Now they have found that, even though it cannot be owned, it can be taken."

"Well, now, at least they didn't copy the British in Ireland, where the land they seized is rented back to the dispossessed at ever-increasing rates. Theft, followed by profits taken monthly from the victims."

Tobias looked at Kele and Rory. "True, you are dispossessed, but you have yet to become property, yourselves."

"Kele," said Rory, "I believe we've just been trumped in this contest of relative injustices. Would y'pass the wine bottle, now?"

"What will you do, Rory?" Tobias asked as he reached to fill Rory's glass.

"I must resign my warrant, my friend. My father and sister will be in the South, I'm convinced, and my brother, too, I'm thinkin'. We shall be on opposite sides, Tobias. If it comes to war, I swear I shall never cause you harm."

"Nor I you, Rory."

"My friends," said Kele, "you are strong, resourceful men. You will endure, and if war comes, it will pass, and you will still have your friendship and your honor."

"Are you a *Kahuna kilo kilo*, Kele, with a vision of the future?" Tobias asked.

"I know dis t'ing," the *Kanaka* said, simply.

"In Ireland, we'd call Kele a *senachie*," said Rory. "I must tell the captain of my decision. Kele, good fortune to you, sir. Tobias, I'll see you aboard."

George Davidson, commandant of the U.S. Coast Survey for the Pacific Coast, sat with James Alden in the great cabin of the *Active*. He had come aboard in Port Townsend, after traveling up the coast in *Northerner*. "When will you tell the crew about your new orders, Captain Alden?"

"I'll announce it this evening, sir, at the change of the watch. I'll tell St. John, beforehand of his promotion to master. He and I will be traveling together, he to the *Preble*, and me to assume command of the *Merrimack* at Norfolk, and refit her. I'm sure he'll request leave to visit Antigua on the way. He always does. I'll grant it, of course. He's done a splendid job for us."

"You've a good crew, Captain. St. John is an outstanding navigator. It's not presumptuous to say that service in the Coast Survey carries a great deal of weight in an officer's record. After all," he smiled, "we are the finest cartographers afloat. And your charting will be in use for years. I'm confident the Haro Strait work will eventually lead to undisputed American possession of San Juan Island."

"That being said, you know my concerns over your wild forays to defend against Indians, or to rescue the shipwrecked. You must stop vacillating, and learn to focus on your mission."

"An officer must do his duty as he sees it, sir," replied Alden.

Alden looked up at a knock on the door. "Enter," he called. It opened and Rory's head appeared. "Sir, may I have a word with you and the commandant?"

"Of course, Dunbrody. Frankly, I've been expecting you. I'd guess you've been wrestling with your future. Have a seat."

"Captain, commandant." Rory slumped into the nearest chair. "This is by far the hardest thing I've ever had to do. My father, my sister, and, I suspect, my brother will all be part of the Confederacy. I feel I cannot leave them. And so I must leave many of the shipmates I hold dear. There's no good solution, at all." He took a deep breath.

"Sure, it's the least of two bad choices. I'm going to resign, sir. Here is my resignation," he said, handing over a folded paper. "I must tell you what a fine commander you've been. I'll always look to your example when I wish to model my command behavior, sir." Rory stood, came to attention, and saluted; even though being 'uncovered', or not wearing his uniform cap, it was not the naval custom to do so.

Alden returned the salute. "This is painful for me, Dunbrody, painful for us all. I cannot condone your decision, but I understand it. May we meet again in better times. You've been a fine officer. Be safe. You may make arrangements to travel as you wish. I assume you'll catch a steamer in Port Townsend. Now, please ask St. John to report. He has orders, as do I. We'll all be leaving together."

"Aye, aye, sir. And, thank you, sir."

Rory sought out Tobias, who had just returned from the fort. "I've told the captain, Tobias, and I'm relieved of duty. He will forward my resignation to the Navy Department. You're to report to him. He said you have orders."

"Wait here, Rory." Tobias disappeared below. A light evening breeze blew from the southwest and to the ships, rippling the calm waters off Ketron Island. Rory leaned on the quarterdeck rail, gazing at the forested shore and contemplating the future.

After some time, Tobias came to the rail and leaned beside Rory, showing him his orders. "I'm to report to the *Preble* in Norfolk. Alden's to command the refit of the *Merrimack* there. And I have a week in Antigua on the way. I'll see Monique. Rory, they've made me master! I'm commissioned! No more 'Master's Mate St. John.'"

"Congratulations, Tobias. You've risen to the top of your rate. And worked twice as hard and twice as well as most to do it, too," he recognized. He turned and looked intently at his companion. "Tobias, we must stay in contact with each other. You're the nearest I have to a close friend, and we knowin' each other for only four years."

"We shall, Rory, but carefully. It will do neither of us any good to receive letters from enemy territory."

"I've thought of that. We can write to each other through my Uncle Liam in Galway. He'll forward our letters." Rory smiled. "You can tell your mates in the wardroom that you're 'Black Irish'."

Tobias laughed. "To use your phrase, Dunbrody, you're daft. But we must be careful, and destroy the letters. The Articles of War call for punishment by death for those convicted of 'holding correspondence with the enemy'. Let's get our sea chests packed. I think the *Beaver* is headed north. Maybe she'll take us to Townsend."

CHAPTER 15
ARRIVAL IN NEW ORLEANS
APRIL 1861

The New Orleans riverfront was crowded with shipping from every corner of the world. Rory stood at the rail of the packet *Mingulay*, sixteen days out from Colon, Isthmus of Panama. From the deck of the ship, one could look down over the crest of the levee into the city streets below, many of which were at an elevation lower than the river.

The packet had ascended the Mississippi River through the Southwest Pass, one of three main outlets of the river. The *Mingulay* drew less than thirteen feet, the depth of the bar in the Southwest Pass. The three passes joined together some eighty miles downriver from New Orleans at the Head of the Passes. Rory had never been to New Orleans and was fascinated by the trip upriver from the Gulf of Mexico. The two great stone forts, Jackson and St. Philip, which guarded the river twenty miles upstream of the Head of the Passes, had commanded his attention as *Mingulay* sailed by. *A steamship might be exposed for fifteen minutes, but no more,* he thought to himself. *Sure, it's hardly a foolproof defense.*

Mingulay moored next to *Bienville*, a U.S. Mail Packet. Rory turned to a fellow passenger. "Apparently, mail service hasn't been suspended, even with secession."

"Ah'd be surprised, 'though, if the grace period were to last much longah. That mail packet's a temptin' target for our new and gallant navy," replied his companion.

"The *Bienville's* captain looks to be of the same mind," Rory observed. "He has his lines singled up, a guard at the gangway, and his steam up."

The *Bienville* was named for the original village on the present site of New Orleans. It lay docked at a wharf on the great sweeping bow of the river as it ran west to east, with the *Vieux Carre*, the old quarter, the core of the city, at the northeast side of the bow, and the wharfs and shipyards of the Town of Algiers directly southeast across the river. The sultry, humidity-laden heat of the Mississippi delta settled heavily on Rory, fresh from the low humidity and spring temperatures of Puget's Sound. He saw his sea chest put ashore through the cargo gangway and moved toward the passenger gangway to retrieve it.

Rory booked a hotel room in the Old Quarter at the huge City Exchange Hotel. He bought a train ticket for Montgomery the next day, took a nap, and awoke to the frenetic activity of the Old Quarter at night. His hotel's long bar, close to the riverfront, was obviously home to merchants, brokers, sailors, and rivermen of all descriptions. French, and the Acadian or "Cajun" patois was frequently heard, as well as the brogue of the more recent Irish immigrants. Rory dredged up the French he'd learned from Grandfather Fearghus, late of the *Armee Francaise*. "*Bon soir, m'sieur. Etes-vous une vin rouge ordinaire, sil vous plais.*"

"One cheap red wine, comin' up, sailor," said the barman, smiling. Rory was dressed in white duck trousers, a light cotton tarpaulin-style jacket, and a nondescript fisherman's cap. His wardrobe had been seriously depleted by his resignation from the U.S. Navy, and his consequent reluctance to wear his old uniforms. He'd given them all to Phil Johnson who'd opted to stay with the USN. What Phil couldn't wear, Rory knew, would end up in the 'slops', or 'lucky bag' for picking over by the crew of the *Active*.

Rory would later find that many of his fellow Confederate Navy officers had kept their navy blues, assuming they could be converted to a Confederate uniform with minimal alteration. Their discovery that the Navy of the Confederacy would wear gray would cause widespread consternation. "Who ever heard of a naval officer wearing anything but blue?" was to become an oft-asked question in the CSN.

Rory stood at the bar and nursed his wine. The bar conversation centered on the shelling of Fort Sumter only this morning by South

Carolina forces under General P. G. T. Beauregard. The U.S. Army garrison at Sumter was being called upon to surrender the fort. An experienced-looking captain in the uniform of the Mail Steamship Company stood next to Rory. "You're brave to attempt French in this town, young man," he said.

"Sure, captain, I learned it from my grandfather, who'd never forgive me for failin' t'try it in this city. And you'd be the captain of the *Bienville*, just a guess, now?"

"A good guess, at that. James Dunwoody Bulloch is my name. And you, by the sound and looks of you, were raised in Ireland and have been to sea." Bulloch looked Rory up and down with a friendly, encompassing gaze. In his forties, he had formidable sideburns and mustache, and a lonely curl on an otherwise bald forehead.

"Yes, sir. I'm Rory Dunbrody, North Carolina born, and on my way to Montgomery in response to the Naval Affairs Committee. I've resigned my U.S. Navy warrant as a passed midshipman. I'm just back from two years in Puget's Sound."

"I'll be on my way to Montgomery, myself, as soon as I return *Bienville* to my owners. But I haven't had to agonize over a resignation and goodbyes to shipmates, as you have. I resigned as a lieutenant in '53, to work for the steamship company."

"You're relaxed, now, sir. You must have found some assurances the Confederates won't commandeer *Bienville*. I noticed your lines were singled up and your steam raised when I came in on *Mingulay* today."

"You're an observant young officer! Assurances have only just arrived, at four bells in the afternoon watch, and from Jefferson Davis, himself. I'd told the governor I was unwilling and unable to sell or surrender the ship. At first his war committee considered taking us by force, but the governor wired the president for guidance. Davis wired back his unwillingness to take private property.

"So I am at last free to have a drink at my favorite establishment before departing in the morning." He raised his glass. "Tell me about your naval career."

"Aye, aye, sir." Rory described his life at sea, and his recent Pig War experience.

"It sounds as if your relations with the Royal Navy were beneficial."

"Oh, aye, sir, and weren't we the lucky ones to have officers like Admiral Baynes and Captain Hornby on that station? I'm lookin' forward to a simple naval ordnance assignment, free from intrigue!"

"Understandable, Dunbrody. With your experience, I'm sure you'll be useful to Mr. Mallory. I'm due back on board now. I hope our paths cross again."

"Thank you, sir. Smooth sailin' to you."

As Rory boarded the train the next morning, he noted that the masts and spars of the *Bienville* were nowhere to be seen. *No sense his lingering and giving opportunity for the War Council's change of mind,* he thought to himself.

A day later Rory presented himself to the Confederate States Secretary of the Navy, Stephen Mallory. The most refined hotel in Montgomery housed, temporarily, the offices of the Confederate government. The accommodations were not luxurious. President Davis occupied a hotel parlor which he shared with his secretary. Navy Secretary Mallory was officed in a series of hotel rooms housing four clerks, a messenger's cubbyhole in a closet, and a larger room for Mallory and his chief clerk, with a large table. This was the Navy Department of the Confederate States of America.

"Rory Dunbrody, Mr. Secretary, reporting as requested."

"Ah, yes, Mr. Dunbrody, I'm delighted to see you." Stephen Mallory was a slightly overweight man with a round and pleasant face, soft-spoken, and with the harried look of someone trying to do twenty things simultaneously. "I've heard about you from several officers. Taylor Wood and Jack Tucker both speak highly of you. And I received a most interesting telegram two days ago from James Bulloch. He said you two met in a bar, and he found you a most perceptive young officer, with a range of experience from hand-to-hand combat to international relations. Quite unusual for a passed midshipman, he thought. Said he has an eye on you for his command, which of course, he doesn't have yet. But I have some other duties in mind first, and time is of the essence."

Rory was taken aback by this avalanche of information and

blurted out a disjointed response. "Aye, aye, Mr. Secretary, sir, but what is my rank to be, and where can I serve, sir, and would it be possible to see my family briefly in New Berne?"

"Well, young man, why don't we both take a deep breath?" Mallory smiled. "On the strength of your recommenders, I offer you a commission as a lieutenant. The Confederate Navy offers commissions to former U.S. Navy officers at their previous ranks. In my view, a passed midshipman who has passed the lieutenant's examination and has served as a watch-keeping officer has served at the equivalent of a lieutenancy.

"I want you to serve initially in New Orleans, helping Commander Semmes arm our first cruiser, the CSS *Sumter*. You have ten days to report. That should give you time to visit New Berne. Say hello to your father for me. He builds good ships. We will need them."

"Aye, aye, Mr. Secretary. I accept, sure and I do. And God save you, sir."

"It is my pleasure, Lieutenant Dunbrody. After *Sumter* is at sea, I suspect we'll still need your talents in New Orleans for a time, keeping the Federal wolves from the door. But eventually, you'll rejoin your mentors Wood and Tucker in Virginia. They'll be arming and commissioning vessels there. I believe I'll be heading there myself. Unless I miss my guess, the capital will shortly be moved to Richmond. My clerk will draw up your orders. And here, sir, is your commission."

"My thanks to you, Mr. Secretary. I'll look forward to seein' you in Virginia." Rory saluted and quickly exited, an unreasoning concern surfacing that it was all too good to be true, and that Mallory might change his mind. *A lieutenant, and in New Orleans,* he thought. *Wait 'til I tell Da.*

CHAPTER 16
VISITING NEW BERNE
APRIL 1861

After several trains which took him through Alabama, Georgia, and South Carolina, Rory entered the "Old North State", home to his family, and came at last to the city of New Berne. He left the big brick railway station on Queen Street and walked down the gentle slope toward the Trent River through elm-shaded streets to his father's house on Hancock, and opened the front door. "Sure, it's your long-lost brother, home from sea," he called.

His auburn-haired sister, Siobhan, ran from the kitchen in the rear of the house at the sound of his voice. "Me own little brother, Heaven save us." Her Irish lilt was softened with an overlay of the middle-South, for she had been raised in North Carolina but with Irish-born parents at home. She was seven years Rory's senior, and still pronounced her name in the traditional Irish way, 'Sha-baan'. She had remained single after her first romance ended in tragedy. While in her early twenties, she had visited her family in Ireland and had met a dashing lieutenant in the Royal Inniskilling Fusiliers. They were betrothed, but he died on duty in Madras before they could be married.

"Are y' passin' through on yer way somewhere, or what are y' about, m'dearest?"

"Sister, y'didn't get my last letter? I've resigned from the Federal Navy. The Confederates have made me a lieutenant. I couldn't bear the thought of bein' on the other side from my family, and Tim's last letter was leanin' to the Secesh." He flung his jacket on the settee.

A rueful look crossed Siobhan's face. "Brother mine, Tim's up and done one of his frequent about-faces." She sighed and wiped her hands on her apron as Rory's face fell at the news. "But, regardless, Da and I can't move the shipyard, so as long as one of you followed the North, we're a divided family. Your brother's a Union infantry captain. Not that that's a strange situation around New Berne. Strong Union sentiment, hereabouts."

"Oh, dear God. Here I am committed to a cause for which I've little passion."

"You're not the first such warrior. Think of all the Irishmen in the Queen's forces, the Royal Navy, the Dublin Fusiliers, the Irish Guards. They're not all serving for the glory of dear old England, to be sure. Food and a place to sleep for most of them." Siobhan had always been the practical sibling in the family, the stabilizer. Tim was the dreamer and idealist, and Rory, the occasional scamp and frequent daredevil, striving for the approval of his siblings and father. His naval service was slowly maturing him.

Siobhan put a light wrap over her shoulders to ward off the April sun and handed Rory his jacket. "Come along, brother. We'll go down to the shipyard and tell our father what's transpired. He's the man to put a good face on it all."

Siobhan and Rory walked the short distance to South Front Street near the confluence of the Trent and the Neuse. The Neuse River was very broad at New Berne, and the Dunbrody shipyard's location on the Trent afforded more protection from the winds off Pamlico Sound. Patrick Conor Dunbrody's office was at the street side of the large building in which ships were framed and planked before being moved outside to be launched and rigged. Siobhan burst open the door without a knock. "Father, dear, it's Rory with a tale t'make th' angels weep," she exclaimed, as she grabbed Rory by the elbow and thrust him into the office.

"And it's your sister, still with her flair for the dramatic. Ruiri, my son. You're a sight for sore eyes." Rory's father delighted in pronouncing Rory's name in the Celtic way. "Tell me what has your sister all a-frazzle."

"Da, after reading Tim's last, I thought he'd be fighting for the South so I resigned my warrant to join him. And the mugwump, he's not here! Now, I'm stuck, I am. With a lieutenant's commission, and orders for New Orleans."

"Son, things could be worse. I don't expect the South to prevail in any war, and there'll be one, without doubt. So, at least one Dunbrody will be on the winning side!" He leaned forward, and his voice grew more serious. "You and Tim must do your best to come through the war in one piece. And look at the two of you. You've both made honorable decisions based on your best judgment, and you now go to serve your causes courageously. No one can do more than that."

"You always make me look for a rainbow beyond the hills, Father. Sure, it's a gift! So you think the South can't prevail?"

"Too many industrial resources in the North, son. Railroads, shipyards, munitions factories, and people. Too many people. And just enough of a core committed to a cause not to waver. But never you mind all of that, now," he said, waving a hand. "It's time for a toast to your promotion. Siobhan, the poteen!"

"The key's already in hand, Da," said Siobhan, marching to a sturdy cabinet behind her father's desk.

Patrick raised his glass. "The Dunbrodies of Connemara!" The aged potato whiskey burned like a beautiful white flame.

"I've just the potion t'ease the naggin' ache of separation from your brother. We'll ship as supernumeraries aboard the *Rose of Clifden*. She's a side-wheel steamer I just built and sold to the State of North Carolina. She's brigantine-rigged for sail as well. Lieutenant Thomas, commanding. He's an old friend and will ship us for sure on his next dash out of Hatteras Inlet, particularly when he finds you're an officer in the navy that he'll next be commissioned in, as soon as North Carolina is admitted to the Confederacy." Patrick Dunbrody smiled and lifted his glass to his younger son. "To our next cruise together!"

Rory awoke the next morning and couldn't think of a reason not to accompany his irrepressible father aboard the North Carolina gunboat. As the senior Dunbrody had pointed out the night before, Rory could send a first-hand report to Mallory on Old North State Navy operations, useful to a department that would soon include those ships in its Navy List. Keeping in touch with Mallory was a wise thing to do. A bit of action would help distract him from his anguish over Timothy, and his choice of causes. And cruising with his father would end in laughter, without a doubt.

The *Rose of Clifden*, named for the Connemara home of the Dunbrodies, sailed at mid-day. After the sixty mile trip, she took station in Pamlico Sound the following morning, just inshore of the Cape Hatteras Light. She was ready to move south and then slip through Hatteras Inlet at the signal of the lighthouse attendants if they spotted a promising sail making its way along the coasts of Hatteras or Ocracoke islands.

The steamer mounted one eight-inch rifle pivot and four 32pounder smooth bores. Rory and his father stood on the starboard bridge wing of the wheelhouse just forward of the paddle-wheel boxes, from which they could see the signal flagstaff of the lighthouse. Rory wore a blue merchant officer's uniform coat borrowed from his father. Rory and Patrick gazed, mesmerized, at the sunlight glittering off the wavelets on Pamlico Sound.

Patrick turned to Rory. "When we were in the midst of our poteen toasts, I forgot to drink t'yer Grandfather Fearghus. Maybe I forgot because he is so larger than life. It isn't easy having a father-in-law who can lay about him and knock down six men in a moment. A terror with a shillelagh as well as a saber, he is."

"No wonder you moved to New Berne," Rory laughed. "Look, Da, the lighthouse is running up a signal hoist." Rory pointed to the signal fluttering at the distant flagstaff. Lieutenant Thomas leaned through the open bridge window.

"Patrick, they're signaling a barque about five miles off the mouth of the inlet on a southerly course," he said to the senior Dunbrody. "We'll take a look." Thomas still wore his U.S. Navy uniform.

"Thank you, Captain Thomas, it sounds like a promising hunt, it does." Patrick Dunbrody addressed Lieutenant Thomas as "Captain;" the courtesy title afforded any ship commander, no matter what his substantive rank.

Turning to Rory, he said, "You'll remember, son, how to get through the Inlet. Port turn five hundred yards southeast of the buoy, with Fort Hatteras bearing north, northeast, and then bear up just to port of the outer buoy."

"Aye, aye, Da, it's coming back to me."

Through the inlet and with the shoals and breakers receding aft, they could see the barque's topsails on the horizon. The steamer pitched and rolled in the Atlantic swells. Rory felt eager for action and apprehensive at the same time. He absent-mindedly hummed the opening bars of "The Minstrel Boy" for reassurance, and sang the words to himself. "The minstrel boy to the war has gone, in the ranks of death you will find him."

His father overheard the tune. "Let's hope that's not prophetic, lad," he said.

Lieutenant Thomas opened the pilothouse door and joined the Dunbrodies on the bridge wing. "Rory, I'd be grateful if you'd command the cutter during boarding. We're short of experienced officers. I'll send Midshipman Abbott with you as your second-in-command."

"Sure, captain, 'twould be my pleasure. My one chance to serve under my state's colors." Rory glanced at the new North Carolina ensign fluttering aft at the staff; a dark blue field with a white 'V' and a white star encircled with the words "sirgit astrum, May 20, 1775." The flag had not been officially adopted, but Governor Ellis, when the state bought the ship from Patrick, had written:

> *North Carolina is, for all intents and purposes, out of the Union. I've forwarded a state flag that was proposed by Colonel Whitford, a member of the convention that adopted our ordinance of secession. It's the only one we have, at present. You may hoist it aboard our navy's first ship.*

The same ensign flew over the two uncompleted earthworks on the northeast shore of Hatteras Island, "Forts" Hatteras and Clark, receding aft into the distance as the *Rose of Clifden* left the coast. The former was a two hundred fifty-foot-square earthen redoubt, mounting twelve 32-pounder smoothbores protected by ramparts, parapets and embrasures. Fort Clarke, seven hundred yards up the beach, mounted two six-pounders and five thirty-twos.

After an hour's chase, the *Rose of Clifden* was within gunshot of the barque. The red ensign flying at the peak of her spanker gaff identified her as a British merchantman. "Let's see if she's who she purports to be," said Captain Thomas. "Mr. Clark, a shot across her bow, if you please." In time of war, ships of belligerents could stop and inspect neutrals to ensure that their cargoes were not intended for other belligerents. After a shot from the *Rose's* eight-inch pivot, the barque came up into the wind, backing her fore course. The foresail or "fore course," was the lowest and largest sail on the foremast. Trimming it so the wind filled it from the front, called "backing" it, was the equivalent of putting on the brakes.

Rory clambered down the ladder to the steamer's cutter, and her eight oarsmen drove her through the Atlantic swells to the side of the barque. "Mr. Abbott, you and I will go aboard while the boat's crew remains here, prepared to board if she proves to be other than British, or with contraband cargo." Rory shifted his scabbard behind him and began his climb up the ladder lowered by the barque's crew. He heard Abbott's muffled "aye, aye, sir" behind him on the ladder.

"I'm Captain Prendergast of the barque *Scioto*," said a portly officer in a blue uniform jacket, the gold insignia of a British merchant captain at his cuffs and on his peaked cap. "Here are my ship's papers. Who might you be, and whom do you represent? I can't say I'm familiar with your ensign."

"Lieutenant Dunbrody of the Confederate States Navy, at your service, sir. This is Midshipman Abbott of the Navy of North Carolina. It's his ensign you don't recognize, sir. I'm on temporary assignment with their *Rose of Clifden.*" It was only a small departure from the truth. *More like a lark with my Da*, thought Rory to himself.

Just then, the most beautiful woman he'd ever seen caught his eye. She came on deck in a Caribbean blue-green dress that matched her eyes to perfection, her golden-blond hair caught back in a sea-green barrette.

"You're Irish!" Prendergast exclaimed.

"Raised there, but born here, captain. Untrouble your mind, sir; we're not the Fenians. May we go to your cabin so I might examine your papers?"

"Very well, lieutenant. Before we do, may I present one of your countrywomen, Miss Carrie Anne Eastman, of New Orleans, homeward bound with us?"

"How do you do, Lieutenant Dunbrody? My stars, Captain Prendergast is carryin' fine linens and broadcloth to New Orleans. Ah don't think he's the game y'all are huntin'." As Carrie Anne spoke, Rory was transfixed by her eyes. He felt a shortness of breath and a visceral blow to his body.

I haven't felt like this since I kissed Mary Kate O'Shaughnessy when I was thirteen, he thought. "Sure, and you've the long and short of it, Miss Eastman. I'll be goin' below and walkin' Midshipman Abbott through the paperwork, and we'll be on our way, without a doubt." Rory literally scuttled below, thinking, *Jasus, I sound like a blithering idjit. What a beauty!*

It was clear from the *Scioto*'s log, manifest, and registration papers that it was a British vessel bound for New Orleans, without contraband cargo. Rory and Abbott returned to the quarterdeck. "Captain, thank you for the use of your cabin. All's in order here. We're sorry to have troubled you. Perhaps we'll meet again in New Orleans. I'm to report for duty there in four days." Rory stole a look at Carrie Anne and saw a demure but definite hint of a smile at his words.

"No trouble at all, lieutenant," said Prendergast. "I've no doubt our paths will cross again. The rumor in Halifax was that President Lincoln is about to declare a blockade. But declaring and enforcing are two different things. It will be several weeks before the Union will be able to have ships on station. We'll have no trouble reaching New Orleans. Good luck to you, now."

"Sail, ho! Two points off the port bow!" The call came from the lookout at the main topgallant crosstrees. "You can see the royals, sir. Looks like a man o' war, and a Yankee at that."

"It appears you're about to have company, lieutenant," Prendergast said.

"And the more, the merrier, captain. A good day to you, sir. Miss Eastman, it's been a pleasure, I'm sure." Rory touched his cap to the captain and the quarterdeck, and he and Abbott were over the side and quickly into the cutter.

As they rowed back to the *Rose*, it occurred to Rory that an escape from the threat of the Yankee man o' war was also an opportunity to entice her into danger. He considered how he'd feel if Captain Thomas rejected the plan he was still formulating in his mind. *I've got a lot of brass,* he thought, *suggestin' a cockeyed plan to a man I've just met. Ah, sure, what can it hurt? Me Da's there to nurse me damaged feelin's.*

Bounding up the *Rose*'s ladder as they reached her side, Rory ran to the wheelhouse bridge. "Captain Thomas, the barque is British, but would y'consider, sir, drawing yon Yankee into your spider's web?"

Thomas and the elder Dunbrody turned to Rory. "And what do you have in mind, lieutenant?" asked Thomas.

"Sir, if we can persuade the Yankee that we're slow, desperate to escape, and that we've run aground and dismasted in our haste, she might be tempted to come within range of Fort Hatteras, or at least send her boats within range to board and burn us."

"A seemingly tall order, lieutenant." Thomas was clearly skeptical.

"Sir, I believe it's a matter of good acting, thick smoke, a drogue or sea anchor overside at the right moment, and a few sheets and braces let fly. May I elaborate, sir?"

"Go ahead, Mr. Dunbrody," said Thomas, "I'm listening." Patrick Dunbrody stepped back, a smile on his face, and watched as Rory outlined the details of his plan with great animation.

When Rory had finished, Thomas said to the Dunbrodies, "I'm inclined to try this. It would be good for the men's morale and for their experience. It would give the Fort's gunners some much-needed practice, too. Mr. Dunbrody, I'm putting you in charge of implementing your plan. Please give the necessary orders and directions to the engineer and the deck crew."

Thomas leaned over the voice pipe to the engine room. "Mr. Mackenzie, I've asked Mr. Dunbrody to tell you what we need from the engine room. We're going to pull the wool over the Yankee's eyes."

Rory spoke down the voice pipe. "Mr. Mackenzie, I'd be grateful if you'll cause the smoke from the stack to look like we're giving her all we've got, but keep her at half-ahead. We're going to lure this Yankee sloop o' war into range of Fort Hatteras."

Rory called to the boatswain, "Mr. Edwards, you've twenty-five minutes to make us a drogue. A reinforced sea anchor might do. Perhaps you'll have a spare dolphin-striker chain. We need to simulate going aground, to help her stop abruptly. It might hold with your heaviest canvas. We'll have our port side to the Yankee, so we'll set it from the starboard fore chains on my signal."

"Mr. Abbott, please put dependable men on the fore tops'l sheets and braces. We'll set the fore tops'l and the fore course. When we set the drogue, we'll let fly sheets and braces. Every telescope from the Yankee will be trained on us. We must convince them we've grounded and damaged the rigging."

Rory left the bridge and put the foretopmen to work preparing for the ruse. Like most steamers of the day, the *Rose* was rigged for sail to augment her steam propulsion. The *Rose of Clifden* was a brigantine, a two-masted vessel with square sails on the foremast, and fore-and-aft sails on the mainmast. The Union warship was hull-up from the *Rose's* masthead and coming into range. Rory returned to the bridge. "Captain, I believe we're ready for our masquerade."

"Excellent, Mr. Dunbrody. We'll back the engines as we set the drogue, to simulate being aground."

"Aye, aye, sir. I've told-off the boats crews for the cutter and longboat. We'd best set an anchor with one, out of sight of the Yankee, so that both can then pretend to be pulling us off our mythical sandbar."

"Very good, Dunbrody. As soon as we're close enough for the fort to read our signals, we'll let them in on our plan."

The Union man o' war's hull was now visible from the bridge. Rory trained his telescope on her. He had seen ships of her type in his U.S. Navy days. She was a "razee", a former 44-gun frigate now cut-down or altered to the next smaller ship configuration in order to improve her sailing qualities.

"She's a twenty-four-gun sail sloop of war; I'd guess the *Cumberland*. She's armed with 32-pounder smooth-bores, and her effective range is about twelve hundred yards," Rory called out to the captain.

The *Cumberland's* bow chaser tried a ranging shot, which fell a cable's length short of the *Rose of Clifden*. The *Rose* was on a west-north-west heading, a half mile from the outer buoy marking the channel through Hatteras Inlet. Rory could see the breakers on the shoals to port, and the North Carolina flag on the flagstaffs of Fort Hatteras and Fort Clark to starboard. The signalman had a hoist ready at the signal halyard that explained the simulated grounding about to occur.

"Captain Thomas," said Rory, "If we pretend to run aground on the north edge of the channel, *Cumberland* must come within range of the fort's guns in order to reach us. Those guns in the fort have a two thousand-yard extreme range."

"Very well, Mr. Dunbrody, see to it."

"Outer buoy to port," Midshipman Abbott reported.

"Ease her two points to starboard, quartermaster, if you please," said Rory. "Stand by the drogue. Clear the foredeck." Rory opened the voice pipe. "Mr. Mackenzie, stand by to back engines."

The *Rose* was at the very edge of the channel. A mile behind her, the USS *Cumberland* yawed, and the twelve guns of her port battery fired a broadside. She was just beyond effective range, and the *Rose* still presented her stern to the Yankee, a narrow target. Two or three 32-pound roundshot skipped harmlessly by. Rory called out, his voice carried by the fifteen-knot breeze: "Set the drogue! Back engines! Let fly sheets and ease braces!"

Without the sheets and braces to trim the foretopsail yard and the foot of the sail, the foretopsail yard swung loose, and the sail flapped and cracked in the wind like a live thing, the sheets flying from the two lower corners of the sail, the clews, like the lash of teamsters' whips. The drogue and the backed engines stopped the way on the *Rose* just outside the north shoals. The black smoke from the *Rose*'s stack made visibility from the *Cumberland* difficult.

"Launch and cutter crews away! Gun crew, stand by the eight-inch pivot gun!" The veteran sailors aboard the *Rose*, led by the boatswain and his mates, carried out Rory's orders swiftly. The men in the launch set the anchor. Topmen re-secured the foretopsail sheets and braces. The cutter crew bent the towline and hauled it aft.

Cumberland had tacked, closed the range, and fired a second broadside. She was now within range of the fort's guns. Spouts of water were springing up around the *Cumberland* as the fort's gunners found the range.

Midshipman Abbott trained his telescope on the *Cumberland*. "She's lowering her boats with boarding crews! I can see Marines."

"Splendid, Mr. Abbott." The captain turned to Rory. "It appears our ruse is working, Mr. Dunbrody. Well done!"

"Sir, if we back the starboard paddle wheel, we'll turn our starboard side to the *Cumberland* and her boats. We can open fire with two thirty-twos and the eight-inch pivot."

Thomas called down the voice pipe, "Back the starboard paddle wheel, Mr. Mackenzie. Bo'sun, cutter and launch crews help haul her stern around so the guns bear on *Cumberland*!" The Yankee had ceased her fire on the steamer as her boat crews approached the paddle wheeler, and had shifted fire to the two forts. The gunners of Fort Hatteras were making good practice on the *Cumberland*. Rory could see splinters fly from her bulwarks and several stays parted by shot from the fort.

The two starboard thirty-twos were run out and their gun captains ready with their firing lanyards. Rory sighted the pivot gun himself. "Gun captains, fire at the boats! Each gun take one boat and fire low. Your round shot will skip and still do damage." The one drawback of a rifled pivot was that, if they fired short and hit the water, the conical shells could skip in any direction. Roundshot, on the other hand, nearly always skipped straight.

"Fire as you bear!" At the captain's command, each of the three guns fired as it bore on the target. Rory could see the round shot from the smooth bores and his shell from the pivot fly just above the two oncoming boats, which were bow-on to the broadside battery. "Depress your guns," he cried to the gun captains. His pivot gun, from the bow, had a good broadside angle on the boat approaching the *Rose*'s stern.

The second shot from the forward thirty-two skipped in front of the first *Cumberland* boat and ploughed through its starboard bank of oars. The eight portside oars completed another stroke, and slewed the boat around broadside to the *Rose*. The longboat came to a stop. The *Cumberland*, realizing her quarry was not helplessly aground, and beleaguered by the fort's fire, hoisted the recall signal to her boats. It was too late. The pivot's second shot had gone wide, but the third blew the bow off *Cumberland*'s launch and the survivors, in the water, began to swim to the longboat, now with only half its oars.

"Well done, gunners," cried Captain Thomas. "Cutter and launch crews, load your bow swivels with grape. I want those men as prisoners. Bo'sun, call away my gig crew to assist. Weigh anchor, and we'll run down on the boats." The *Cumberland*'s overloaded longboat, filled with the half-drowned crew of *Cumberland*'s launch, afforded little resistance to the *Rose*'s boat crews.

Rory shifted targets with the pivot from the boats to the *Cumberland*. Alone of all the guns engaged, the pivot had ample range to reach the *Cumberland* consistently. The *Cumberland*, still under fire from the fort's thirty-twos and helpless to aid its boat crews, fired an angry and desperate broadside as it withdrew. One stray cannonball, a "parting shot", reached the deck of the *Rose*, killing the helmsman and decapitating Midshipman Abbott, who was standing just behind the helm.

Rory made his way aft, and he and his father laid the bodies near the quarterdeck rail. With boat crews and gun crews at work, there were no others left to deal with the dead.

"Sure and it's a terrible waste," said Patrick. "He was a promisin' lad, and that's a fact."

"Mr. Dunbrody, have the gun crews stand by to secure the prisoners as we bring them aboard." The dispirited Union sailors and Marines came up the ladder one-by-one. The *Rose*'s crew secured each of them, their spirits more elevated than the Yankees', but tempered by the sight of their dead comrades.

Late the next day, after the *Rose* had returned to New Berne with her prisoners, Patrick, Siobhan, and Rory sat in the drawing room of the Dunbrody house. "Dammit, Da, I hated to lose young Abbott. What a bright and amiable fellow!"

"The vagaries of misfortune, according to Plutarch, lad. The world's a hit or miss proposition, 'tis." Patrick said. "But you have the satisfaction of saying you were among the first and last of those who were in action for the Navy of North Carolina. Their little fleet will be enfolded by your Confederate States Navy as soon as the Old North State is admitted to the Confederacy."

"Captain Thomas is a steady commander, to be sure," said Rory. "He'll do well in the CSN."

"He's writing a letter of commendation for you to Mallory. He told me." Patrick looked at Rory in fatherly pride. "You did well, and the capture of Union sailors from a man o' war, even one without steam, is an important boost to Confederate morale. I hope the Confederacy knows enough to shore up those forts with rifled guns. The next time the Union Navy fires on them, 'twill be from steam frigates that can circle, keep up a steady fire, and present a moving target. They'll pound those forts to pieces unless the forts get longer-range armament like your pivot gun."

"True enough," said Rory. "Da, if they strengthen the forts, you'd think privateers could carry out the interruption of commerce along the coast, and free up the navy crews for the ironclads and raiders Mallory's building."

"Oh, now, brother, 'twould be true if the Treaty of Paris hadn't been signed," said Siobhan. "But all the world save the U.S.A. has ended the rewards for privateering, and the Yankees now wish they had. The privateers can't flourish without the profit denied them by the Treaty." Siobhan smiled confidently.

"Your sister knows her nautical finance, Rory. She's been doing the shipyard books almost since the day we lost your Ma."

"Sure, she's a bright one, Da," Rory said, beaming at his sister. "Like Ma, there's no doubt. Mark you, I missed being away from you and Siobhan, growin' up, but I'm glad you sent me to Ireland to be raised by the rest of the family. I feel I got to know Ma through knowin' Uncle Francis. And havin' Uncle Liam was as close to havin' you as could be."

"They did a fine job of raisin' ye, lad. I think you're equipped to make your way in the world! But as you do, remember my advice on talk of slavery with your fellow officers. Avoid it. Your views won't jibe with theirs."

"I'll remember, Da. Maybe this war will end the 'peculiar institution'."

"There's the wee irony, lad. Many white southerners are

embarrassed by the institution and might not be upset to be rid of it. But north or south, most whites believe the Negro to be inferior, slave or no. Your friend Tobias has a tough row to hoe."

"Da, Tobias is going to write me care of Uncle Liam, who'll forward the letters to you. If you'd be kind enough to send them on, and forward my replies, we can keep track of each other, with a built-in four month delay."

"We're glad to, son. Aren't we now, Siobhan? And when the war is through, you'll be home tellin' me again of sailin' that Galway Hooker into Galway Bay at sunrise with a load of hay aboard and my brother makin' sure you're trimmin' the sails just so! Off with ye, now, son. The train will be leavin' soon."

Rory stood, and hesitated. "Da, I didn't have time to be afraid before the fight, but I was shaken afterwards," he confessed.

"Oh, son, you'll never be free of that reaction. Best you be treatin' it as an old friend."

A month later, Confederate Navy Secretary Stephen Mallory sat in his office amid boxes of books and papers being packed for the move to Richmond. He finished reading the second of two reports he'd received from New Berne. *It surely looks like I made the right appointment with Mr. Dunbrody*, he thought to himself. The first report was from Captain Thomas of the North Carolina Navy, which began, "I'm pleased to report the diligence and ingenuity of one of your officers, Lieutenant Rory Dunbrody..." The second was Rory's report that had mentioned his father's observations on the condition of Forts Clark and Hatteras.

I must speak to Secretary of War Benjamin about upgrades, Mallory thought. *Captain Semmes will surely be well-served by Dunbrody's help with the Sumter's ordnance.*

CHAPTER 17
THE WEST INDIES
MAY 1861

Tobias stood outside the westernmost brick wall protecting Nelson's Dockyard in English Harbor, Antigua. Behind him, overlooking Tank Bay, was Admiralty Public House, a venerable establishment that had catered to the British sailor since the mid-1700's. Tobias wore the blue uniform coat of a master in the U.S. Navy.

So fine to see my cousin Mitchell after the voyage from the Isthmus, he thought. The Navy had afforded him ten day's leave before taking ship for his new assignment as master of the U.S. sloop of war *Preble* in Norfolk. He'd landed at St. John's, the principal city on Antigua, and gone straight to the home of his mother's nephew, Mitchell, his childhood companion 'til the age of ten, when his parents had emigrated to New Bedford. His cousin was taking him to Terre de Haut aboard his schooner which lay anchored in English Harbor after its sail down the leeward coast of Antigua during the day.

Bless Mitch for arranging my passage to Les Saintes tomorrow, Tobias thought. *I'll see Monique within twenty-four hours. This calls for a drink in the 'Admiralty'. I'd never have dared this five years ago, and odds are I'll regret it, but I'm a master, USN, man of color or no.* He strode resolutely to the swinging doors of the pub and stepped to the bar. There, a black Antiguan bartender looked up with a mixture of surprise, admiration, and dismay.

"Mon, what are you t'inkin'? I ent served no colored here in all my ten years of tendin' bar!"

"Sorry, brother, but this I must do. I'm celebrating my promotion to master. What kind of man am I if I can't do so on the island of my birth?"

"Oh, yes mon, I see, I truly do, but sit at dat table back in the shadows. Maybe my clientele dis evenin' won't be the worst I can draw, maybe even a mellow officer or two." The bartender smiled wanly.

"A pint of ale, if you please." Tobias took a seat at a back table. The bartender brought his ale and whispered, "we all dam' proud of you, Mr. St. John." Antigua was a small, close-knit community, and Tobias' navy success was known to many.

"Most kind of you, mon, God bless you." Tobias relaxed in his chair, took a deep draught of his ale, and smiled. At that moment, three officers from among the Royal Navy ships in the harbor entered, and took a table near the bar. "Edward," one called to the bartender, "three gins, my good man!"

"Comin' right up, lieutenant," Edward replied.

Having ordered, the British officer placed his cocked hat on the table and glanced toward Tobias' table. He looked, and then stared. "I say, fellow, are you lost?"

"I would hope not, lieutenant, as I'm the navigator of the USS *Preble*," Tobias replied good-naturedly.

"Astounding! I must say, whatever strange appointments the colonies may be making on their Navy List, you, my good man, are a black in a white man's bar."

"Accurate as far as it goes, lieutenant, but I am further, a commissioned naval officer of a sovereign nation in a bar which traditionally caters to naval officers. And, I have the decency not to raise a brouhaha worthy of a Billingsgate fishwife over the fact."

"Score one for the Yankee Navy, Ludlow!" The newcomer to the argument looked familiar to Tobias. "Not only are you damnably lacking in decorum, you're addressing a man mentioned in dispatches for valor by none other than Captain James Prevost, RN."

Tobias suddenly realized why he recognized the British officer. "Lieutenant Tremaine? First of *Tribune* and *Satellite*? And now promoted, I see."

"The same, Mr. St. John, I'm now master and commander, commanding Her Majesty's brig of war *Querulous*. Let me introduce you to two fine officers of the Royal Navy. You've already locked horns with Lieutenant Bertram Ludlow, second of the frigate *Irrepressible*. He's testy, but a damn fine sailor. And the quiet contemplative fellow here is my younger brother, James Tremaine, first of the *Bristol*."

Tobias rose from his table and shook hands with the elder Tremaine. "How do you do, gentlemen," he said to the others. "It's a pleasure to see you again, Commander Tremaine."

"For me as well, Mr. St. John. We had some fine times in the far Northwest. How is Midshipman Dunbrody?"

"Gone to the Confederate Navy, I'm sad to say. But, no doubt he's a lieutenant by now. So many friends and brothers will be on opposite sides. It's tragedy, indeed."

"Quite so, Mr. St. John. And now you're master of the *Preble*. Here's a toast to our promotions!"

"To our promotions, sir. She's only a small sailing sloop of war, not a steamer; one hundred seventeen feet, with seven thirty-twos and two eight-inch rifles, but she'll be home to me. I'm grateful for your cordiality, sir. I'm visiting friends in Bourg de Haut tomorrow, before I report to Norfolk, so I'd best be going."

"Good luck to you, St. John." Tremaine rose to shake hands with Tobias. Tobias then nodded to the others, and with a "gentlemen" to bid goodbye, walked to the door. "Good evening, mon, and thanks," he paused and whispered to the barman as he left. "Oh, yes, mon," Edward smiled and whispered in reply, "we bot' dodge de bullet tonight. Drop in again nex' time you 'pon lan'."

"Damn the cheek of that brazen black," blustered Lieutenant Ludlow as Tobias left the pub. "If he were a gentleman, I'd call him out!"

"I'd be careful there, old boy," said the elder Tremaine with a hint of a smile. "He kills Indians, hand-to-hand."

"I'll find some way to teach him where he belongs, should opportunity arise," muttered Ludlow into his gin.

"*Pointe de la Grande Vigie*, Papa," called eleven-year–old Daniel, Cousin Mitch's son, as they came abeam of the towering headland on the north end of Guadeloupe's eastern half, Grande Terre, far to port or larboard, in the distance.

"How does that translate to English, Cousin Daniel?" Tobias smiled at the boy.

"Big look-out, Cousin Toby." Daniel and Monique were the only individuals Tobias ever allowed to address him as 'Toby'.

Tobias could remember climbing to Shirley Heights on Antigua's south shore as a boy, and gazing toward Grande Vigie beyond the Guadeloupe Passage as he schemed of ways to persuade his father to take him to Les Saintes to see Monique. Mitch's big schooner had made a fast transit across Guadeloupe Passage, having caught a strong breeze as they approached the leeward island of Guadeloupe, Basse Terre. In May, the tradewinds became fluky and variable. It would have been a gamble to take the longer, windward course around Guadeloupe to The Saints at this time of year. The leeward passage down Guadeloupe's west side was shorter, but the Trades, if blowing, would diminish somewhat in the lee of the island.

The Trades, blowing strong at the moment, allowed a fast passage, but not so quick as to allow Tobias any respite from Daniel's inexhaustible supply of questions. "How did you meet Monique? What's she like?"

"I met her when our dads fished together. She's tall, she has light hair and blue eyes, she is very independent and loving, she speaks Breton, French, and English, and she is a free black."

"Why is she not dark like us and the Guadeloupe blacks?"

"Terre-de-Haut, where she lives, was settled by blue-eyed Breton fishermen. A few, like her father, intermarried with blacks who worked the plantations on the other Saints main island, Terre-de-Basse. The Bretons are Celts, very passionate. Her father saw her mother who was very beautiful, fell in love, bought her, freed her, and married her. And to anticipate your next barrage of questions, the Celts are remnants of a race that once lived from the Black Sea across Europe to Gaul. They're now in Ireland, Scotland, Wales, Cornwall, Brittany, Galicia, and the Isle of Man."

"Daniel, leave your cousin alone for a while." Mitch smiled from the helm.

"It's all right, Mitch. He's keeping me from anxiety over seeing her after so long."

The town of Basse-Terre was now visible to larboard. They had experienced periodic sustained gusts of wind roaring down the volcanic "chutes" that traversed the slopes of the towering central mountain range which culminated in the 5000-foot volcano La Soufriere. The schooner would soon round Pointe de Vieux Fort at the southern end of Basse-Terre and tack into the head wind that blew for a mile off the point. Then they'd relax on the six-mile reach to Les Saintes' port, Bourg des Saintes, on the largest of the Saintes, Terre-de-Haut.

Dinner with Monique and her family was a reunion replete with laughter, song, sea stories, and serious discussion of life's most perplexing questions. Her father, her brothers, and their families all treated Tobias as a family member, honored as one of her oldest friends, and quietly recognized as her cherished lover. They spoke French when Tobias was present, as he did not understand Breton. "*Le Marine Americaine*! *Et notre Navigateur*, Tobias!" Pierre Duvalliere, the patriarch of Monique's family, toasted Tobias and his navy. "How is your father, *mon fils*?"

"Still teaching at the academy in New Bedford and glad not to be at sea, *mon pere*."

"He was wise to leave Antigua in '38 when the British abolished slavery on the island. We were slower here, I regret to say. Our Alsatian friend, Schoelcher, could not persuade the French to free the slaves for another ten years."

The conversation turned to Tobias' new ship, the *Preble*. "She's a sloop of war, a 'corvette', 117 feet in length," Tobias told them. "She mounts only nine guns, but we will be part of a large blockading squadron with many larger *bateaux*, I'm sure. She has no engines, just sail."

Tobias then told them the story of his encounter with Tremaine and his colleagues in English Harbor, to appreciative nods.

"Ah, 'Tremaine'. Perhaps a good Huguenot, *n'est-ce pas*? Monique's brother, Etienne, clapped Tobias on the shoulder. "But, *mon ami*, what of your good friend Dunbrody? He has gone to the South, *n'est-ce pas*? What great *tristesse*!"

"Yes, it is most sad, Etienne. But the war will pass, and, if we both live, we shall still be friends, and still live with honor for the betterment and the freedom of our peoples." He looked up from his reverie. "My, that sounds grave. I believe I have had too much of this excellent wine."

"When will you leave, my son?" asked Pierre.

"In four days time, *mon pere*, from St. John's, on the packet."

"Excellent! Etienne, we will take him to St. John's in our schooner, *mais oui?*"

"*Oui, Papa.*"

After dinner Tobias and Monique walked through the village to her shop as the light faded on Terre-de-Haut. "Your father has not aged a bit," said Tobias. "Still the sailor seeking to learn more of his world."

"You are much alike," said Monique as she put her hand in his. She opened the gate to the courtyard behind her fabric shop, a white house with the traditional blue and red trim of the village and a carved balcony over the courtyard. She lived upstairs. "Sit in the courtyard while I go upstairs to the kitchen and bring some cognac."

Tobias watched her climb the stairs to her living quarters. *Lithe and bonnie, a Celt might say,* he smiled to himself. *So tall, so slender and beautiful.* Monique soon descended the stairs, cognac snifters in hand, but clad in only a loose-woven sarong, an earlier gift from one of Tobias' whaling voyages. "My God, woman, you stir me as nothing else can!"

"That's the idea, *ma chere.*" As Monique set the glasses on the table, Tobias stood, embracing her and trembling. "Oh, love, if we seize the moment, the cognac will wait. I know I cannot." Lifting her in his arms in the twilight, Tobias took the stairs two at a time, and they left the courtyard to the evening birds and the brilliant hue of the bougainvillea.

CHAPTER 18
RETURN TO NEW ORLEANS
APRIL 1861

Rory left the train at the New Orleans station and returned to the City Exchange Hotel where he had stored his sea chest while in New Berne. After getting settled in his hotel room, he took one of the several ferryboats running across the Mississippi to the port of Algiers, where the CSS *Sumter* was fitting out.

The former packet ship *Habana*, a "fruiterer" from the South American fruit trade, had been renamed as the CSS *Sumter*. Rory found her around the point of Algiers, at the yard of Atlantic Dry Dock Company, at the foot of Atlantic Street. She was a small propeller steamer of five hundred tons, with a low-pressure engine, and was being fitted out to carry five guns. Rory saw that her rig had been altered to that of a barque, with square sails on the fore and main masts and fore-and-aft sails on the mizzen. Work crews were below strengthening the main deck with the addition of heavy beams to support the weight of her battery.

Rory inquired at the shipyard office where he encountered the owner, James Martin. "Sir, I'm reporting to Captain Semmes for temporary duty. Where might I find him?"

"The captain may be aboard their tender, *Star of the West*. She's berthed nearby, up the levee at the quay."

"Thank you most kindly, Mr. Martin," Rory said, and walked down the levee to the side-wheeler *Star of the West*. She had been renamed CSS *St. Philip* after the Confederates captured her off the Texas coast, but everyone still referred to her by her Union name. Going aboard, he saluted the quarterdeck and turned to the boatwain's mate at the gangway. "I'm reporting for duty. Where may I find Captain Semmes?"

"Sir, the captain's ashore, but the first lieutnenant, Mr. Kell, is in his stateroom, aft."

Rory found the cabin of Lieutenant Kell. "Sir, Lieutenant Rory Dunbrody reporting for duty." Rory handed Kell his orders.

Kell glanced at the orders. "Welcome, Mr. Dunbrody. You're here to assist us in equipping *Sumter* with our ordnance. We could use the help. We're still waiting for our four thirty-twos and our eight-inch pivot. Lieutenant Chapman is scouring the rail lines between here and Norfolk, to find where they were thrown off the trains to make room for more 'important' cargo."

"Aye, aye, sir. Perhaps I can be helpin' with the gun carriages and the pivot slide and circle while we're waitin'. Would there be quarters available aboard *Star of the West*, sir? I'm at the Exchange Hotel, and it's a bit dear for navy pay."

"Check out in the morning, Lieutenant, and move your dunnage aboard *Star*. I'll have a cabin ready for you. I'll get you started on the carriages and pivot today. A Mr. Roy, a local ironworker, has agreed to try his hand at constructing a pivot slide and rails. You can see him this morning. He's at the Customs House. Be back aboard *Star of the West* by two bells in the first dog watch, and my guess is you can see the captain then."

"Aye, aye, sir. And thank you, sir. I'll talk to Mr. Roy directly."

Rory returned to the main deck and re-crossed the river. After a short walk, he opened a set of tall double doors on the Canal Street side of the massive Customs House, and found a portion of the interior converted to an ironworker's shop and foundry, with several mechanics at work.

Rory introduced himself to Mr. Roy, a short and rather bemused-looking man, bald; wearing round spectacles perched on the end of his nose, and examining a set of plans for a gun carriage. The plans showed that the traditional wheels at the back of the carriage had been replaced with a wooden bar, which slid on the deck after the gun was fired. The resultant friction reduced recoil.

"A good afternoon to you, Mr. Roy. I see you have the drawings for a Marsilly 'dumb-truck' carriage."

"Indeed, I do, young man, and you seem to know something of ordnance. Who might you be?"

"Sure, I'm Lieutenant Dunbrody, CSN, at your service, sir, and under orders from Secretary Mallory to assist Captain Semmes in getting ready for sea. I've not met the captain, as yet, but thought I'd see if I could be of assistance to you while I'm waiting to do so."

"You certainly may. I'll have you work with that group, crafting the carriage walls. I'd be obliged if you'd check the port sill measurements. But, first, tell me a bit more about you. You sound Irish. We've had many Irishmen come to live in the city these last few years."

"Aye, it's the effect of the Great Famine, to be sure. When the potato blight struck, millions starved, and millions left Ireland. Twelve years later, conditions are still unbearable, and Irish are still leaving. I, myself, was born in New Berne, where my father still builds ships, but I was raised in Galway by my uncle, who is a ship owner there."

Rory and the mechanically gifted Mr. Roy exchanged personal information for a time, and then Rory went to work on the carriage fabrication. At 4:30, he finished for the day and returned to the *Star of the West*.

There he found Raphael Semmes, in a new uniform of steel-gray, standing near the taffrail and talking to a foreman of Atlantic Dry Dock. Semmes wore his dark hair combed in a pompadour and had an imperial mustache with its ends upturned and heavily waxed. He fixed his imperious gaze on Rory who came to attention, saluted smartly, and reported for duty.

"Dunbrody, yes, I've been expecting you. I received just today from Secretary Mallory your report on the engagement with the *Cumberland*. Fine work, lieutenant. Let me finish here, and we'll talk in my cabin."

Semmes asked Rory to be seated when they entered his cabin. Rory returned the gaze from Semmes' steel-blue eyes and stared at the captain's high forehead. "We've much to do with the ordnance here, lieutenant. Are you innovative? We're reduced to building everything but the cannons themselves."

"Yes, sir, I'm used to fending for meself for repair and replacement. There was every opportunity to learn self-reliance with the Brazil squadron, and aboard *Active* in the Northwest. Both stations were far from any ordnance depot. Mr. Kell mentioned that Mr. Roy was fabricatin' your gun carriages, sir, so I took the liberty of spendin' the day with him t' help any way I could. He had me verifyin' the port sill measurements for starters."

"Excellent. I like initiative in my officers, Mr. Dunbrody. I'll rely on you to see that Mr. Roy's work is properly completed."

"Aye, aye, sir. When do you wish the batteries to be mounted?"

"The third week of this month is the date I have in mind, if Mr. Chapman can find our guns between here and Gosport."

"Aye, aye, sir. 'Twill have my central energies, sir."

"Secretary Mallory tells me you're North Carolina born. Is that the genesis of your decision to come south?"

"Yes, sir, and my assumption that my brother Timothy would leave the Union Army and come south also. Unfortunately, I was wrong. He stayed with the North. But my father and sister live in New Berne, and I could not raise my hand against my father. I pray Tim will make it through the war unhurt."

"I'm sure your Tim felt his loyalty well-placed." Semmes leaned back in his chair and gazed out the port at the river traffic. "I cannot give the same credit for motive to those hypocrite politicians and merchant rascals who twist the Constitution and the Articles of Confederation to create something that never was: a federal government. Ours has always been a government of sovereign states, each with the right to secede from the confederation. Secession is not treason, as Lincoln maintains, but exercise of state's rights!"

"I've not heard it put so clearly as that, sir. Are you an attorney?"

"Yes, I'm a member of the Alabama Bar with a practice there at the times I'm ashore and not on active duty." Semmes leaned forward, obviously pleased to have an audience.

"Let me give you a further example of the hypocrisy of our northern foes. At the time the U.S. Constitution was adopted by the Constitutional Convention and then referred to the states, all of which were signatories to the Articles of Confederation, each state left the Articles of Confederation for the new constitution piecemeal, one at a time. Rhode Island retained separate sovereignty for two years before joining the new 'constitutional' Union. No one accused her of treason. The flag that we both served as a symbol of states' rights now waves over yelling and maddened majorities, whose will it is to be both constitution and law over any state asserting its rights. What treachery!"

"Aye, aye, sir." Rory could think of no other response that would not serve to continue the discussion, and he knew that continued discourse would inevitably lead to the topic of slavery. He decided to follow his father's advice and avoid the subject, if possible.

"It's a pity our Southern officers did not bring some of their ships with them," said Semmes. "We'd not be reduced to fashioning a navy out of baling wire. But, I suppose they followed the military principle, having been personally entrusted with their commands. A naval man cannot go far astray who abides by the point of honor."

Now, there's a point I can agree with, thought Rory to himself.

"Have you ordered your uniform, lieutenant?"

"I plan to do so in the morning, sir, before I come aboard *Star of the West*. I'm booked for tonight at the City Exchange."

"My officers have been grumbling at the gray, to coin a phrase. Can't say that I blame them, but regulation is regulation. It's probably for the best. I suspect indigo dye will be in short supply soon throughout the South. It's in very short supply here, thanks to the threat of blockade. So, I've taken steps to make the new gray uniforms available in advance of the rest of the navy. I suggest you go to Boudreaux on Magazine Street. They're doing the uniforms for most of my officers."

"Aye, aye, sir. I'll see them directly in the morning and then stow my sea chest and rejoin Mr. Roy."

"Tell them you'll need it in a week. We've been invited to a soiree at one of the finest plantations on the river near Audubon Park. I want my officers well dressed. Our hosts wish to show their appreciation for our willingness to go in harm's way. I'm told they'll present us with a Stars and Bars ensign sewn by patriotic ladies of New Orleans."

"Aye, aye, sir. I'll be sure t' be well-turned-out." Rory left

Semmes and made his way to the ferry landing where he waited, standing next to a lieutenant of Marines in the new Marine-gray officer's frock coat with double-knotted gold shoulder insignia, gray cap, and sky-blue trousers. As they boarded the ferry, Rory introduced himself.

"Lieutenant Beckett Howell, commanding the *Sumter*'s Marines, sir. I'm on my way into the old quarter to greet some friends. Would you care to join me?"

"Sure, that's most kind of you, sir. But I must be up at the peep o' day to move my gear to the *Star* and work with Mr. Roy on the gun carriages. It's a great disappointment not to accept your invitation."

"Not at all, lieutenant, perhaps another day. So you've met Captain Semmes, have you?"

"Indeed. He seems a very dedicated officer."

Howell smiled. "Nicely put, Mr. Dunbrody. He's quite passionate about the Cause. As are we all, I'm certain. But I dread the day we must confront our classmates and friends from the academies."

"To be sure, Mr. Howell. A case of 'the enemy: our friends,' I'm thinkin'." They bade each other goodbye until the morning as the ferry docked in New Orleans.

Day-by-day, Rory labored on gun carriage construction in Roy's shop. Gun size had increased during the first half of the century, enabling larger charges, increased velocity, and a consequent greater recoil. The old four-truck or four-wheeled carriages had given way to the two-truck Marsilly carriage. The rear trucks had been replaced by a solid wood brace or 'dumb-truck,' which sat flat on the deck. The resulting friction gave more resistance to recoil. Neither Mr. Roy nor any of his workers had ever constructed gun carriages. It was a trial-and-error process.

Rory's uniforms were ready the day before the soiree. The ensemble included a gray peaked cap, a gray frock coat, white waistcoat and trousers for summer, and gray for winter. The sleeve lace showed the one looped gold bar of a lieutenant with light-blue shoulder bars edged in gold with one gold star.

On the evening of the trip to Etienne de Bore's plantation, Semmes assembled his officers to inspect their turnout. Howell, the Marine, wore a red sash about his waist beneath his patent leather black sword belt. The lieutenants and Semmes were in summer white trousers and waistcoats and white high-collar shirts with black ties. All wore their dress sword belts and sabers in dress scabbards.

They traveled in two carriages on St. Charles Street, up-river to the beginning of the New Orleans crescent. Liveried servants took their caps when they arrived. They were greeted by their hosts and received the eager welcomes of jewelry-bedecked New Orleans society. Zouave and other colorful Confederate Army uniforms were everywhere. "Our gray and white looks rather drab compared to these peacocks," Howell whispered to Rory.

"After a cruise in the Atlantic sun, you'll be swarthy enough to counterbalance that, Beckett. Besides, you've already been in action, and they haven't!" In early May, Howell had commanded a company of Marines confronting Union troops at Fort Pickens, Pensacola, Florida.

Rory, Howell, and the others passed through the receiving line as a small orchestra played and officers and civilian men danced with women in gowns of every hue. Rory noticed a lieutenant colonel in the red, white and blue-striped pantaloons and crimson shell jacket of the Louisiana Tiger Zouaves, modeled on the uniform of a French-Algerian regiment in keeping with Louisiana's Gallic heritage. He was dancing with a young blonde in a pale blue gown. As they turned toward him, Rory recognized Carrie Anne Eastman. She smiled instantly in recognition.

Beckett Howell, Rory, and Captain Semmes stood by the punch bowl as the music ended. Carrie Anne clasped her dancing partner by the hand and led him to Rory and Beckett.

"Lieutenant Dunbrody, how nice to see you. May I introduce my fiancé, Colonel Thomas Donovan of the Louisiana Tiger Zouaves, and my cousin, Miss Natalie Farwell."

"Delighted to meet you, Miss Farwell. Colonel, a pleasure, sir. And a pleasure, too, to see you again, Miss Eastman." Rory realized he had strung a 'too' and a 'to' together. *Idjit*, he thought.

"May I introduce Captain Raphael Semmes of the CSS *Sumter*, and my friend Lieutenant Beckett Howell III, of the Confederate Marines, commanding the *Sumter*'s Marine detachment. Colonel Donovan, Miss Eastman, Miss Farwell."

Donovan's eyes grew wide in recognition. "Oh, yes, lieutenant, you're President Davis' brother-in law. I heard you were stationed here." Obviously impressed with Beckett's connection to the president, Donovan rudely ignored Semmes, who did not take kindly to slights, real or perceived.

"Thomas knows everyone in New Orleans," said Carrie Anne, in a voice tinged with resignation. *Readin' between the lines*, thought Rory, *I'd guess she thinks her fiancé's a shameless namedropper. She may be right.*

"Were you raised in Mississippi, Lieutenant Howell?" Carrie Anne asked.

"No, Miss," answered Howell. "My youth was spent in Virginia. My sister and her husband, Mr. Davis, raised me and sent me to school in Alexandria when he was in the Senate."

"What a wonderful opportunity for learning, lieutenant! At the seat of government, raised by a Senator in the thick of debate on the most weighty of issues. You were most fortunate! Welcome to New Orleans, Lieutenant Howell." Carrie Anne turned to Semmes, and with her smile, contrived to melt his frosty glare. "Captain, I hear that your efforts will soon have the *Sumter* at sea."

"Yes, Miss Eastman, we're hopeful of a late-May departure, but fashioning the accoutrements of war from scratch is proving a challenge."

"I'm sure you will prove necessity the mother of invention, Captain. A group of our New Orleans ladies has been sewing an ensign for the *Sumter*. Would you accept the Stars and Bars from the ladies of a grateful city as a gift?"

The thaw was complete. "Old Beeswax" (after his waxed mustache ends) melted like an ice-block in a bayou July. "The *Sumter* would be delighted to receive such a gift, Miss Eastman."

Rory was the next to bear the Eastman irradiation. "I am glad, Lieutenant Dunbrody, to see that you escaped from that Yankee ship."

"Sure, I'm even more delighted, learning that you are glad of it, Miss Eastman. But the crew of the USS *Cumberland* might say that they escaped from us."

"Oh, my stars, lieutenant, what on earth happened?"

"We pretended to run aground and tricked her into launching

her boats to board us. We sank her boats, captured her Marines and crews, and the Hatteras fort guns and our pivot drove the *Cumberland* off."

"What an incredible tale," said Donovan with a withering look. "Being of Irish stock myself, but having lifted myself out of the bogs, I'm compelled to observe that no one is here who could lend the credible to your story."

Rory rose to the challenge. "And isn't it the truth, what you say, colonel? The Irish bards embellishin' as they do? Of course now, we could be askin' the *Cumberland* prisoners at New Berne, or the Fort Hatteras garrison, or Captain Thomas of the North Carolina Ship *Rose of Clifden*, who wrote the report to Secretary Mallory. They might shed some light, t' be sure. Or perhaps 'tis just an Irishman's dream. Would y' be takin' offense, now, if I asked for the honor of this dance with yer fiancée?"

Donovan tensed but maintained his composure. "No, it would be churlish to do so, lieutenant."

"Well, yes, Thomas," said Carrie Anne, "it would be, with the lieutenant so courteous and professional when he boarded the *Scioto*. Come along, Mr. Dunbrody."

Carrie Anne gave just a hint of a flounce on her way to the dance floor. As Rory put his right hand upon her waist and guided her into the waltz, she grinned at him. "Thomas is just a wee bit jealous!"

"Aye, just a wee," Rory agreed. "Your cousin Natalie seemed amused at that exchange."

"Oh, yes. Natalie is my chaperone when needed, and my confidant, always. She knows as much about Thomas as I do."

"And is that an interesting study, now?"

"Demanding, at times. Thomas' family is quite prominent. He can be, well, rather forceful," she said, resignedly.

At the punchbowl, Donovan found himself the target of the notorious Semmes glare. "I'll have you know, colonel, that Mr. Dunbrody's bona fides come from Secretary Mallory himself."

"Still, captain, you'll concede that Dunbrody's story verges on the tall tale, taking into account his youth and obvious inexperience."

"On the contrary, colonel," said Semmes, menacingly.

"Dunbrody's file contains independent confirmation of his actions. His verisimilitude is unquestionable, and his experience is extensive for one so young. A word of warning to you, sir. His record contains commendations for successful hand-to-hand combat with the North Coast Indians. I'd be most careful, sir, voicing doubts of his honor."

Donovan departed from the group at the punchbowl, a scowl upon his face. On the dance floor, Rory and Carrie Anne were obviously enjoying each other's company. "I was very grateful for your reassurances aboard the *Scioto*. Do I detect your planning in the ruse that fooled the *Cumberland*?"

"Sure, 'twas the captain's plan. Anyone who says otherwise is just being overly kind. And have you and the colonel set a date?"

She laughed. "So nice of you to be interested, lieutenant. We've decided to wait for the war to end. Thomas thinks it will be quick."

"Then I'll pray for a long war, Miss Carrie Anne Eastman. The dance is ended. I hope to see you again."

"It could happen, Lieutenant Rory. New Orleans is such a small place." She squeezed his hand as he bowed to her.

Rory rejoined Beckett Howell at the punch bowl. Howell was talking to a small young man about fifteen years of age, dressed in a U.S. Naval Academy midshipman's uniform with the buttons covered and minus the fouled-anchor insignia. "Rory, let me introduce James Morris Morgan, late of the Naval Academy and looking for a midshipman's warrant. Jimmie is a native of these parts."

It's a pleasure to meet you, midshipman. When the *Sumter* sails, I'll be looking for a berth right alongside you." Young Morgan reminded Rory of himself in his first days at Annapolis, a fourteen-year-old plebe midshipman.

"Yes, sir," replied young Jimmie, "but at least you already have your commission. I'm frankly envious of you, and of your uniform. I'd heard the gray can't be found here. In fact they're still debating its adoption as the uniform color."

"Sure, that's true, but Captain Semmes is sure 't will be adopted and has arranged for a special shipment to Boudreaux. A very purposeful man, the captain."

"Yes, sir, he's already gaining a reputation for singular and passionate devotion to the Cause."

"Jimmie's quite the diplomat," said Howell. "I've heard others call it self-righteousness and arrogance."

I've heard the same, Beckett," said Rory. "'Tis true his disdain for the Yankees is profound. Perhaps he calls upon his hatred as a means to his achievements. I'm loath to criticize a man who creates a warship out of a packet in six weeks' time."

"You have a point, Rory," said Beckett. "I feel constrained to point out that young Morgan, here, is a remarkably considerate individual. He's been most courteous to me, despite the fact that my older brother, William, was a second to James Sparks in a duel last month in which Sparks killed his brother, Harry."

"Dueling is a way of life here, Mr. Howell," Jimmie responded. "And Harry chose shotguns as the weapons. No guilt can attach to your brother. It's a sad part of New Orleans culture. Dozens of fencing salons are crowded with young men seemingly eager to be tested in a duel. Brother Harry might have been better off with the sword."

"Sure, I could use some polishing upon my technique," said Rory. "Can you recommend a salon, Jimmie?"

"Sir, the best in the city is Pepe Lulla's in Exchange Alley. He is reputed to be a master shot and swordsman, particularly with small sword."

"It sounds a good place to start despite my weapon of choice being the saber. Thank you most kindly for the recommendation, Jimmie."

"Jimmie, you are most gracious to absolve my brother of blame," said Beckett. "If I can find a way to aid you in your quest for a warrant, I will do so without hesitation."

"Thank you, Mr. Howell. As I am without a warrant, and therefore not officially a subordinate, I would like to invite you two gentlemen to join me for dinner at my brother's, Judge P.H. Morgan's house. The judge makes no bones about his Union sympathies, but with two brothers serving the South, and another one trying, his inclination is treated as the eccentricity of an otherwise-beloved public figure."

"Do I speak for you, Rory, in accepting with pleasure?"

"To be sure, friend Beckett."

"On Tuesday, then. My brother will send a carriage to *Star of the West*."

A drum roll from the orchestra's percussion section called everyone's attention to a small lectern where their host, Etienne de Bore, introduced a bevy of ladies, including Carrie Anne, to present their Stars and Bars ensign to Captain Semmes. "A splendid end to the evening, Rory," said Beckett. "Now you can stare at her without being thought rude."

On Monday following the weekend, Rory sought out Captain Semmes to ask permission to visit a fencing salon twice weekly. "I need to maintain my skills, sir, as a fighting officer. I'll make up time lost on producing the traverse by work in the evenings."

"Permission granted, lieutenant. You're a hard-working officer. I appreciate your attention to duty."

On Tuesday, Rory presented himself at the Lulla Fencing Academy in Exchange Alley, which extended four blocks from Canal to Toulouse Street. "Señor José Lulla, *por favor*," he said to the slender, middle-aged Hispanic gentleman at the reception desk.

"I am José Lulla, but I am usually called Pepe," the *salle* master replied in English. "What can I do for you, lieutenant?"

"*Muchisimo gusto, Maestro*," Rory responded. "The Morgan family recommended you as the premier sword master in the city. I need to maintain my fencing skills while attending to my other duties. And it's certain I could use the physical exertion and the concentration of mind."

"I have a vacancy at present, and I am happy to accept you to the salon. Have you a moment now, that I may assess the breadth and depth of your experience? Then we can discuss my fee."

Rory and Señor Lulla entered the spacious great room of the salon and took positions on one of the many *pistes*. Donning masks, they exercised with foil, *e'pe'e*, and saber. Rory explained that the saber was his weapon of both choice and necessity as it was such a close cousin to the navy cutlass.

"You have a high level of skill, lieutenant. I can assign you to *salle* opponents of like levels, and we can work on the aspects of your swordsmanship as you wish. Have you freedom of schedule?"

"Yes, sir. I have my commander's permission to adjust my schedule to accommodate your requirements." They settled on a Thursday session each week. Rory walked back to the imposing granite bulk of the Customs House and to his labors with Mr. Roy in constructing the traverse for the *Sumter*'s pivot gun.

The next evening Beckett and Rory were met by carriage at the *Star of the West,* crossed the river, and were taken to the home of Judge Philip H. Morgan, eldest of Jimmie Morgan's eight older siblings. The Judge was a gigantic figure, in both stature and reputation, and was respected in the city in spite of his Union leanings. "Welcome, lieutenants. You've been most kind to young Jimmie. I'm most grateful, although he seems to me far too young to serve."

"He's a determined young man, Judge. I'm sure he'll have his warrant soon. And many naval officers and Marines begin their careers at his age," Beckett answered. "You're gracious to invite me, given my brother's unfortunate involvement with your late brother Harry. My condolences, sir."

"Those who embrace the duello flirt with fate. Harry would have been a fine medical officer for the Confederacy. However we feel about the Union, this will be the cruelest of wars, with so many families divided. I have a dear brother-in-law in the Union Army. Yet, I must stay with my State, dismayed 'though I am over her secession. I understand Lieutenant Dunbrody faces a similar family division. Well, let us not dwell upon the negative. Please come into the parlor. What may I give you to drink?"

The dinner party included a jurist and his wife in addition to the Morgans and the officers of the *Sumter*. Rory's natural inclination was to join the conversation, and shape it to his interest. He had learned in his naval career that a safer and more productive approach was to listen, contribute sparingly, and observe his evening's companions. The conversation ranged from the difficulties of the combatant governments to droll accounts of life at the Naval Academy, an experience shared among Beckett, Rory, and Jimmie.

"Was Major Lockwood on the faculty when you two were there?"

asked Jimmie. "He had a stammer," Jimmie explained to the other guests. "We had been admonished never to execute a command until the word of command had been completed. We faithfully and mischievously followed that order written when Major Lockwood became our drill officer. The major was marching our company toward the sea wall when he tried to give the command 'halt', and lapsed into a fit of stammering. All we heard was 'ha-ha-ha,' as we gleefully marched over the sea wall and into the Bay, rifles, bandoleers, and all. Of course we were punished for this, but it was worth it."

As the guests left, Beckett said to the judge, "I have written to Secretary Mallory on Jimmie's behalf, sir."

"That's most kind of you, lieutenant. I wish you the very best, and thank you." Rory and Beckett rode back to the Algiers ferry in silence, each preoccupied with the war's effect upon their families. The warm and glowing lights of the Morgan home receded in the distance, and a mist rose from the river.

On Rory's next visit to Lulla's Salon, Señor Lulla paired him with an engaging planter, Georges Dupree. Dupree was wiry and strong and very quick. Rory had more saber experience, and it was an even match of benefit to both. Rory was careful not to resort to unorthodox moves taught him by his grandfather. They both enjoyed the encounter and each other. "Next week, *mon ami?*" Dupree asked.

"*Mais oui*, Georges", Rory replied. "With great pleasure."

After Dupree had left, Señor Lulla said, "You use the very traditional sequences, Rory. You do not employ the unusual."

"Sure, it may be best to save those for our sessions, Señor, or for occasions of a more pressing need." Rory and Lulla smiled knowingly at one another.

As Rory exited the salon, he glimpsed a blond-haired woman walking ahead of him down Exchange Alley. Recognizing Carrie Anne, he quickened his step and overtook her. "And isn't the day immeasurably brighter, just seein' you, Miss Eastman?" he said as he came abreast of her.

"I declare, lieutenant, that must be the 'Blarney' I've heard so much about. What brings you to Exchange Alley?"

"Tryin' to improve my meager fencing skills, like a good sailor.

You've been shopping, I see. A fatiguing activity in its own right. Could I interest you in a sit-down and something cool, now?"

"I'd be delighted, Rory. I'm to have lunch with Thomas when he finishes at the fencing academy he attends, and cousin Natalie is due to meet me here. Thomas will be another hour. Something cool in the shade is just what I need."

"What master does Thomas take instruction from?"

"Croquere, I believe the man's name is. Thomas sets great store by him. Sometimes I believe he loves that sword more than he loves me," said Carrie Anne, her lips in a mock pout.

"Well, now, that's a misplaced affection, if ever I've heard of one. How could the man take his eyes from you for a moment? What kind of sword would the colonel be so deeply taken by that he would spurn New Orleans' foremost beauty?"

"Oh, la, lieutenant, 'spurn' may be too strong a word. And from your inquisition, I suspect you may be another so taken with swords he'd assign love to second place."

"Never in my life would you find yourself in second place, my dear. And isn't it the most natural thing for me, so clearly interested in you, to know all I can about one who shares my interest. How grand it would be if you elevated me to the level of 'rival'".

"If it were not for the charm of your brogue, you'd border on the glib, handsome Rory. Very well, I think it's a foil Thomas favors. Here, we can find an ice in this shop and a place to sit."

As they sat and talked, Rory clearly felt the tug of desire between them. He knew his giddiness was no friend to prudence, but decided to ignore caution when she said, with a sigh like one about to leap from a precipice, "I must tend to my friend's garden next week at her home on Felicity Street while she has gone to the shore. Do you like gardens, Rory?"

"Sure, I've always fancied a fine garden. So many grand and gorgeous blossoms. The thought of the scent overwhelms me as I think of it." They grinned at one another like school children contemplating a prank, and then her expression changed to one of wistful regret.

"Tuesday week might be a good day for gardening," said Carrie

Anne. "It's the two-story pink house on the corner of Robertson and Felicity. And now I must look for my cousin. It's not seemly that I am unchaperoned with a gentleman." She smiled, rose, and extended her hand which Rory took in his and pressed to his lips in fine European fashion.

"It's countin' the hours I'll be, then, lovely Carrie Anne," he said, laughing as they took their leave of one another. *Jasus*, he thought to himself. *I'm on course for what Uncle Liam would call a 'fine contretemps'. But I do not care. In fact, I'm lookin' forward to it. Maybe it's the Southern climate.*

CHAPTER 19
FITTING OUT THE SUMTER
MAY-JUNE 1861

The ensuing week was tumultuous. The water tanks were delivered and installed aboard the *Sumter*. The wooden Marsilly carriages for the thirty-twos were completed and tested as much as possible without an actual firing drill. The circular pivot rails or 'racers' for the eight-inch pivot gun were laid down and the bolts emplaced. The pivot, weighing four and a half tons, was slung by a crane alongside the drydock and mounted on the bows.

On the third of June, Semmes formally commissioned the ship, hoisted the colors of the patriotic ladies, transferred the crew from the receiving ship, and required the officers to mess aboard. Rory was assigned temporary quarters aboard, until such time as the ordnance had been thoroughly tested. The *Sumter* was hauled off from the dockyard and anchored in the stream. Semmes scheduled a series of day cruises up the river to test the engines, guns, and sailing qualities of the ship. Before the day sails began, Rory was able to go ashore for his fencing practice and for his appointment with Carrie Anne which his active imagination had daily turned into a tryst.

Sure, but she's of two minds about seein' me, Rory thought to himself as he walked up Felicity Street. *One moment she's as gleeful as me, and the next, she's pensive as can be. Guilt, I'd venture. Ah, there's the house.* He rang the bell-pull, unmindful of the momentary parting of the curtains drawn in the house across the street. Light footsteps, a door opened, and smiling sea-green eyes greeted him.

"I do so love time in the garden, lieutenant. How nice of you to join me." Carrie Anne took his hand and led him through the house and down the back steps into a secluded back-yard garden centered around a gazebo. "I've been workin' so diligently this morning, I just must sit for a spell."

Gale-force winds, thought Rory of his emotions as loneliness and desire overwhelmed any thoughts of caution he might have entertained in thinking of this moment. He took her in his arms, feeling warmth and response, her arms tightly around him. "I must move us inside, my dear, please, I beg you."

"Oh, Rory, I can't keep up with my emotions. Please, not this quickly; give me time." They sat back suddenly on the gazebo bench, their hands entwined.

"We must be very, very careful, my dear. You must think me a flirt without scruple to behave so while betrothed. And I wouldn't blame you, not a bit."

"Ah, for me, dear, it's a rush of delight, but I sense for you that you're drawn where you'd rather not be."

"I want to be here with you, but I feel so fenced in by circumstance. My family is beset with financial problems, my mother widowed, and with only minimal help from her sister in Richmond. When I met Thomas, and he proposed soon after, he offered my brother, Beau, a job with his father's firm. Beau is an accountant, and his withered leg precludes his military service. Mother was delighted and not just for fiscal reasons. She sets great store by society's viewpoint, and the Donovans are very prominent here. I felt I couldn't refuse his proposal even with my doubts about him. And they turned out to be well founded. He is so domineering!"

"Sure, and I must have looked good by comparison!"

She smiled warmly. "My attraction to you, Rory dear, is quite independent of relative merit."

"Then you'll not refuse me another visit, out of hand?" Rory paused, expectantly.

"My fear is I'll not refuse you at all. But I know I cannot stay away from you. Such a sweet dilemma!"

"Ah, now, wouldn't you know the navy is about to call the tune in our lovely gavotte for a few measures? I'll be at sea, or at least on the river, these next few weeks, until the ship is ready to run the blockade. I can't bear the thought of a day away, much less the month of June."

"I'll be here, my love, and we will find another quiet garden."

"With a more comfortable bench, if it's not too much trouble. I'm due aboard. One small kiss for this poor lad with his knees a-quiver?"

"Gently, dear. Captain Semmes does not strike me as tolerant of tardiness." Carrie Anne embraced him for a moment, and led him back through the house.

"Don't worry, love," he said. "We'll find a way through this without jeopardizing your family." She smiled uncertainly as she closed the door.

Back aboard *Sumter*, Rory sat in the wardroom reading the ordnance stores list. His attention strayed to thoughts of Carrie Anne. *She is so bright, and so knowledgeable of things that matter to me, the war, life at sea. I've not met women who can match her mind, nor her beauty, either. And isn't she in the damnedest quandry, terrible, altogether, her family all but hostage to the influence and goodwill of the Donovans? How can I help her out of the briar patch of Southern society without scratches?*

The captain's clerk, Breedlove Smith, appeared at the hatchway. "Captain's compliments and he would like to see you in his cabin, Mr. Dunbrody."

"I'm on my way, Mr. Smith," said Rory, rising and walking aft. The Marine sentry opened the cabin door and Rory entered, coming to attention and announcing, "Lieutenant Dunbrody reporting, sir."

"Be seated, lieutenant. As part of our shakedown day-sails upriver, I'm planning to invite some of the principal citizens of the city to observe a gunnery exercise and partake of a collation. I assume you would not object if I include Colonel Donavan, his fiancée, his father, and his brother Grenville?"

"Not at all, sir. It would be a pleasure to see the colonel and Miss Eastman again, and to meet his family."

"Yes, I'm sure it would, at least in part. Your private life is your own, Dunbrody, but I'm told the Donovans are a powerful and unforgiving family, so, be careful as your relationships unfold. I would hate to see the navy lose so promising an officer."

"Aye, aye, sir," said Rory, not knowing quite how to respond and taking refuge in the navy's safest answer.

Semmes smiled at Rory's obvious bewilderment. "There are no secrets in New Orleans, lieutenant, and assuredly none aboard *Sumter*. Are the gunpowder and shot records in order?"

"Yes, sir. You are ready for sea. May I make a request, sir?"

"You may."

"I know my work is nearly complete, sir, but I would like permission to stay aboard until you have cleared the Passes. I could return with the pilot."

"Request granted. Your performance for me has been excellent, lieutenant. It will be useful to have you on board to assist with any last minute ordnance problems. And, given the large numbers of Irish in our crew, I'm certain it's salubrious for them to see an Irish officer. Our collation for the patriotic citizens will be day after tomorrow. If there's nothing else, you're dismissed."

"Aye, aye, sir." Rory returned to the wardroom, his mind preoccupied with the thought of seeing Carrie Anne sooner than he'd expected, notwithstanding the presence of the Donovan family.

Forty-eight hours later, the *Sumter* sailed upriver toward Baton Rouge. A group of twenty citizens stood on the quarterdeck as the gun crews labored in the waist, firing at barrels set out by the *Sumter*'s launch. Rory was forward, near the pivot gun, discussing its ease of traverse with Lieutenant R.T. Chapman, who had tracked down the *Sumter*'s guns along the railroad tracks of the Confederacy where they had been unloaded in favor of cargo more desirable in the view of the Confederate States Army. The pivot gun crew was alternating its fire between barrels to port and to starboard, traversing each shot. "The mechanism seems to be working well," said Chapman. "Would you convey that observation to the captain with my respects, Lieutenant?"

"With pleasure, sir," Rory replied. "I'm delighted it's finally performing to expectations." He made his way aft through the waist and up the ladder to the quarterdeck. Touching his hat to Semmes, Rory reported. "Lieutenant Chapman's respects, sir, and the traverse mechanism is working well."

"Excellent, Mr. Dunbrody. You and Mr. Roy may be justly proud of a job well done. Ladies and gentlemen," Semmes announced to the citizens clustered on the quarterdeck, "may I present our very fine ordnance liaison officer, Mr. Dunbrody. I'll ask my clerk, Mr. Smith, to introduce him to y'all individually as I must return to my duties."

W. Breedlove Smith, mustachioed, heavily sideburned, and darkly handsome, took Rory by the arm and carried out the introductions. When they came to the Donovan party, Smith said to Rory, "I believe you've met Colonel Donovan and Miss Eastman, sir. May I present the colonel's father, James O'Kerrigan Donovan and the colonel's brother, Captain Grenville Donovan."

The senior Donovan wore round-lens wire-rimmed glasses and a waistcoat too small for his corpulent body. He glared haughtily at Rory, who decided in the face of Donovan's obvious dislike to deepen the Donovans' distaste. "Sure, and it's always a pleasure to meet another son of the Emerald Isle," he said in his best stage-Irish accent.

"We are Louisianans, suh, not Irishmen." James Donovan sniffed and turned away from Rory who smiled warmly at the colonel and Carrie Anne. Grenville Donovan, a shorter version of his good-sized brother, merely glared.

Rory's stage-Irish demeanor vanished, and he turned to Thomas Donovan with military formality. "Welcome aboard, colonel. I remember now you telling me as we met that your family had raised itself out of the bogs. My apologies for my forgetfulness. Would you and Miss Eastman care to observe the working of the pivot gun at close hand? I'd be interested in your professional observations."

"I can observe quite well from here, thank you," replied the red, white and blue-pantalooned Zouave.

"Well, I confess I am curious about the gun, lieutenant." Carrie Anne, a twinkle in her eye, took Rory's arm and they descended the ladder to the waist and walked forward to the pivot.

"Thomas has been a perfect bear recently. I'm quite tired of it.

Thank Heaven I have cousin Natalie to commiserate with me. She told me from the first her reservations about Thomas. I declare, with you about to leave for a month, I don't know how I'd manage without her to confide in."

"Could he have heard we've been together, now, do you suppose?"

"Well, my friend Beth Marie said she'd heard such a rumor, so that could be the cause of his surly behavior. But then, he's always surly. I denied to Beth Marie that we'd done anything but have an ice together in Exchange Alley, of course."

"I had given up hope of seeing you for the month when the captain surprised me with his party plans. What a treat for me to find you aboard, love, even under these strained circumstances."

"When I hear that the *Sumter* has cleared the passes, Natalie and I will meet you at ten the following Tuesday at the same spot in the Exchange. It will all be very proper. Will that work, my dear Rory?"

"It will, love. Ah, the fine girl you are, to follow shipping news so closely, now. No other woman in New Orleans knows half as much, to be sure. I'd best return you to the quarterdeck. It's quite grand that you'd be expected to hold my arm this way against the motion of the ship and all. Not even your fiancé could gainsay that!"

"No, he can't, but he'll grumble all the same. I'll see you at month's end." Carrie Anne left Rory and joined Captain Semmes and a group that included the Donovans. "My goodness, captain, that pivot will be a formidable weapon!"

"Why, indeed it will, Miss Eastman. I'm so glad you could observe Lieutenant Chapman and Lieutenant Dunbrody and their work at close hand."

Indeed she has, captain, thought Rory as he passed out of earshot and returned to the foredeck.

CHAPTER 20
ESCAPE OF THE SUMTER
JUNE 1861

The *Sumter* lay in the river between the two forts, Jackson and St. Philip, just a few miles above the Head of the Passes, the point where the mouths of the river began; to the east – Pass a l'Outre, Northeast and Southeast Pass, to the south – South Pass, and to the west - Southwest Pass. Southwest and l'Outre were the two deepest, and so were the ones most used by deep-draft sea-going vessels.

Shortly after sunrise, a boat from Fort Jackson rowed to the *Sumter*, and the messenger was sent below to the captain's cabin. Captain Semmes appeared on the quarterdeck.

"Mr. Kell," he called to the first lieutenant, "Fort Jackson has just sent word that Governor Moore and former Senator Slidell are inspecting the forts this morning. Call away my gig. I'm going ashore to invite them for gunnery exercise and lunch. Have Chapman and Dunbrody ready the gun crews at six bells in the forenoon watch."

As the dignitaries enjoyed a mid-afternoon lunch in the captain's cabin after watching the *Sumter*'s batteries sink several barrels, a dispatch from the forts arrived with word that the USS *Powhatan*, blockading the Southwest Pass, had left station to chase two ships. Semmes immediately began to raise steam, hoping to reach Southwest Pass before *Powhatan* returned.

Two hours later, *Sumter* hove-to at the lighthouse that marked the Head of the Passes. "Mr. Kell, signal for a pilot, if you please." Semmes waited impatiently for a response and finally dispatched a boat to summon the pilot. The boat returned and its midshipman reported to Semmes.

"Sir, there is no pilot at the lighthouse. The lighthouse keeper said they're all at the pilot station at l'Outre Pass."

"Very well, Mr. Hicks. Mr. Dunbrody, my information from the New Orleans squadron is that most of the pilots here are Yankees. You're a supernumerary aboard and your duties aboard are concluded. Take the launch, and row to the pilot station at l'Outre. Bring me back a pilot. Mr. Hicks, return to the lighthouse and stand by its telegraph in case Mr. Dunbrody sends a message. Mr. Kell, as night is falling, we must wait to see what morning brings."

Rory's boat crew included eight oarsmen and a coxswain. "Cox'n," said Rory, "I'll be needin' four carbines, and a navy six pistol for every man, just in case we encounter the Yankees venturin' upriver, d'ye see?"

"Aye, aye, sir," the coxswain responded, with a slightly confused look.

"Not t' worry, cox'n," said Rory with a reassuring smile, "we just want to be persuasive, if need be."

In the dark of the mid-watch, the bow oar of the launch leaped to the quay at the l'Outre pilot station, and grabbed the painter flung to him. Leaving the coxswain with the boat, Rory led eight men armed with carbines and pistols up the path to the pilot station. Rory knocked and knocked again more forcefully. No one responded. He forced the door and entered just as the several pilots stumbled, bleary-eyed, from their bunks. Rory's men lit the kerosene lamps.

"Gentlemen, we are in need of a pilot for CSS *Sumter* at the Head of the Passes. Would one of you be so kind as to accompany us back up the pass?" Rory smiled at the hastily assembling pilots.

The senior pilot, a tall and spare man with a drooping mustache and a New England accent, stepped forward, his face contorted in rage. "How dare you barge into this station, and order professional pilots about, you damned pirate!"

Rory turned to his men and nodded discretely. Each man then cocked his carbine or navy six, and held his weapon at the ready. The clicks of the cocking mechanisms echoed in the silence of the station. Rory trained his revolver on the senior pilot. "Pirates, gentlemen? Surely you know that a true pirate would not hesitate to shoot a resister in cold blood, so as to encourage a volunteer from the rest? Don't test me, gentlemen. I'm an Irish hooligan without the restraints of New England courtesy." Rory glowered menacingly. "As you seem to be unsure as to which of you should go, I'll take you all."

Morning brought the *Powhatan* back on station, and a telegraphic dispatch from Rory at the pilot station.

> *Sir:*
>
> *The pilots refuse to accompany me voluntarily. I am returning with the captain of the Pilots' Association and several pilots so that you may impress them at first hand with the gravity of the situation. Your obedient servant.*
> *Lt. R. Dunbrody, CSN.*

Semmes read the dispatch and laughed. "Mr. Kell, I'm even more convinced that we have an officer with some initiative."

Later, in the captain's cabin, the pilots sputtered their excuses for their recalcitrance, but in the end, confronted with Semmes' threat to detain them all aboard *Sumter*, they reluctantly agreed that one of their number would stay aboard until *Sumter* cleared the river. They left three additional pilots at the lighthouse at the Head of the Passes. As the launch receded into the distance with the others, Semmes said to his officers, "It appears that all but one of the pilots on station are Northerners. We'll have to see if our new plan bears fruit."

They lay at the Head of the Passes for nine days, awaiting the chance to slip by the blockading Union warships. Rory occupied part of the first few days in organizing the dozens of national ensigns of foreign nations that *Sumter* carried. They were to be used when a *ruse d'guerre* would be useful

The officers fell to speculating on the speed of the various blockaders. One, having served on *Brooklyn*, claimed she could do fourteen knots. "Nonsense," scoffed Semmes. "Maybe in her trial

trip, but ten to one, she's no faster than *Sumter*." His officers remained
unconvinced.

"Regardless of relative speed, gentlemen, what amazes me is
that *Powhatan*, *Brooklyn*, and the other blockaders have neither sent a
cutting-out expedition to take our little steamer, nor lightened their vessels
enough to draw them over the Southwest bar, and taken our position here
at the Head of the Passes. Why guard three routes when you could guard
one?" Semmes shook his head in disbelief at what he considered blatant
dereliction of duty.

"Let's hope it doesn't occur to them 'til we escape, sir," said Kell.
Rory stood by the break of the quarterdeck, observing the set of officers
aboard *Sumter*: Kell, the tall, middle-aged first lieutenant, affable, efficient
and equal to any situation. Next to him, Semmes, his intelligence and
commanding presence overshadowing his arrogance and acerbic nature.
Chapman, the second lieutenant, witty and good-natured, and Beckett
Howell, the Marine lieutenant, competent, disciplined, dependable, and,
having been raised in Jeff Davis' household, possessed of a remarkable
grasp of national affairs. *I wish I were assigned with them permanently,*
thought Rory.

On June 30, the steamer *Empire Parish* brought coal and
provisions to *Sumter* on her way to provision the pilot station at Pass a
l'Outre. Commodore Rousseau, commanding the New Orleans station
for the Confederate States Navy, had become concerned that stores were
running low aboard *Sumter* because of the long delay. Several hours later,
Empire Parish returned and when passing *Sumter*, cast off the tow of a
boat she'd been towing. A single oysterman rowed quickly to *Sumter*, and,
when aboard, told Semmes that *Brooklyn* had steamed out of sight of Pass
a l'Outre in pursuit of a strange sail. Quickly, the boats were slung in,
steam was raised and the anchor heaved-up. The on-duty pilot stood next
to Semmes, agitated and noticeably nervous.

"Pilot, you look about to faint," Semmes declared. "What
troubles you so?"

"Captain, please, I know nothing of Pass a l'Outre. I'm a
Southwest bar pilot, and ignorant of the other passes."

"What," said Semmes angrily, "did you not know that I was lying here for the very purpose of taking any of the outlets through which an opportunity of escape might present itself? How dare you now tell me you know only one? You have been deceiving me! Get out of my sight! Mr. Kell, hoist the Jack to signal for another pilot. If no pilot appears, I'll run the bar myself!"

As *Sumter* came down the pass, the *Brooklyn* appeared eight miles distant, having sighted *Sumter*'s smoke from her stack, and having then broken off her chase of the strange sail.

Rory trained a telescope on the pilot station as it came in sight. "Sir, a four-oared crew putting off from the pilot station. Looks to be a pilot in the stern sheets."

"Very good, Mr. Dunbrody, This may be the one southerner on station. I see a woman waving a handkerchief at him from the porch of a home next to the pilot station. She's a beauty, too. Mr. Kell, engines ahead half while we toss them a line and bring him on board. Mr. Dunbrody, get your dunnage. I'll send you ashore with this pilot when we've crossed the bar. Take that other miserable excuse for a pilot back with you, if you please."

"Aye, aye, sir." Rory ran below to get his small sea bag. Upon returning to the quarterdeck, Beckett Howell gave him a firm, two-handed handshake.

"Stay out of trouble, Rory."

"God save ye, kindly, Beckett. I hope we meet again."

"Gentlemen," said Semmes, "this war will last long enough for us all to meet again. You've done fine work, Mr. Dunbrody. It's been a pleasure to have you aboard."

"Thank you, sir. Smooth sailing and a soldier's wind to you all, sir."

Sumter swept past a Bremen merchantman lying aground on the bar and was, at last, on the high seas. The young pilot said to Semmes, "Now, captain, you are all clear; give her Hell and let her go!" *Sumter* slackened speed, hauled the pilot's boat close aboard, and Rory and the two pilots joined the four black oarsmen for the row back to the pilot station. *Brooklyn*, four miles distant, was still out of range. By the time they reached shore, only the smoke from the stacks could be seen.

CHAPTER 21
CSS MCRAE, ARMED AND READY
JULY 1861

CSS *McRae* lay anchored in mid-stream, off New Orleans
to the northwest, and Algiers to the southeast. Ten days had passed
since *Sumter* had reached the high seas, time enough for word to reach
Secretary Mallory, and for new orders to be transmitted to Lieutenant
Rory Dunbrody, CSN. Rory approached the barque-rigged steamer in the
stern-sheets of a 'water taxi', a four-oared, two man rowing wherry which
came alongside *McRae* in a most seamanlike fashion, enabling Rory to
step to the boarding ladder effortlessly and report almost immediately to a
mildly surprised lieutenant-commanding, Thomas Huger.

"Welcome aboard, lieutenant," said Huger. "I'm one lieutenant
short of complement. Your timing is excellent. We could have used your
experience when we mounted our nine-inch Dahlgren pivot, but I know
you were busy doing the same work for Captain Semmes. In a few days,
we'll be ready to sail to the Baton Rouge arsenal for our ammunition. Let
me introduce you to some of your fellow officers."

On the quarterdeck, Rory met C.W. 'Savez' Read, sailing master,
a slight, intense Mississippian, First Lieutenant Warley, and Second
Lieutenant Eggleston.

McRae was scheduled to depart for Baton Rouge on Wednesday.
On Tuesday, Rory received permission from Captain Huger to continue
his fencing exercises, and after a session with Pepe Lulla, he relaxed over an
ice in the shop in Exchange Alley. Carrie Anne arrived, in the company
of cousin Natalie. A very worried frown dimmed Carrie Anne's usually

bright eyes.

"Hello, Miss Farwell. What ill wind has blown trouble your way, my dear Carrie Anne? You look as though you've heard the banshee."

"Oh, Rory, I've just left Thomas, and I'm so troubled. He's been impossible to be near since we met on the *Sumter*. He insults you constantly. I'd break off the engagement, but my brother, Beau, and indeed, my whole family, depend on his father's goodwill for our livelihood. What shall I do?"

"There must be other opportunity in the city for a junior accountant, sure?"

Natalie responded. "Yes, but the Donovans would be deeply offended if Carrie Anne broke the engagement, and Mr. James is not above making it impossible for Beau to find other work."

"Let me try to find a solution, ladies. We sail for Baton Rouge for ammunition tomorrow, and then back here for coal in ten days. Let's meet here at the same time in a fortnight." Though they stood in a crowded alley, Rory impulsively leaned toward Carrie Anne and kissed her gently on the cheek, an action that did not escape the notice of several passers-by.

McRae sailed upriver to the arsenal at Baton Rouge, and lay ten days taking on ammunition. A red flag flew at the fore yardarm, giving notice to the unwary that *McRae* was loading explosives. The black powder, placed in the magazine in canisters, was particularly volatile. The men wore worsted shirts, clothing without buttons, and cloth slippers. Pockets were emptied. Everyone was vigilant in avoiding the chance of a spark.

On July 17th, Rory, serving as officer of the deck, was surprised to see Jimmie Morgan come aboard in his Annapolis uniform, with the covers removed from the buttons. "Lieutenant Dunbrody, sir. Midshipman Morgan, CSN, reporting for duty."

I see you've received your warrant, Mr. Morgan. Congratulations to you, young man."

Captain Huger appeared on deck. "Ah, Morgan, you've found us. I see you've met Mr. Dunbrody."

"I had the pleasure of meeting Mr. Morgan ashore, sir, before I was assigned to the *McRae*."

"Excellent, lieutenant. He'll be in your division. Ask Mr. Warley to assign him his duties, if you please."

"Aye, aye, captain. Mr. Morgan, have you been visiting your father here?"

"Yes, sir. I believe he's pleased that I'm back in uniform, albeit in a different service."

The *McRae*, her ammunition aboard at last, dropped downriver to the coaling station at New Orleans. Rory sat at his usual table in Exchange Alley the following Tuesday. He had stewed for hours over the dilemma he and Carrie Anne found themselves in. He had reached the conclusion that he must leave her life unless her family was willing to leave New Orleans, a sacrifice he was reluctant to ask them to make.

He glanced up, expecting to see Carrie Anne. Instead, he was confronted with a very angry Thomas Donovan, in full Zouave uniform, with a major from his regiment alongside. "Sir," spat Donovan, "you've trifled with the affections of my fiancée for the last time. You are a blackguard, sir, a scoundrel, and no gentleman. Permit me to introduce my second, Major Rochambeau."

"How do you do, major? If you will be kind enough to provide me your card, I will see that my second is in touch with you immediately. I believe, as this imbecile has issued the challenge, that the choice of weapons is mine. Is that your understanding, major?" Rory had not risen but sat reclining casually in his chair, a slight smile on his lips.

"Uh, yes, no, that is, the choice is yours," sputtered Major Rochambeau, wishing to respond without seeming to agree that his principal was an imbecile, and handing Rory his card.

"That being the case, major," continued Rory, studiously ignoring Donovan, who stood, seething, "know that my second will inform you that my choice is sabers. Good day to you, sir."

Now, who am I to ask to be my second? Rory asked himself as the two Louisiana Zouaves departed. *I'm thinkin' I'll not be seein' Carrie Anne today.*

CHAPTER 22
THE DUEL AND AFTERMATH
JULY-OCTOBER 1861

Back aboard *McRae*, Rory first informed the captain, asked permission to seek a second from among the ship's officers, and assured Huger that he intended to fight within twenty-four hours so as not to delay the ship from proceeding downriver. "This Donovan is reputed to be a crack swordsman, lieutenant. Are you good?" Huger waited hopefully, dismayed at the prospect of losing an officer.

"Yes, sir, I'm very good with a saber. And he fights usually with a foil. Not the same, at all, at all. There's no whackin' about the head and face with the foil. Ah, but the saber, now. Considerable head-whackin' goin' on. Never you worry, sir. I'll be back in time for tea, sure as I'm a Dunbrody, sir." Rory smiled what Huger had to admit was a very confident smile.

Rory was feeling much less confident than his smile conveyed. *I hope Donovan's not of the caliber of von Klopfenstein. I'm in deep trouble if he is,* he thought to himself. *Damn, I wish Tobias were here. I'd somehow feel more confident if he were.*

Rory went forward to the wardroom where he found Savez Read and Jimmie Morgan seated at the wardroom table. In the few days since Morgan had reported, he and Savez, both young, bright, and below average height, had struck up a friendship. "Gentlemen," said Rory, "just the lads I'm lookin' for. It seems I was called out by Colonel Thomas Donovan today, for bein' no gentleman and other assorted shortcomings. I'm in need of a second. Would either or both of you consider appearing on my behalf to make the arrangements?"

"Yes," they chorused. "We can't hardly have the Army spreading lies about, now can we?" said Read.

"Thank you most kindly, gentlemen. I'm eternally grateful. I need all the support I can muster. His second is a Major Rochambeau of his regiment, the Louisiana Tiger Zouaves. Here's his card," said Rory, handing the card to Savez. "Jimmie's just gone through this with his brother, Harry. My friends, I want to fight as soon as possible. Tomorrow would be splendid. Sabers are my choice of weapons."

"Mr. Read," said Jimmie, "I can arrange for the venue. The 'Dueling Oaks' customarily sees a dozen duels a week."

"Fine, Mr. Morgan. I'll contact the major now. Let's meet this afternoon."

When the three officers met again aboard *McRae*, the sun was in the west, and a duel was in the offing for daybreak.

"Major Rochambeau and I have agreed on a doctor, who will join us in the morning," said Savez, "and because you have two seconds, Donovan's brother Grenville will join the major."

Savez, Jimmie, and Rory talked into the evening. They all tried to avoid talk of the duel. As the conversation for a time centered on other topics, it helped to keep Rory's natural nervousness in check. "Savez, according to the watch bill, your first name is Charles. How came you by 'Savez'?"

"Well, Rory, while in my third year at Annapolis, two years before young Jimmie entered, I fell to the lower half of my class in academics. I was done in by French, my worst subject. I knew one word; savez, 'you know.' I used it constantly. I've been 'Savez' ever since; but everyone, including me, pronounces it 'savvy' instead of 'savay.'"

"Sure, that's the most unusual nickname tale I've ever heard," said Rory.

"I've asked the watch to call us at eight bells in the mid-watch," said Savez. "That gives us an hour and a half to reach the Dueling Oaks near Lake Ponchartrain. Jimmie tells me we can get coffee nearby at a shop that caters to dueling parties."

"Jimmie, I thought it was coffee afterwards, 'pistols for two, coffee for one,'"

"I'm sure you'll be having coffee both before and after, Rory. Have you planned a strategy? My brother was foolish enough to choose shotguns. It didn't leave much room for an alternative approach if things went wrong at first."

"Well, now, young Morgan, I'll be disclosin' me strategy, you bein' so persuasive, and all. He's very strong, Jimmie, but the saber is a demanding sword, very heavy, much more so than the foil he's used to. And he'll be more comfortable with thrusts, rather than slashes, as that's the way of the foil. The foil's a torso weapon, but the *sabreur* cuts at the head, the arm, the legs, like a proper cavalryman is trained to do. He's not used to that, but I am. And I'll avoid his thrusts by moving. This is not fought on a *piste* where the convention is not to move one's feet. This is the woods, the 'Dueling Oaks'."

"You may know what you're about after all," said Savez.

"We'll hope so, Savez. But I'll not try to kill him. The South needs its soldiers, and I'm only interested in preventing his family from harassing Carrie Anne's."

As they turned in, Rory gave his seconds a reassuring smile, which belied his fears for the morning. This was his first actual duel. His previous travels in harm's way had included enemy broadsides and boarding parties, the possibility of drowning, and hand-to-hand action with the Haida war party, but no duels. He fought several in his mind's eye that night and was a long time getting to sleep.

"Eight bells, Mr. Dunbrody." The boatswain's mate of the watch paused outside Rory's compartment until he saw Rory sit up with his feet on the deck, looking through the latticework bulkhead that constituted the 'wall' of Rory's quarters.

Rory and his two sleepy seconds rowed ashore in the jolly boat and were met on the quay by the carriage Savez had engaged. A ride north through the deserted streets of the Crescent City and into the countryside surrounding Lake Ponchartrain brought them to an extensive grove of oaks. They had stopped just before the grove for coffee at a small shop nestled in a curve of the road and were now wide-awake, adrenalin making the smallest motion crystal-clear. Leaving the coach, they found

Donovan, his brother Grenville in his infantry captain's uniform, the major, a doctor, and his assistant already on the grounds.

"Gentlemen," said Rochambeau, "do either of you wish to offer an apology at this point and obviate the need for the duel?"

"I have nought for which to apologize," said Rory.

"I reiterate," said Donovan, "this man is no gentleman."

"Then, we may move forward." The doctor's instruments were laid out on a linen tablecloth covering a table he had brought in his carriage. The seconds examined each principal's saber and pronounced it acceptable. Donovan and Rory, each in uniform, took off uniform jackets and stood in shirtsleeves, the Zouave distinguished by his flowing and voluminous pantaloons. "*Engarde*," said Rochambeau, and the two touched sabers and began.

Donovan delivered the first blow, a powerful downward slash that indicated his appreciation of the saber and its effective use. Rory parried easily, with his sword fist raised in the high left or "quince" position, but the power of Donovan's blow numbed Rory's sword arm. Rory stepped back, feinted a backhanded slash to Donovan's right side, and when Donovan's arm rose to parry on his right, Rory moved to Donovan's left with a lightning-quick cut that Donovan could parry only partially. Rory drew first blood from his cut over Donovan's left eye. Like most head-wounds, it bled profusely.

Donovan gave a cry and thrust powerfully toward Rory's torso. Rory leaped to his left, and the point of Donovan's saber tore his shirt, the edge grazing his chest and drawing blood. As Rory landed on his feet, his body at right angle to Donovan's, Rory's sword-fist was raised over his left shoulder, and he slashed down on Donovan's right shoulder, through Donovan's ineffective parry, with a riposte which cut deeply. Rory pulled his saber toward him in a 'draw', cutting more deeply yet, parried Donovan's next thrust, and cut underhanded at Donovan's right leg, cutting deeply once again.

Rory stepped back. The morning sun shone through the oaks, warming his body but leaving his face in shadow. "Surely, colonel, your honor has been maintained. Your wounds need attention. I have no wish to kill you by forcing you to bleed to death."

Donovan snarled at Rory. "Damn you, you blackguard, fight on!" He struck an awkward blow at Rory, his sword arm severely hampered by the deep cut in his right shoulder.

Rory struck a quick blow to Donovan's forehead, causing blood to obscure the Zouave's vision. "Now, you daft bogtrotter, you can't see, you can't swing, and you can barely walk. Major! Reason with your principal, sir!"

Donovan sank to the ground as Rochambeau, Grenville, the doctor, and his assistant all rushed to his aid.

Savez and Jimmie appeared at Rory's side. Jimmie took his saber from his hand, while Savez, towel over one shoulder, opened Rory's shirt to look at his chest wound. "It's not very deep, Rory," said Savez. Press this towel on it. I'll ask the doctor to see to you when he finishes with Donovan."

"It appears to me that Donovan's the one who's finished," said Rory, lightly. Overcome with a sudden elation, he thought, *Thanks be, I survived!* His adrenalin level then began to subside, and in its place, he felt tired, but still quite relieved to have endured. "Jimmie, once we've returned to *McRae*, will you take a note to Carrie Anne? I'll square it with the captain."

"Aye, aye, sir. It will be my pleasure. I'm already trained. I've been carrying messages to Captain Huger's fiancée this last week."

The doctor looked briefly at Rory's wound. "This needs to be sewn up, but it can wait 'til you get to the hospital. I must move the colonel quickly. He's very weak from blood loss." And with that the doctor ran to his waiting carriage, Donovan already inside, slumped on the seat and attended to by the doctor's assistant. Rory stood away from the seconds as they bowed a farewell to one another. He heard Grenville Donovan say to Rochambeau, "That mick bastard will pay for this!" Rory smiled to himself at the irony of being called a "mick" by a Donovan.

Rory, stitches sewn in the shallow cut on his chest, rested in the wardroom after dispatching Jimmie with a note to Carrie Anne, explaining the events of the last twenty-four hours, and promising to meet her at his first opportunity. He had assured Huger that his wound would not keep him from duty. Huger was determined to move *McRae* down to the forts, and to watch, with the help of the armed side wheel steamer CSS *Ivy*, for an opportunity to escape the river and get the *McRae* on her way as a commerce raider.

The engines, which had broken down in Baton Rouge, broke down once again in New Orleans. Coaling had been going on, and the crew was hot, sooty, and parched. Engine repairs added to the discomfort. The day after the duel, coaling was finally complete and the engines repaired once more. The officers sat in the evening around the wardroom table. A scuttle had been rigged over the skylight to catch the cool evening breeze.

"Dunbrody, you should have contrived a bit more serious wound. You would have missed the coaling entirely." Lieutenant Warley smiled as he wiped his brow and sipped the lemonade being served by the steward.

"Sure, sir, I tried, but that pantalooned colonel was not cooperative. D'ye think we'll move down-river tomorrow?"

"I think the captain will move us just to calm the citizenry," said Lieutenant Eggleston. "I was ashore today, and all the talk is of your duel. The doctors hold out little chance for Donovan's recovery. Half the town is pleased, and the other half, outraged. He was not universally loved, nor is his family, but I would not be surprised if the Donovan family contrived at some manner of revenge. Watch your back, Rory."

"We know we'll at least move our anchorage to Jackson Square. The captain's fiancée lives near the Cathedral of St. Louis." Warley's little joke evoked smiles all around the table. With the hard work done, they were ready to relax. But, professional concerns were always a part of wardroom talk. "If our engine problems continue, we won't stand a chance as a raider," Warley said.

"Not to mention our limited coal capacity," said Rory. "I'll be surprised if we can get one of those Yankee pilots to try to take us out."

The *McRae* moved down-river to just above the Head of the Passes, but experienced ten days of false starts and pilot recalcitrance. On a day when it appeared Pass a l'Outre was clear, *Ivy* appeared towing a French merchantman who reported that USS *Water Witch* had added her five guns to the blockade and lay off the mouth of the pass. Huger decided to return *McRae* to New Orleans the next day.

Aging and ailing Commodore Rousseau was replaced with the already aged, but aggressive Commodore George Hollins. With the withdrawal of *McRae* from the Head of the Passes, Semmes' earlier prediction was fulfilled, and the blockading squadron lightened its deeper-draft ships, towed them over the bar, and anchored at the Head of the Passes.

Back in New Orleans, the officers of the *McRae* assessed the strength of their enemy, pursued their love lives, and enjoyed the gaiety that was New Orleans in 1861. Donovan had succumbed to his wounds. Carrie Anne and her family had attended the funeral, and had been ostracized by the Donovans and many of the mourners. Mrs. Eastman insisted that her family engage in mourning although it rankled Carrie Anne to do so.

Rory, when ashore, sensed from those he encountered sometimes respect, often enmity, and on occasion, both. He visited Carrie Anne at her mother's home. Their passions were checked, but not diminished, by the altered circumstances under which they now met. *Black does become her, to be sure,* he frequently thought to himself.

"My stars, Rory, it is so discouragin' to shop in this city, and be snubbed by half of those I counted as friends."

"Y'must focus, my love, on the half that still are friendly, and count that as a great blessing." Rory, listening to himself, thought, *Faith, it's my father speaking. I'm turning into Da.*

"Do y'think I'm right, now, Mrs. Eastman?" Rory asked Carrie Anne's mother.

"Right as rain, Rory. Still, my son, Beau, has lost his job with Donovan senior, and we have no alternative but to seek the mercy of my sister's family in Richmond. I fear we'll be moving within the week. My niece, Natalie, has decided to leave her teaching position here and return to her parents' home with us."

"Oh, Mother, I'll miss Rory so!"

"Carrie Anne, as a navy officer, I could be halfway around the world in a few weeks' time. As it happens, Secretary Mallory told me at my commissioning that he'll soon be transferring me to the James River

Squadron. We'll see each other more there than here, I've no doubt. But give me your aunt's address, so I know where to write in the meanwhile. The 'first luff' tells me Commodore Hollins has a special endeavor in mind for the *McRae* this week, so I'm unsure of seeing you before you leave."

Mrs. Eastman wrote her sister's address on a card for Rory. "You've been a great solace for my daughter, Rory. That Donovan family was impossible to be around. They're a dangerous lot. With Thomas dead, his father and brother are both threatening revenge on you. Be careful. They have the wealth and connections enough to make your life miserable."

"I shall, Mrs. Eastman. I'm sure the move to Richmond will be good for your family. I look forward to seeing you all there."

CHAPTER 23
THE TAKING OF THE MANASSAS
OCTOBER 1861

Back aboard the *McRae*, preparations were being made to lead the "mosquito" fleet of smaller war craft that constituted the CSN's Mississippi Squadron into battle against the blockading Union vessels at the Head of the Passes. Commodore Hollins had moved his command pennant to *McRae*, which would serve as flagship. He met with Huger and his officers in the captain's cabin.

"Gentlemen, let me outline our task and its challenges." Hollins knit his prominent eyebrows beneath his bald crown. He was in his sixties, but a bold, resourceful and sometimes bellicose leader, nonetheless. Rory remembered Tobias telling of his service aboard USS *Cyane* under Hollins in 1854 when Hollins brazenly bombarded helpless Greytown, Nicaragua. "We've assembled five steamers, with *McRae* the largest and best armed," said Hollins. "Several of the others mount only one heavy rifle. Yet, with all our vessels under steam, we have a maneuvering advantage over the Federals. Two of their ships are sail-only, most unsuitable for riverine warfare."

"Commodore, are you familiar with the Yankee commanders?" Huger leaned forward in his chair.

"Yes, captain, I've served with several. *Richmond*, a twenty-two gun screw sloop of war, is commanded by 'Honest John' Pope and is the most powerful of their fleet. She draws seventeen feet and can't move easily over either of the bars. Pope is a rather unimaginative commander. *Vincennes*, twenty guns, Captain Handy, and *Preble*, ten guns, Captain

French, are sailing vessels with no engines. French is a solid commander but Handy leaves much to be desired. I don't know Lieutenant Winslow of the *Water Witch*. She's a side-wheeler, mounting five guns."

"Sir, it sounds as if we may be close to a match for them," said Rory.

"Under the right circumstances, lieutenant, but I'd like a further improvement of our chances," Hollins replied. "Which brings me to the subject at hand: the tug *Enoch Train*, now converted to an ironclad privateer and renamed *Manassas*. She's got a cast-iron ram forward, below the waterline, and a 32-pounder mounted right above it in a gunport so narrow you can barely train it, let alone aim. But, still, she's an ironclad. She's owned by John Stevenson of the Pilot's Association and several other investors. Her crew are not man o' warsmen, but appear to be largely undisciplined and rowdy longshoremen. When I politely requested that she join our sally against the Federals, I was summarily refused. When I informed him that I would have no choice but to take her by force, I was told I 'didn't have enough men to take her'. We're about to find out. She's moored over at John Hughes Shipyard in Algiers. We'll take her this afternoon."

"Sir, may I suggest Lieutenant Warley lead the cutting out effort," said Huger.

"What say you, lieutenant"?

"Aye, aye, commodore. I'd like the launch, eight oarsmen, Midshipman Morgan, and Lieutenant Dunbrody, if you please. He's been in 'action' most recently of all of us," he said pointedly.

"Yes, so I understand." The men exchanged amused looks before continuing with business. "Do you concur, Captain Huger?"

"Yes, sir. Eight bells in the afternoon watch should give us time to prepare, sir."

"Very well, gentlemen. With *Manassas* in the fleet, we'll see what the Yankees are made of."

The *McRae* moved across the river to Algiers, where *Manassas* was found anchored in the stream off Hughes Shipyard. She resembled an iron-gray turtle; railway iron 'T' rails dovetailed over an arched back, with two tall smoke stacks the only contrast to the convex 'turtleback'.

McRae ranged up along side her, and when Hollins told her crew through his speaking trumpet, that *McRae* was about to board and take possession, he was greeted with a chorus of catcalls from the boisterous crew that continued until Warley's launch came alongside.

Rory whispered to Warley as they sat in the stern sheets of the launch. "I'd say they've a drop of the drink taken, sir."

"No doubt you're right, Mr. Dunbrody. You and Morgan keep the men in the boat until I call for you," said Warley, revolver in hand, as he bounded up the ladder extending from the waterline to the top of the deck. The crew of thirty, most of whom had been standing at the top of the arched deck calling out insults only moments before, pushed, shoved, and scuttled down the hatch. Warley followed them down and seconds later they emerged from an after hatch, shorn of their bravado, and dove into the water, swimming to shore.

"Gentlemen, we have a new squadron member." Warley, revolver still in hand, climbed out the forward hatch and stood, grinning, at the men in the launch. "Mr. Dunbrody, bring four men aboard with you, if you please. We'll get CSS *Manassas* squared away. They've left a bit of a mess. Mr. Morgan, I'd be obliged if you'd return to *McRae*. Report to the commodore we've a new ship. My respects to the captain, and could he spare four more men for clean-up?"

That evening *McRae* posted a guard boat for the *Manassas* in the event the owners attempted retaking. The two ships were anchored 150 yards apart, and the watch aboard *McRae* kept a sharp lookout. Rory and Lieutenant Alexander Warley talked late into the evening after inspecting the *Manassas*. "Well, Mr. Dunbrody, she's a bug-bear," sighed Warley. "No power, no speed, no armament, and no visibility."

"Sure, you've the right of it, sir," said Rory, "yet, she's armored, she's got that big ironclad underwater ram up forward, and firing the 32pounder should scare the bejesus out of anyone even if we can't see to aim it."

"Just steering by squinting through the four-inch opening in the forward hatch would be enough of a challenge," said Warley. "At night, it's impossible. I have the suspicion Hollins will ask me to command her. If he does, I'd like you as my first lieutenant."

"I'd be honored, sir," said Rory. "I'm thinkin' we'll need to ask 'round the fleet for volunteers to man her."

"If my prediction is correct, lieutenant, that will be your first assignment."

The two officers were summoned aboard *McRae* in the morning and met with Hollins and Huger in the captain's cabin. "Gentlemen," began Hollins, "your report on the condition of *Manassas*, please." Warley outlined the strengths and shortcomings of the ironclad. When he'd concluded, Hollins asked, "Would you accept command of her, lieutenant?"

"With pleasure, sir. Captain Huger, could I have Dunbrody as my lieutenant? I need his gunnery experience and his recruiting skills if I'm to find a crew. Lots of Irish sailors in New Orleans."

Huger glanced at Hollins, who nodded. "Very well, Mr. Warley, but it's a lot to ask."

"I appreciate that, sir," Warley replied. "Commodore, may we ask for volunteers around the fleet as part of our efforts?"

"I'm reluctant to say yes, but, dammit, I want to attack the Federals at the Head of the Passes as soon as *Manassas* is ready, so yes, you have my permission. I'd like to be ready within two weeks."

"Aye, aye, sir," replied Warley. "Mr. Dunbrody, get me my crew!"

CHAPTER 24
USS PREBLE, HEAD OF THE PASSES
OCTOBER 1861

The sailing master of the sailing sloop of war USS *Preble* stood on the quarterdeck by the mizzen shrouds, gazing upriver in the gathering twilight. Commander Henry French, the *Preble*'s captain, stood beside him, telescope to his eye. "Still no sign of the Rebels, Mr. St. John," said French.

"No, sir," Tobias replied, "and the longer they wait, the better off we are. One or two more steamers of ours would make me breathe a lot easier, captain. *Preble* and *Vincennes*, with no engines on a river, are fish out of water."

"Well, at least we have two pivots aboard, even if we can't bring our broadside guns to bear. Are you feeling a bit constrained, yourself, sailing master? With no need to navigate by the stars, and your charts out of date, owing to the daily shifting of the Mississippi sands?"

"It's a definite concern, sir, I admit. But I'm more concerned about the maneuverability of the Rebels, every ship a steamer."

"Well, Mr. St. John, at least we finally moved to the Head of the Passes after months of dilly-dallying. The Porter and Du Pont strategy board recommended that in June. Now, if I only had a first lieutenant!"

"When were you told a replacement would arrive, sir?"

"Any day now, Mr. St. John. In the meantime, you'll have to continue standing a watch."

"My pleasure, captain. My navigational duties are not onerous at anchor. In fact, I've been able to read off watch all the materials we have on board regarding the navies of France, Spain, and Britain. Since they just agreed to jointly intervene in Mexico, I'm sure we'll encounter their ships in the Gulf."

"Good luck to them trying to collect the debts owed them by the Mexicans in the middle of their civil war. The Mexican Conservatives and the Juarez Constitutionalists have better things to worry about than paying debts to Europe." said French. "But you're right, St. John. The Gulf will be full of European naval vessels. Meanwhile, we need to keep a sharp eye out tonight. The Rebels have to be encouraged by our performance three days ago. That little steamer, with an eight-inch rifle, opened fire on us and after we fired three rounds, *Richmond* signaled 'cease fire'. We could have reached him easily."

"It appears Captain Pope prefers to err on the side of caution, not to be critical, sir."

"You may speak freely, master. I was right there, and saw with my own eyes. We'll just have to redouble our efforts aboard *Preble*. I'm going below. You have the morning watch as well?"

"Yes, sir, I do."

"That's reassuring. Please call me when you come on watch again. I suspect Johnny Reb will attack in the dead of the morning, when he does."

At four a.m., or eight bells in the mid watch, Tobias came on deck as officer of the watch. Captain French joined him. "No moon, sir, and this mist has cut visibility considerable. *Richmond's* been coaling all night. You can just see the coaling schooner forward on her port side."

"Very good, Mr. St. John. I'm going below again. Call me if you need to."

"Aye, aye, sir." Tobias looked away from the USS *Richmond*. The lanterns being used to light the coaling operation were diminishing his night vision. He looked upriver. A low form loomed out of the mist.

"Quartermaster, fire a flare! Midshipman of the watch, wake the captain! Beat to quarters!"

As the turtle-backed CSS *Manassas* approached the USS *Richmond*, Tobias could see her stacks silhouetted against the lanterns of the coaling schooner. Gun crews ran to their stations, loading and running out the broadside guns. The captain called to the pivot gun crews, "Don't fire until the Rebel is clear of *Richmond*!"

The CSS *Manassas* had rammed the USS *Richmond* and fired her 32pounder at the moment of impact. Tobias watched as the *Richmond's* first broadside passed harmlessly over the low hull of the Rebel ironclad. *Manassas* backed away, the current carrying her toward *Richmond's* quarter. She rammed *Richmond* again, but at such low speed as to cause little damage, and drifted down river. Tobias noticed her stacks lying across her curved deck.

"See *Manassas'* stacks, sir. Must have jarred loose or sheared when she rammed. She'll be filling with smoke." He glanced upstream. "Fire rafts coming downstream, sir." Dawn was lighting the river, as well as the glow from the three barges filled with combustibles. "The rafts look like they've grounded on a shoal."

"*Richmond's* showing a red light at the fore, sir," cried the signal petty officer.

Damn, thought French, *that's the signal to slip cables and run for the pass. What can he be thinking? We've got twenty-eight broadside guns! Well, orders are orders.* He shouted to his crew. "Mr. St. John! Veer to the thirty-fathom shackle on the chain, slip the cable, and make sail."

"Aye, aye, sir. Topmen and sail trimmers, set jibs and topsails! Anchor detail, veer and slip! Quartermaster, when you have way on her, the wind will be dead aft."

The four Union ships fled down the Southwest pass, followed, but not too closely, by CSS *McRae*, CSS *Ivy*, and CSS *Tuscarora*, a third Rebel side-wheeler. "They're firing, sir, but not making good practice," said Tobias, as they reached the bar. "I can see the ironclad. She's aground, just out of range, on the west bank. *Water Witch* is over the bar. Captain, it looks as if *Vincennes* and *Richmond* can't make it over the bar. They draw too much water."

"I'm aware of that, St. John. We'll no doubt have to come back and provide covering fire while they lighten ship and tow over." Tobias, realizing he'd been mildly chastised for stating the obvious, looked busily at the sails.

"Sir, shall I set topgallants and the fore course?"

"Very good, Mr. St. John."

Just after day broke, USS *Preble* and USS *Water Witch* found themselves across the Southwest Pass bar. Tobias watched through his telescope as USS *Richmond* approached the bar.

"She's luffing up," announced Tobias to those in hearing on the quarterdeck. "She's taken aback! She's aground on the bar! She's swinging broadside to the channel. *Vincennes* is right behind her, now she's aground! Her stern's to the enemy." Lowering the telescope, Tobias turned to Captain French. "*Vincennes* is about two hundred yards upriver from *Richmond*, sir. I can see the three Rebel steamers and the ironclad about two thousand yards upstream. *Manassas* must have drifted this far before going aground."

"Very good, Mr. St. John, thank you." He called to his second lieutenant, on deck since the cable was slipped. "Mr. Fredericks, anchor us just outside the bar and lead another anchor cable out the stern gallery and back forward to the spare small bower. Set the small bower astern. I want a good field of fire for the pivots. We'll need to help *Richmond* keep them at long range. *Vincennes* can't bring her broadsides to bear."

The bower anchors were the two largest aboard ship. Setting both anchors enabled USS *Preble* to present her broadside and both pivots to the Rebel ships.

"Aye, aye, sir. The Rebels have opened fire from their anchored position, sir."

"Very good, Mr. Fredericks."

"Signal from *Richmond*, sir," said Tobias. "Retire from action."

"Very well, Mr. St. John. Acknowledge, if you please. I'm sure that's directed at *Vincennes*, aground. I don't suppose that means we should cease fire, do you Mr. Fredericks, Mr. St. John?"

"No, sir," they chorused.

"Very well, then. Continue with the anchor details."

"Boat approaching from *Vincennes*, sir," reported Lieutenant Fredericks.

"See what they want, Mr. Fredericks." The USS *Vincennes'* jolly boat lay off *Preble*'s quarter. The young midshipman in the stern sheets plaintively asked, "Sir, Captain Handy's respects, and may we have your longboat to help transfer our crew, in response to the 'abandon ship' signal?"

Captain French rushed to the rail. "You, youngster! Get that boat back to Captain Handy and tell him there is no 'abandon ship' signal. The hoist says 'retire from action'. Get you gone, now!"

The middie saluted and the boat returned to *Vincennes*, the oarsmen pulling like madmen. "What can that man be thinking?" French asked no one in particular. "Mr. St. John, keep that glass trained on *Vincennes*. I don't like what I'm hearing."

"Aye, aye, captain." Tobias sprang into the mizzen shrouds for a better view and trained his telescope on *Vincennes'* quarterdeck. "Sir, they have their boats slung out and taking off the crew. Captain Handy is waving off their jolly boat. He's, he's wrapped in the flag, sir. The national ensign. He's wearing it like a cape! He's talking to a petty officer with a slow match in one hand and a slow fuse in the other. The fuse leads below, sir. I think he's firing the magazine, sir!"

"The man's gone mad," exclaimed French.

"Sir, please," said Tobias, returning to the deck, "let me take the launch and cut that fuse. We're about to lose a sloop of war, sure as a gun, sir."

"Mr. St. John, that magazine could explode at any time." The captain's face showed his inner struggle between safety for his sailing master and the need to avert disaster.

"Sir, I'm sure it's a slow fuse. He'd allow time to get his crew off. The sooner, the better, sir. The launch's crew can put me aboard and stand off 'til I call them."

"Very well, Mr. St. John. Good luck to you, young man! Clear away the launch! Look lively, now!"

As the *Preble's* launch passed *Richmond*, Captain Pope called out through his speaking trumpet, "What'r you about, Mister?" Tobias stood in the stern sheets as Midshipman Jones steered onward. "They've fired their magazine, sir. Keep clear!" Great spouts of water leaped around them from time to time as they approached *Vincennes*. The Confederate steamers continued their long-range fire, but came no closer.

The eight-oared launch met the boats from *Vincennes* pulling toward *Richmond*. Robert Handy, still wrapped in the Stars and Stripes, waved frantically and cried out, "Stay away, she's going to explode!"

Tobias ignored him. "Pull, you Prebles, pull as you've never pulled before. The faster we get there, the safer you'll be!" The stroke oar laughed, a wild look in his eye. "Pull, you lubbers," he cried. "Mr. St. John's on a holy mission!"

They swung alongside of *Vincennes* with Tobias balancing on the balls of his feet in the bow. He leaped to the boarding ladder as Midshipman Jones called "toss oars," and swept away again on the strength of the boat's momentum, leaving Tobias clinging to the ladder. "Out oars," called Jones. "Give way together."

"Stand off one hundred fifty yards, Mr. Jones," called Tobias as he reached the deck. Tobias rushed below deck, following the fuse past the gun deck to the orlop deck. *Oh, Monique*, he thought, *may I live to hold you again.* Racing aft, he saw the fuse extending through the curtains of the magazine. The fuse was burning six feet from the curtains. On the other side were the powder canisters and bags.

No time to worry about my shoes creating a spark, he thought. He reached the curtain and with his knife cut the fuse three feet in front of the glowing section. Reaching for the fuse behind the fire, he pulled it to a fire bucket and plunged the smoldering glowing section into the water. He sat below the bucket, hanging on the bulkhead, and gulped great breaths of air.

Rising, he removed his shoes, and in his bare feet, parted the magazine curtain, removing the fuse end from the canister full of powder where it had been placed. He carefully carried the fuse end out of the magazine, and climbed the companionway to the main deck. Walking to the rail, he waved to the launch, and shouted, "All clear! Well done, Prebles!"

A cheer went up from the oarsmen in the launch, and Midshipman Jones brought her back alongside *Vincennes*.

As they came under the counter of the *Richmond*, on their way back to *Preble*, Tobias called "way enough!" He could see Captain Pope and Captain Handy peering over the rail. "Sir, the fuse is cut and damped. It's safe to return to *Vincennes*."

"Thank you and well done, sailing master," Pope replied. "What's your name?"

"St. John, sir."

"Carry on, then, 'Sinjin.'" Tobias watched, fascinated, as Pope turned and gestured emphatically to Handy, pointing at *Vincennes*, while officers of both ships looked on, wearing thinly concealed smirks.

"Give way, Mr. Jones. We shan't see a sight like this again in our careers, I'll warrant."

Jones laughed. "I believe you're right, sir. Stand by to give way together, there. Give way all."

Alongside the *Preble*, Tobias ran up the ladder to report to Captain French. After hearing a terse description of the action aboard *Vincennes*, the captain said, "Well done, Mr. St. John. My report will commend you in the highest degree. Secretary Welles will receive a copy."

"Thank you, sir. I'm very appreciative."

The signal midshipman had a glass trained on *Richmond*. "Boats putting off the flagship, sir. They look to be the *Vincennes*' crew returning." Lieutenant Fredericks looked through his telescope. "Did you ever see a more hang-dog gang of sailors? They'll be the laughingstock of the fleet."

"So they will, lieutenant, and all because of the inexplicable actions of their commander," said French.

"Sir," said the signal midshipman, "*Santee* signaling, 'have on board your first lieutenant'." USS *Santee*, a huge fifty-gun sailing frigate, had been watching the action from a mile outside the bar, where her deep draft had consigned her.

"It's about time," was French's only response.

"Sir," said Fredericks, "the Rebel steamers appear to be withdrawing upriver."

"Very good, Mr. Fredericks, I'd be obliged if you'd call away the cutter, launch, and longboat, with relief crews. I anticipate that *Richmond* and *Vincennes* will need help getting off the bar. After the boats are launched, you may weigh anchor."

As the *Preble* bore away from the Southwest Pass, Captain French chose a course to bring her close to *Santee*. "Mr. Fredericks, signal the frigate that we're sending a boat for our new first lieutenant. Have him report to me when he comes aboard. I'll be in my cabin."

"Aye, aye, sir. Call away the captain's gig!"

Fredericks greeted the new first lieutenant as he returned with the gig from the *Santee*. "Welcome aboard, sir. I'm Fredericks, the second lieutenant. May I introduce two of our officers, sir? Sailing Master St. John, Midshipman Jones."

"How do you do, sir," they chorused.

"Gentlemen," replied the new "First", with the hint of a smile not echoed by his eyes. Those were somewhat beady and too close together, set in a pockmarked face under close-cropped hair. "I'm Daniel Fell, your first lieutenant."

"Sir, Captain French asked that I escort you to his cabin," said Fredericks. "With your permission, sir."

As Fell entered French's cabin, the captain half-rose from behind his desk and shook Fell's hand. "Welcome aboard, lieutenant. I'm sorry you missed an interesting day of action, but I'm glad to see you. We've been shorthanded for weeks.

"I'm glad to be aboard, sir." Fell's expression was guarded.

"I'm sure you want to get right to work. We'll need to replenish the shot and powder we expended today. I've asked the officers to assemble in the wardroom. I expect you're eager to meet them."

"Yes, sir. I've met Mr. Fredericks, the master, and a midshipman already. It's unusual to find a Negro on the quarterdeck. Sir," Fell added, after a pause.

"Like most of our navy vessels, we have many negroes aboard, almost a fifth of the crew," French replied, a quizzical look on his face.

"Yes, sir, as landsmen, stokers, stewards, and the like, but one rarely sees one of those people as a commissioned officer, even if only a master."

"Mr. St. John is an exemplary officer, Mr. Fell. He single-handedly saved *Vincennes* from being blown up by her own captain!"

"Aye, aye, sir, I'll bear that in mind." French couldn't tell from Fell's expression whether the master's exploit had made any impression upon him at all.

A boisterous babble of spirited conversation quieted as Lieutenant Fell entered the wardroom. "At ease, gentlemen," said Fredericks. "Our new first lieutenant, Mr. Fell," he continued by way of introduction. "May I introduce the officers, sir?"

"By all means, Mr. Fredericks," Fell replied.

Fredrickson went around the table with his introductions - the third lieutenant, the warrant officers, the purser, boatswain, gunner, and surgeon, remarking that he'd already met the master, and then the midshipmen in addition to Mr. Jones.

When Fredericks concluded, Fell cleared his throat and cocked his head to one side in a mannerism soon to become familiar to the officers and crew of the *Preble*. "Gentlemen, I look forward to knowing each of you well. We must all depend upon each other's skills for the safety of the ship. And it's my responsibility to the captain to ensure that your skills are sufficient to meet the challenges this ship will face."

Fell looked around the table, smugly folding his arms. "Now, tell me what happened with the *Vincennes*. It sounds like quite a story."

"It was the most amazing thing, sir," said Fredericks. "Captain Handy misread the signal to discontinue the engagement. We saw him abandoning ship, and lighting the fuse to blow the magazine. Mr. St. John and Mr. Jones took the launch, and Mr. St. John went aboard and cut the fuse just in time. It was a hangdog group of *Vincennes* sailors who returned to their ship, I can tell you!"

"Embarrassed, were they?" Fell asked.

"Extremely, sir," said Fredericks. "Captain Handy had sent a boat to us asking for help in getting his men off. Captain French told the middie in charge of the boat to tell Captain Handy he'd misread the signal. Handy ignored him, sir."

"It was as if he wanted to blow her up at all costs, sir," said the third lieutenant.

"And the other ships' crews were laughing?"

"Yes, sir; with cause, sir," Jones chimed in.

"We were under the *Richmond*'s counter, sir," said Tobias. "You could tell the *Vincennes*' own officers were having difficulty in keeping from laughing at their own captain."

"Mr. Saint John, is it?" Fell's countenance changed suddenly from amused disinterest to malevolence. "I believe we have an unfortunate situation here. You've crossed the line, and have voiced disrespect for a superior officer!"

Tobias' face registered shock. "Sir, I intended no such thing!"

"Nonetheless, your utterance was made. The bell can't be unrung. I'll be discussing a court martial with the captain."

"But, sir," said Fredericks, "we were all commenting on Captain Handy's conduct. Even Captain French remarked on it at the time!"

"Be that as it may, lieutenant, it's my responsibility and obligation to see that the Articles of War are not contravened aboard this ship. And, in my judgment, the master has done so. You're confined to quarters, Mr. Saint John. You're dismissed."

Tobias rose and left the wardroom, making his way aft to his tiny, eight-foot by six-foot compartment. As he did so, he could hear Fell's dismissal of the other officers. "That will be all, gentlemen. I'm confident you'll all remember a proper deference to your superiors, a hallmark of a good officer."

Tobias was dismayed beyond all measure. A scant hour ago, he had been the hero of the moment, acclaimed and exalted by all on board for his courage and skill in saving the *Vincennes*. Now, he faced the prospect of a court-martial, or at the very least, service under the watchful eye of a man who obviously had undertaken to harass him. *A bigot, of a certainty,* he thought to himself, *and a clever one at that. I'd best watch my step, or everything I've worked for will be lost.*

Tobias languished in his compartment for two hours, agonizing over the summons certain to come from Captain French. The wait seemed an eternity, when at last the captain's secretary appeared at the latticework door of Tobias' compartment. "Sir, the captain's compliments, and would you report to him in his cabin?"

"My respects to the captain, I'm on my way." Pausing only to put on his uniform jacket, and straighten his tie, Tobias hurried all the way aft and up a deck to French's cabin. The Marine sentry opened the cabin door. "Sailing master reporting as ordered, sir." The Marine sentry closed the cabin door after Tobias entered, and resumed his post in the passageway.

The captain was alone in his cabin. "Mr. St. John, please sit down. Mr. Fell has told me that he wishes to bring you before a court martial for disrespect to a superior officer. I'd appreciate your version of the incident which precipitated this." The captain looked exasperated, but Tobias was uncertain just what was the center of French's exasperation; Tobias, Fell, or just the awkward situation.

"Sir, we met him as you directed, in the wardroom. He steered the conversation to the Captain Handy incident. Mr. Fredericks described it in detail. The third luff chimed in and then Mr. Jones, sir. I described the difficulty the *Vincennes'* officers were having in disguising their mirth, sir."

"Then he said it was disrespect, but only on my part, and told me he'd recommend court, and confined me to quarters. I'm sorry, sir. I meant no disrespect. I was just describing the reaction of the officers on the deck of the flagship. Maybe it was disrespectful, sir, but it wasn't my intention."

"Mr. St. John, when Mr. Fell brought these charges, I commended him for his zeal in monitoring the actions of our officers under the terms of the Articles of War. After all, that is what one expects of one's first lieutenant."

"Yes, sir," Tobias could think of no other response, but he was fascinated by the captain's train of thought. *Where is he going with this,* he wondered, *to my destruction or absolution?*

"As Convening Authority, of course, my obligation is to ensure that the facts underlying the charges are sufficient to warrant a formal court-martial proceeding. I've decided, under the circumstances, to be my own 'court of inquiry', as it were."

The naval court of inquiry was a court fewer in number and less formal than a court-martial, but complete with a judge advocate, or prosecutor. It was used to determine whether charges made were of sufficient substance to require a court martial.

"Yes, sir."

"After conversations with the second and third lieutenants,

and Midshipman Jones, I've concluded that the facts of the case do not warrant a court-martial proceeding. Informally, I admonish you to be careful of your comments regarding Captain Handy. I will give the same admonition to your fellow officers, whose comments, I found, were in precisely the same vein as yours."

"Sir, thank you. I'm very grateful."

"Mr. St. John, a word of advice even more informal than your admonition. I have no doubt that Mr. Fell will be a dedicated and effective first lieutenant. He is intelligent, even shrewd, and has the ability to keep from straying outside the letter of Regulations, even if his actions are beyond the spirit of Regulations."

French adjusted in his seat and cleared his throat. "Some officers with those talents are not capable of accepting similar merit in subordinates when skin color or background differs. I'm tip-toeing here."

Resigned, Tobias said, "Your meaning is quite clear, sir. I appreciate the awkwardness of the circumstance."

French sighed and continued. "In my experience, St. John, there is no good solution to this kind of problem. People do not change their minds easily regarding race. I hate to lose you; you're a fine master and leader. But I think it best for the ship and your career if I write to my close friend in the Navy Secretary's office to find you a more suitable ship. Of course, the same set of dispatches will carry my account of your brave actions in saving the *Vincennes*, addressed to Secretary Welles himself."

"Aye, aye, sir. I thank you for being so candid, sir."

"In the meantime, until I can arrange a suitable transfer, I ask that you be most careful of your interchanges with Mr. Fell."

"Circumspection will be my middle name, sir." Henry French smiled.

"I'm sure it will, St. John. You'll come through this shining like brass work, I've no doubt. Dismissed." As Tobias left the cabin, French drew three sheets of letterhead toward him. The first letter he would frame to his good friend, Gustavus V. Fox, Assistant Secretary of the Navy, asking his help in resolving a personnel problem. The formation of an Office of Detail in the Navy Department to handle personnel was still months away.

The second and third identical dispatches he'd already begun in his mind.

> To: The Honorable, the Secretary of the Navy, Gideon Welles:
> To: Flag Officer William W. McKean, commanding the Gulf Blockading Squadron, Through: Captain John Pope, USS *Richmond*, commanding the Mississippi Inshore Squadron:
>
> Sirs: It is with great pleasure I commend to your attention the indomitable courage and leadership of Sailing Master Tobias St. John for his action in saving USS *Vincennes* from certain destruction on the 12th instant...

CHAPTER 25
WARDROOM OF CSS MCRAE AFTER THE BATTLE
OCTOBER 1861

The wardroom of the *McRae* was crowded with officers and near-giddy enthusiasm. The sight of four Union warships fleeing in the face of gunfire from the rag-tag little squadron charged with defending New Orleans had heightened the camaraderie and resolve of the band of Confederate Navy officers crammed into the wardroom's confines. Captain Huger sat at the head of the table. Lieutenant Warley, commander of the *Manassas*, and Rory, his first lieutenant, together with *Manassas'* sailing master, Austin, and Chief Engineer Hardy sat on one side, with the *McRae*'s officers on the other. Officers of the *Calhoun*, *Tuscarora*, *Ivy*, and *Jackson* occupied the foot end of the table.

"Gentlemen," began Huger. "Commodore Hollins is ashore on business and has asked that we discuss a draft of a report on the recent action for Secretary Mallory. The commodore extends his congratulations to us all for our successful pursuit of the first fleet action of the war, the first ever lost by the Union, and the first fought under steam and including an armored ship! Midshipman Morgan will be our scrivener. Captain Warley, would you begin with the ironclad's experience?"

"Aye, aye, sir. Near four bells in the mid-watch, quarter to four, sir, we approached USS *Richmond* without being seen and rammed her. Unfortunately, we couldn't see either, visibility being so limited from our pilot casement, and we didn't discern the coaling schooner alongside her. The effect of our ram was diminished as we glanced off the schooner before hitting *Richmond*. The collision sheared off our smokestacks, and reduced the draft to the engine room and our subsequent speed as well, sir. We struck *Richmond* again as we passed down her length, but our way was so reduced we did little damage. We then drifted to the far bank, quite a way down Southwest Pass, and went gently aground. We sustained no real damage from any of the broadsides *Richmond* fired. The rest of the squadron was in our vicinity as they pursued the Yankees, sir."

"Very good, captain," Huger glanced at the officers of the smaller steam gunboats. "Let me summarize the actions of the remainder of the squadron, gentlemen. Please interject if I leave something out. We set fire to the three fire rafts and cut them adrift. The current took them toward the Federals, and they all slipped cables and headed down Southwest Pass. We pursued from a safe distance, being seriously outgunned, and kept up a sustained fire as they fled. Morning showed USS *Preble* and *Water Witch* across the bar, but *Richmond* and *Vincennes* aground. How am I doing so far, gentlemen?"

"Very complete, sir," said the captain of the CSS *Tuscarora*. "I did note that *Water Witch*, under steam, was able to stand across the river and back to cover the retreat of the others."

"Quite so, captain. Well worth noting, for the record." Huger turned to Rory. "Mr. Dunbrody, I saw from *McRae* that you had the glass on the grounded vessels in the morning. Please recount what you saw."

"Aye, aye, sir. We experienced a desultory fire from *Richmond* and *Vincennes*, closest to us. A signal from the flagship, which from my U.S. Navy experience I'd judge as 'discontinue the action', created a flurry of activity aboard *Vincennes*."

"Sure, it was like ants around honey, sir. Boats puttin' off, puttin' crew aboard *Richmond*, and goin' back for more. I saw *Vincennes'* captain wrap himself in the Stars and Stripes, like a toga, sir. I saw a quarter gunner light a slow match fuse leadin' below, and then the captain and the quarter gunner went over the side into a boat. "

"Well, sir, he'd obviously misread the signal, thinkin' it 'abandon ship' or some such, because as soon as the fuse was lit, a boat from the *Preble*, which'd been firin' on us all the while, made for *Vincennes*." Rory paused for breath.

"Excellent, lieutenant. Please continue," said Huger.

"Yes, sir. I'm sure I recognized the *Preble*'s boat officer. He was a Negro master. Not too many of them in the Union Navy. It was my old shipmate from USS *Active*, Tobias St. John, sure as a gun! And he's a good 'un, sir. Sure enough, I saw him go aboard *Vincennes*, go below, and come on deck with the fuse end in hand. The tugs took us in tow about then, captain, but the last I saw, the *Vincennes*' crew was goin' back aboard."

"Thank you, Dunbrody. Tersely described. Questions, gentlemen?"

"Captain Huger," said *Ivy*'s captain, "the newspaper this morning reported a telegram from the Commodore sent after the battle which mentions our sinking of the *Preble*. Has that been confirmed, sir?" His question evoked a look of surprise from several of the officers present.

"To the best of my knowledge, Captain, *Preble*'s still afloat. But, gentlemen, regardless of any typographical errors from whatever source, I think we can applaud heartily the commodore's leadership and the achievement of routing a squadron of the enemy far superior in force to ours, with nought but some slapped-together, made-over warships and our own courage."

"Steward! Wine for these gentlemen." As the steward poured the wine glasses full, Huger raised his. "My friends, a toast to Commodore Hollins and the New Orleans Squadron of the Confederate States Navy!"

"Hear, hear," each and every gray-coated officer cried as the glasses were lifted and grins exchanged.

"Mr. Midshipman Morgan has been recording our comments. I'd like a draft for the commodore this evening, Jimmie."

"Aye, aye, captain," said Jimmie Morgan, putting down his glass and picking up his notes.

"That will be all for this session, gentlemen," said Huger. "Enjoy the *McRae*'s hospitality for a while longer, please. We all deserve it. I'm afraid that doesn't extend to you, Mr. Morgan, until you have a fair copy made."

"No, sir, I understand, sir," Jimmie replied, gathering his notes and leaving the wardroom.

Huger followed Morgan into the companionway. "You may omit the last exchange regarding the Preble and the telegram, Mr.

Morgan."

"Aye, aye, sir." When Jimmie replied, Huger nodded and rejoined the others.

As the wardroom emptied, Rory left the *McRae* and returned to *Star of the West*, where the crewmembers of the *Manassas* were making their temporary home until battle damage repair to the ironclad could be completed. Entering his small stateroom, he opened the letter just received from Carrie Anne in Richmond, one he'd not been yet able to read.

> *My Dear Rory,*
>
> *I hope that this finds you in good health and safe from dangers of the war. Mother, Beau, and I have settled in with my Aunt and Uncle in their spacious home. They are glad that their daughter Natalie has returned with us. They are so kind to us. My uncle, who is somewhat advanced in years, owns a very successful mercantile business, and has hired Beau as a junior accountant. Beau is able to work sitting, which alleviates the pain in his leg.*
>
> *My uncle and aunt live in Church Hill, a wonderful neighborhood of older homes. Mansions, really. We have been befriended by one of their neighbors, Elizabeth Van Lew, and her mother, Eliza.*
>
> *The Van Lews are prominent and rather controversial. The newspapers have taken them to task for giving small comfort, food and clothing and such, to wounded Union prisoners in Howard Prison. Yet, their home is always full of wounded Confederate soldiers, mostly privates, to whom they extend the same aid. They often visit the Confederate hospitals and bring solace to the wounded there. Sometimes I accompany them. We have had long talks about the war, and its confusing causes, so many of which seem just, on either side.*
>
> *I count the days until you report to the James River Squadron. I miss you, and remain,*
> *Your Carrie*

CHAPTER 26
MR. ST. JOHN'S REPRIEVE
LATE OCTOBER 1861

Tobias sat alone at the wardroom table, and was enjoying a rare moment of off-watch relaxation, when the captain's secretary appeared.

"Captain's compliments, sir, and would you report to him in his cabin?"

Fredericks had the watch, and Lieutenant Fell was on deck as well, observing the mail and supplies being transferred from the dispatch schooner alongside. The inshore squadron of five vessels had been standing off the three main passes of the Mississippi River mouth for the past two weeks, seeing nothing but the thick foliage of cypress which grew to the water's edge. The Rebel steamers had not ventured out, and the blockade seemed at last to be preventing escape from the river.

As Tobias made his way to French's cabin, his mind replayed the last two weeks. First Lieutenant Fell had persuaded the captain of his need for a fourth lieutenant. Until one reported, he insisted that Tobias continue to stand a watch, in addition to his full-time navigational duties, now critically important with an inshore blockade effort. Moreover, Fell permanently assigned Tobias the mid-watch, from midnight to four a.m. Tobias was exhausted. At one point, out of hearing to anyone else, Fell had told him, "you may have slipped out of a court martial, but I know the kind of officer you are. You'll fail in your duty one day, and I'll be there to note the occasion."

Tobias had replied with a noncommittal "aye, aye, sir," but his every working moment was plagued with over-concern for his performance and conduct.

Henry French greeted Tobias with a smile. "I believe I have good news, Mr. St. John. The dispatch schooner brought orders cut by Gustavus Fox himself, transferring you to USS *Wabash* as master. C.R. Perry Rodgers is her commander, and she's a fine ship! I hate to lose you, but, under the circumstances, I think this is a good move."

"Yes, sir. Thank you, sir, for all you've done for me. It's been a pleasure serving under you. I'll enjoy rejoining the *Wabash*. I was aboard her in the fifties, under Captain Paulding."

"I see smooth sailing ahead for you, Mr. St. John. I'm holding that schooner for you. You've fifteen minutes to gather your gear and say goodbye to shipmates. The *Wabash* is on her way with the fleet to take Port Royal, South Carolina. The schooner will rendezvous with her there."

Tobias quickly packed his sea chest, grabbed his small sea bag as two seamen thoughtfully dispatched by the captain arrived to sway his chest into the cutter alongside, and made his way on deck.

Fredericks stood by the gunwale as the cutter waited below, his hand extended in farewell. "It's been a pleasure serving with you, Tobias."

"Thank you, sir. Good luck to you."

"We'll meet again, St. John," a voice called. Tobias looked up and aft to see Fell standing at the break of the quarterdeck, glowering over the rail.

"Aye, aye, sir," Tobias replied, saluting, and descending the ladder to the cutter. *Never would be too soon,* he thought, relaxing for the first time in three weeks.

CHAPTER 27
PRELUDE TO HAMPTON ROADS
OCTOBER 1861

Rory descended the ladder from the turtle-backed hull of CSS *Manassas* to the dry floor of the drydock. He walked forward to take one last look at the minimal damage caused by the grounding during the Battle of the Head of the Passes. His report to Lieutenant Warley, commanding the *Manassas*, was due in the morning. After the hull damage had been repaired, the ironclad would be re-floated, and her smokestacks, lost in the ramming of the USS *Richmond*, would be replaced.

Rory climbed the ladder to the side of the drydock, and walked to the office of Atlantic Dry Dock Company. He put his notes in his briefcase and took the ten-minute trudge to the receiving ship *Star of the West*, secured to the Algiers quay. The crew of the ironclad was quartered aboard during repairs. A Confederate Navy lieutenant stood on deck talking to Alexander Warley, Rory's commander.

As Rory came aboard, he heard Warley say "Ah, here's Dunbrody now, lieutenant. I'm about to lose you, Rory!"

"How so, sir?"

"This is Lieutenant Robert Minor, fresh from Richmond, and Secretary Mallory," said Warley, a rueful smile beneath his neatly trimmed mustache. "He's orders for you to report to Commander Tucker in Norfolk aboard CSS *Patrick Henry* in two weeks' time, after you've assisted him with an ordnance audit here."

Minor shook hands with Rory. "At least I won't have to uproot you twice, Mr. Dunbrody. I'll have one of the larger staterooms aboard *Star of the West* fitted out for our office. I'll be taking the train back to Richmond with you in two weeks."

"Sure, that eases the pain of leaving my leader here," Rory said, smiling at Warley. "I'll have the hull report on *Manassas* for you in the morning, sir."

"Very good, lieutenant, it's painful to lose you, too, but Minor tells me of great things happening in Norfolk."

"Thank you, captain, I'll be interested to hear what's in store. But, first, I owe you a report." Rory turned to Minor. "Shall we meet in the morning, lieutenant, after I turn in the hull report?"

That would be fine, lieutenant," replied Minor. "I'll see you then."

At nine the next morning, after Rory's report was in Warley's hands, Rory met with Minor in a large stateroom that had been converted to an office. "I think first names will suffice, being we're of equal rank," said Minor. "Call me Bob."

"Bob, I'm Rory, and I'm mindful of your high position as Director of the Naval Ordnance Laboratory of the Ordnance Bureau."

Minor waved a hand in dismissal. "I regret to say it's more of a facade for a dilettante than a lofty post, Rory. Mallory has me responding to every trouble spot in the navy, a different one every week. Two weeks ago, I was here reporting on CSS *Louisiana*'s buoyancy problems during construction. Next week, I'm to conduct tests on mobile torpedoes at Hampton Roads, while serving as a watch officer aboard *Virginia*."

"And this week, I'm here under false colors. You and I, under the guise of ordnance experts, are to audit runaway expenditures for ship construction by Commodore Hollins. We're also to look at Lieutenant Beverly Kennon's Ordnance Department budget, apparently well overdrawn. Mallory wanted you involved as someone on the scene."

"Sure, this doesn't sound as exciting as torpedo testing. What does the secretary think has been happening with the commodore and Mr. Kennon?"

"Kennon's been in charge of the Ordnance Department here. His reputation is of a daring and resourceful officer who is something of a bungler. Mallory's office has received billings for ordnance far in excess of the budget here. The commodore, as you no doubt know from serving under him, is aggressive to the point of recklessness, which makes a fine officer in battle, but gives the secretary pause as far as spending for gunboat construction. We're to look at his expenditures for conversion of seven riverboats to gunboats."

"Reckless, he is, Bob! A friend of mine from the USN, St. John, who I just saw in action on the *Vincennes*, once told me of being aboard the *Cyane* under Hollins in 1854 at Greytown. The Navy Department gave Hollins carte blanc to quell a riot which threatened US citizens there after an American murdered a Nicaraguan black. His response was to remove the Americans and then level the town with gunfire!"

"We'll see if he's mellowed with respect to budgeting," said Minor.

"Well, now, Bob, let's change the subject to something more exciting. We've been hearing of a conversion in Norfolk to create an ironclad monster vessel. What can you tell me?"

Minor lit up. "Rory, the *Merrimack* is the most compelling project I've been associated with, and the most daunting, too. Mallory, I think, erred in not appointing one man to be in charge. The responsibility for constructing this ironclad on the hull of USS *Merrimack* is divided between John Porter, the Chief Constructor, and John Brooke, the Surveyor of the Work. So we've had fits and starts. Lieutenant Catesby ap Jones, the doughty Welshman, he's helped a lot since being assigned as first lieutenant. He's an effective mediator between Brooke and Porter!"

"And I'll be seein' it at first hand in two weeks! I'm ready to tackle these mounds of paper now," said Rory with enthusiasm as he pointed toward the stacks of invoices on the table.

"Fine, Rory, let's get to work."

After two days' examination of the invoices, Minor decided to suspend authorization of any further purchases from Hollins or Kennon, under the authority given him by Mallory.

"My God, Rory, Kennon's spent $146,000 of a $40,000 budget! And Hollins has ordered $250,000-worth of light wooden, paddle-wheel gunboats. They'll never stand up to the ironclads the Yankees are building in Cairo, up the Mississippi!"

At the end of their audit, they discussed their report. "Rory, I'll ask you to carry this to Mallory in Richmond, yourself. I need to stay on for a week to bring some order to the chaos Kennon has left in the Ordnance Department."

"Aye, aye, lieutenant. But I'd like to temper our comments on the fiscal disaster with our respect for Hollins as a fighting officer. Leaders, after all, are frequently flawed."

"I concur, Rory. He was the right man to lead the first fleet action of the war. But he's dug himself such a financial hole, I don't think his combat record will mitigate that. He's on borrowed time. One more mistake, and I'll bet he'll be recalled. Mallory's under pressure from the Treasury already. The report will be ready for you in the morning. I'll see you when I rejoin the James River Squadron."

CHAPTER 28
USS WABASH ATTACKING PORT ROYAL, SOUTH CAROLINA
NOVEMBER 1861

Tobias stood on the foredeck of the dispatch schooner, surveying the invasion fleet anchored off Port Royal Sound. It was the greatest collection of ships he, or any observer of the U.S. Navy, had ever seen. More than seventy transports, colliers, and warships were anchored as close to the entrance of the Sound as possible, having escaped a severe six-day gale on their passage from Hampton Roads. The flagship *Wabash* was anchored close to what was apparently the main channel, now being re-buoyed by a number of boats watched over by the US Coast Survey steamer *Vixen*, a side-wheel gunboat steaming slowly close to the bar off the Port entrance. The schooner hove to near the *Wabash*, and Tobias was soon in a cutter on the way to his new ship.

Captain Perry Rodgers welcomed Tobias in his cabin aboard *Wabash*. "I'm glad to have an experienced master aboard, Mr. St. John," he said, gesturing toward an empty chair. "You've an extensive and impressive record. James Alden is a former shipmate."

Tobias gratefully took a seat and relaxed. "He was a fine commander and mentor, sir. I learned much of charting in the three years I served aboard *Active*."

"It's a shame he was entangled in the Gosport Yard fiasco. Even a good man is not proof against a befuddled commander."

"Yes, sir. We've all heard how Captain McCauley ordered Alden and Captain Isherwood to draw the *Merrimack's* engine-room fires and prevent her from leaving Norfolk."

Rodgers sighed. "McCauley apparently feared that moving *Merrimack* would drive Virginia out of the Union. He didn't know that the legislative assembly had secretly voted to secede the day before. Even though we finally burned her to the waterline before abandoning Gosport, intelligence reports indicate that *Merrimack's* about to be rebuilt into a Rebel ironclad.

"But," he said, adjusting in his chair, "we can't go back, so let us go forward. It's a fine group of officers we have here, but rather short on experience under fire. I've been forwarded Captain French's report on your gallantry at New Orleans. We can use your leadership, and your navigational experience."

"I'm eager to assume my duties, sir. It's nice to rejoin a ship I served aboard in '58!"

"You're senior in experience to many of our watch-standing officers, and in rank, too, for the time being. Many of them are warrants, either midshipmen, or recently promoted to acting master. Most of those are the upperclassmen from the Naval Academy, whose classes were moved to active duty before graduation, at the outbreak of secession and the firing on Fort Sumter. They'll soon be lieutenants, at the rate the navy's expanding."

Tobias could hear clearly the unspoken addendum to the captain's description of future promotions. *I'm as high as ever I will go in this navy, merit notwithstanding,* he thought. *Still,* he mused, *I'm a commissioned master, it's better than whaling, and as long as I'm not captured in a slave state, I need not fear seizure.*

Rodgers continued. "We'll be moving the squadron in tomorrow now that we've re-buoyed the channel. In a matter of days, we'll sail to the forts and begin our bombardment, with landing parties ready to seize them. I'll ask you to lead a company of 'naval infantry' from our crew. But first, I'll require your assistance in getting us over the bar. I'll ask that you meet with Captain Boutelle of the *Vixen* this afternoon, as they will lead the squadron over the bar. You Coast Survey veterans can put you heads together and make sure of a safe passage!"

"Aye, aye, sir."

"I've had your gear stowed in your stateroom," said Rodgers. "The first lieutenant will introduce you to the wardroom officers. This is the flagship, so I'll arrange for you to be introduced to Flag Officer Du Pont and Fleet Captain Davis in the morning."

In the row of compartments off the wardroom, Tobias' was next to Acting Master Roswell Lamson, in charge of the forecastle gun division. Lamson was a tall, slender officer with the broad shoulders of a man raised on a farm. He had a piercing gaze, eyes set in a handsome face framed by dark hair parted on the left, and a well-trimmed goatee and mustache.

Recently promoted from midshipman, Lamson had exchanged his hammock near the gunroom for his new stateroom, seven feet by six. The *Wabash* was the newest of the navy's screw frigates, forty-six guns and six hundred men. Lamson commanded a gun division of eight eight-inch broadside guns forward, and the ten-inch rifled Parrott pivot gun, a muzzle-loader with a wrought-iron band around the breech to withstand the incredible forces generated by its firing. He was well liked by the sailors of his division, and an excellent battery commander, who often was called upon by the captain to lay the forward ten-inch pivot himself, aiming and firing it. Lamson was a dead shot with the massive Parrott.

"How do you do, Mr. Lamson," said Tobias, after First Lieutenant Corbin had introduced them.

"A pleasure to meet you, sir."

Tobias smiled at the young sailor. "We're virtually of the same rank, Mr. Lamson. My name is Tobias."

"Well, yes, sir—Tobias, I mean—but you're the ship's navigation officer, commissioned, and I'm merely a jumped-up midshipman," Lamson stammered in reply. "My Christian name is Roswell."

Tobias laughed. "We'll all be cut from the same bolt when we fire on the forts."

"True enough, Tobias," Roswell sighed, dropping to his bunk. "Mr. Corbin said you'd been stationed in Washington Territory. That's near my home in western Oregon."

"A beautiful country, I found," said Tobias. "I have much to do this afternoon, so I'll see you tomorrow, I'm sure."

Tobias left for his stateroom, lost in thought. *No harm in*

---

minimizing the difference in rank with Lamson. He seems to be a nice fellow, and bright. All the more quick-witted recent midshipmen are being made acting masters now, and as soon as they pass their exams, they'll skip a master's commission, and be made lieutenants, no doubt in my mind. Then they'll be superior to me. Good relations now, good relations later.

The jolly boat took Tobias to the *Vixen* where he met with her commander, Charles Boutelle, and her sailing master, Robert Platt. Boutelle was a permanent member of the Survey, and his title in that organization was "assistant." Boutelle explained that the squadron would take advantage of an extraordinarily high tide the next day, caused by the rare alignment of the sun, earth, and moon when the latter was in its closest approach to the earth, the so-called "syzygy" effect.

At sunup, the midshipman of the watch found Tobias awake and dressed, poring over a chart of the entrance to Port Royal Sound at the wardroom table. "Captain's compliments, sir, and you're to report to his cabin in fifteen minutes. You're to meet the flag officer."

"My respects to the captain, midshipman."

Flag Officer Samuel F. Du Pont's cabin was the spacious one usually occupied by the ship's captain. Since the *Wabash* was currently designated as a flagship, Captain Perry Rodgers now occupied the "day" cabin just forward of Du Pont's more spacious quarters. From a wealthy family, Du Pont had furnished his cabin beautifully, with comfortable easy chairs and a handsome mahogany table serving as both desk and dining surface.

Flag Officer Du Pont and his chief of staff, Fleet Captain Charles Davis, rose from their chart-strewn table and greeted Tobias and Captain Rodgers. Du Pont had finely-chiseled features, substantial sideburns, and hair combed in the fashion of a Roman consul. "So," he said to Rodgers, "this is the officer we're trusting to bring us safely into the Sound?"

"Yes, sir. We're glad to have him, sir, both for his fighting record and for his navigation."

"I've been looking at Commander French's report on Head of the Passes," said Du Pont. "Most impressive work, Mr. St. John. You took quite a chance going aboard with that fuse lit."

"Thank you, sir. I had great confidence in the boat crew from the *Preble*, sir. And Captain French was a decisive commander."

"We'll be sure to give you more opportunity for action, Mr. St. John," said Du Pont.

"I'll look forward to it, sir."

"Your navigation credentials are certainly impressive, Mr. St. John. I have the greatest respect for the Coast Survey, having served on the Blockade Strategy Board with its superintendent, Alexander Bache, a fine man. Did you know that the Washington budgeteers tried to cut the Survey's budget in half at the beginning of the war, on the grounds that we'd lost half our coastline?"

"No sir, I hadn't heard."

Du Pont laughed, remembering. "Dr. Bache gently reminded them that the Rebels had removed all bouys and lights from the very harbors we needed to attack, and that Survey personnel were the only pilots available to take our fleets in. They restored the budget!" Davis, Rodgers and Tobias all smiled as Du Pont finished his anecdote.

Wabash led the fleet over the bar in the morning, following *Vixen*. Tobias stood on the foredeck, listening to the calls of the leadsmen in the chains as they swung the lead lines overhead and flung them forward. "By the deep six!" intoned the port leadsman. *Wabash*, drawing twenty-three feet, was in thirty-six feet or six fathoms as she entered what all hoped was the channel, freshly buoyed.

"And a half five," called the starboard leadsman, timing his cast of his lead to follow the port leadsman at an even interval. Tobias noted the shoaling bottom, half a fathom, in the space of one cast of the lead.

Each leadsman stood on the chain plates of the foremast shrouds, which supported the foremast from each side. The shrouds were attached or anchored to the chain plates, small platforms protruding from the hull of the ship, ideal for standing on to cast the lead. The lead was a cylinder five inches in length. Its concave end had wax applied to it, which as it was bounced by the leadsman on the bottom, picked up a sample. Sand, gravel, shell, and mud all helped the master determine the relative position from the type of bottom indicated on his chart.

"By the deep six, with coarse black sand," the starboard leadsman called. As a master's mate on whaling ships, Tobias had served under some masters who could sniff the lead's bottom and announce their position!

The leadsman whirled the line around with his outboard hand for momentum and cast the lead ahead of the ship. As the lead sank, the ship advanced so the line was perpendicular and vertical. The line was marked with specific knots, rags, or leathers at six-foot intervals. The leadsman could identify the depth marks by feel even in the dark. Depths measured at these indicators were called 'marks.' In-between fathoms, which were measured where the ropes had no marks, were known as 'deeps'. "By the mark two" ('mark twain' on the Mississippi River) was distinguished by two strips of leather. The 'deep six' had no mark, but was in between 'mark five' (white duck), and 'mark seven' (red bunting).

"By the mark five!" came the next call from portside. "And a half five!" from starboard. They were too far to the left side of the channel. It was shoaling faster there.

"Starboard half a point," Tobias called aft to the helmsman. The ship responded gradually to the helm during the next sixty seconds. She eased to the right, into deeper water.

"Well done, Mr. St. John," the captain called. "We'll anchor here. Bo'sun, drop the hook!"

They anchored at more than extreme range from the guns of Fort Walker (to the south on Hilton Head Island) and Fort Beauregard (on St. Phillip's Island to the north of the entrance to Port Royal Sound). The Sound, four miles wide and six deep, was an ideal base for the South Atlantic Blockading Squadron. The fleet prepared for the next day's assault on the forts by 'sending down' their topgallant masts, to reduce themselves as targets and avoid injury to those on deck from falling spars. The ships' boats were towed astern to avoid damage from the forts and to be ready to send with landing parties. A violent gale arose the next day, and precluded the attack.

The *Wabash* led twelve steam frigates and sloops of war to attack Fort Walker the next morning after the gale abated, with the frigate *Susquehanna* next astern. Across the entrance to the Sound, northeast, the smaller gunboats opened fire on Fort Beauregard. The larger ships steamed past Fort Walker to the northwest and then circled back to concentrate fire on the fort's northwest side. Fort Walker's huge Columbiads, ten-inch cast-iron guns weighing fifteen thousand pounds, scored a number of hits on the fleet. One of Lamson's broadside eight-inch shell guns was dismounted and its gun captain killed.

The sustained fire from the fleet at last drove the defenders from Fort Walker. Both squadrons of the fleet, frigates and gunboats, had circled continuously, broadsides firing on the forts. A small squadron of Confederate tugs, lightly armed, had steamed out from the Beaufort River to the north, but were quickly outgunned by the gunboats and retired.

"Captain Rodgers," said Du Pont. "Fort Walker has ceased fire. Land a shore party, if you please."

"Captain Smithson," Rodgers called to his captain of Marines. "The garrison is fleeing Fort Walker! Take your Marines and Mr. St. John's company of seamen and secure the fort."

"Aye, aye, sir," Smithson replied. The fifty seamen and fifty Marines were soon in the boats, pulled from astern and loaded in succession, and were rowing for Hilton Head. The sailors going ashore as infantry wore leggings, shoes, and sword belts with cutlasses and ammunition pouches, and carried muskets.

Tobias' sailors were distributed among three boats. "Bo'sun's mate," he said to his second in command, "be sure when we reach the beach that the men have five yard intervals between them. We're the middle boat. The man on each end of our line needs to take station on the nearest man from the other boats."

"Aye, aye, sir." replied the boatswain's mate. "You heard the master. Five yard intervals. Munro, Fisher, take your bearings off the nearest man in the other boat," he called to the man on each flank.

As the boats grounded in the small surf on the broad, sandy beach, the men splashed through the shallows and formed a line abreast. Tobias stood in front and to the left-center of the line within hearing of Smithson, whose Marines were to the left. At Smithson's command, the line moved up the slope of the beach to the fort. It was still, the earthworks shattered by the fleet's exploding shells. Cannon, still loaded, stood unattended, while others had been dismounted by the barrage.

Tents still stood within the enclosure. Most were tattered and ripped by the bombardment, and muskets and swords lay scattered about. A few dazed Rebels, some with physical wounds, were taken prisoner. "Mr. St. John," said Smithson, "would you be so kind as to secure our perimeter? I'll send out skirmishers for a distance to preclude counterattack and take charge of the prisoners."

"Aye, aye, captain," Tobias replied. He reached for his telescope in its case, suspended from his sword belt. As Tobias surveyed the terrain around the fort, he glanced at the low outline of St. Phillip's Island, across the Sound. "Look," he called to Smithson. "*Seneca* is sending boats to Fort Beauregard. The Rebels have abandoned it too!"

CHAPTER 29
JOINING THE JAMES RIVER SQUADRON
MID-NOVEMBER 1861

Rory gazed out the window of the train, listening to the monotonous melody of the tracks and wheels, and watching the winter woods of Virginia give way to isolated homes and brick buildings on the outskirts of Richmond. His sea chest was in the baggage car, his sea bag and his portfolio with the Hollins-Kennon report, above him in the rack.

Rory's thoughts were miles away, on the banks of the Neuse River at New Berne. Rory knew that in late August, Federal navy and army forces in a joint amphibious operation had seized Hatteras Inlet, and later Roanoke Island on the Pamlico Sound side of Hatteras Island. It was only a matter of time, Rory knew, until Union forces would attempt to seize ports on the Neuse River and Albemarle Sound. His father's home and his livelihood, the shipyard, would soon be in jeopardy. Sister Siobhan had written that brother Timothy had recently been in action at the Union defeat in the Battle of Leesburg, Virginia. "Sure and all," thought Rory, "there's no haven for us in this war, not for any Dunbrodies on the west side of the Atlantic."

The train crossed the James River and made its way slowly through the city to the station. Rory stored his gear with the baggage office, and began the walk west to the Navy Department offices, housed in the former Mechanics Institute at Franklin and Ninth streets, a huge brick building that had once been a library and lecture hall. Walking beneath the bare limbs of the trees on Capitol Square, Rory entered the building and took the staircase to the second floor right.

"The secretary will see you now," the clerk announced to Rory after a fifteen-minute wait. Rory entered Mallory's office overlooking Capitol Square.

"Lieutenant Dunbrody, Mr. Secretary, with a report from Lieutenant Minor."

"Come in, come in, Dunbrody. Have a seat." The smile on Mallory's rotund face was genuine. Rory relaxed, and sat in a chair across the desk from Mallory. *He's actually glad to see me,* Rory thought, with some degree of wonder. *That's a good sign.* He removed the report on the New Orleans Department fiscal status and handed it to Mallory.

"I'll read this in its entirety this evening, lieutenant. Please summarize for me."

"Aye, aye, Mr. Secretary." Mallory looked pleased with Rory's nautical acknowledgement. *Probably as close as the poor fellow gets to the salt sea air*, Rory thought. "Lieutenant Kennon is seriously unfamiliar with the concept of a budget, sir. He's spent three times more than he has, with little to show for it in the way of useful ordnance. Commodore Hollins has invested $250,000 in converted wooden riverboats, which he hopes will suffice for gunboats to oppose the Union ironclads. We are not sanguine about his chances of success, sir, although we acknowledge he's a fine and daring commander."

"Very succinct, Mr. Dunbrody. You have the makings of a good staff officer." Mallory gazed into the middle distance and continued more to himself than to Rory, "I'll have to crawl to Treasury in supplication to cover the overspending and get more funds. But this time the additional money will go direct from me to ironclad construction."

He turned back to Rory. "And we'll find activity for Mr. Kennon, far removed from spending authorizations. We must make do with what we have. Good work, Mr. Dunbrody. You and Mr. Minor will be seeing each other again, on the James." He reached into a pile of orders on his desk and handed Rory his. "You'll be under the command of John Randolph Tucker, senior officer of the James River Squadron. Right now, it consists of one side-wheeler, the *Patrick Henry*, ten 32-pounders, five to a side, and a ten-inch pivot forward with an eight-inch pivot aft.

"We'll be augmenting Tucker's command with three more small

ships, and one will be yours, the one-gun tug *Old Dominion*. She's being refitted at Rockett's Wharf here in Richmond. Take a look at her this afternoon. Tomorrow, take the Norfolk and Petersburg train to Norfolk. I've telegraphed Commander Tucker to have a launch ready to take you upriver to his headquarters on Mulberry Island."

Rory was stunned. His first command! "Sir, Mr. Secretary, sure and you've taken the wind from my sails. I'm grateful to you for my command, sir." The words tumbled out one after the other. Rory felt his face redden, and he broke into an insuppressible grin.

"Now, now, lieutenant, you've done well these last months and deserve the opportunity. Semmes and Huger say you're a steady and reliable officer. Now, if we can just keep you away from duels for a while," he grinned, knowingly, "I see a splendid future."

"Aye, aye, sir. I'll avoid that kind of confrontation in favor of confronting the Yankees." Rory gave a self-deprecating chuckle. "I'm delighted to be under Commander Tucker. I was aboard the receiving ship *Pennsylvania* in 1855 while awaiting orders after my Academy graduation. He was in command. And wouldn't he spend hours with the middies in the officer's mess, educating us on life at sea, now? His tales of landing and fighting naval guns ashore in Mexico were fascinating, sir."

"Excellent, lieutenant. And now, I have a surprise for you. My next appointment is with a gentleman whom you met, briefly, at the start of the war in New Orleans, and whom you impressed deeply enough in that brief encounter so that he mentioned you to me. Commander James Bulloch is in the conference room. Please accompany me, and say hello."

"Aye, aye, Mr. Secretary." They walked to the conference room, and Bulloch, in civilian clothes, greeted Rory warmly.

"I'm delighted you've done so well since we last met, Mr. Dunbrody," Bulloch said, rising from his chair and extending a handshake. "Secretary Mallory has told me of your work in New Berne and New Orleans, and of your new assignment here. Congratulations on your upcoming command!"

"Thank you, commander. It's a pleasure to see you again."

"Ah, yes, the secretary has told you of my new rank. It will be useful in England, where store is set on status. I'm concerned about those who've not interrupted their service, as I did, and therefore would be above me in seniority among lieutenants, but," he exhaled, "exigencies of war, I suppose."

Rory smiled. "I'm thinkin' we ought not to question the secretary's judgment, sir, seein' as he's just promoted the both of us."

"An excellent point, lieutenant." Bulloch smiled in return, as did Mallory.

"I'm here for a brief visit to report to Mr. Mallory before returning as I came, aboard the *Fingal*, a ship I purchased for the Confederacy in England," explained Bulloch. "We brought war supplies through the blockade, which seems to be tightening."

"Surely it will, sir. Your remark reminds me of an observation Captain Semmes made regardin' the blockade. He's a lawyer, the captain is, and he noted that only belligerent nations are blockaded by others. The Union argues that we're not really a separate country, and that therefore our naval men are pirates, instead of legitimate combatants. Yet, they blockaded our ports instead of 'closed' them as a country would if it considered a port part of its territory. I'm sure the Union's minister to the Court of Saint James is ignoring that point as he tries to make building our ships there more difficult."

"Indeed he is, and a point well taken, Mr. Dunbrody," said Bulloch. "You're more knowledgeable about the diplomatic situation abroad than most lieutenants, I'd wager. I'm hopeful we can put more vessels to sea from England as raiders, but it must be done carefully and in accordance with British law. I seem to remember you've a number of good contacts with the Royal Navy and that you speak French. Does my memory serve?"

"Yes, sir, you've the right of it, although my French is best described as marginal."

"There may come a time when we can use a man of your talents overseas. In the meantime, good luck with your new command."

"Thank you, Commander Bulloch, and a safe voyage back. Mr. Secretary," said Rory, "I truly appreciate your confidence. May I take my leave?"

"You may, and good luck to you, Mr. Dunbrody." Mallory

extended his hand.

"Thank you, Mr. Secretary, for everything. Good bye, commander."

After Rory left the room, Bulloch and Mallory naturally fell to discussing him. "The young man has a brain and acts decisively under duress, that's my evaluation," said Mallory.

"I agree, Mr. Secretary, and he has a diplomatic way about him in addition."

"Have you seen the newspapers on the Trent affair, commander?"

"Yes, sir, on the train up. It seems Commander Wilkes is living up to his reputation for precipitous action." Charles Wilkes had commanded the U.S. Exploring Expedition from 1838 to 1842, in which James Alden was a participant. Wilkes had been in command of USS *San Jacinto* in early November, and had taken Confederate Commissioners to Great Britain off a British packet in international waters. Initially hailed as a hero in the North, Wilkes was now facing criticism for bringing Great Britain to the brink of war with the Union. Confederates, of course, were delighted. In late December, commissioners Slidell and Mason would be released to proceed to Great Britain, and the Union would acknowledge Wilkes' action as "illegal".

"Perhaps," said Mallory, "this will move Britain closer to recognizing us."

"I have my doubts, Mr. Secretary, unless the Union allows British honor to remain besmirched. Any apology, it seems to me, will suffice to prevent Britain from going to war or to burn her diplomatic bridges with the North. The Union is too important a trading partner to discard out of hand. And the British, I've observed, are a cautious and commercial people, not overly given to passion."

Rory walked down to Main Street and found a hotel close to the train station. He took a cab for hire to Rockett's Wharf just downstream of the city proper, where three ships destined for the squadron were being refitted: *Jamestown*, a side-wheeler, and *Teaser* and *Old Dominion*, two tugboats. *Old Dominion*, the larger of the tugs, was a screw-driven tug with a low bow and a powerful engine. Her wheelhouse was being moved aft to accommodate a pivot gun. Rory could see the racer tracks of a pivot being installed on the foredeck. Just aft of the taller wheelhouse was a lower, long deckhouse, which held the galley and the officers' quarters in four small staterooms. The stack rose just abaft the wheelhouse. Aft the deckhouse, a spacious afterdeck held ample room for towing bitts and hawsers.

Rory made his way to the wharf and found the foreman of the works. "A good afternoon t' ye, sir." The foreman looked up to see a tall young lieutenant in navy gray, with a regulation overcoat, collar turned up against the late November wind.

"I've just received orders for *Old Dominion,* here. Can y' spare a moment to talk of your progress, now?" Rory smiled at the workman, whose frown faded in the face of genuine interest in his work.

"When we're done with her, suh, she'll do Virginia proud," the foreman drawled. She'll do seven knots, and we're moving the wheelhouse aft to take the eight-inch Parrott rifle we scrounged from the Norfolk Navy yard after the Yankees abandoned it. She should be ready in two weeks' time, cap'n."

"Sure, and I'll count the days, Mr. Foreman," said Rory.

"Would y'all like to step aboard for a quick look around, cap'n?" The foreman took obvious pride in his work, and was more than glad to accommodate someone who appreciated the efforts of the work crew.

"And isn't it a kind fellow you are, t' be takin' time with an excited youngster and his first command?" Rory was all smiles, as he'd been all day since encountering Mallory. The mood was contagious.

"Watch your step, here, cap'n," said the foreman as they peered into the wheelhouse. "We're putting a two-inch plate at the wheelhouse forward bulkhead. Not much, but it'll stop a minie ball. We're moving the bulkheads for your quarters further aft, too." Rory looked through a square port into a ten-by-ten stateroom, more space than he'd ever had aboard ship. It struck him then: this was his. He suddenly felt the weight of the charge he was being given.

Daunting, to be sure, but exhilarating too, he thought. He looked up at the tall smokestack abaft his deckhouse quarters.

"The crew's quarters are forward, below deck, and the engine room is under your cabin. Damn' fine engine, too. It'll get passin' warm in your stateroom in summer, but for now, you'll be mighty comfortable, cap'n. Y'all sound Irish t'me, sir. How did you come to the Rebel Navy if you don't mind me askin'?"

"Born in North Carolina, raised in County Galway, trained in the U.S. Navy. And here I am, ready to drive the Yankees from Virginia's shores." He laughed, unable not to. "With a tug boat, that is!"

"Have you ever served on a tug before, sir?" the foreman asked.

"I'm confessin' it's my first time, Mr. Foreman."

"Let me show you a few more details, then, captain," the foreman said with obvious enthusiasm. It was clear he was a craftsman and subsumed in his trade. "Tugboat wheelhouses are traditionally narrow, sir," he said, "because the captain's alone in the wheelhouse. Most tugs can't afford a helmsman and a captain both, so the skipper has to be able to look aft to his tow out either side of the wheelhouse without taking his hand off the wheel. Y'see, we're fixin' to widen the wheelhouse so your mate, you and a helmsman can all fit inside, this bein' a warship now." The foreman pointed to the chalk marks on the deck where the new wheelhouse bulkheads would rise.

"Fascinating, it is," said Rory. "I never knew that."

"And you'll find the wide, bluff bow and stern give the hull double the normal buoyancy fore and aft, sir," the foreman continued. "That's handy when pushin' a ship or towin' a barge with a cable because both actions tend to force the hull down. Without the increased beam, and the convex bow and stern below the waterline, the boat would tend to swamp."

Rory clapped the man on the shoulder appreciatively. "You've added a great deal to my store of knowledge about tugs which was around the zero mark, Mr. Foreman. Thank you for your time. I'll get out of the way, and hope to see you again."

"I wish you good luck, sir." As Rory stepped ashore, the foreman waved.

Rory returned to his horse-drawn cab and gave the driver Carrie Anne's address on Church Hill. After an up-hill ride, the cab drew up in front of a large, Federal-style mansion just off Broad Street. *I guess Carrie's aunt and uncle are indeed well off,* he thought, looking at the size of the home. He paid the cab driver, now having his bearings for a return walk back to his hotel, a mere eleven blocks. *I'm not paid enough for carriages,* he reflected. *I hope one of the Eastmans is at home.*

He rang the bell, and a Negro butler answered the door. Rory handed his card to the servant. "Lieutenant Dunbrody to call upon Miss Eastman," he said.

"Come in, sir, and please have a seat in the vestibule, while I see if Miss Eastman is at liberty to receive you." The butler vanished into the inner recesses of the mansion.

A well-dressed woman with silver hair and a twinkle in her eye appeared, a more humorous version of Carrie's mother, without the years of concern that Mrs. Eastman showed. "Good afternoon, lieutenant. I am Mrs. Farwell, Carrie Anne's aunt. She begs you to wait while she makes herself presentable". She smiled and asked him to join her in the parlor, a well-appointed room with comfortable chairs and a beautiful, deep-pile sea-green carpet. Natalie Farwell sat reading by a window.

"Miss Farwell, I'm delighted to see you," Rory exclaimed with a smile.

"It's good to see you, lieutenant," she responded.

"Are you familiar with Richmond, lieutenant?" Mrs. Farwell asked.

"Please call me Rory, ma'am. I've only passed through before. Now, I've just been to the banks of the river to see my new ship. She should be refit in two weeks. Just a little tug, but she's my first command."

"How exciting for you. We've heard so much about you from Carrie Anne; it's a pleasure to finally meet you. Why, here she is now." Carrie Anne stood in the doorway, looking lovely in a sea green frock that accentuated the hue of her eyes. Mrs. Farwell made no effort to leave the room, but greeted her niece with a smile.

Rory rose and kissed Carrie Anne's hand. "Oh, my," she laughed. "Such a proper fellow, you are."

"Sure, you're a beautiful sight for these eyes. You have found a safe harbor."

"Oh, yes, dear Rory. Beau is working and is even now on a

business trip for Uncle Fred. Mother is making new friends, and we're helping with the wounded. Natalie is happy to be home, and Aunt Harriet and Uncle Fred have saved us from a terrible fate."

"You were right to leave New Orleans. It will be in Federal hands soon."

"But you won the battle," she said, lowering herself onto a settee with a puzzled look.

"Oh, now, Carrie, the Union was so poorly led, with the wrong ships. Wait 'till they get a commander like Porter or Farragut, and steamers like *Brooklyn* or *Hartford*. They'll win the race. We can't build enough ironclads fast enough, not that we won't try."

"Well," she said with assurance, "I'll go on believing we'll win although it's such a shame that so many young men must suffer. When I visit the hospital and the prisoners of war with Mrs. and Miss Van Lew, my heart wants to break at the plight of those young men, of both sides."

"Tell me about the Van Lews, Carrie, dear. You seem very taken with them."

"Well, they've been harangued in the newspapers. Aunt Harriet told me that there were editorials criticizing them, before we moved here. Yet they're so calm and purposeful in the face of all that vituperation."

"They are among the very best of families here, Rory," said Aunt Harriet. "And while they've comforted the Union prisoners, they've done the same for our own boys. They even brought Commandant Gibbs, of the prison, into their home for a month of convalescence from illness. There's no doubt in my mind that they're fine Southern patriots."

"Yes, and Miss Van Lew, Elizabeth, says she aids both sides because it's the Christian thing to do," added Natalie. "She's quite devout!"

"Sure, I can't fault anyone being merciful to Union prisoners in need, what with a brother in the Union Army. They sound very kind, Carrie Anne."

Rory glanced at Aunt Harriet. "Mrs. Farwell, might your niece and I excuse ourselves for a short stroll about the neighborhood? Such a nice day, not raining and all."

"Of course you may, Rory. And I'm sure Natalie will be glad to walk with you, won't you, dear?" Natalie nodded her assent. Aunt Harriet turned to Rory. "How long will you be in Richmond?"

"And isn't it a pity I report tomorrow to Commander Tucker aboard the *Patrick Henry* on Mulberry Island? I'm betwixt and between, wantin' time with Carrie Anne and excited over my new duty station."

"Dear boy, torn between love and war. At least have dinner with us, Rory," said Aunt Harriet.

"I think I'll be needin' to trudge back to the station and me hotel, now, it being eleven blocks and all. But you're most kind to offer, ma'am."

"Nonsense," Aunt Harriet responded with consummate authority. "Our coachman will drive you back after dinner. I expect to lose our horses to the war effort eventually, but it's not upon us yet. Now, you all have a pleasant walk!" The discussion was obviously at an end.

As the three began their walk, Natalie said, "I believe I shall walk a bit behind, they sidewalk bein' so narrow. Did I mention I've had trouble with my hearing and vision of late?" This last was delivered with a wink and a conspiratorial grin.

The dinner was remarkable for its nuanced sauces and for spirit, and its occasional sparkle of conversation. Uncle Fred was a voracious reader, and as the owner of a successful import-export concern, he had a wide understanding of international affairs. The plight of the Irish peasantry, the arguments surrounding the question of support by Britain and France for the Confederacy, and the paucity of Southern industrial capability were exhaustively discussed.

Aunt Harriet, Natalie, Mrs. Eastman, and Carrie Anne were far more knowledgeable and contributory on those subjects than the norm for women, at least the norm assumed and expected by most men. *Beauty and brains*, thought Rory, *my cup runneth over.* Aunt Harriet was a kind and thoughtful conversationalist, making sure that each dinner guest had opportunity to participate and shine. At one point she drew Rory into a discussion of sea life.

"The sea seems so remote, so separate from our lives here ashore," she said to Rory.

"And, yet, ma'am, everyday, shore folks use nautical expressions without even realizing they do so."

"And what might an example be, Rory?"

"Ma'am, how many times have you been 'taken aback', or remarked that 'the cat's out of the bag', or felt 'between the devil and the deep blue sea', or even used mayonnaise?"

"Well, yes, 'taken aback' seems faintly nautical, though I can't be precise regarding its derivation."

"When a ship is taken aback, the wind shifts to fill the sails from the wrong side and sends the ship backwards. Backing a sail has a braking effect. The others, now, are much more obscure," said Rory, realizing he was about to show off to an appreciative audience and enjoying the prospect.

"The cat in question is the cat o' nine tails, nine cords as punishment that are bound together and used for lashing a man's back. The lash is kept in a red baize bag. When the bo'sun's mate takes the 'cat' out of the bag, dire punishment ensues."

"Oh, dear," said Harriet. "I always envisioned a tabby."

Rory smiled. "Yes, ma'am. The 'devil' is the seam of the deck board or strake nearest to the gunwale or railing. Fall from there and you're in an untenable condition, between the devil and the deep blue sea. Now, we're in debt to the French for my last example. Admiral Richelieu, in the 1700's, won a great battle with the English off Port Mahon, in the Balearics. Bein' French, he had his saucier aboard, and commissioned him to create a celebratory sauce, named for Port Mahon: Mayonnaise! The sea is always with you, Mrs. Farwell."

"I'll surely be more aware of it after our little seminar, Rory, than I have been heretofore!" Her eyes twinkled, and there was a hint of a smile on her lips. Carrie was giggling behind her napkin. "Thank you ever so much, Professor Dunbrody," she said.

After dinner, the Farwell's coachman returned Rory to his hotel. As Rory left the carriage, he thanked the coachman. "Cicero, take care of those kind people. I suspect their lives will change drastically in this war."

"Yassuh, lieutenant, they'se kind folks, fo' sure. Ah'll look out for 'em, suh."

"God save y'kindly, Cicero."

CHAPTER 30
ABOARD THE PATRICK HENRY,
MULBERRY ISLAND
DECEMBER 1, 1861

Rory woke from an exhausted doze as the train left the Dismal Swamp and slowed, gradually entering the outskirts of Portsmouth, home of the Gosport Navy Yard, across the Elizabeth River from Norfolk. The yard, late of the United States Navy, was now the locus of Confederate ironclad construction and the repository of Confederate naval ordnance recently acquired from the Union. In April 1861, Commodore McCauley, commandant of the Navy Yard, against orders from the Secretary of the Navy and the pleas of his subordinates, had failed to defend the yard against minimal Confederate forces. McCauley, awash with indecision, cowardice, and inebriation, had refused to safeguard the five frigates and sloops of war in the yard by moving them across Hampton Roads to safety at Newport News.

Rory's old commander and mentor, James Alden, had been given command of the largest of the yard's ships, the 4300 ton *Merrimack*, with instructions to bring it safely out of Norfolk. But Commandant McCauley, in a vacillating alcohol-induced stupor, ordered the *Merrimack's* fires drawn. Alden carried out the order. Days later, *Merrimack* was scuttled and burned as the Union forces abandoned twelve hundred heavy cannon and retired without a fight. Her hull, intact near and below the waterline, was the foundation upon which the South's great ironclad, ultimately to be named *Virginia,* was being built.

Poor Captain Alden, thought Rory. *He should have defied the sot and taken Merrimack across to Fort Monroe. Ah, well, his compliance with a senseless order is the Union's loss and our gain.* Rory sighed. *We have the hull of the Merrimack and thirteen hundred pieces of ordnance. What a windfall for us!*

Rory met the steam launch from Mulberry Island at Gosport Yard. As they left the navy yard, on their way down the Elizabeth River to head up the James, Rory could see the workers laboring on *Merrimack* in the huge drydock that the Federals had also failed to destroy.

Fifteen miles up the James River, the launch pulled into the dock where the CSS *Patrick Henry* lay. Mulberry Island was on the north shore of the James, a low island covered with sycamore and oak among the scattered pines. Commander John Randolph Tucker, captain of the *Patrick Henry*, greeted Rory in the captain's cabin. "You've come a long way in six years, Dunbrody. I've been reading your file."

"Thank you, captain, I was hoping you'd remember me!" Rory was delighted at Tucker's enthusiasm. "Handsome Jack" Tucker was one of the most respected officers in the prewar U.S. Navy. Fifty years old and a widower with nine children, he was a dynamic leader and a student of the new technologies in ordnance and propulsion.

"Remember? Why, Dunbrody, I've gone so far as to arrange for a party in your honor tomorrow!" Tucker, who actually did love a party, could scarcely contain himself. "I've had the damndest time bringing enough seamen aboard for a full crew. But I must train the ones I have up to snuff. So, short-handed or no, we're going downriver to trade broadsides with our old colleagues at Newport News in the morning!"

Rory laughed. "Captain, y'shouldn't have gone to all the trouble. What a treat!"

"I'll ask you to command the forward ten-inch rifled pivot. It's a Parrott, a gift from Captain McCauley."

"Aye, aye, sir. We've all heard about McCauley's generous nature. Would I be havin' time this afternoon t'meet my gun crew, and do a drill or two?"

"I know that can be arranged, Mr. Dunbrody. Let me take you to the wardroom and introduce you to whomever might be there."

The *Patrick Henry* was a graceful side-wheeler, her foremast stepped equidistant from the tall 'midships stack and the mock-clipper bow. The mainmast was stepped just aft of the paddle wheels whose cover box bore a likeness of Patrick Henry himself. The captain conned the ship from a high catwalk between the two paddle wheel covers. Ship's boats were cradled in davits, two to the side, fore and aft of the paddle wheels.

Two officers sat at the wardroom table as Rory and Tucker entered. "A family gathering, Mr. Dunbrody," said Tucker. May I introduce my clerk, Mr. Charles Douglas Tucker, and our Third Assistant Engineer, John Tarleton Tucker. Gentlemen, our new gunnery officer, Mr. Rory Cormac Dunbrody; at least until his new command, *Old Dominion*, is ready. Mr. Dunbrody, two of my sons."

"Welcome, sir," said John and Charles. The first lieutenant, Rochelle, and two junior officers, Mason and Dornin, joined the group. The enthusiasm in the wardroom was at the level Rory remembered from his days with Tucker aboard *Pennsylvania* in 1855. *Sure, there's nothing as stimulatin' as a disciplined and happy ship*, thought Rory.

Rory assembled the forward pivot crew for a live firing drill in the late afternoon. "Well, now, gentlemen of the gun," said Rory, "would y'be givin' yer new officer a lesson in how this ten-inch gun handles?"

The men grinned back at him and stood ready for command. "Stand by your gun. Cast loose!" The ten-man crew removed the covers and attached the training and side tackles.

"Serve vent and sponge!" The gun captain cleared the vent with a wire and stopped the vent. The seaman assigned as sponger-rammer inserted a wet sponge on the end of the rammer, twirled it in the bore, and removed it, examining the sponge for any burning fragments. There were none, of course, as the gun had not yet been fired, but it was critical that each step be repeated in the same way, no matter what the drill circumstance. This, so that in the heat and tumult of battle each movement would be automatic, and none would be omitted.

"Load!" A crew member put the bagged powder charge into the muzzle by hand, and the rammer pushed it firmly but gently to the end of the bore, mindful of the mark on the rammer handle which indicated he had pushed to "full bore", so as not to mash or damage the charge. The shell's fuse cap was removed, and it was placed in the bore and forced firmly down to rest on the charge.

"Prime!" The gun captain punctured the charge by inserting a priming wire through the vent, and then inserted a fuse, the "primer," into the vent.

"Point!" Men on the training and side tackles moved the gun left as it rotated on the pivot tracks until it bore on the sycamore tree Rory had indicated was the target of the drill, on the far bank of the James, twelve hundred yards distant.

"Raise!" The man at the elevating screw responded without delay.

"Fire as she bears!" The gun captain pulled the lanyard, igniting the fuse, and the shell arced toward a distant tree, landing twenty yards short in a geyser of James River water. On a ship at sea, the gun captain would wait until the ship rolled or pitched, and the gun barrel lined up at the proper attitude to the target depending on its distance from the ship.

"Well laid and fired, gun crew!" Rory said. "According to Captain Tucker, we'll have a live fire exercise downriver tomorrow. Cease fire and secure." Captain Tucker had obviously been exercising the men at the guns, and the crew was honed to perfection.

"Cast off bow line!" Jack Tucker stood on his bridge catwalk the next morning as *Patrick Henry*, bow upriver, got under way. "Ease the stern spring." The "spring" or diagonal line leading from the bow to the dock opposite the stern was slacked off. It served to pivot the bow out into the stream while holding the stern to the dock. As the bow swung out in to the stream, Tucker called, "Cast off spring and stern line. All ahead, two-thirds. Ease the helm to port and bring her on a downstream heading."

"Helm a port to a downstream heading," repeated the quartermaster at the big-wheeled helm. It was critical that all helm orders were repeated back to the commander, to avoid confusion in storm or battle. The officer of the deck repeated speed orders through the voice pipe to the on-duty engineer in the engine room and then the orders were duplicated by the engine-room telegraph.

A light rain was falling. Mist clung to the banks of the James as *Patrick Henry* churned downstream, making close to eight knots with the current. She was very fast for a paddlewheel steamer. When they reached a point in the river three miles distant from the shore batteries at Newport News, Tucker could see the Union frigates *Savannah* and *Louisiana* and several small gunboats lying off the batteries. Rory and the other deck officers stood on the catwalk near the captain.

"Gentlemen," said Tucker, "we'll come broadside-to at a range of a mile and a half, extreme range for the broadside 32-pounders. We'll steam at that range across the river and back giving each broadside battery a chance for practice. The two pivots will fire continuously, regardless of which side we present to the enemy."

Rory glanced to port and saw the tents of the Union infantry garrisoned along the riverbank north and west of Newport News.

"Sir, will you assign targets for the various gun divisions?" Rory asked.

"Just getting to that, Mr. Dunbrody," the captain responded. "Pivots concentrate on the frigates, unless the gunboats approach and shorten the range. Broadsides, target the gunboats. Your round shot won't have much effect on the timbers of those big frigates, especially at this range."

"At the mile and a half range now, sir," the midshipman of the watch reported.

"Very good, Mr. Mason. Gun division commanders, to your divisions, if you please."

Patrick Henry opened fire as her bow turned toward the mouth of the Nansemond River on the southwest bank of the James. Most of the roundshot from her 32-pounders fell well short of the Union ships as did the countering fire from the Federals. Rory marked the fall of the pivots' exploding shells and was certain that at least one hit *Savannah*. One of the paddle wheel gunboats moved toward the *Patrick Henry*, shortening the range to a mile and a quarter. The pivots centered on her as a new target, and a shell exploded on her starboard side. Her starboard paddle wheel dissolved into splinters and wood fragments, and she was quickly towed out of range by another gunboat. *I wonder.* thought Rory, *which of my old classmates we're maiming aboard her?*

After two hours, Tucker took *Patrick Henry* back upstream to Mulberry Island, well satisfied with the exercise, which had avoided any casualties aboard his steamer.

On the upstream leg, Rory posed a question to Tucker, one that had troubled him since watching his smoothly functioning gun crew in the two-hour engagement.

"Sir, the forward pivot crew performed well."

"I noted that, Dunbrody. They're our best!"

"Sir, if I'm to take command of *Old Dominion* in two weeks' time, I should be recruiting a crew now. Sure, it'll take me months to bring them up to current squadron standards."

"Very astute of you to realize that, Mr. Dunbrody. As you've noticed, we're still shorthanded after four months. Lieutenant Barney of the *Jamestown* accuses me, and rightfully so, of siphoning off all the available new hands. He's so shorthanded he's been unable to join the squadron." Tucker smiled seraphically at Rory.

"So you, my young lieutenant, have a vexing command problem. You are the most junior commander in the squadron, with a ship to man in two weeks and no men in sight. The whole navy's short of good seamen. 'The devil to pay and no pitch hot.' When you find the solution, let your commander know how he can help."

"Aye, aye, sir. With your permission, sir, I'll go below and ponder."

"Carry on, Mr. Dunbrody."

Rory appeared on deck the next morning as Tucker was enjoying a cup of coffee. "Sir, I have a plan I'd like your permission to undertake."

"Go on, Dunbrody, let's hear the effect of your enlightenment."

"Sir, the Federals took the Hatteras forts and the forts at Ocracoke and Oregon Inlets. Roanoke Island is next, and not receiving much help from the Norfolk Army command. Just a mosquito fleet of small inland craft is standing by the defenders at Roanoke. The bigger ships, like *Rose of Clifden*, are caught in port. They've effectively closed down Pamlico Sound and much of our naval activity on Albemarle Sound. The North Carolina gunboat crews are ashore and bottled up, sir, with no prospects for action.

"Talk in Norfolk is of an impending Federal attack up the Neuse River on New Berne. That's my home, sir. I have lots of contacts there.

Let me take a short recruiting trip and see if those lads would like to fight up here. Sure, I'd be glad to share some of the spoils. Some, sir," he grinned.

"I knew you'd find a way, Captain Dunbrody," said Tucker, using Rory's new command honorific for the first time. "Good command thinking. Permission granted. Good hunting. I'll provide you a letter asking the cooperation of the commanders in the North Carolina Naval Department. You have one week."

CHAPTER 31
RECRUITING IN NEW BERNE
DECEMBER 1861

Rory took the train from Norfolk to Petersburg, then traveled aboard the Wilmington and Weldon Railroad south to Goldsboro, N.C., and on to New Berne aboard the Atlantic and North Carolina Railroad. From the New Berne station, he went directly to his father's shipyard on South Front Street for a heartfelt reunion and a base of operations.

"Rory," shouted Siobhan over the din of the yard. "What a sight you are, and what brings you home in the midst of war?" Rory's father appeared at that moment, and Rory shared his mission with both of them.

"Oh, lad, 'tis a grand idea to ask for men here now," said Patrick Dunbrody. "Captain Thomas from the *Rose* has command of his crew ashore as the *Rose* daren't poke her nose into Pamlico at all, at all. He also commands men from two other gunboats stranded ashore. They're building shore batteries along the north bank of the Neuse River, they are, and they're hungry for sea duty."

"D'ye think I could approach Captain Thomas today, Da? The sooner I find a crew, the sooner I can train them and have my new command ready."

"We'll cross over the river this very morning. But first, a sit-down, a cup of coffee, and you tellin' us of New Orleans, the James River, and your new lady. Then we'll tell you of brother Tim's latest."

Patrick Dunbrody talked of the Federal landing at the Hatteras forts. "Sure, as I predicted, the earthworks dissolved under the fused shells from Yankee steamships. Now that they've swept the Confederate

Navy from the waters of Pamlico, I'm guessin' that they'll attack New
Berne within months. But, I'm also guessin' they'll attack Roanoke Island
first, and try to close Albemarle Sound and the Dismal Swamp Canal to
Norfolk."

"What will y'do, Da, if they take the town?"

"Ah, sure, your ol' Da is a step ahead of the Yankees. I've a friend
in Scotland Neck, Peter Smith. I built a boat for him years ago. He's a
farmer and owns a big field right on the Roanoke River, at Edwards Ferry.
We've been talkin' about a craft that could hold its own with the Yankees
in the Sounds. He knows a brilliant young shipwright, Gilbert Elliott,
from Elizabeth City. The three of us have written to Stephen Mallory
encouragin' him to contract with us to build a casemated ironclad at
Edwards Ferry.

"If the Yankees take New Berne, your sister and I will leave our
house and yard with our foreman, and tell him to do what he has to do
to survive and maintain the structures. We'll get started preparin' the
cornfield t'be a shipyard, and hope we get a contract. At least we won't be
in occupied North Carolina."

"Won't I breathe easier about you two, knowin' this plan, Father?
And what of Timothy?"

"Oh, the letters come slow as we're using your Uncle Liam as
a courier. As of September, his unit's with the Trans-Mississippi forces
under General Grant at Cairo, Illinois. No action as yet."

Rory and Patrick crossed the Neuse to Fort Anderson, and with
borrowed horses, rode downstream to the log and earthwork fortifications
under construction directly across the river from Fort Thompson on the
southwest bank of the Neuse.

Captain Zachary Thomas, late of the North Carolina Navy and
now a lieutenant in the Confederate Navy, commanded the men of the
small squadron that included the *Rose of Clifden*. It was a squadron in
name only, as its ships were blockaded in New Berne, and its crews were
wielding shovels as they built parapets at the river's edge.

"Patrick, and young Mr. Dunbrody!" Thomas beamed with
delight. "You must tell me, Rory, of your adventures since you left us. I've
had bits and pieces from your father. I need to hear of the sea, as this may

be as close as I get for a long while."

"Sure, it's a delight to see you, captain. I've been busy at sea, there's no doubt. But first, I've come asking for your help. I think you're the only one who can assure I'll have a crew for my first command."

Rory handed Thomas Captain Tucker's letter of introduction. Reading it quickly, Thomas said, "Captain Jack Tucker, he's a fine one. You're fortunate to be under his command, Rory. And with your own ship!"

"Would you let me ask for volunteers among your crews, sir? I know it will leave you short of men."

"Ah, any lubber can handle a shovel, Rory. You need seamen, and I've got 'em. Besides, I'm in your debt for that idea of the ruse which caused the *Cumberland* so much trouble."

"I'm thinkin' *Cumberland's* bound to return to Hampton Roads, sir, when we launch the new ironclad. If some of your lads come with me, they can get another whack at her."

"I'll assemble the men, Rory, so that you may make your pitch. Then, we'll tell some sea stories. Come on, Patrick, and we'll watch Rory speak to my crews. It's not every father that gets to see his son at work."

Sixty-five men assembled next to the rampart being built along the riverbank. The nearest Federal steamer was twenty miles distant, patrolling the mouth of the Neuse. Thomas introduced Rory and spoke supportively of his request. Rory recognized a number of the *Rose's* crew, including Edwards, the boatswain, and MacKenzie, the chief engineer.

"A good mornin' to you, gentlemen. As Captain Thomas said, I'm lookin' for lads eager for action afloat. And I'm hopin' you're mighty tired of shovelin'." Smiles and nods greeted that statement.

"Captain John Tucker commands a squadron on the James that's short of crewmen. The flagship is his *Patrick Henry*, a ten-gun side-wheeler. The *Jamestown*, a smaller steamer, and my tug, the *Old Dominion*, are the rest of the squadron, at present. I need nineteen men for the tug. The rest will go to *Patrick Henry*. I've sailed with many of you against the *Cumberland*. You're seamen, and battle-tested. Just two days ago, the *Patrick Henry* engaged the Federals off Newport News. We damaged a gunboat and the frigate *Savannah*. How many of you will take the train back to Norfolk with me for a little more action like that?"

Some men tossed their shovels to the ground immediately and stepped forward. Others talked to one another and milled about, then joined the first group. In the end, forty-five men, including most of the 'Roses', were dismissed to put their affairs in order and pack for the next morning's train. Edwards and MacKenzie were among them.

"Lieutenant, I'll have these men at the station in the morning, in formation." Thomas looked a bit wistful. "I wish I could go myself, but I'm the navy in New Berne for the present. I'll be harassing my army counterpart for replacements."

"Sir," said Rory, "you've been the soul of generosity. I hope I haven't gotten you in trouble with the army."

"Never give it a thought, lieutenant. They'll have to give me the men; otherwise, their batteries won't be protected. And I've actually done something offensive for the war effort instead of our usual Old North State defensive posture. Please remember me to Commander Tucker. Patrick, good to see you. We'll talk soon. You go home and enjoy your family, Rory."

"Aye, aye, sir. And God save you, sir, we'll make good use of the men."

Patrick Dunbrody invited Captain Thomas to stop by the shipyard for drinks and re-acquaintance with Rory after his crew had finished for the day. After he left, the Dunbrody family talked far into the evening, realizing that the opportunities for family gatherings would be few for the duration of the war.

"Old Zach Thomas would rather be anywhere than ashore digging fortifications, I can tell you that, son." said Patrick. "He'd really like to be with the mosquito fleet at Roanoke Island, even though none of them are big enough to stand against the ships the Yankees will bring when they attack. What he did for you today was tonic for his soul. He thinks the world of you, Rory, after the *Cumberland* engagement."

"What a fine thing it was to release these men. Captain Tucker will be astounded, sure, he will. Siobhan, we've not heard from Tobias, I'm guessin'?"

"Not a word, Rory."

"It's my fault. I've been so busy, I've not written him. It was October twelfth I saw him swashbucklin' aboard the *Vincennes*. It'll take seven weeks for a letter to get to him via Uncle Liam."

"Well then, son, y'd best be getting to writin'. Friends are a fragile commodity," Patrick observed.

After goodbyes in the morning all 'round, Rory marshaled his men aboard the train, and settled down in a day coach, seated across from Chief Engineer MacKenzie and Boatswain Edwards. "It's grand t'be travelin' with old shipmates again, Mr. MacKenzie, Mr. Edwards!"

"We feel the same, Mr. Dunbrody," said MacKenzie.

"I'll be askin' Captain Tucker for your services aboard *Old Dominion*," said Rory. "No guarantees, for he'll do what's best for the whole command, but when we show up forty-five strong, I'm hopin' he'll give way to my request."

Rory had telegraphed Tucker from New Berne, requesting boats to meet the train at Portsmouth. A coxswain from *Patrick Henry* met the train, and soon the steam launch, towing two ship's boats from the flagship, was chugging upriver to Mulberry Island. A smiling John Tucker stood aft on his quarterdeck as Rory reported. "If I'd known you were such a recruiter, I'd have asked Secretary Mallory for you months ago, lieutenant."

"Just a few North Carolina lads, sir, gettin' together for old times' sake."

"Auld lang syne has never been so fruitful, Captain Dunbrody."

"Yes, sir. I've assembled them in front of the barracks ashore, captain, so you may greet them altogether, as it were."

"I'll do just that. Captain Dunbrody, please take station on me." Turner walked down the gangway, Rory following.

Rory called the North Carolinians to attention. Tucker stepped forward. "The spirit of North Carolina you've shown in volunteering for service in the James River Squadron tells me that no one will prevail against us. Soon we'll be sailing in support of a mighty ironclad, built on the hull of the old *Merrimack*. We'll all get our share of action. Captain Dunbrody, Captain Barney, and I will sit down to assign you your ships. By tomorrow evening, you'll have your new billets. Rest, eat, and be prepared for duty tomorrow."

Boatswain Edwards stepped forward. "Three cheers for Captain Tucker!" Resounding calls of "hip, hip, hooray" echoed off the barrack-side.

CHAPTER 32
THE CAPTURE OF BEAUFORT, SOUTH CAROLINA
DECEMBER 1861

Fleet Captain Davis, Acting Master Roswell Lamson, Sailing Master Tobias St. John, and a party of Marines and seamen from USS *Wabash* proceeded cautiously up the Beaufort River, north from Port Royal Sound. Their boats were under tow by the gunboat *Seneca*, aboard which they took their ease through the broad and placid reaches of the Beaufort stream.

Presently they came to Beaufort, South Carolina, a city of four thousand souls, now totally devoid of its upper echelon, the aristocracy of the Sea Islands, as this part of the state was known. The stately plantation homes had been abandoned by their owners who had fled inland. Most of their slaves remained, the majority continuing in their previous labors without supervision or direction.

Captain Davis put several parties ashore to assess the conditions on the plantations and in the town. Tobias commanded one boat crew which secured its cutter to the town wharf in front of the Cotton Exchange, a handsome, brick-front building with sandstone pillars and capstones, and a white-railed veranda off the upper story. Tobias divided his crew into two squads to explore the riverfront. Tobias and four seamen wandered east along Bay Street and soon came to several fishing boats and a steam launch secured to the quay. The crews, all black, talked, standing or lounging on deck or in the pilothouses. Not a white person was to be seen.

Tobias asked a crewmember of the steam launch, "Is the owner aboard?"

"Oh, no sah," the man replied, "he skedaddled wif all de plantation owners when de soldiers landed."

"Did he use the launch often?"

"Oh, no, he stayed in de office. I'se de pilot. We carry the supplies and mail all up an' down de river and back through de branches in de islands," he said, pointing east across the river.

"Do many of the boats in the Sound have slave pilots?"

"Yas, suh, most all of dem."

"Would you guide us upriver from here? We'd pay you, of course. And we'd like to meet other pilots, too."

The man's eyes sparkled, and he grinned widely. "I know dem all, suh. I show you all de bays and creeks. Hallelujah, suh, I do it for free!"

As the *Seneca* returned to the Sound, Tobias reported to Fleet Captain Davis. "Sir, I talked to a pilot, a slave who guided our boats up the river above Beaufort. I met two other pilots. They all know these waters. They have a communications network, a grapevine that extends far into Rebel territory hereabouts. I think they could be very useful to us as we mount the blockade disclosing Rebel ship movements and other information, sir."

"Very good, Mr. St. John. I'll bring this up with Flag Officer Du Pont. Now that it's safe to land the troops, we'll be taking General Stevens' command up the Beaufort and the Broad River."

"Aye, aye, sir. Would that be General Isaac Stevens, sir?"

"Yes, it is. Are you acquainted?"

"Oh, no, sir, but we've been introduced. In the San Juan Islands, sir. He's quite notorious, er, well-known, there. He was the first territorial governor and then Washington Territory's representative to Congress."

"Notorious, Mr. St. John? An interesting word to use to describe a territorial governor."

"Yes, sir, just repeating what some of his Army colleagues had to say of him. Colonel Silas Casey of the 4th Infantry and Stevens were at odds during the Indian War in Puget's Sound in the mid '50s, sir. One of Casey's officers told me Governor Stevens arrested white settlers he thought were too friendly to the Indians and charged them with treason. Colonel Casey refused to jail them at Fort Steilacoom."

"Stevens also tried Chief Leschi of the Nisquallies as a murderer for action he took as a war leader. Casey told Stevens that Leschi should be treated as a prisoner of war, and when Leschi was convicted by Stevens' civilian court, Colonel Casey refused to hang him at the Fort. The civilian authorities built gallows just east of the Fort and hanged Leschi there. When a civilian judge cited Stevens for contempt during the proceedings, Stevens pardoned himself, sir."

"Perhaps 'notorious' was a reasonable choice of words, sailing master." Davis nodded. "It's always interesting to know something of those we must work with in this war."

"Yes, sir. Casey's now a general, too, sir. Who knows, we might run across him in the course of the war."

"We live in interesting times, Mr. St. John. Thank you. You're dismissed."

CHAPTER 33
A LOST CONFEDERATE COMPANY ON
VIRGINIA'S EASTERN SHORE
MID - DECEMBER 1861

Rory's hopes for a promising crew to commission the CSS *Old Dominion* were realized when he, Tucker, and Barney of the *Jamestown* divided the men he'd recruited from New Berne. Boatswain Edwards, Chief Mackenzie, and seventeen gunners, seamen and engine room stokers were assigned to the tug. He also was assigned Lieutenant Quentin Glendenning as executive officer, and Midshipman Archibald Ormsby, altogether a remarkably complete crew for a ship not yet in commission.

Rory drilled his gun crew aboard the flagship for the week prior to the commissioning of *Old Dominion*. Chief Engineer Mackenzie did the same with his engine room crew, the "black gang," as deck sailors had begun to call them. They were usually covered with coal dust. When commissioning day came, the officers of the squadron, the tug's crew, and invited family members who lived near Richmond, including Carrie Anne and her family, were unexpectedly joined at Rockett's Wharf by Secretary Mallory.

Captain Tucker, the main speaker, prevailed upon the Secretary for a few words. Mallory was quite complimentary of Rory's record. The tug's black hull, deckhouse, and the Parrott pivot were handsomely set off by her white holystoned deck, white deckhouse trim, and gleaming brass fittings. Multi-colored signal flags flew from her backstay and forestay. Carrie Anne broke a champagne bottle over the bow watched by her family and the Van Lews. It was an occasion!

A bit later in the pilothouse, Rory showed Carrie Anne the flag locker near the starboard pilothouse door. "I'll share with you my little conceit, dear Carrie," said Rory, showing her a Kelly green flag with a golden harp in the center. "Long ago, I promised myself that if I ever commanded a ship, I'd hoist Ireland's oldest ensign after my ship's first victory. This is the ancient flag of Brian Boru, the first king of all Erin. I'm ready. Now all I have to do is win!"

The next day Rory moved the tug downstream to Mulberry Island. Rory reported to Tucker aboard the flagship.

"Mr. Dunbrody, I have just received an urgent dispatch from Colonel Charles Smith, late commander of Confederate forces on Virginia's Eastern Shore. It's through General Huger, his commander. Smith escaped with about four hundred men late last month from Union forces invading from Eastern Maryland. He disbanded the other eleven hundred of his command. Those men laid down their weapons and went back to their homes. I think their war is over. Eastern Virginia has been annexed to Maryland."

Tucker continued. "It seems the good colonel left his rearguard, a company of forty men, ashore near Cape Charles. They're hiding but still together as a unit to the best of his knowledge. He'd like us to rescue them, if it's not too much trouble. Just the assignment for the *Old Dominion*, wouldn't you say?"

"Aye, aye, sir. Does he know how near to Cape Charles, sir?"

"He embarked from close to the mouth of Old Plantation Creek. The colonel's best guess is that they're holed up around the farm and the wooded area south of the creek near Capeville." Tucker paused. "The bad news is, the Union Navy has increased its offshore patrols nearby on the Chesapeake side. You may have trouble avoiding them, and they doubtless outgun you." Tucker pointed to the chart on his cabin table.

Rory examined the chart of the Cape Charles, Cape Henry, and Hampton Roads area. "Sir, we'll need to be lucky indeed to make contact with these men and dodge the Yankee patrols. Does Colonel Smith have a man he can spare who knows the area and can reach the lost company through partisan contacts?"

"I'll make the request."

"Thank you, sir. I suggest, sir, that we leave Norfolk after nightfall. We'll hug the shore to Cape Henry, then cross the mouth of the Chesapeake to Cape Charles and go east, up the Sea Isles waterway until we're opposite the Capeville area. The Yankees won't be patrolling that side, and it's only four miles across the peninsula. We'll have to squeeze those forty men in and wait for decent weather to bring 'em back."

"I like this plan, captain. You be cautious coming back. I'd hate to lose the tug, and lose the company for a second time. I can afford to have you gone for a few days."

"Tomorrow we are getting the tug *Teaser* under Captain Webb, added to the squadron. More family. He's my brother-in-law." Tucker grimaced. "I know it's not a good practice to command one's kin but in this war, what can one do?"

Rory was in his stateroom aboard *Old Dominion*, secured just aft of the flagship at the Mulberry Island quay when Midshipman Ormsby knocked on his door. "Sir, Lieutenant Drummond of the Confederate Army, accompanied by a corporal, has come aboard and desires a word with you."

"Fine, Mr. Ormsby, please show them in."

Rory introduced himself to Lieutenant James Drummond, CSA, a member of Colonel Smith's Eastern Shore unit now under General Huger. "Are you a 'Drummondtown' Drummond, lieutenant?"

"I am, sir. My family has been on the eastern shore for many generations. I opted to accompany Colonel Smith when he decided to continue the fight in this part of Virginia. I've taken the liberty of bringing my brother, Wilfred. We'll be more effective searchers with two of us who know the country."

"A pleasure to meet you, Corporal Drummond." Rory shook the young man's hand. "It must have been painful to leave the ancestral home, lieutenant."

"Yes, sir. We knew we couldn't prevail against a 4500-man Yankee force but the colonel did not wish to give up. We decided to follow him."

"Sure, if you can help me find your rearguard, you'll add some familiar faces to what's left of your unit."

"We'll do our best, sir."

"I intend to go up the Sea Isles passage to a point near Mill Creek on the east shore as we have word the Federal cruisers are patrolling the west shore. Will that suffice as a jumping-off point to our search for your lost company?"

"Yes, sir. We'll be only a mile from our cousin's house there. He'll know their whereabouts, without doubt. And he has the horses we can use to meet them."

"Excellent, lieutenant. My plan is to leave Mr. Glendenning, my first lieutenant, in command. I'll ride with you so as to signal Glendenning if something goes amiss. I'm a good horseman. I won't slow you down. If all goes well, we'll march the company to the tug and be able to load within a half hour. If we're discovered, or pursued, or have to abort the enterprise, I'll fire a flare. Mr. Glendenning will get under way and rendezvous with us at peninsula's end. If we make it, well and good. If not, he'll proceed to Norfolk, and we'll reassess our chances. How does that strike you, lieutenant?"

"Most workable, sir. My most salient concern is the possibility of betrayal. Northampton and Accomac Counties are now annexed to Maryland, and many folks bear stronger allegiance to profit or survival than to their home state and its cause."

"Sure, and that sounds familiar to me. Ireland, my childhood home, is still rife with informers. We'll hope our caution and good fortune can overcome the threat of betrayal. We'll sail at noon, gentlemen, for Norfolk. I'll want to leave there at nightfall. Come below with me to our little wardroom and meet our officers as we share our plan. We'll have to squeeze in." Rory smiled apologetically. "Everything's small on *Old Dominion*."

As night fell over the Gosport Navy Yard, the *Old Dominion* eased quietly downstream to the river mouth, rounded Point Sewell, and moved along the Ocean View shore east toward Cape Henry at half-ahead. The powerful engine of the tug was somewhat muffled at this speed. The watch officers on deck were vigilant, searching the waters to the north for any signs of Federal cruisers closing on the tug. Several Confederate batteries on Virginia's north shore usually served to keep the cruisers at a distance. It was a cloudy night, the wind at ten knots, perfect for moving along shore without being seen. No lights shone aboard; save for the tiny binnacle light which illuminated the compass rose.

Reaching a point abeam of Cape Henry, the southern "gate" of the mouth of Chesapeake Bay, *Old Dominion* turned due north. The first lieutenant stood outside the starboard door to the pilothouse, straining to see through the dark and the wind-blown spray. He slid open the pilothouse door. "Wind's freshening, sir," said Lieutenant Glendenning. "East, nor'east, a half east, at fifteen knots, sir."

"Very good, Mr. Glendenning." The door slid closed again. Without the wind's howl, relative quiet returned to the pilothouse. The muffled thrum of the steam engine could be heard once more. Rory glanced at Glendenning's figure on the deck outside the pilothouse, visible as a dark silhouette. *He could be my biggest obstacle to success with this ship,* Rory thought. Glendenning had offered little but veiled disagreement with Rory's orders since coming aboard. Rory also found Glendenning's relations with the crew to be too familiar, given that he was the ship's disciplinarian. Rory sighed as he gazed ahead into the dark. The fate of forty Confederate infantry depended on him. He could feel, almost physically, the weight of his first command as he crossed the mouth of the Chesapeake. That weight was easily matched by the exhilaration of facing the challenge ahead.

CHAPTER 34

THE SECRET SERVICE AMONG THE ISLANDS OF PORT ROYAL
JANUARY-FEBRUARY 1862

Tobias sat writing at the deserted wardroom table aboard *Wabash.*

Dear Rory,

The Wabash has been moored in Port Royal Sound the month of January and into February. I have your letter of November 1861 telling how you sighted me going aboard Vincennes last October. I hope this finds you well, and anticipating action that will result in promotion and awards not posthumous.

At first, I was put in command of landing parties to secure position against attack by Rebel forces attempting to retake the ground we have secured. The attacks did not materialize, but I learned much about pickets and perimeters. Lately Flag Officer Du Pont has employed me ashore among the freed slaves of the Port Royal plantations.

Most of these new freedmen are quite at a loss to know how to deal with their freedom. They are used to being told how to spend every moment of their day, and at present, there is no one to fill that void. They have also been prohibited, for the most part, from learning to read, write, or do arithmetic. I have heard that volunteers from the Union will soon be here to teach and guide the new freedmen. Until then, some of my duties entail helping them to get through each day by just surviving. It's a far cry from navigation, but

> *fascinating in its own right. I must go for I have the watch.*
> *With a fervent wish for your well being, I remain,*
> *Your great friend,*
> *Tobias St.J.*

Tobias addressed his letter to Mr. Liam Dunbrody, of Clifden, County Galway. Rory's uncle Liam would forward it to Rory. Tobias posted his letter with the purser, and stood his watch without incident. A fast steamer had entered the Sound during the morning, anchoring nearby. A boat from the steamer brought a nondescript man in civilian clothes and a derby to the accommodation ladder and float at the *Wabash's* port side. Fleet Captain Davis was on hand to greet the visitor.

At the conclusion of Tobias' watch, the secretary to the flag officer appeared on deck and asked that Tobias report to Du Pont's cabin. As Tobias entered the cabin, he found Du Pont, Davis and the civilian visitor waiting, seated around the large cabin table.

"Sailing master reporting as ordered, flag officer," said Tobias.

"Have a seat, please, Mr. St. John," said Du Pont. "Let me introduce Mr. Allan Pinkerton of President Lincoln's Secret Service."

"How do you do, Mr. St. John," said Pinkerton in the particular burr of a Glasgow native. "Flag Officer Du Pont has told me of the general information you've been able to gather from the recently-freed slaves hereabouts. I'm interested in your assessment of its worth and what you think its possibilities might be in other areas similar to Port Royal."

Pinkerton's rumpled appearance would make it easy for him to avoid notice in a crowd, *unless,* Tobias thought, *one would look into his eyes.* They fixed Tobias with a steady and unrelenting gaze. Tobias could imagine interrogation from this man and guessed that it would not be a pleasant experience.

"Mr. Pinkerton, the slaves throughout the South have a grapevine, the so-called 'Black Dispatch', which can provide timely and accurate information on troop movements, shipping schedules, commodities moving on the railroads, and the like. I was astounded at what was available and freely given until I realized that this system has been in place for three hundred years. Some of the freedmen refer to the methodology as 'below the porch', the place where slaves traditionally sit and listen to their masters discuss any and all of their plans and opinions."

"Aye, Mr. St. John, that coincides with my experience in interviewing 'contrabands'. I've also found their information to be astoundingly accurate. Flag Officer Du Pont has told me of your specific efforts tae ascertain blockade-runner sailing dates, efforts you've begun through local pilots here. Have you ideas on how we might expand the use of this intelligence, extend the grapevine, as it were?"

Tobias paused, sorting out his thoughts. "Sir, we might begin with a Georgia pilot I've just befriended named Isaac Tatnall. He's near Beaufort, helping the more elderly freed slaves to work the plantations. He's young and quite strong, and I know he wants to do more for the war effort. I think he has a network which extends far beyond the Port Royal area."

"Flag Officer Du Pont," said Pinkerton, "this could be a real break-through for the secret service. Heretaefore, I've relied on implanting agents in Rebel territory. I've no' been very successful," he admitted, looking at his hands. "They're frequently identified, captured, and sometimes, executed. Finding agents in place, already within Rebel areas, och, tha' could be hugely effective."

"Mr. St. John," said Du Pont, "why don't you pay this Tatnall a visit and report back to me. I'll keep Mr. Pinkerton apprized of developments."

"Aye, aye, sir. Isaac Tatnall came to the squadron with a group of slaves and asked for shelter shortly after we'd taken Great Tybee Island near Savannah, Georgia, in December. Around Beaufort, many of the slave-owners who fled took their able-bodied slaves with them, and left the weak and elderly. Isaac has been a great help to them."

"Make sure, however you expand your present network, that you build one whose members are capable of working under great stress," said Pinkerton. "It's a frightening endeavor, spying."

"Mr. Pinkerton," said Tobias, "the ones I've met have been living under threat of physical and emotional harm all their lives. I believe they're virtually inured to danger. I'm not as inured, yet I'd like to volunteer to go behind enemy lines to help what you called 'an agent in place'. For instance, if I could masquerade as a slave pilot, assisting an agent already in a southern port, I'll wager we could cut out a blockade runner with the right kind of luck."

Pinkerton fixed Tobias with a quizzical look. "Be careful what ye wish for, sailing master. But with the flag officer's permission, I'll be alert for the right opportunity."

"No harm in trying, if St. John is willing,' said Du Pont. "He seems to have a flair for the dangerous."

Tobias could read the determination in Pinkerton's eyes. "There's nae doubt," the Scot said, "that if we could bring off the capture Mr. St. John envisions, it would be a great boost tae navy and northern morale and a great help to President Lincoln! We'll meet again when ye return from talking t'yer friend Tatnall."

As Tobias left the cabin, his thoughts raced. *If nothing else, this would be in keeping with the tradition of John Paul Jones; 'in harm's way'. No turning back now.*

TO BE CONTINUED IN
"GRAY RAIDERS, GREEN SEAS"

The "running survey" method of triangulation and charting developed by Charles Wilkes in the 1838-1842 U.S. Exploring Expedition reduced the time required to chart an island by more than half.

The Pig War had its share of drama, each country taking turns teetering on the brink of a shooting war. Geoffrey Phipps Hornby, Admiral Baynes, Winfield Scott, Silas Casey, even the hot-headed George Edward Pickett each exercised restraint and calm judgment at crucial times during the crisis.

The US Coast Survey played a huge part in the eventual resolution of the "main channel" controversy in the San Juans. The Coast Survey, elite among world cartographic organizations, was instrumental in the mapping and charting of the western United States and its coastal waters. James Alden, USN, on loan to the Coast Survey, was notorious for suddenly suspending his charting activities to react to Haida and other tribal raids or to rescue shipwrecked sailors. His Coast Survey superior George Davidson was bitterly critical of this penchant, and their rivalry for recognition hindered their efficiency as survey officers. Although my story line has the *Active* briefly in Puget Sound during 1860-61, she actually remained on the Oregon and California coasts in those years.

I transplanted the Haida Raid chapter details from an actual confrontation between Chief Jefferson of the Skidegate Haidas and the British in northern Vancouver Island. The circumstances and the quote are accurate.

The Wilkes Expedition (the "US Ex Ex") left a legacy for both the Pig War and the Civil War. James Alden first saw Puget Sound with Wilkes, and no fewer than eight officers of that expedition later achieved flag rank. Many more were commissioned in the Confederate Navy, as was also the case for the officers, army and navy, involved in the Pig War. One of Wilkes' lieutenants, William L. Maury, cousin to Matthew F. Maury, commanded the CSS *Georgia,* and Alden gained fame or notoriety when he stopped his USS *Brooklyn* because of torpedoes (floating mines) at Mobile Bay, evoking the signal (perhaps apocryphal) from Farragut's USS

Hartford astern of him, "Damn the torpedoes, full steam ahead."

Many tugs were armed on both sides as the war began. They were available, and their abundant buoyancy fore and aft enabled them to accommodate heavy cannon. Three took part in the Battle of Hampton Roads, and the CSS *Manassas* was a converted river towboat.

All accounts of the USS *Vincennes* debacle at the Battle of the Head of the Passes agree that Captain Handy misread the signal, abandoned ship, wrapped himself in the flag, and tried to blow up the ship. No two accounts agree on the reason she didn't explode. I've simply added one more possible (albeit fictional) explanation.

Gray uniform jackets for Confederate naval officers caused quite a controversy among the officer corps. Blue was the accepted hue for all navies. Scarcity of indigo dye in the south helped the ease the transition from blue to gray. I've accelerated the date gray uniforms were available by a few weeks so as to present a more striking visual contrast.

Midshipman James M. Morgan was present in Lt. Alexander Warley's boat as he took the *Manassas*. Morgan described the action in his "Recollections of a Rebel Reefer." Rory is my only addition to that scene. No photos exist of the CSS *Manassas*, but many sketches depict her with one stack, like the one on the back cover of this book. James Morgan, who was there, describes her "smokestacks" (plural), so I have likewise described her thus.

Henry Martyn Robert, author of Robert's Rules of Order, did construct the redoubt over Griffin Bay on San Juan Island, and later rose to command of the Army Corps of Engineers.

Pickett never visited son Jimmie in Arkata (or anywhere else) but sent money instead. I contrived the visit to south Puget Sound so that he and Rory could talk once more before they left for the Confederacy.

When Rory delivers his lecture on nautical expressions at dinner in Richmond, he fails to mention that flogging (the cat's out of the bag) was abolished in the USN in 1850.

The spelling of New Bern with an "e" on the end (New Berne) was in use until the late 19th century. Peter Smith's cornfield still exists on the banks of the Roanoke River. The CSS *Albemarle*, constructed there by Smith and Gilbert Elliott (with Patrick Dunbrody's fictional help) was later commanded by Alexander Warley, the CSS *Manassas* commander at Head of the Passes. She was sunk in 1864 by a steam launch bearing a spar torpedo, commanded by Lt. Will Cushing, USN, who you will meet in "**The Wake of the Woonsocket**."

The incidents in Greytown (San Juan del Norte, Nicaragua) referenced by both Rory and Tobias involved a contest extending from 1853 to 1858 among the Cornelius Vanderbilt industrial empire, Charles Morgan, Vanderbilt's former corporate associate, William Walker, an American "filibuster" or freebooter who managed to get himself elected President of Nicaragua, and the Costa Rican government. Rory and Tobias served aboard US ships in the thick of the conflict.

APPENDIX B:
SHIPS

Most of the ships appearing in this novel were actual vessels, and most of the officers noted were historical characters aboard these ships. The following are the only fictional ships:

Canute: Pacific Northwest side wheel packet

Mingulay: Panama to New Orleans packet

Pride of the Mystic: New England whale ship

CSS Old Dominion: One-gun screw tug, Rory's first command.

CSS Rose of Clifton: Dunbrody-shipyard-built paddlewheel gunboat.

Scioto: British barque. In 1864, an actual British ship of the same name bore the first Japanese plantation workers to Hawaii (see the Hilo Museum).

MAJOR CHARACTERS

Rory Dunbrody, CSN, and father Patrick, sister Siobhan, brother Tim, Uncle Liam, and the Dillon side of the family.

Tobias St. John, and his family. Antiguan-born former slave, whaler and now a Union sailing master. Cousins Mitchell and Daniel of St. John's, Antigua. Father Carlyle St. John of New Bedford.

Kalama, Kele and son Kekoa - Hawaiian seafarers. Kekoa becomes a master's mate in the US Navy.

Other Important Characters   "*" denotes an actual historical figure.

* Commander James D. Bulloch, CSN – Commanded the packet *Bienville*, then joined the CSN and directed Rebel raider acquisitions in Europe.

* Jefferson Davis – President, Confederate States.

Colonel Thomas Donovan, CSA (& family)– Confederate officer of the Louisiana Tiger Zouave Regiment, betrothed to Carrie Anne Eastman whom Rory kills in a duel,

*Admiral Samuel Francis "Frank" Du Pont, USN – commanding the South Atlantic Blockading Squadron (and therefore, Tobias) in the first years of the war.

Monique Duvalliere – Tobias' lover and childhood sweetheart in les Isles de Saintes. Monique's father Pierre, brothers Etienne and Claude.

Carrie Anne Eastman - Rory's Southern love interest. Her mother, her brother Beau, her aunt and uncle Harriet and Fred Farwell, her cousin Natalie Farwell.

*Gilbert Elliott – Brilliant young shipwright who constructed the CSS *Albemarle* in the cornfield on the Roanoke River mentioned by Patrick Dunbrody. The field is still there.

Lieutenant Daniel Fell - bigoted Union naval officer, Tobias' occasional tormentor.

*Commander Henry French, USN – commanding USS *Preble* at the Battle of the Head of the Passes.

* Gustavus Fox - Assistant US Navy Secretary, confidant of President

Lincoln.

Quentin Glendenning, CSN – Rory's subordinate lieutenant.

*Commodore George N. Hollins, CSN – mercurial and feisty US and then Confederate officer

*Sir Geoffrey Phipps Hornby - Royal Navy officer who befriended Rory in Puget's Sound and helped him in England. Later, Admiral of the Fleet (Britain's highest naval rank).

*Lt. Beckett Howell III, Confederate States Marine Corps – Brother-in-law of Jefferson Davis, commanding Marine detachments aboard CSS *Sumter* and later CSS *Alabama.*

*Lt. Catesby ap Roger Jones – Welsh-named first lieutenant and later commander of CSS *Virginia.* Ap is Welsh for "son of."

*Lt. John Kell, CSN – First Lieutenant of CSS *Sumter* and later CSS *Alabama.*

* Acting master Roswell Lamson, USN – Outstanding US Navy officer from Oregon whose assignments are often coincident with Tobias'.

* President Abraham Lincoln

Lieutenant Bertram Ludlow, Royal Navy – Blockade runner, bigot and general trouble-maker in Tobias' world.

* Confederate Secretary of the Navy Stephen Mallory – ran the Rebel navy with creativity and determination.

*Lt. Robert "Bob" Minor, CSN – Mallory's "trouble shooter" for several navy projects. Wounded at the battle of Hampton Roads.

* Midshipman James Morris "Jimmie" Morgan, CSN – his assignments in New Orleans, Richmond and Great Britain were coincident with Rory's. The portrayal of his father, Judge Morgan, is taken from James Morgan's "Recollections of a Rebel Reefer," as is the involvement of Beckett Howell as a second in the duel where James' brother Harry was killed.

Archibald Ormsby - South Carolinian naval officer often under Rory's command.

* George Edward Pickett - US Army captain and later Confederate major general. Last in his class at West Point. Charming. Flamboyant. He and Rory cross paths frequently.

* Allan Pinkerton – Secret Service Chief for General McClellan and Lincoln's protector. Tobias impresses him with his clandestine abilities.

*Lt. Charles W. "Savez" Read, CSN – dashing and irrepressible officer later famous for his attacks against Northern shipping while in command of CSS *Tacony*.

*Raphael Semmes - Confederate naval officer who commanded CSS *Sumter* and later CSS *Alabama*.

*General Winfield Scott – Hero of the Mexican War, mediator of peace with the British over a border dispute with Canada, and hence the "Great Pacificator," he advanced the "Anaconda" plan to isolate the South by blockade, and he negotiated the joint occupancy of San Juan Island until that new border dispute could be resolved by arbitration.

Wickstrand Tremaine - Royal Navy commander who befriended Rory and Tobias in Puget's Sound and later assisted Rory in England.

*Tatnall, Isaac – Freed slave pilot of Georgia coastal waters who became a leader among newly-freed salves in South Carolina.

*Tattnall, Commodore Josiah, CSN – Commander of CSS *Virginia* (the old *Merrimack*) after the Battle of Hampton Roads. A former US Navy officer in his sixties, he was known as "Old Tat."

*John Randolph Tucker – senior US and Confederate naval officer in many theaters where Rory fought. Later an admiral jointly commanding the Chilean and Peruvian navies.

*Van Lew, Elizabeth (and her mother Eliza) – Controversial yet proper southern ladies who aided both wounded Confederates and Union prisoners while operating a Union spy ring in Richmond.

Klaus Dieter von Klopfenstein – aide to George Pickett, formerly a Prussian army officer and duelist, Rory's antagonist.

*Lt. Alexander F. Warley, CSN – Commander of the CSS *Manassas* in 1861, later, in 1864, commander of CSS *Albemarle* when she was sunk by Lt. William Cushing, USN, with a spar torpedo delivered from a steam launch.

* Gideon Welles - Union Secretary of the Navy, cabinet adviser to President Lincoln.

* John Taylor Wood – dashing Rebel navy commander and cavalry colonel. Formerly assistant US Naval Academy superintendent. Commanded a "naval cavalry" unit specializing in the capture of Union blockader gunboats. Gunnery officer aboard CSS *Virginia* at Hampton Roads. Jefferson Davis' nephew and aide.

Appendix d:
Glossary

ABAFT: Toward the stern of the ship, used relatively, e.g., "the gun was abaft the mizzenmast."

ABEAM: Beside, next to, abreast. At the side of, as opposed to in front or behind.

AFTERGUARD: Seamen whose station is on the quarterdeck.

A HUI HOU: In Hawai'ian, until we next meet.

AVAST: A shipboard order: hold, or stop hauling.

ARMS: Cannon: Smoothbore cannon had no rifling or grooves inside the barrel, and fired roundshot (solid cannon balls) as well as grapeshot (bags of musket balls) or chainshot (two roundshot bound together by a chain) very harmful to rigging. They were muzzleloaders, and usually mounted on wooden gun carriages with wooden wheels to accommodate recoil. Sometimes, they were on Marsilly or "dumbtruck" carriages, on which the back two wheels were replaced by a wooden bar sliding on the deck to more effectively reduce recoil. They were classified by the weight of their roundshot, e.g., 32pounders, 24-pounders. These cannon were used afloat and ashore. Swivels were small smoothbores mounted or set in the gunwales of ships or ship's boats and rotated in any direction. Smoothbores were most often mounted in broadside, firing from only one side of the vessel, through a gunport.

Rifled cannon fire shaped shells, either exploding or solid, with rims so that the rifling causes them to spin through the air for better accuracy. They are classified by muzzle diameter, e.g., 8-inch, eleven-inch, and inventor or manufacturer, e.g., Parrott, Dahlgren (Union), Brooke, the British Whitworth, Blakely, and Armstrong (used by the Confederacy). Their effective range was a bit more than a mile. Most are muzzleloaders, except the breechloader Armstrong. These cannon were used afloat and ashore. So were howitzers, smaller wheeled cannon with elevated muzzles. Columbiads were huge 15,000-pound guns used in shore fortifications, with a range of three miles. Rifled cannon were frequently mounted as pivots, on tracks secured to the fore or after decks that enabled the gun to be trained in any direction. A pivot might have three gunports through which it could fire, rather than the one customary for a broadside gun.

Excellent sources for some of the above are Paul Silverstone's **Civil War Navies 1855-1883** – Naval Institute Press, and **Ironclads and Columbiads** by William R. Trotter – John F. Blair.

<u>Swords</u>: Sabers and cutlasses were the most common used by Civil war armed forces, and were used more often to cut and slash than to thrust, with a single edged blade. <u>Rapiers</u>, including epees, were double or triple edged and used more to thrust. They were common in dueling.

<u>Sidearms</u>, handguns and revolvers: Very popular was the 1851 Colt .36 caliber Navy Six, a six-shot revolver light in weight and favored by cavalry and the navy.

ARTICLES OF WAR: The disciplinary code for the navy. The US Navy code was adopted, virtually verbatim, by the Confederate Navy. The armies' articles were similar. The modern equivalent is the Uniform Code of Military Justice (UCMJ).

AT ALL, AT ALL, or more commonly, ATALLATALL: a 19th century "paddyism" - not at all (emphatically).

BAD MOR, pronounced "bawd moor," "big boat": The largest type of Galway Hooker. "Hookers," or "huickers," from the Dutch, are cutter-rigged freight boats used in the waters of western Ireland. Bad Mors are from 35 to 44 feet long and carry livestock, turf or peat, hay and other bulk goods. They are now used sparingly for transport, and an association exists for their preservation as a type. Today, they often are raced in Hooker regattas. But in the 19th century, with its poor roads in western Ireland, they were a most effective means of transportation. In addition to the Bad Mor, there are three other smaller types of Hookers, used often for fishing.

BEAR UP: In a sailing ship, to sail closer to the wind, or in a steamer, to head for.

BEAT TO QUARTERS: A drum rhythm from the ship's drummer that called the crew to battle stations.

BELL TIME: The striking of the ship's bell to mark the passage of time. Time at sea is divided into four-hour "watches." One bell is struck at each half hour, for a cumulative total of eight bells at the end of the fourth hour. From midnight, the watches are Mid, Morning, Forenoon and Afternoon, bringing the day to 4:00 pm, or "eight bells in the afternoon watch." To preclude sailors from standing the same watch each day, two two-hour watches span the 4:00 to 8:00 pm time. They are known as the First and Second Dog Watches. Four bells are sounded at the end of the First Dog Watch, but in the Second we hear one, two, three, and then at 8:00 pm, eight bells once again. The seventh watch is the Evening Watch, ending when eight bells sounds midnight.

BEST BOWER: The starboard of the two anchors carried at the bow, as opposed to the SMALL BOWER, the portside anchor, which was, peculiarly, the same weight as the best bower.

BLATHERSKITE: In Ireland, a nonsense talker, a useless individual who talks "blather."

BLOCKADE STRATEGY BOARD: This forerunner of the Joint Chiefs of Staff was comprised of a senior Corps of Engineers officer, a navy captain as secretary, the Superintendent of the US Coast Survey, Alexander Bache (Benjamin Franklin's great grandson) and was chaired by Francis Du Pont, later admiral commanding the South Atlantic Blockading Squadron. Du Pont admired Bache's skill in implementing Winfield Scott's "Anaconda" plan to blockade and isolate the South.

BRIAN BORU'S FLAG: Brian Boru was the 11th century King who united all Ireland. His flag (probably apocryphal) was green with a gold harp. It is now the navy jack of the Republic of Ireland. It was known as "The harp without the crown" to distinguish it from the Irish Harp in the British coat of arms. The British had placed a crown above the harp as a symbol of their dominance over the Irish.

BROAD REACH: A point of sailing with the wind abeam or slightly abaft the beam.

BULWARK: The side of the vessel above the level of the top deck. Its top is the gunwale.

CAISSONS: Two-wheeled wagons carrying artillery ammunition.

CAPOEIRA: A martial art often disguised as dance and frequently practiced to music, developed first in the slave plantations of Brazil, emphasizing striking with the legs. When slave masters would appear, the participants would subtly shift from confrontational movements to dance form.

CAPSTAN, WINDLASS, CAPSTAN BARS, WINCH: A vertical cylindrical barrel on the main deck of a sailing ship, capped by a drumhead with square pigeon holes in which wooden capstan bars were inserted and pushed by the crew to raise the anchor or yards or boats. Hawsers or cables were wrapped around the drum and held by pawls. With the advent of steam and electricity, a powered horizontal drum, or windlass, performed the same function. The more modern horizontal winch is likewise steam or electrically powered, and a vertical winch is turned by hand on yachts.

CHANTIES: Work songs and by extension ballads of the sea. The work songs, to help sailors with the rhythm of raising the sails (halyard chanties), raising the anchor (capstan chanties) and pumping ship, were used only in the merchant fleet, but both work songs and ballads were sung by off-duty navy men and officers for their own enjoyment. The ballads were often sung on the foredeck where it was cool, and were known as fore-bitters because they were sung close to the fore bitts, the vertical timbers used to secure lines.

COUNTER: The underside of the after-overhang of a ship, below the transom.

CONTRABANDS: escaped or freed slaves during the Civil War, so termed by Union general Benjamin Butler (a lawyer) when asked by southern slave owners under a flag of truce to return their "property" under the Fugitive Slave Act, still in effect in the Union. Butler brilliantly evoked the slave owners' declaration that if returned, their slaves would be used in the war effort, digging trenches, etc. Butler then declared the slaves "contraband of war" the same as guns or ammunition, and therefore exempt from the Fugitive Slave Act. The term stuck.

CRIMP: A keepers of seamen's lodgings who doubled as a procurer of seamen for ships needing sailors, at a price, of course. Crimps most commonly used spiked drinks as the means to render sailors insensible and easily delivered to ships about to sail.

DALTHEEN: (Irish) impudent fellow.

DAVIT: A set of two small cranes fitted with tackle to lower the boat slung between them along the side or the stern of a ship.

DEVIL TO PAY AND NO PITCH HOT: being unprepared for a task. The "devil" is the outboard seam on the deck. Sailors "payed" or caulked the seam with hot pitch.

DOUSED HER GLIM: Put out the lantern or other light showing aboard a ship.

DRAFT or draught: The vertical distance between a ship's waterline and her keel. The depth of water a ship "draws" is her draft, e.g., "she drew 22 feet."

ENFILADE: Sweep (with gunfire) along a line of troops or a trench.

FALLS: The tackle (tackle; two blocks [pulleys] and the rope between them) for lowering and raising boats suspended from davits.

FENIANS: Originally, an American brotherhood of Irish dedicated to the freedom of Ireland from Great Britain, led by John O'Mahoney (1859). They were named for the ancient Gaelic warrior Fiona MacCumhail and his elite legion, the Fianna. Later, James Stephens' Irish branch of the organization adopted the same name.

FORTIFICATIONS: Forts or fortresses consist of ramparts, the outer walls, surmounted by parapets, upward extensions of the ramparts behind which guns are mounted and fired through embrasures or openings in the parapet. Corners of the fortification may project beyond the main walls in hexagonal outward extensions called bastions, which contain chambers called casemates in which guns are housed. Sally ports are chambered entrances with two doors, an inner door closed after defenders are in the sally port, and an outer door that then is opened to let the defenders "sally forth." Redoubts are earthworks outside of main forts and independent of them.

FREE QUAKER: An offshoot of the Society of Friends which, in the American Revolution, and beyond, made exception to the Quaker abhorrence of war and violence for situations in which man struggles against intolerable tyranny.

GLEOITEOG: A type of Galway Hooker (see above), pronounced "glochug," 24-30' long, used often for fishing.

GOMBEEN MEN: Rural Irish usurers who exacted exorbitant interest on loans to the Irish peasantry.

GROG: A mixture of rum and water served daily to the ship's crew in the

Royal and American navies. Named for British Admiral Vernon, whose nickname, after a coat he wore, was "Old Grogham." Drink too much and you were "groggy." The Royal Navy continued the custom through the 20th century, but the Union (US) Navy discontinued it in 1862.

GUNWALE: The upper edge of the side or bulwark of a vessel. Pronounced "gun'l."

GYBE: or "jibe": While wearing a vessel with a fore-and-aft mainsail (moving the stern through the wind), the moment when the boom and sail swing from one side of the craft to the other. Depending on the force of the wind and the area of the sail, this action can put a great strain on the rigging and spars. It can be mitigated by strong control of the mainsheet. If unexpected (e.g., a sudden wind-shift) the swinging boom can knock a man overside.

HAWSE HOLE: The aperture in the bows of a ship through which the anchor cable passes. "Stay clear of my hawse hole!" is a admonition to keep out of my way.

HAWSER: A heavy rope or cable greater than five inches in circumference. Used for towing, some anchor lines or to secure to a dock.

HOKU: In Hawaii, a star.

HOOLEY: In Ireland, an extended celebration usually with "too much of the drink taken." From a Hindu word for festival, brought back by Irish soldiers in the Honorable East India Company's army (the "John" Company).

INU: Hawaiian – drink, to drink.

KAHUNA: In Hawaii, a priest, wizard, minister, expert in any sprofession.

KANAKA: The Hawaiian word for human being, man, person, individual. In the world outside the Hawaiian Islands, frequently used to denote a Hawaiian.

KEEL: The principal member or timber extending the length of a ship's bottom. The ship's "backbone."

KERNES or KERNS: Irish light infantry, originally around the 13th century.

KILO: In Hawaii, a stargazer, seer, reader of omens.

LANYARD: A short length of rope used for a variety of purposes, including the release of the hammer on flintlocks when they were used as firing mechanisms for cannon.

LEAD LINE: A 25-fathom (150 foot) line with a lead weight cylinder attached, used to find the depth of the water. The lead's lower end is cupped and "armed" with tallow, to bring to the surface the nature of the bottom, mud, sand, pebbles, shingles, etc. The line is measured in six-foot lengths or fathoms. The leadsman heaves the line ahead of the ship so that it is vertical as it reaches the bottom. He is positioned in the chains, a platform to which the fore shrouds are attached. The line is marked with specific knots, rags or leathers at most of the six-foot 'fathom' intervals. The leadsman can identify the depth marks by feel, even in the dark. Depths measured by indicators are referred to as marks. Unmarked fathoms in between marks are called out as deeps. "By the mark two" was distinguished by two strips of leather. The "deep six" had no mark but was between "mark five" (white duck cloth) and "mark seven" (red bunting). The deep sea or "dipsea" lead measures depths up to 100 fathoms. It is extended along the length of the ship and held at intervals by sailors who drop their segment of the line in succession.

LEE: The side of a ship or promontory away from the wind.

LIGHTERS: Barges used to convey cargo from ship to shore in shallow waters. They are shallow draft and very steady in calmer water.

LUFF: 1. Slang for lieutenant, from the French and British pronunciation "leftenant." "First Luff" is the first lieutenant or executive officer of a ship. 2. The leading edge of a fore-and-aft sail. To "luff up" is to bring the vessel into the wind so that the luff shivers and the sail spills the wind.

MAHALO NUI LOA: In Hawai'i, thank you very much.

MALAMA PONO: In Hawai'i, be careful, watch out!

MOKU: In Hawai'i, an island, a ship (because the first European ships suggested islands). Sailor is kelamoku, or in pidgin, sailamoku.

MOULINET: In fencing, a circular saber stroke or swing at head level.

MONKEY FIST: An intricately constructed knot, round, and weighty, attached to the end of the light heaving line first tossed from a ship to another vessel or to a dock. Once the lighter, more-easily-thrown heaving line was in hand, the ship's end was tied or "bent" to a heavier line that secured the originating ship to the other vessel or to the dock.

ORLOP DECK: The lowest deck in a ship. Usually, the location of the surgeon's operating compartment, called the "cockpit." "Orlop" and "cockpit" were sometimes used interchangeably when referring to the surgery.

PA ELE: In Hawai'i, a Negro.

PAINTER: A line at the bow of a boat used to secure to a dock.

PALU: In Micronesia, a navigator-priest.

PAWLS: A series of metal protrusions at the bottom of a capstan barrel that dropped into slots and acted as a brake on the anchor line. "Heave a pawl": take in the line by the distance of one more pawl by heaving or pushing on the capstan bars.

PELORUS: An instrument for taking bearings, with two sighting vanes, fitted to the rim of a compass and giving the bearings of two objects from a fixed point, usually a ship or boat.

PILIKIA: In Hawai'i, trouble, bad business, bother, adversity.

POINTS OF THE COMPASS: The circumference of the magnetic compass card is divided into 32 points. In the 19th century, they bore names. The four cardinal points were north (N), east (E), south (S), and west (W). Using the northeast quadrant as an example, the names of the seven points between N and E were: N by E, NNE, NE by N, NE, NE by E, ENE, and E by N. In that century, points were used to express the bearing of an object from the ship's heading, e.g., "two points off the starboard bow," or "one point abaft the port beam."

QUOIN: A wedge used to elevate the angle of fire from a ship's cannon.

RUCTION: In Ireland, a disturbance, fight, uproar.

RUSE d'GUERRE: An artifice or trick of war, accepted practice within the rules of war, such as flying a flag not one's own until opening fire. Just before opening fire, one's actual flag must be hoisted.

SASANACH: In Ireland, an Englishman, sometimes, a Protestant. A term of derision

SCHOELCHER, VICTOR: Parisian abolitionist originally from Alsace appointed head of a committee to enforce emancipation in Guadeloupe after an uprising in 1848.

SCREW: A nautical propeller.

SCUPPERS: Drains for the weather or upper decks.

SCUTTLEBUTT: 1. A cask of fresh water for daily drinking use, located in a convenient part of the ship. 2. Gossip. As many members of the crew would use the scuttlebutt and pause during the ship's work day, talk and gossip were exchanged there. Gossip exchanged at the office water cooler is a direct descendant.

SHEET: A single line used to trim a sail to the wind and attached to the clew. The clew on a fore-and-aft sail is the lower aftermost corner. On a square sail, the clews are the two lower corners.

SHENANIGANS: In Ireland, tricks or trickery, japes – a practical joke.

SHIP'S BOATS: The dimensions and characteristics of the boats described herein varied with the passage of time and the size of the ships they served. For instance, a cutter, a beamy boat that sailed well, but rowed less well, could be 34 feet long and carry 66 men on a ship of the line or a large steam frigate, but measured 18 feet long on a brig. Smaller vessels had difficulty in hoisting out larger boats using their main and fore course yards. The invention of davits in the 1790s helped the smaller craft to hoist out boats more easily. Generally, the size of a boat from large to small followed this order: Longboat, launch, pinnace, barge, cutter, yawl, gig, jolly boat, skiff, dory, wherry, dinghy. Double-ended whaleboats of 28-30 feet length came into naval use in the mid-19th century. A quarter boat often was one of the above hung in davits at the ship's quarter or after part. The following list from the 1817 Royal Navy Rate Book shows the variety of boats sizes within small boat nomenclature. It is taken from W. E. May's excellent "The Boats of Men of War," Naval Institute Press 1999, the definitive work on the topic:

Launches: in 17 varying lengths – 16 ft to 34 ft.
Barges & pinnaces: 8 different lengths – 28 to 37 ft.
Cutters: 17 different lengths – 12 to 34 ft.
Gigs: 6 different lengths – 18 to 26 ft.

Ship's boats were designed for sailing qualities, rowing qualities, or a compromise combination. Rowing configurations were termed single banked or double banked. Single banked boats had one rower to a thwart, seated all the way across the thwart from the oarlock. For wider or more beamy boats, double banking put two men each with an oar, on each thwart. Oarlocks were first thole pins, upright pegs in the gunwales that the oar pulled against as a fulcrum, with a lanyard around the oar to secure it. Next, a second thole pin was added and the oar set between. Later, notches were cut in a strake above the gunwale and the oar set in. In 1826, metal swiveling oar crutches were introduced.

SHIP TYPES: Beginning with the system of the Royal Navy's Lord Anson in 1751, warships of sailing navies were divided into six divisions or "rates" according to the number of broadside guns carried. A "first rate" carried 100 guns or more. A "fourth rate" carried from 50 to 70 guns, and was the smallest ship of the line, or line-of-battle ship. Fifth and sixth rates were brigs of war, sloops of war, corvettes or frigates carrying up to 50 guns.

Steam power brought additional and changing classifications. Ships carried more powerful pivot guns that fired in any direction, in addition to broadside guns. Steam ships came to be classified by how they were powered or armored. Ironclads, sidewheel frigates, screw frigates, sidewheel or screw sloops, sidewheel or screw gunboats, and armed sidewheel or screw tugs were some new types. Specialty vessels, such as spar torpedo boats and hand-propelled submarines were introduced in the American Civil War. River combat spawned cottonclads, tinclads, timberclads and rams.

It's interesting to note that "second-rate," now connoting low quality, originally meant a ship of the line carrying from 84 to 100 guns, with nothing low-quality about her.

SHUILER: In Ireland, a vagrant, a wanderer.

SIDEBOY: A sailor assigned to attend the gangway when officers or other dignitaries are boarding the ship. The rank of the boarding officer determines the number of sideboys.

SPALPEEN: In Ireland, an itinerant farmhand of dubious reputation or low degree. A rascal. A derogatory term.

SPOKE THE SHIP: at sea one "speaks" another vessel, one does not "speak to" a ship.

STERNSHEETS: In an open boat the section aft of the after thwart, usually fitted with seats for the coxswain, boat commander or passengers.

STOP HER COCKS: To plug any below-waterline pipes opening to the sea on a vessel.

STRAKE: A line of planking in a wooden vessel. The hull is made up of rows of strakes.

SURE, TO BE SURE: "paddyisms" expressing certainty, "without a doubt."

TEAGUE: A common Irish surname which came to be used as a derogatory term for an Irishman in the USA and Great Britain of the 19th century, like "mick" or "paddy." The "tea" is pronounced "tay." Sometimes, "Taig" or "Teig."

THWART: The transverse wooden seat in a rowing boat on which oarsmen sit.

TIDES: The states of the tides include: slack water, when the tide changes from ebb to flood or the reverse; ebb, outgoing; flood, incoming; high, the greatest level, and low, the lowest level.

TOP HAMPER: A ship's superstructure and upper-deck equipment.

TRANSOM: The athwartship timbers bolted to the sternpost, constituting a flat stern.

WARDROOM: The mess and common room for the senior officers (except the captain) in a larger warship, or for all officers (except the captain) in a smaller ship. The gunroom in a larger ship serves the more junior officers.

WAY and WEIGH: Way is to be in motion over the sea bottom. A ship has "way" on her, or is "under way." The command for rowers to begin rowing is "give way all." To weigh anchor is to lift the anchor from the sea bottom. "Under weigh" is an incorrect usage.

WAY ENOUGH: A command to stop rowing.

"WILL NAE BE KENT": In Scots dialect, "will not be known."

YARD: A large wooden or metal spar crossing the masts of a ship horizontally (or diagonally to bear lateen sails), from which a sail is set .

YAW, PITCH AND ROLL: Yaw is the motion of the bow to the left or to the right of the course. Pitch is the up and down motion of the bow caused by wave action ahead or astern of the ship. Roll is the up and down movement of the side of a ship due to wave action from the side or abeam of the ship.

ZOUAVE: member of a French-Algerian regiment uniformed in colorful pantaloons and short shell jackets. Many Civil War regiments adopted similar uniforms (and the name), notably those from Louisiana and New York.

In addition to the sources cited above, the author is indebted to **The Oxford Companion to Ships and the Sea**, Peter Kemp, Oxford Reference, **Ship to Shore**, Peter D. Jeans, McGraw Hill, **A Sea of Words**, Dean King, Henry Bolt, **Origins of Sea Terms**, John G. Rogers, Mystic Seaport Museum, **Hawaiian Dictionary**, Mary Kawena Pukui and Samuel H. Elbert, University of Hawaii Press, **The Green Flag, Volume II**, Robert Kee, Penguin and **Slanguage, a Dictionary of Irish Slang**, Bernard Share, Gill and Macmillan.